Libretto

a novel by

ANN WADSWORTH

Libretto

Published by Wheatmark®
2030 East Speedway Boulevard, Suite 106
Tucson, Arizona 85719 USA
www.wheatmark.com

ISBN: 978-1-62787-986-6 (paperback)
ISBN: 978-1-62787-987-3 (hardcover)
ISBN: 978-1-62787-988-0 (ebook)
LCCN: 2022910235

Bulk ordering discounts are available through Wheatmark, Inc.
For more information, email orders@wheatmark.com or call 1-888-934-0888.

For Pam Hoyle

One

If I hadn't been dispatched to central Italy some years ago to cover a story in Perugia—an assignment I never asked for and tried vigorously to reject—I would never have thought of exploring this ancient hilltop city on my own. I had been hoping for an assignment in Salzburg, possibly, or Bayreuth, or Aix-en-Provence; I can't remember. I do remember feeling very bitter. I had expected a tedious stay, an unenlightened cuisine featuring various dishes made of wild boar meat, and an uninteresting population made up mostly of students. But this was before I wandered into Perugia's *passeggiata* for the first time, tasted *baccalà* at La Taverna, and lost myself in the city's ghostly passageways at night. What really happened couldn't have been farther from what I had imagined. I thought I was too old to learn patient ways of looking at old perceptions of love and loss. I was mistaken.

As a freelance commentator on the esoteric world of opera, I've grown accustomed to temperamental singers who don't show up, complicated pieces of stage machinery that suddenly collapse, and performances that go completely off the rails in ways that might be tragic if they weren't so absurdly entertaining.

But I'm an observer—I stress that point—not a critic, and anything that makes a performance more comprehensible provides ink for my pen, as it were. Almost every bit of an operatic production is based on spectacle, which is why Italians love it. And are so good at composing music for it. But for the rest of us there exists something about spectacle that is discovered only after learning to ignore the words. Because—except in rare instances—words can get in the way. And when they do—in art as in life—they can cause a great deal of trouble.

This tale begins in September, late on a mild afternoon, as I was navigating my rented Fiat through a succession of switchbacks toward the icy cold Garibaldi I hoped was waiting for me in the bar at the Hotel Brufani, Perugia's magisterial hotel in the upper city. This treat would be a reward for a forgettable afternoon in the small town of Beata Colomba that had concluded in the massive traffic jam from which I had just managed to make a precipitous exit.

"Ah, Signora!" the older of the two bartenders called out to me. "*Buona sera!* There is a seat for you here! You prefer the terrace this evening?"

"Not yet. Thank you, Ercole."

"A Garibaldi for you?"

"As fast as you can make it." I stashed my briefcase under my bar stool, brushed the travel dust off my jacket, and began a text to my editor in London: *Gail: DiBrufa didn't show up. Any other wild geese up your sleeve? If so, count me OUT. Love, Ally (with a heart).* I sent it off with a hard punch.

A deep breath. Now the evening could begin. Now I could watch the passeggiata in peace, the sun could shed its corals and vermillions into the blue-gray clouds waiting behind the hills west of the city. And after that, the long evening. Food. Sleep. I'd decide the rest tomorrow.

Ercole knew just how to make a perfect Garibaldi, just the right balance of Campari and orange juice, just the right amount of foam lingering near the rim of the glass. A quarter-moon orange slice balanced on top of it all. I had grown to like this bar in the Hotel Brufani during my brief sojourn in Perugia, although my expense account would never come close to enabling me to sleep in one of its beds. The bar was mostly quiet and allowed me to answer emails and organize my notes in peace. I looked around. So where was Italo Montecalvo, my newfound oracle, who would doubtless enjoy the sordid details of my afternoon?

At that moment his cane fell to the floor behind the adjacent bar stool.

"Forgive my cane," he said. "You must retrieve it for me, please, Signora Crosbie. Once I was tall as an oak, but now my lower branches do not bend so easily."

I unwound my long legs from around my own seat and hung his cane over the back of the stool on which he had settled.

"Ercole!" he called out to the bartender.

"Signor Italo?"

"Vermouth cassis for me, *per favore.* And you, Signora Crosbie?"

"I'm still working on my Garibaldi, thanks."

The doors to the outside terrace had been opened wider, admitting the diminishing glow of the setting sun, and a soft breeze drifted over from the Carducci Gardens across the way. The evening passeggiata walkabout had begun, and the street had become busy with strollers headed for the far side of the gardens to reassure themselves that the sun would disappear behind the hills to the west, as it did every evening.

"You had an enjoyable afternoon?" Montecalvo asked me.

"As you predicted, Maestro DiBrufa did not show up."

"So sorry. But ..."

"No, I'm relieved. I was never enthusiastic about this assignment."

"Well, someone must talk to him. He has prepared himself for immediate fame."

"Well, it won't be me. He had his chance today. I'd like to take a look at this libretto he's created just out of curiosity, but so far all I have are rumors. The score, for example, would be a help."

"You may have been spared a disappointing afternoon, Signora. This libretto is worse than terrible, as I told you yesterday. In fact, the poor composer has now fled the city."

I turned on my stool and looked at him. "When did this happen?"

"Late this morning." He sipped his drink. "Did anyone, any substitute, appear at your appointment in Beata Columba?"

"His sister. We had a curious and, I must say, unfriendly encounter. Very brief."

He crossed himself and kissed the tip of his thumb. "The unholy Monica. Frightening, è vero?"

"Intriguing, more like. She was wearing an Elsa Peretti snake ring."

He smiled. "Those are your standards, Signora?"

"My reporting standards, Signor Montecalvo, don't shy away from the worse than terrible. But the point is presently moot. Monica DiBrufa has barred the door to any future contact with her brother Piero. Other than having a small curiosity about what they might be concealing, I'm personally happy to abandon this project. Although my editor may not feel the same."

"She will fire you?"

"It's not a fireable offense."

Ercole stood before us, listening carefully. He was a dark,

quiet man who generally stayed out of the way. "Signor Italo?" he asked.

"Another for me, please."

"One Garibaldi is my limit," I said. "But maybe soda water and lime."

After a little while, Montecalvo said, "So you will be leaving Perugia now?"

"That remains to be seen."

"You might do a follow-up investigation of the bloody murder trial Perugia has just suffered through."

I laughed a little. "It might be easier. But that's not my line of interest. And *Opera World* wouldn't buy it in any case."

"Too bad." He shook his head thoughtfully. "Such disorder. The BBC alone required two floors of a hotel."

I finished my drink and began to think of dinner.

"There is something else," he began, "that might be of interest to you."

"And that would be?"

"My musical friends in the city—not always accurate with their facts—tell me that Piero DiBrufa has begun to stir some trouble up at the opera house. 'Interfering' is the word they chose, with the preparation of his opera. And the stage director's ready to throw in her towel, I think you say. Or something heavier."

"Go on."

"And if that's true, the production may have real trouble. This director is world class, and the company doesn't want to lose her."

"That would be Elaine Bishop, I think."

"I believe that is her name."

"She is world class. But she's had some recent professional troubles, if I'm not mistaken."

"Piero will find a way to have his libretto used. No matter

how bad it may be. Or who's standing in his way. He forgets that a libretto is only one small bright star in the grand firmament of opera."

"Do you know him? I forgot to ask you yesterday." I regretted leaving my notebook in my book bag, which was out of reach beneath my feet.

"We were boyhood friends." He gave a little sigh and finished his vermouth. "What will happen now? To you? If all stories fail?"

"It won't be the end of the world. I lead a peripatetic life, Signor Montecalvo. I'll be sent along to some other story."

"You have no one tending a fire, waiting for your return?"

I smiled. "Sadly, no. Sorry to disappoint." I retrieved my bag and prepared to depart. "If I'm still around tomorrow, I'll see you here. Thanks for the drink. And the information."

He fumbled in his pocket and produced his card. "If I can be of any other assistance to you, please find me in my bookstore. In Via Oberdan."

"I'll remember that."

We walked slowly across the terrace and parted on the sidewalk. The sun had set, and the passeggiata had reversed. Everyone was now heading back down the corso toward dinner.

I left the Brufani behind me and took an indirect route to my own hotel through the gardens of Piazza Italia, where the lamps had come on in the early darkness. Across from the piazza was a wide, semicircular overlook where one could view the entire width of the Tiber Valley stretched out toward the western flank of the Apennines, with small villages on the plain far below that in the dusk seemed to be lit with handfuls of little stars. In the distance a small radiance rested against the shadowed base of a mountain—Assisi, I guessed. Somewhere in that direction, Piero

DiBrufa was preparing for his evening meal, perhaps, while Monica, in her rooms, might be combing her dark tresses out of the severe twist that had clung to her head like a cinematic alien during my brief afternoon encounter with her. At dinner they would no doubt spend some time congratulating each other for keeping an unwelcome foreign journalist from the gates once again. I thought about that as I watched the evening settle in. A wandering breeze carried the faint aromas of olive oil, garlic, and wine, the base of a good sauce. A swallow dipped and darted away, looking for his own dinner.

I was just sliding toward sleep that night when my phone buzzed. Gail Graham, my editor/agent, had decided to respond to my text.

"Asleep?" she said. "Sorry. I had a list of calls to return. I should have called you first." A pause, while she poured something into a glass. "Ally? Still there?"

"I'm here."

"I don't know where to begin. I've gone over your message and all I can say is, who the hell is this Monica DiBrufa that she can roll you over and turn you into a dying lily? You were there to enlighten the world about her brother's work, and he doesn't even show up? That was simply rude. And I don't understand her excuses at all. What threat could she possibly have made that would cause you to pack up your bags and get out your timetables without putting up some sort of fight? Surely you have enough Italian to do that at least."

"She didn't threaten me. She'd already made her decision, Gail, before she even got to me."

"*Opera World* has you blocked in for their February issue. Remember that. And I have one of our photographers on standby."

"Look, I had no great desire to do this interview. I'm more or less relieved Piero didn't show up. He refused to collaborate with the composer, who has now fled the city. As far as DiBrufa was concerned, everything about this opera was supposed to revolve around his libretto. His words. For him, the music was incidental. I'm not even sure *Opera World* would have accepted anything I wrote."

"Where does that leave me, then? Or you, for that matter? You've got an advance. Can you pull *anything* out of this mess?"

"I don't know if it's worth it now. And it wasn't my idea to begin with."

"When has that ever stopped you?"

"I'm tired of interviews, Gail. They're dead ends. I'm established enough now to write for the more musically enlightened."

"Yes, well we all know how those experiments have turned out. Goethe and Massenet? *Opera Magazine* laughed in my face."

"That essay was pretty well put together, I thought."

"It was a freak reaction to your forty-third birthday. It's over and done with. Wait while I freshen my drink."

"It was one of my best," I said into a yawn. "There was meat on its bones."

"Now," Gail said as she returned. "Number one ..."

"There is something else that might work."

"Be quick about it. I've got some decisions to make."

"If Piero DiBrufa's libretto for the new opera is out of the question, at least for the moment, let it rest. Elaine Bishop is here. She's directing *Sirius,* that's the DiBrufa opera that may fall on its face. She's brilliant, but she's run into some professional trouble over the past year or so. Maybe she's trying to reinvent herself in Perugia, I don't know. But DiBrufa, so I've been told, is part of her problem. It could be something, I don't know. More of a profile than an interview. It might be worth looking into."

"And who put you onto this track?"

"Someone I met here."

"Oh, no. No, no, no."

"He's an old man but he's local, and I have a feeling he knows a thing or two."

"Maybe it's time to send you back out on one of your travel junkets. For your Plan B readers, as you call them."

"Oh, yes, I really see myself climbing a volcano right now, or in an Argentine tango bar."

"Well, you do have your talents, but let's see if we can save something from this project—for which you've already been partially paid, I say again. I'll give you Piero DiBrufa or Elaine Bishop. Both, if necessary. Can you get me something by November or early December?"

"Possibly."

"You'll have to do better than that, Ally. I don't understand what's happened to you. You're wandering around following some plan of your own—or no plan at all that I can figure out. Are you stalking someone? Or do you just decide to go somewhere and wait to be inspired? Half the time I don't know where you are. You speculate; you're off in a dream. I'm running a business here. I have to send my writers to interesting places, and to people who want to be written about, not hiding to avoid it."

"I get it."

"You'd better. Here's my bottom line: find some*thing* or some*one* in Perugia to write about as long as you're there, or move on. For the moment I'll leave the DiBrufa family in limbo. They'll either come around or they won't. If you can get an audience with

Bishop, do it. I won't renege on my advance, but you'll have to find a cheaper way to live. No five-star hotels. Or four. Or even three. No nights on the town on my dime. Pull yourself together or it's the tango bars for you."

If I hadn't decided to take my breakfast at one of the streetside tables on the corso the following morning, I would have missed her. Our tables were close, but not conspicuously so, and the woman was, at the moment, alone. She was making notes in a large, yellow-bound book that looked suspiciously like a score. The wind had picked up since yesterday, and it played and lifted her hair off her face. She absently brushed it back. Salt and peppery. Professionally styled certainly.

I took a long look while I waited for my cornetto, my coffee still too hot to drink.

She seemed to be one of those women who always seem to be well put together: never dressed to stand out but perfectly comfortable in her body and what she was wearing. A quality I lacked. Fiftyish. But she was troubled, tapping her pen against a plate of leftover crumbs. The wind worried her hair. The day was warming up.

When the waiter delivered my cornetto, I asked for another coffee. I'd had a rough night. Around three o'clock I'd gotten up and begun to repack my bag. Then, hearing some commotion in the street, I'd opened my window and looked down. Only quiet laughter, footsteps passing by. Even at that hour there was some activity, and over the tiled roofs across the street, a nearly full moon was peering down into the ancient alleys. I needed to make a move out of this muddled little hotel, with its buzzing neon sign blinking below, its lumpy mattress, and the shower down the hall.

"Morning, Renato," the woman said, as a dapper gentleman

with a pencil moustache joined her. "Want coffee?" She lifted her arm, and a waiter was instantly attentive.

I looked up. Her accent was American. Her voice moderately mellow. Precise. She was used to being listened to.

"Yes, coffee," he said. "Elaine, I've had a call ..."

Whatever else he told her was lost in the hubbub of a chattering tourist group that had chosen this moment to walk by on its way to the duomo.

I stretched to see across the tables, but they had their heads together. She of the tapping pen was talking now, but it was impossible to hear her. He was writing everything down.

As my coffee arrived, the woman abruptly slammed the score closed; her pen fell to the pavement. "Damn that man!" she said loudly. I smiled. *Elaine Bishop,* I thought. *Has to be.*

"I need a place to stay for a while," I said to Montecalvo later in the day. "Not too costly."

Ercole stood before us, patiently awaiting my order. "A glass of Torgiano white," I told him finally. "And something to eat. Something like a sandwich."

"A *tramezzino?*" he offered. "Prosciutto? Cheese?"

"Anything."

"I am eating later," Montecalvo said.

When Ercole had quietly arrived with my food and wine, he lingered for a moment. "Signora," he began.

"Thank you," I said. "This is perfect."

"Signora," he said quietly, "you look for a place to live?"

"Yes. For a while. Not too long."

"My wife," he said quietly. "My wife rents some rooms in our house. In Via Rocchi."

"Ah, yes!" Montecalvo said. "Yes, she does!"

"She keeps a good house. No students. All women. She does not serve meals, but tenants have free use of her kitchen. Perhaps you would care to speak with her?"

"You must do this, Signora Crosbie," Montecalvo said. "Bravo, Ercole, for this thought! This would be a perfect solution to your problem!"

Ercole wrote an address on an order slip and passed it over to me. He nodded and smiled. "We have two children," he said. "Two girls. They behave well."

I did not ask about rent or what the room was like or anything else. "I'll go to see her," I said. "I'll go later this afternoon."

"Yes, yes," Ercole said, looking over his shoulder.

"Thank you."

"Well," Montecalvo said. "A stroke of luck. Via Rocchi is on the hill behind the duomo, toward the Stranieri University."

"But no students," Ercole said.

"Stefania has rules that are not broken," Montecalvo added. "No students."

"No students," I said. "That point has been made."

My tramezzino suddenly tasted like a three-course lunch.

Two

Number 40, Via Ulisse Rocchi. I rang the bell and waited. Then firmly knocked. The door was opened by a dark-haired, Anna Magnani look-alike in a limp, flowered apron. In one hand she carried a knife; the other held a fistful of carrots. Around her waist a heating pad was strapped, attached to a heavy-duty electrical cord that disappeared into the room behind her.

"Pazienza," she said. "The soup must be stirred."

I took a deep breath. English? Italian? "I ask about the available room, Signora. Oh, *scusa*. Buona sera." Greetings first.

She gave me a dark, curious look. "Who sends you here?"

"*Suo marito, Signora Caccini.* Your husband."

"*Ah, si.*" She relaxed a bit. This was not like dealing with hotel desk clerks, with whom I could get along in any language.

Eventually, having made her decision, she opened the door fully. "*Avanti.* A single room remains."

I followed her into the apartment, trying to avoid the cord that swayed behind her like a reptilian tail. I also kept an eye on her knife, which she was using as a pointer: "*La cucina. La sala da pranzo. Il bagno.*"

The available room faced the street, which lay far below. The bed was somewhat larger than a single, and a rather grand desk faced the window. A modest wardrobe stood against the corner wall. Some chairs. A lamp or two. Simple, but comfortable enough. I tried to get a sense of the place. And, as if in answer to a question I might have asked, the recorded voice of the late diva Renata Tebaldi rose faintly from within the bar below. "*Ah, si, si!*" she sang, and launched into, I believe, something from *Gioconda.*

The signora shrugged. "In evenings the noise is more quiet," she said.

I was already reaching for my passport and cards, euros, whatever she would take.

"*Allora,*" she said. "I am Stefania Caccini. Owner and wife."

"Allyn Crosbie."

She counted my deposit and slid it into her apron pocket. "We now have a full house."

My living quarters were more or less what I expected. I was pleased that Signora Caccini had a policy of not renting to students, and the other residents of her good-sized apartment were a mixed bag of adult women who hailed from as far away as Abu Dhabi, Mexico City, and Buenos Aires. They all had "professional interests," in the signora's words. We had no common language among us, but when we had an urgent need for the bathroom or wanted to discuss the mysteries of the microwave, we managed to make ourselves understood. And we did not get in one another's way, for which I was grateful. If I showed no signs of wanting company, I was left alone.

The signora had made one exception to her no-student rule, and that was in the person of Jo, the only other American in residence, who was a brilliant young beauty from Atlanta with, as it developed, a floating history of melodramatic romantic entanglements with members of Il Grifo, Perugia's professional soccer team. The signora was proud of this association with her home, and it was probably the reason she'd rented Jo a room. Ercole, her husband, was especially pleased. The delightfully dissimilar Caccini daughters, Maria Rosa and Teresina (aged twelve and nine), made up the rest of the household.

I occasionally attempted to find excuses to converse with Signora Caccini, who was happy to provide me with a great deal of information about Perugia's history and some of its current inhabitants. She claimed, for example, to have attended school with the current female chief of the Perugia homicide squad, a tough cookie (my translation) as she described her, who was notoriously fashion conscious—black stiletto boots and tight jeans in winter; baby-doll blouses and sandals in summer. This story seemed to be true, and I found it intriguing. In fact, under different circumstances I might have pursued it. But she had been deeply involved in the recent murder trial, so I had to let it go. Gail would have rejected it out of hand.

By late September it was dark by six thirty and getting colder. The wind came up in chilly gusts from the valley as I climbed up Via Rocchi with my notebook to stroll the evening passeggiata. The corso was bright with lights, and shop window displays seemed more elegant than they had at midday, with their collections of red cashmere by Luisa Spagnoli, glittering earrings, and chocolates (the pride of Perugina) on tiers of paper lace.

I'd decided to write a little about the city before I tackled the opera house and activities that involved Elaine Bishop. And there was much to describe in this city full of foreigners. I didn't find it strange to find purveyors of drugs hard at work around the ancient piazzas or in the shadows under Etruscan-built arches that had once been the scenes of savage medieval bloodbaths. But as much as this urban melodrama appealed to me, I hadn't forgotten my mission, and I would linger after lunch across the street from the Teatro Morlacchi, watching for the appearance of anyone looking even vaguely operatic. Until, that is, I realized I was watching for Elaine Bishop, at which point I put the lingering on hold. I had one frightening near-encounter with Monica DiBrufa but in the end lost the courage to follow her through the side door of the theater to see what I could discover.

And I tried to have a nightly drink with Montecalvo when I could.

These activities, I'm sure, are what Gail Graham would call spinning my wheels. Waiting to be inspired? I didn't think so. I would know when I was ready to begin to write. And now I guess I was simply exploring.

But I couldn't excuse what happened next.

Three

One night about ten thirty, I was walking back to Casa Caccini when a figure stepped out of the darkness by the duomo and spoke to me in Italian. Her Italian was nearly unintelligible—even I could tell she wasn't a native—but I did understand that she was asking for directions to Via Baglioni, which was quite nearby. I responded in Italian and pointed the way, whereupon she said in English, "Your Italian is awful."

"Maybe," I said, "but the longer I stay, the better I get."

In that way Senta Farrar, from Syracuse, New York, stepped into my life.

Bar Centrale, across the piazza, was still open, so we walked over to get something to drink. My legs are long and hers were—well, not so long, and she bumbled along beside me in worn-down boots and well-traveled jeans. She had a head of dark, curly hair. She first stood at the bar, then changed her mind and put her small computer case on one of the metal tables. She was clearly exhausted.

I bought Senta a coffee and myself a limoncello. She was not a student, at least not in Perugia, but had come to Italy to do research on early Italian labor unions for her postdoctoral work at Syracuse. It was hard to guess her age. Early thirties, I guessed. But postdoctoral? It had been a long time since I'd been an academic.

"Why are you headed for Via Baglioni?" I asked.

"I want to rent a room over there." She took a slip of paper from her pocket. "Signora Martinelli. Via Baglioni, number ten."

"You won't find anyone up at this hour."

"Where are you staying? Is there any space?" She used her spoon to scrape the grains of sugar around in the bottom of her coffee cup.

"We're full up. Do you have a place for tonight?"

"I left my bag with the Oblate Sisters on Via della Cupa. They gave me a bed."

"You really came to Perugia to study labor unions? How do you manage? Your Italian is worse than mine."

"Believe it or not, I've already been to Bologna and Naples. Ciro told me to come to Perugia for a while. It's a very political city, he says. Lots going on. And two big universities."

"Who's Ciro? A politician?"

"Hardly. I met him in Bologna. He's back in Naples now, with his family." She was having difficulty keeping her eyes open.

I finished my drink. "Maybe you should head back to your nuns."

"Maybe I should do that. My Italian is terrible, you're right, and I'm having to read all these labor tracts. I'm bored out of my mind."

Although I was enjoying talking easy English with someone for a change, I didn't feel like going into my life story at this time of night. "Right now I'm trying to imagine the Tiber Valley at the bottom of a deep prehistoric lake, which is where it used to be."

"You're doing this for fun?"

"No, it's part of something I'm thinking of deleting from a piece I'm writing."

She was quickly alert. "Are you a writer? This is a lucky break. Do you have a publisher?"

"I have a very impatient editor."

"But have you published something? Would I know any of your work?"

I was ready to head home and stood up. "Not likely, unless you read travel magazines. Or *Opera World.*"

She shook her head. "Nope."

"I'm putting together a piece on a production the opera company here is doing. With some side notes on the city."

"Not the murder trial," she said.

"God, no."

"Do you write other things? Fiction maybe?"

"No. Some of my travel pieces were collected in a book last year. That's about it."

"What was it called?"

"*Boarding Passes.* Not my idea. I wanted to call it *Escape Routes.*"

"Because I think I've got a novel in me."

"Everyone thinks they have a novel in them." She was attractive in an aggressive way that I usually found off-putting. So I surprised myself by asking if she'd like to have dinner the next night.

She gave me a small scowl. "No place expensive, my grant money's running out."

"My treat. I'll meet you on the steps by the cathedral about seven. Just there." I pointed out the door of the bar toward the long flank of steps that ran along the southwestern façade of the duomo. "By the fountain," I added.

I offered her my hand to get her on her feet. “Okay,” she said. “You say your name is Allyn? First or last?”

“First. It’s a family name. Call me Ally, if you like.”

“So you’re Ally and I’m Senta,” she said outside. “Thelma and Louise. *Ciao*, then, see you tomorrow.”

The rainy season was stubbornly refusing to begin, and despite the ritual cups of herb tea consumed daily by Signora Caccini, the skies remained cloudless. But the mornings had grown chillier, and the chimneys in the Porta Sant’Angelo quarter and poorer neighborhoods in the city began to issue gray, pungent streams of wood smoke with the bells at dawn and at sunset. The sun rose daily in a pale mist, but by ten o’clock it was beating down as if it was July. But if there was no rain, there were certainly the brisk winds blowing down off the Apennines, and midday meals were now taken behind half-closed shutters. On the mountains to the northeast, behind the Monteripido monastery, one could even see snow on the tallest peaks. Residents of the city wore sweaters and jackets now if they went out at night, when the wind would gust up the streets, pushing against the doors of the cafés and rattling glass windows. They were more than half-hoping for rain, to get the autumn underway.

I began to spend late evenings in Senta’s room discussing the novel she had impulsively started to write, which would have nothing to do with labor unions. This novel, which apparently had been germinating for a while now, would focus on her Jewish heritage, a variety of radical social philosophies, and her development as a liberated sexual woman. She made me feel ancient.

She had rented the topmost room of the building on Via Baglioni owned by Signora Martinelli, which overlooked a terrace and a hilly cascade of dusty-rose roof tiles that descended into the lower neighborhoods of the southeastern part of the city. Across the valley was Assisi, which on clear days we could see flung up against the base of Mount Subasio like a chalky stain. Early one evening a strange man with a patch on one eye delivered cans of kerosene, and after some inquiries, Senta figured out how to light the stove in her room without blowing it up. From that point on there was heat when we needed it, which was usually after ten at night after we returned from dinner.

About eight thirty we would leave Signora Martinelli's and walk over to Da Peppino, a *rosticceria* on Via Danzetta, a street that was no more than an alley between Via Baglioni and the corso. We would choose our supper from whatever was displayed behind a glass display case, Senta usually opting for a cold spinach-looking mess, upon which she would lavish oil and vinegar. She would also have several slices of roast veal, bread, and white wine, into which she would squeeze a lemon, a habit she claimed to have acquired in Bologna. I usually had pasta or a cooked tomato stuffed with rice and some slices of roast chicken. White wine too—good, local Umbrian wine, without the lemon. We talked, but it was easy talk, and from time to time Peppino's little son, who was learning English, came over and joined the conversation. Senta showed him how to make animal figures out of toothpicks.

After a while we would wander over to the corso for coffee at Lunabar Ferrari and then return to Senta's, sometimes walking up and through the Carducci Gardens if the wind was not too fierce. Back in Senta's room, the kerosene odor would be so overpowering after she lit the stove that she would have to open the window for five or ten minutes to allow the air to refresh itself. While that was happening, we would stand in the dark watching the lights of the cars far below on their way to join the main road to Assisi or the E45 highway south. On several occasions she reached over to hold my hand, a move that startled me, but not enough to disengage myself. If something was beginning, I had no immediate objection. I liked beginnings. I preferred them, in fact. But I usually avoided that sort of complication when I was on assignment. I'd had enough of emotions edging into my work routine in my younger years.

Senta was short—almost a head shorter than I was. Her eyes were crinkled as if she laughed a lot, which she did, although she took herself very seriously and was more often excited than smiling. Her curly hair was usually in a tousled state, as if it had been blown about by a great wind. Our relationship had remained on a friendly level, but as time passed it gradually became more complicated, mainly because of Ciro, who had reappeared for a brief visit and quickly become convinced that I "played for an opposite team," as Senta described it. From Naples, he was now attempting by email and *telefonino* to persuade Senta to use me to expand her sexual horizons. He was unusually interested in the progress of this plan and phoned Senta several times a week to see how things were moving along.

"He's wrong, as usual, about almost everything," Senta said, after confiding these details to me. "I've already expanded my horizons with women. He just wants to be involved too."

"In what way? I'm past the age of finding boyish fantasies like that entertaining." The problem was that although Ciro was slowly beginning to bore Senta, she had fallen in love with his enormous family, which had gathered her in and seen her through a particularly lonely period she had experienced during the summer. She was determined not to return to Syracuse before she absolutely had to, and Ciro's family had become her refuge from this possibility.

As I departed her little garret one night, she handed me the first twenty pages of her novel to read, a responsibility that I didn't really want to accept. I had come to look forward to my late-night walks back to my room from my evenings with her, and the manuscript weighed heavily in my bag. Generally, there weren't many people about in the streets at that hour, and it was lovely when the moon was high enough to shed its pale light against the old stones of the city. I smelled autumn in the wind. As I crossed the central piazza, the bells from Palazzo Priori would be tolling one, or one fifteen, and the majestic Great Fountain was playing for the sole delight of the marble figure of Pope Julius III, who was keeping a watchful eye on any creatures of the night who might pass through.

If any emotions were edging into my routine at all, they were focused on the city, to which I seemed to be responding on a personal level I hadn't felt in a while. My night walks were beginning to feel like falling slowly in love, much as, I suppose, Senta had fallen in love with Ciro's family.

I had made it a point not to sleep over at Senta's, in part because I preferred to sleep in my own bed. But I also knew Signora Caccini kept a casual eye on the hour each of her tenants returned to her premises. Although she often forgot that her tenants were adult women, she remained alert to the watchful eyes of her neighbors. But things happen. One evening I was propped up on Senta's bed, reading a week-old *New York Times* while she was at work on her laptop. I must have fallen asleep, for I eventually sensed that she had turned out the light and opened the window a bit wider. She quietly removed the newspaper from where it had fallen across my face and lay down beside me. Half asleep, I made no move toward her, although I became aware of the scratch of her wool sweater against my face (I am fiercely allergic) and the sweet smell of her hair. For a while I drifted in and out of sleep, although I could hear the distant sound of cars on the highway below, muffled applause from the television in Signora Martinelli's rooms, and a low conversation that had begun on the terrace below Senta's window. I was pleasantly aware of our breathing, Senta's and mine, and we gradually began to shift a bit to make room for each other in her narrow, single bed. The length of my legs was not making it easy. At one moment I probably kissed her, but then we both dropped off to sleep. When I woke and looked at my watch, it was four thirty, and through the window I could see light forming behind the mountains east of Assisi. I slipped away without waking her and speedily made tracks for Via Rocchi. I later appeared in the kitchen with one side of my face aflame in red welts.

"What has bitten you?" the signora asked me, touching my cheek with concern. "This needs a treatment." She hurried out of the kitchen to fetch something from her supply of various ointments. If she had heard me creep into the apartment at five o'clock, she never mentioned it.

Senta and I had made plans to go to dinner at a restaurant in the lower part of the city a week or so after that, but when I returned to the apartment the morning before, the signora handed me an envelope with my name on it, in Senta's unmistakable scribble. "A friend knocks on the door," the signora said firmly in English. I carried it into my bedroom. *Cara Ally,* the note began. *Io sono qui ma tu non sei. Basta.* She gave up on Italian and went on in English.

Today is a very bad day and I'm sorry you're not at your house. I was frightened walking beside you in the street last night, not because of you, but because I've been a little uneasy about showing you my writing and all it will tell you about me. I just came by to ask you to convince me not to go down to Ciro's in Napoli. It's really like a compulsive eating disorder, this business with Ciro and me and his family (especially his mother). Maybe if I just sit here and go on writing I will miss the train and I won't have to make a decision. You can tell I'm not thinking straight, and so maybe it's time to step backward into the bosom of the Mariotti family again, at least for a few days. The train for Rome leaves in forty-five minutes, and I have to get down the hill to the station. Or not. Please don't think I'm crazy, even though I might be. Sorry I can't go to dinner. I will miss that and miss you. I'm sorry you're not here because I wanted to kiss you again. See you in a few days, or in a few weeks, or who knows? S.

So that was the end of that interlude, perhaps. I was curiously relieved but also a little disappointed. I had been left with a cluster of days that just hung there. I knew exactly how I should use the time: the first draft of my city profile had been glaring from my computer screen for a week. And it was time I made a contact with Elaine Bishop. But I was restless. On top of that, Gail Graham had chosen that moment to send me a hair-on-fire email demanding a status report and some written results "with no more delays."

So when some friendly Australians I'd met asked me to go to up to Vienna with them, I thought it was a fortuitous moment to leave my collection of Italian frustrations in the stew pot and go north to see what was happening in the City of Music.

During our days in Vienna, it rained every day and was remarkable for one major event: a brilliant performance of Strauss's *Elektra*, where I sat in the highest, cheapest seats of the redolently perfumed Vienna State Opera House and watched as Elektra danced herself to death while the orchestra brought this wonderful blood bath of an opera to a breathtaking conclusion in a decisive C major key. Even the soprano singing the role of Chrysothemis, whose name I wrote down but have since forgotten, remained in a sort of stunned shock during the ovation that followed, perhaps still under the fearsome spell of her mother, Klytemnestra, the unhappy queen who would dream no more. It was a thoroughly satisfying performance. The kind that assured me that my love of the operatic art form was still very much alive.

The following day, still bewitched by Strauss's evocative music, I found myself wandering through the rain, up and down Mariahilferstrasse, my libido apparently reawakened. Humming Sondheim's "Pretty Women," I followed several of them into the dark interiors of coffee houses, where I lingered over huge bowls of coffee or hot chocolate piled with blown cream, and dove into buttery pastries that shed their flakes all over my damp rain jacket. Back outside I was nearly overcome with new stimulations: "*Pretty women...fascinating...sipping coffee...dancing!*" It seemed to be spring, fall, and New Year's Eve all at once. And the leaves blowing. Music was everywhere. As the trams rumbled by, their bells sounded like Christmas chimes.

Lawrence Durrell has written of his "panic spring." I, instead, seemed to be in the midst of my own "manic October." After a day or two in this state, I realized that this high degree of excitement was beginning to do some damage. It would not work. I could not happily participate in trips to the Vienna Woods or spend endless afternoons traipsing through museums. So I made my excuses and bid my new friends goodbye. I bought water, a ham sandwich, and a couple of hardboiled eggs, and after only four days in Vienna, I fled onto a train bound for Venice, where I would change for points south.

This brief sojourn north of the Alps had passed as quickly as an explosive flashbulb on an ancient camera, but its series of afterimages was difficult to get out of my mind. I had made the journey to avoid work I should have been doing, and it had succeeded after a fashion. But my experiences in Vienna had also pulled the trigger on a surge of erotic feverishness. Before I departed for Vienna, Montecalvo had said to me one afternoon—after I'd put away two Garibaldis instead of my usual one—"Go and live your life! Do your job! The situation will resolve itself!" I wondered whether I had waited too long.

Four

I returned to find fall in Perugia, completely and at last. The rains had begun, but only at night, and most of the trees were bare, their branches moving sinuously in the hard winds. Evenings were coming earlier and earlier. The ubiquitous city cats lurked in doorways, their golden eyes gleaming at the affront of the rain that poured from gutters onto the slick streets. Assisi and the mountains beyond disappeared in mist, and the sounds from the highway below the city rose in a constant wet hiss.

And then followed days of flawless sunshine, warm, mild days, with crisp, chilly nights.

On my second night back, Senta appeared at the Caccinis' door, having come directly from the station. Back from Naples. My signora, somewhat taken aback, led her to my room and shut the door. I had been leaning against my pillows, trying to read a short story by Natalia Ginzburg in hopes of improving my Italian. Senta dropped her bag on the floor and collapsed on my desk chair. She'd decided I should take her to bed.

"So Ciro has won," I said, closing my book. But I was glad she had come by, either because I had finished the excerpt from her novel or because I was still under the spell of Vienna. The answer at that moment was to go out to dinner.

A draft from one of my notebooks, only to show that I was observing, not simply waiting for something to happen:

There was a point during the early days of my sojourn in Perugia when I became preoccupied with a couple I often saw who were residents of some note in the city. I compiled quite a file on them, in fact, unaware of the roles they would later play in the drama of my life in the city. But that part of the story was yet to come.

The Contessa, Her Companion, and the Dogs

I followed them one day as they made their way through the midday passeggiata because what they had to say to one another, when I could get close enough to overhear it, created a new layer of intrigue as my impressions of Perugia expanded. The midday passeggiata would begin about twelve thirty, and the contessa had joined the throngs of people who were beginning to navigate the corso. With her were her two spaniel dogs, on leashes, and her companion, a tall woman with dark hair severely pulled back from her face and a ruddy, alcoholic flush about her cheeks. She wore a dark blue cardigan flung over her shoulders and pursued the contessa and the two dogs as they wound their way through the crowd. The contessa was a solidly built woman, dressed boldly in a full, almost street-length skirt. She had an uncanny resemblance to Picasso's well-known portrait of Gertrude Stein, and a vocal attitude that I imagined was much like that of the writer's. She generally carried a cane, although she didn't seem to need it; she used it mainly to salute someone she knew, or to hold it high, much as a Venetian tour guide would do, in order for her companion to keep up with her. She made no verbal or visible response to the men who removed their hats and bowed slightly as she passed, or to the women who softly said, "Buon giorno, Contessa," as she strode through the crowd, pulled along—so it seemed—by the lively pair of dogs. When she reached the Hotel Brufani terrace, she stopped and turned about, and I quickly placed myself in the angular shadow cast by the ATM across from the hotel entrance.

"Margit?" she shouted, as she yanked the dogs to a quick halt.

Her friend emerged from the crowd in the middle of the street. "Will you have something to drink?" she asked her companion.

Margit was gazing out over the Carducci Gardens toward the distant lower hills, an unlit cigarette between her fingers.

"Margit!"

Margit turned and sank quickly and quietly into a metal chair. "Must you shout so, Renata?" she said softly.

"Come now," the contessa said, settling the dogs. "We'll have a coffee."

A waiter appeared and bowed respectfully.

"Caffè corretto, per favore," Margit said, as she lit her Nazionale.

"I will have one of those shaker drinks," the contessa said with a smile.

"Un caffè shakerato, Contessa?"

"Just so."

The two women sat in companionable silence for a while, the smoke from Margit's cigarette eddying around her head in a blue haze. She had turned her gaze toward Piazza Italia, across the way, her mind clearly elsewhere. The contessa had her eye on the crowds passing in the street and finally reached down to pat the dogs. "Those Americans arrive from Rome tomorrow, you remember. What have you planned?"

"For which night?"

At this point my account abruptly ended. Possibly because I suspected that Margit had spotted me. Nevertheless, I found it important enough to send a copy off to Gail (who was puzzled).

Five

My experiment with Senta—or hers with me—had turned into a passionate little affair, and it was immediately apparent that she had indeed "expanded her horizons" with women before. Her body was younger than mine, certainly more flexible, and although she was shy about removing her clothes at first, I convinced her that if she didn't take off her wool sweater, at least, I would quickly erupt in a rash. Everything else rapidly followed. To tell the truth, my mind was half on the possibility that Ciro might appear, and on one occasion I even checked under her bed.

But she was easy, easy to please and easy to give in to—and a delicious relief. I had a bit of an advantage over her, of course; having read detailed sections of her novel, I was very much aware of what she liked—and even what her fantasies might be. But I wasted no time being smug and she, in turn, knowing nothing about what might be in my mind, was a natural at just doing what felt best. It was not love—I never expected that—but it was somehow more than just sex.

After our first night, I didn't make it back to Via Rocchi at all. When I carefully opened the Caccinis' door around ten the next morning, I realized with relief that the signora was already off at the market. I had a quick sponge bath and was back outside in forty-five minutes. I bought a tramezzino and coffee at Bar Etrusco and took them out to the end of Corso Garibaldi, where I found a peaceful little olive grove just beyond the Porta Sant'Angelo. I lay down in the grass, ate my food, and dozed in the sun for an hour.

As time passed, of course, I tried to return to my regular schedule, but my continuing lack of sleep made me feel as if I was in constant jet lag. My appetite decreased, and I was easily irritated. There were issues on my mind other than sex, and although I had developed some genuine affection for Senta, somehow this girlish fling was beginning to seem like just exactly that. Something had to change, and something did: like a deus ex machina, Ciro reappeared.

I can't say Ciro's arrival was entirely unexpected, although Senta hadn't spoken about him for a week or so. But one evening I came out of Casa Caccini to find them pacing about in the street. Or rather Senta was pacing, Ciro was lounging coyly against a No Parking sign, a colorful wool scarf draped around his neck against the evening chill. He was an attractive man, and knew it, and took special care of his luxurious head of wavy hair. So far I had seen him use two different types of comb and one little brush with a bone handle.

He put his arm around Senta's shoulder, and then mine, and led us off toward the Etruscan Arch and up Via Rocchi. "Ah, me," he observed cheerfully. "Let us leave this place. I have two beautiful women to take to dinner."

I'd had no time at all to exchange a glance with Senta, and we joined the passeggiata without speaking. He eventually steered us toward an outdoor table at the Lunabar Ferrari and went off to get us something to drink.

"What a surprise," I said to Senta. "What does he want?"

She shrugged. "Don't know. I went out to buy a bottle of wine, and when I came back he was in the salotto with Signora Martinelli telling her a sad story about the death of his sister, who, by the way, is very much alive. The signora now wants to adopt him."

"He does have charm."

"He wants to take us to dinner."

"So he said. Is this part of another plan?"

She turned her head aside.

"Did you call him?" I asked her.

"I may have."

"Why? Do you need to be rescued again?"

"He wants to take us to Sóle. Let's get one good meal out of him, at least."

I wasn't really concerned, but I was certainly curious. I leaned back and watched the parade of people in the street. "You might as well tell me what you have in mind," I said after a while.

"I called him because I felt the ground falling away under me. I called him because I got an email from Syracuse; they want written reports about what I'm doing. I called him because I let you read my novel. I called him because I think I love you. I called him because there's no room for me in your life here."

"You called him because you're too young for me," I said. Before I could explain, Ciro was back with a tray of everything I had no immediate desire to drink. Some small bottles of warm Campari soda, two shakeratos, a small carafe of red wine, and a tall glass of beer.

"*Ecco,*" he said proudly. "Dig out."

"Dig in," I corrected him. "Thank you."

"*Oddio,*" he said to Senta. "*Cara,* you cry." He wiped her cheek with his thumb, then turned to me. "What have you said?"

"Are you really taking us for dinner at Sóle?" I asked him. I finally poured some Campari into a glass and took a drink.

"I won a lottery," he said with a smile. "Back in Napoli. You will have everything on the menu tonight, if you wish."

The prospect of a meal at Sóle was tantalizing, but I didn't see the evening ending in any sort of satisfying way. If Ciro had won Signora Martinelli's maternal heart, he would certainly be allowed a bed in her house. Whether he had additional plans for me, or for me and Senta, I could not guess. I think I knew now that Senta was not strong enough to turn him down, and I didn't at this moment have the inclination to persuade her to stay. She had been an intense, and very pleasurable, physical exercise for me. That might sound unfeeling, but in fact I would be sorry to see it end.

I leaned down and gave Senta a long kiss. "I'm going now," I said.

"You're not coming to eat?"

"I've got some work to catch up on." I could see tears in her eyes. "Don't worry," I said. "You've got a plan. Stick to it." I ruffled her hair with what I hoped was an affectionate touch.

Ciro, for once, was speechless. So I kissed him too. For some reason, that made me feel better.

Six

I missed Senta, but not all the time. I missed her as if I had misplaced something—a book or a ring of keys. Something was missing. And she was definitely gone. I've never been good at self-analysis, but I did attempt to figure out exactly why I'd allowed myself to become involved with her—or perhaps diverted—but my behavior had not been so unusual, so I simply let it go. What did remain nagging at my mind was the thought that somewhere in me a story was developing, and when the time was right, it would emerge. Gail called this a "passive excuse for delay"—among other things—but she was losing patience and reminded me that I was not on vacation, and that if this opera production should collapse completely—and this was a real possibility—so would any story in the pot I seemed to be idly stirring.

Meanwhile, the weather turned progressively colder, the rains came and went, and the food in some of the cheaper trattorias became less identifiable and tasted foully of game.

I began to take late-night walks, following the route I had habitually used to return to Casa Caccini from Senta's room, and occasionally spotted the contessa walking her dogs through Piazza IV November. I was sitting on the steps of the cathedral one night when one of her dogs broke from his leash, dashed over to me, and bit me on my right calf. I didn't think it was a deep bite, but it startled me. My relationships with animals had always been friendly ones. When I looked at my leg, however, I saw that my pants were torn and wet with blood.

With a great shout, the contessa rushed to my side and grabbed her dog by his collar. I took some Kleenex from my pocket and attempted to staunch the bleeding, while she bent her full frame over me and examined my leg. "I cannot explain this," she said. "You have my deep apology. Are you badly hurt?"

"I don't think so," I said, glancing up at her. I was sitting toward the end of the steps in a dim pool of light thrown from a jewelry shop window across the street. "The bleeding may be slowing up."

She turned to settle the dogs. The culprit lay down at her feet with a chagrined look and put his muzzle between his paws. "The dogs are not sick," she assured me. "They have their vaccines."

"They look very happy," I said, rising shakily. "I just need to clean off the bite and put some medication on it." My leg was beginning to throb.

"How is it?" she asked me. "Can you walk?"

I took a few steps and figured I could make it down the hill. "Yes, I think so."

"I cannot explain this. Federico is without evil thoughts." She watched me as I took several hesitant steps toward the fountain. "Do you have a distance to go, signora, to return to your house?"

I shook my head. "Not far. Down Via Rocchi a bit."

I had now moved back toward the jewelry store window and was walking up and down in front of it. She moved in front of me to block my path. "Signora, my name is Renata Grillo, and my house is in Via Bontempi. Quite nearby." She yanked on the dog leashes. "You must come home with me for a small drink of something, as apology. Also, my friend is there. She is a doctor, and I will ask her to see to this wound."

I smiled. "Thanks, but no need for that." I bent down and patted the head of the guilty canine.

"I must insist. It is only a short distance, and I, of course, am responsible for this accident."

I reconsidered. "All right. But it's very late."

"No one in my house will be asleep except the cook, and we will not need her." She turned, her long skirts moving airily about her, and allowed the dogs to pull her back toward Piazza Danti. I followed, limping only slightly. We moved up into the darkness of Via Bontempi, which was lit by an occasional streetlight and a series of somewhat brighter bulbs that swung from a wire above the center of the street. Along the way flickering candles in votive niches served to intensify the darkness. At Arco dei Gigli, where Via Bontempi becomes Via del Roscetto, the paved street morphed into broad descending steps, and when I realized there was no longer any movement ahead of me, I stopped. I could hear nothing except some faint music from a window beyond the arch.

"Sssst! Signora! Here! *Vieni!*" I wheeled about to see her silhouetted in an open doorway. The interior light was so very dim that it only served to confound my senses. Was the hall lit at all? But once I was inside and had shut the heavy door behind me, my eyes adjusted, and I saw a couple of Vespas and a wheelbarrow parked to the side of the stairs. The contessa was already on her way up, presumably aiming for a distant apartment, and the clanking of the dog leashes and the sound of her rustling skirts were quickly receding. As I started up the stairs, my leg began to throb again, and I felt fresh dampness on the leg of my pants that I hoped was not more blood. As I climbed, the light became a bit brighter and the air perceptively fresher, and on the fourth floor landing I found myself catching my breath in a covered loggia, which gave out onto darkened rooftops below. In the distance I could hear cars on the *raccordo*, the superstrada that bypassed the city on the south. It was a familiar view, close to the one Senta and I had often watched from her room, but from a different angle. The stars were brilliant, and the air was crisp and smelled of fallen leaves.

"Signora." The contessa spoke from within a doorway on my left. "It is here." She stepped onto the loggia and stood beside me. "Beautiful, no?"

I nodded.

"In Perugia one must live high up. Above the jumble. The town carries you along then on its shoulders." A dog barked from somewhere within. "Come in. I welcome you."

We entered a lengthy hallway that led through darkness toward a lighted room. The dogs had already begun to trot toward it, their nails clicking on the tiles. From within the room came the sound of a piano. She shut the door behind me and hung the dog leashes somewhere to the side. I followed her down the hall and into a spacious drawing room, squinting against the light.

"Margit! Margit!" the contessa called. The music continued, but it was not the woman called Margit who was playing. The contessa indicated a colorful brocaded chair that sat under a lamp. "Sit, sit," she said to me. "Margit! We need you here." I observed movement from around a corner in another part of the room, which I now determined was L-shaped, and from within a haze of smoke, Margit emerged. Although her face appeared flushed, she had the same look of exhaustion about her that I had observed in front of the Hotel Brufani. She carried a cigarette between her fingers. A sweater was thrown over her shoulders.

"Margit, there you are. Margit, this is Signora ..." She glanced at me. I had not given her my name.

"I'm Allyn," I said. "Allyn Crosbie."

"Yes, Signora Crosbie. In the piazza, Federico, for unknown reasons, chose to attack Signora Crosbie's leg."

"It wasn't really an attack," I protested.

"I wonder if you could examine this injury and tell us what the damage is." Following Margit's gaze, I saw that the contessa was busy behind me and turned to see her ushering the dogs through some double doors onto a terrace. "Meanwhile, I will bring a restorative drink."

"Is it serious, this bite?" Margit spoke in a surprisingly soft voice. She extinguished her cigarette in a Deruta ashtray decorated with blue and red birds.

"I don't think so." I shook my leg. "Just a bit sore now." The piano music had continued more softly from a far corner of the room.

"I'll get my kit and wash my hands. We'll take a look. One moment."

"Is there something that would please you?" the contessa asked me. "A brandy, perhaps?"

"Anything would be fine."

She disappeared through yet another door.

I took a deep breath of the night air that was drifting in from the terrace and settled back to listen to the music, which now seemed to be approaching a heady climax. The pianist was attacking the keys as if he were in graceful combat with the instrument. Despite the movement of his arms and hands, his head remained perfectly still, his back straight. He seemed to be whispering to himself, and as the crescendo concluded, he gave a quiet shout and threw one hand into the air. With his free hand he took a pencil from behind his ear and made some notes on a score, took a breath, and began a soft, downwardly sweeping phrase that seemed to be breathing in small waves, which were followed by sweet, falling diminuendos that eventually trailed off into silence. When he stopped, I held my breath for some moments, afraid to break the spell that had settled in the room.

When he abruptly turned to face me, I think I gasped.

"It won't work," he said in English.

"Sorry," I said. "I'm catching my breath."

"So am I. Not in a good way." He removed his glasses and squinted at me. "Were you holding your breath?"

My leg gave a throb, and I resettled myself on the chair. "I sometimes stop breathing when I'm listening to music. Yours was actually breathing on its own. My breathing would have been, well, redundant."

He smiled at me. "I'll take that as a compliment." He took a thoughtful look at the score and touched it briefly with his hand. "I'm afraid the breathing you heard may have been a bit of a death rattle. This is part of an aria for soprano, but right now it's clumsy. Ungracious. She might as well be singing a grocery list. No one would believe her, not as it is." I heard a soft Scottish lilt in his voice.

"That music was meant to be sung, even as a grocery list. What text are you using?"

"Well, that's the problem, you see. For now, I'm trying to piece something together myself. I'm adapting a novella by William Trevor."

"You mean "*My House in Umbria?*" I asked. "It's a wonderful book. And you're turning it into an opera?"

"I'm trying. But I'm working backward. I don't have a real libretto yet, or even a librettist, and that's the wrong way to do it. The words should always come first. At the moment, I'm using random sections from the book in order to compose the music, and nothing fits." His finger struck one key, but then he decided to stand up. "You're nice to like the music, though." He was tall, maybe a bit younger than I had first thought, with light brown hair that was brushed back over his forehead. He had a sweet face and a strong jaw and a mouth that lifted into a boyish half-smile when he spoke.

He approached me now, rubbing his hands together in a friendly way.

"So it's to be an opera, then," I said. I was beginning to feel a little better. Finally—a live musician.

He looked down at me. "Well ... it's not grand enough to be called an *opera* opera, but I'm hoping it's a step above Shaftesbury Avenue." He laughed. "Pardon me. I have endless illusions. It's my first serious try in this form. Songs are what I usually write."

"You want to bounce *Phantom of the Opera* off its throne, then."

"Nay, not a chance. I write on a more intimate scale. More formal, maybe. Or I try. What I'm writing now is probably a chamber opera. I think of it in a much smaller venue, with a much smaller orchestra."

I was beginning to feel real pain in my leg again. "Well, you know what they say, it's the process that makes the difference."

"I know that's what they say, but it never helps much." He gazed up at the wall of books beside us. "I don't have any trouble writing songs. I can write them in my sleep. But now I'm having to think of drama. And musical progression that has to make sense in a plot!" He gritted his teeth and grinned. "I should have paid more attention during my conservatory days. Are you a musician? Or possibly a bloody critic?"

"I do write occasional reviews."

"Sorry. No offense meant."

"None taken. I write features—musical commentary, production histories, singers, stage directors, that kind of thing. But I'm a great opera fan, and I like musical theater too, for that matter. When I was in grad school, I supported myself as a supernumerary for a while."

"A super! That must have been fun."

"It was. Tell me, what do you know about the opera company in Perugia?"

Margit chose that moment to return with her medical bag. "Vincenzo, let me attend to my patient here. Federico attacked her by the fountain. Renata brought her home." My attempt to argue with the word "attack" was again dismissed, and she went on. "Place your injured leg on the footstool there, signora. And turn your trouser up." The pianist came closer and watched with some puzzlement. "This is Signora Crosbie, Vincenzo. Signora, this is Vincent Norrie, a friend. A Scottish person. He's tutoring at the conservatory and assisting at the theater." She removed some instruments from her bag.

"I'm Allyn Crosbie," I said, tightening my shoulders. Whatever she had begun to do to my leg was stinging, and tears had sprung into my eyes.

"That doesn't sound like Federico," Vincent said, settling down on his heels to watch what Margit was doing. "He's usually a calm fellow."

Margit finished cleaning my wound with great care and said, "Quite a lot of blood. But not too deep." One of the dogs sighed on the terrace, turned himself around, and lay back down. "You will feel more discomfort now," Margit said, and daubed something cold against the skin of my leg. I flinched and for the first time wished for the drink the contessa had left to find over half an hour ago.

"Does it need a stitch?" I asked her.

"Not at all." She finished bandaging my injured calf. "There," she said, rising to her feet. "That should do it." She handed me a tube with a German label and several small packages of wrapped gauze pads. "Clean it once a day. Afterward use the ointment, then put on a fresh pad." She gave me a little smile. "This adventure will leave no permanent damage."

"Well, thank you," I said.

"*Cattivo cane.*" She directed this remark toward the terrace, but she was still smiling a bit. Then, looking back at me, she continued. "Are you able to walk to your home?"

I stood up and paced around the room a bit. "I think so."

"I'll walk you, if you like," Vincent said. He was putting on a dark jacket that had been thrown over a chair.

Margit looked at him. "You are finished for the evening?"

He gathered his papers into a briefcase. "Yes. It's late and I'm stuck, so I'll leave it for now."

"Good." The contessa had permanently disappeared. As we walked down the hallway toward the door, Margit said, "We expect you on Saturday, Vincenzo. Do not forget." She turned to me and continued, "We are having a small dinner for some members of the production staff to discuss the spring opera at the Morlacchi. Saturday evening. Would you like to join us? As an additional apology for Federico's behavior."

I could hardly believe my good luck.

"Bring a guest, if you like," she added.

"I'd like to come," I said. "But I'll be alone."

"Saturday evening, then, any time after eight."

"I'm grateful for your ..."

She raised her hand. "It was nothing. I shall have a talk with the dogs."

She shut the door firmly behind us.

When we reached the street, there was a predawn stirring in the air, and although there was no sign of light, Via Bontempi no longer seemed so dark. Across the street a votive candle sputtered in a dim niche, and I went over to it and emptied away the liquid wax.

"You like to tend to the saints?" Vincent asked over my shoulder.

"I like to tend to the wax." We began to walk back down Via Bontempi toward the cathedral. "What part of Scotland are you from?"

"Edinburgh. The accent, right? I've spent some time abroad, so there are times when I think I've lost it. Your name has a Scottish background, doesn't it?"

"Crosbie? No, oddly enough. The spelling is English, according to my father. Crosby, he says, spelled with a *y*, is Irish."

"I might argue with him there."

"What can you tell me about this upcoming opera production?"

"Truth? It's like a rattling car full of Keystone Kops headed for the edge of a cliff."

I laughed. "Can you be more specific?"

"Not unless you have a couple of hours."

"Who's singing?"

"That's not the problem. Right now there's nothing much to sing. We've lost our original composer and our stage director is about to lose her mind."

"And the librettist ..."

"I really shouldn't be talking about DiBrufa. Why are you interested?"

"I'd like to interview him." I briefly explained my mission in Perugia.

We stopped at the edge of Piazza Danti. After a moment he said, "I'm not too comfortable talking about him. I can get you an interview with the stage director, if you like, she's a friend. I'm helping her out a bit with the production. She's the one to talk to, I think."

"Would that be Elaine Bishop?"

"Well, yes."

"Then wonderful, if you can arrange it. That would be very helpful."

We turned toward the top of Via Rocchi, which began its steep descent behind the cathedral. "So where are you from?" he asked as we began to descend the hill.

"From?"

"Where's your home in the States when you're not traveling about?"

"I'm not sure I have one. I went to school on the West Coast and lived in Boston once upon a time. But now I'm more used to hotel rooms or short-term rentals in all sorts of places."

"You and our stage director have something in common. She owns a condo in New York that she hasn't occupied in years."

As we passed through Piazza Ansidei, I said, "My door's just down there." Via Rocchi was very steep at this point, and my leg was beginning to hurt badly.

"Do you think you'll join this get-together on Saturday evening, then?" he asked.

"Maybe. I'll see how I feel."

"Well, that would be the place to meet some opera people."

Dawn had brightened the sky above the street. The early-morning air was cold, and he began to cough. His cough reminded me of one that had stubbornly remained with me after a bout with pneumonia several years ago. He struggled mightily for breath and just couldn't seem to catch it.

After a while he took out a handkerchief and wiped his face. "Sorry," he said, and made no further comment.

I took out my key.

He cleared his throat. "I hope you'll come," he said. "On Saturday."

"I used to dislike gatherings like that. Now I think I could use one."

It was growing lighter, and a Vespa sputtered to life across the street. "Good night," he said. "I hope to see you." He turned away and began a slow walk back up the hill.

I didn't know what to expect when I entered the apartment, but I spotted the signora immediately. She was asleep in her favorite television chair, her heating pad strapped tightly around her midsection. As I quietly entered my room, I remembered it was my day for a bath (we were allowed two full baths a week, prearranged), but I thought it would be best to wait until later in the day for that challenge.

Seven

By the weekend the weather had turned decisively toward late autumn. There had been occasional sprits of snow, but it was the wind that had become fiercer almost overnight and took one's breath away if you walked against it. On the night of the dinner, a blustery gale was sucking up the streets, pushing into the city's narrow alleys and courtyards. It leaned against wooden doors, wailed under window sills, and shook the glass fronts of bars and restaurants. Children shivered in their beds; men paced about inside their houses and went out. Women stood by the windows, grasping their elbows, watching for fires. The smell of wood smoke was everywhere, sharp in the chill of the air. As I entered Via Bontempi, a dog howled, maybe one of the contessa's on patrol? The sky was black, the stars like icy, gritted teeth.

Vincent had waited for me at the contessa's, and I was relieved to have him with me as we began to climb the stairs.

"I thought you might need a wee boost," he said.

"What should I expect?"

"It's just a collection of music people. No murderers or other evil sorts." Vincent was wearing a black leather jacket, and he'd taken some trouble with his hair, which looked recently trimmed. "You look fetching tonight," he said. "All in black."

"And you smell very ... Parisian," I said. "Nice."

"Well, you never know when you'll meet another love of your life."

The sounds of a gathering in progress were beginning to drift down the stairwell. As we arrived at the third floor landing, I stopped, alerted by the freshening night air from the loggia above.

He braced his arm against the plaster wall and held out his hand. "Come on," he said. "This is no time for cold feet. You need some contacts. Here's where to find them."

I started up the last flight of steps. "Just say you'll make sure I get home."

"Of course. But I've got someone I think you'll like to meet."

"Oh, please," I said. "Don't try to organize anything."

"Why would I want to do that?" He smiled.

"Will you be playing tonight?" I asked as we reached the top landing.

"I doubt it, unless it's something from the opera. Elaine's hired me on as a pro tem *répétiteur*."

We neared the apartment door, which stood slightly ajar, and Margit's face appeared out of the darkness, startling both of us. "Who is there?" she demanded.

"It's Vincenzo, Margit. And I've brought along Signora Crosbie, your patient."

"Well. I'm pleased to see you," she said, opening the door fully. "Do come in."

We headed down the hall toward the light and conversation, and as we entered the room, Margit took my arm and said,

"Forgive me, Vincenzo, but I must take Signora Crosbie aside to examine the dog wound. As you say, she is my patient. And it was my dog who bit her."

So Vincent and I were quickly separated, and I found myself in a pantry with Margit before I had time to get my bearings.

I had to remove my boot and one red sock for her to get a look at the bite, which was healing nicely, I thought. She agreed. "All right," she said. "I'll give you another tube of ointment before you leave. There may be a small scar, just a small one. I extend our apologies again."

"No need, but thank you," I said, pulling my sock back on.

At that moment a thunderous crash resonated from within the adjacent kitchen, and the sound of falling china shards followed.

"Excuse me," Margit said, "I must see to this." And she left me completely alone. In the pantry. I was briefly tempted to stay there and see what happened, but then the swinging door opened and a woman's face peered in. I recognized Elaine Bishop instantly.

"Margit?" she called.

I pointed toward the kitchen.

"Do you speak English?" she asked as she came in. "Are you part of the staff?"

"I speak English, and no, I am not staff."

"Well, maybe you can help me find some vodka. They're calling for vodka." She gave me a long, easy look. "Just hanging out in the pantry?" she asked. "In one red sock?"

I struggled with my boot and finally got it on. "I don't seem to be able to get out of here. Margit's in the kitchen. I have no idea where the liquor is."

From the kitchen Margit's voice could clearly be heard, berating some poor soul in both German and Italian, her invectives becoming louder with each exclamation.

"Well, hell," Elaine said. "I'm not going to bother her while *that's* going on." She leaned back against one of the cupboards. "Are you here with someone?"

And right on cue, the door swung open again and Vincent entered. "What's going on in here? Are you holding her hostage, Elaine?"

She laughed. "I was looking for vodka, but the lady in the red sock can't help me."

Vincent rummaged around in one of the cupboards and extracted a bottle of Stoli. "Well, I'm happy you've met," he said as he turned to face us.

"We haven't," Elaine and I replied in unison.

"Elaine Bishop." She extended her hand, which was cool and firm.

"Allyn Crosbie. And I'd love a drink. Anything at all."

"Elaine is—" Vincent began.

"So would I," Elaine interrupted. "And you shall have one. But let's get the vodka out there."

The guests were conversing in various groups and paid no attention to Vincent and me as we made our way across the room to an elaborately carved cherry table stocked with a mixed collection of wines and harder alcoholic beverages, *acqua minerale*, cut glass bowls of lemons and limes, and a container of ice. Standing alone in pride of place were several open bottles of Brunello.

"Do you see any prosecco?" I asked him.

"On the floor in its own cooling device. I'll have some too."

Drink in hand, I turned to face the room. Elaine had been waylaid by an older man with a pencil moustache and sad eyes, dressed in somber Armani, wool and silk, it looked like. I recognized him as Elaine's breakfast companion. Gazing up at him was a handsome dwarf. Or midget. A little person. In full formal attire. Elaine towered over him, clinging to the bottle of vodka as if it were a club, and he was keeping a careful eye on it. As I watched them, he and Elaine shared a joke and a laugh. The older man remained impassive.

I allowed myself a good look at Elaine, and she was easy to look at. Her face possessed some fascinating angles that seemed to change with every tilt of her head. Her eyes were soft but steady. I got the impression that if you were talking to her, she would give you her full attention. Her salt-and-pepper hair was cut in a short shag that she tossed out of her eyes from time to time as she continued her conversation with the two men.

I turned to Vincent and found him smiling. "Thought so," he said.

"What is the difference between a dwarf and a midget?" I asked him.

He tilted his head. "I believe a midget is a little person with so-called normal body proportions. With dwarfs there is some other genetic element involved. Maybe I'm wrong. Davide Della Bella, who's talking to Elaine there, is technically a midget, but don't call him that. The term is offensive these days."

"Why would I call him anything?" I said. "Who is he?"

"Davide is in charge of casting at La Scala. His mind is like a Rolodex; he can access details about conductors' neuroses, singers' temperaments, their failures, sexual preferences, production fiascos, design disasters—he holds mighty sway over who is hired for what. Right now, I'm afraid Elaine is going to clobber him with that bottle of Stoli she's swinging around." He paused and looked at me. "You want to know more about her?"

"Are you friends?"

"Old friends, from way back. Aha, here she comes."

I immediately said, "Excuse me, I haven't said hello to the contessa, and I don't want to be impolite. See you later."

Prosecco in hand, I made my way across the room to where the contessa was seated on a couch. She had gathered a small group around her, all of whom seemed to be talking quietly at the same time. But as I approached, she raised her head and smiled.

"Welcome, Signora Crosbie," she said. "I hope you're enjoying yourself."

"I am. Thank you for inviting me."

She didn't introduce the others, who had turned their attention to the words of a man in jeans and a short tunic, who was concluding, "… the betrayal of values, the lack of will, and a tendency to drift."

"How is your injury?" the contessa asked me.

"Healing well, thank you. Dr. … Margit took a look at it earlier."

"Fine, fine." She stood up. "I believe we need some music. I'll search for Vincenzo."

Once again I was alone. This is why I disliked large parties. Standing alone I felt like a lighthouse. At that moment I wished a "tendency to drift" was available to me.

A short, dark-eyed personage in glasses appeared at my elbow and stood looking at me for several long moments. "Do I know you?" I finally said in English.

"Well, you might," he replied with an Oxbridge intake of breath between his teeth. "I'm a tenor."

"I thought this was a production party," I said.

"I'm allowed to attend," he said archly. He lightly caressed his chin, which was attempting to produce what might become a goatee at some future date.

Piano music drifted our way, and I assumed the contessa had located Vincent.

He looked around. "When do you think we'll eat? I'm starving."

I finished off the last of my prosecco. "Don't know." I held up my empty glass. "I think I need more of this."

"I'm Atticus Griest." He didn't wait for me to offer my name but went on. "They may ask me to perform later. Maybe. I'm trying to decide what to sing, if Elaine will let me. But I must have food. And very soon."

I turned to face him. "Elaine?"

"Yes, Elaine Bishop, our stage director. She's a demon."

"A demon, you say. Really?"

"Do you live here? Are you part of the management?"

"I'm interested in this opera. Who's the composer?"

"Well, the original composer withdrew. He and the librettist had some issues. We're rehearsing with some version of his original score, but the libretto seems to change from day to day. It's all a bit odd."

"In what way?"

"I'm not sure what it's about. The libretto was originally by ..."

"Piero DiBrufa."

He looked at me in surprise. "Yes. Who is this chap? What is his power? Elaine's supposed to be running this show. But it seems quite out of control."

I excused myself again and headed for the alcohol table. I ran directly into Elaine and the Armani man, who were attempting to make themselves martinis.

Elaine turned as I reached for the prosecco. "Hello again," she said. "Sandro, here, turn around. Sandro Colonna, meet Allyn, a friend of Vincent's. Sandro is our company's managing director."

Sandro bent and kissed my hand, and Elaine smiled at me over his head. When he straightened up and looked at me, I thought of a wounded animal waiting to be overtaken by a forest fire. "I see you've been talking with Atticus Griest," Elaine said to me as she screwed the cap back on the gin bottle.

"Your tenor."

"Not *my* tenor, not in any way. His role is minor. I have no idea what he's doing here."

Sandro's eyes were wandering about the room, but he didn't seem to be looking for anything in particular.

"Was he complaining about the production?" she asked.

"He thinks it's out of control."

"It is."

"I heard there were some problems with the DiBrufa libretto."

"Well," she tilted her head, "that continues to be true."

"His poetry has a fine reputation, doesn't it?"

"Yes, but he has no experience in writing librettos. Writing librettos is a collaborative enterprise. It's not something you do alone in a garret with a candle by your bed. He drove the original composer away. We're trying to find someone to rework the score, but I'm not hopeful." She shrugged. "It's a mess."

"Isn't it unusual for the librettist to have such clout?"

"In this particular situation, there are other powers at work. I've been thinking of removing myself from the whole thing. More frequently, in fact, during the past ten days." Then, with a little cry, she said, "Sandro! Please!" Tears were rolling down Sandro's cheeks. Elaine wasn't carrying a purse, but she was rummaging around in her pockets for a handkerchief. I grabbed a handful of paper napkins and thrust them into her hands, and she dabbed at his cheeks and neck. "Come now," she said to him.

"She's dying," he said. "Dying."

At that moment the contessa appeared in the doorway to an adjoining room. "*A tavola tutti!*" she announced.

The contessa had carefully seated us, placing me on Margit's right, with Vincent on my other side. I relaxed a bit. Sandro was seated on Margit's left; he was holding two glasses and drinking out of both. Elaine was at the other end of the table, next to the contessa. Across from Elaine several pillows had been placed on a chair and Davide Della Bella had nimbly climbed up. There were twelve of us.

We began with a thin pasta with truffles and porcini in a light cream sauce. I could happily have eaten two plates of that and gone home, but we still had the *porchetta* to deal with. Or so Vincent had told me.

Sandro pushed his pasta plate away untouched and got up to refill one of his glasses—he seemed to be eschewing wine—simultaneously with the entrance of the pork, which was carried in on a silver platter and daintily decorated with parsley and flowers.

Poor thing, I thought.

I turned to Vincent and asked, "Do you know Sandro?"

"Sandro Colonna? Of course. Managing director. He's across from us there."

"He seems to be drinking his dinner. And he's constantly in tears."

"His mother is dying."

"Should we do something?"

"Elaine looks out for him."

"That tenor, Atticus, told me Elaine was a demon."

Vincent gave a little laugh. "Well, yes, she almost has to be, given her job. But she's a demon with a sentimental soul and a brilliant knack for creating innovative productions."

The pork was carved and distributed, and the *contorni* were delivered. We all, save Sandro, fell to our food. The pork was strongly flavored, and I carefully cut my pieces into little bites. I'm usually quite fond of *porchetta* when I can buy it still warm from a roadside truck, on a soft bun that has absorbed its juices and little bits of its crust. A formal presentation like this seemed to bring forth some of the gaminess of its recent past. Out of the corner of my eye, I saw Sandro's full plate, his knife and fork lying beside it.

"Oh, please!" Atticus exclaimed from farther down the table.

"Hell's teeth," Vincent swore quietly. Then more loudly, "Let it rest, mate."

The contessa and Margit exchanged a calm glance.

Sandro set down one of his glasses with great force, and a circle of lime flew out and settled like a transparent coin in the middle of the tablecloth.

"Could someone pass along those lovely beans please?" Elaine said.

Della Bella wiped his lips. "Is there more *porchetta* carved?"

Sandro drained his second glass, and the salads arrived.

"*La morte di Caravaggio* had a mixed reception in New York, that's true," Elaine said, in response to a comment from someone on her right. "There's no need to go over it again, Signor Guzman. I'm sure it's not of general interest."

Signor Guzman threw his arms wide. "Of course it is! We are patrons of this production you're staging here. And anxious about its fate. The professional history of our esteemed stage director has everything to do with its success." He clasped his hands before him in a gesture of sincerity.

Elaine now looked a little sick, and I had a momentary urge to interrupt. But she was holding her ground. "It's ancient history now," she said firmly. "Ancient history. Let's move on."

"But were the critics wrong?" Della Bella inquired. "Just as a point of interest, Elaine. Critics can be so unfair." He was holding his fork upright beside his head.

Elaine sat back in her chair and took a sip of wine. "*Caravaggio* collapsed because it had no musical or dramatic center. Or if it was there, Maestro Fracci wouldn't allow me to discover it. I had to make some decisions on my own, and they weren't always the best ones. You can place the responsibility wherever you choose." She stood up. "Excuse me," she said, and left the room.

"As I thought, the fault was with the composer," Della Bella said. "She's had a run of bad luck. Now she's wrestling with this idiot DiBrufa, who seems to be a resident of another planet. If she's trying to get her career back on the rails, this is not the way to do it." He slid off his pillows to the floor. "I'll go and find her."

The contessa reached down and put her hand on his shoulder. "No, Davide, leave her in peace. She will return." She patted the pillows. "Come and eat your salad."

I turned to Vincent. "Will she be all right?"

"Yes. She knew this was coming; she's been through it all before. Sandro should have backed her up."

Sandro was sitting across from us, glassy-eyed, his uneaten food before him.

While the salad plates were being removed, I excused myself and went to look for her. I found her on the terrace with the dogs.

"You discovered my hideout," she said, her hands on the terrace railing. The night had grown colder. The streetlights below lay in pleasant urban patterns, and a half moon was beginning to appear behind the mountains east of Assisi. I wished for my jacket, which had disappeared into some other part of the house.

"I don't mean to intrude."

"You're not intruding. I'm just cooling down."

The dogs turned in their beds and sighed.

"One of those dogs bit me," I said, because I felt some conversation should begin.

"The darker one can be mean."

"Your friend Sandro seems to be in trouble."

"His mother is dying. And she's taking her time about it. I'm not sure what anyone can do about that. I thought tonight might be a diversion for him."

Behind us the guests had left the dining table and were reassembling in the larger salotto, accompanied by the fragrant aroma of very good coffee.

"Maybe some coffee would help."

"Coffee as an antidote to drunkenness is a myth," she said, and turned to face me. "But it might be a good idea to get him out of here. Why are you concerned?"

"He looks unhappy."

"He is unhappy."

We stood and looked at each other for a few moments, not speaking. Then as she moved her head, I breathed in a light, complicated whiff of her scent: citrus, lavender, sandalwood. I couldn't put my finger on it. My nose was born unusually sensitive to scents, from food, weather, or more subtle human aromas, a weakness that has led me into both trouble and delight. I now looked at Elaine with growing interest.

She had returned her gaze to the lights below us in the valley. "What did you make of that conversation at the table?"

I took a small step away from her. "I thought it was a little nasty."

"That New York disaster follows me around like a dream I can't wake up from."

"I don't know anything about the situation, of course."

"No, why would you?" She paused. "You're not from the musical world, then."

"Well, I write about it."

"You're a critic? Please say no. And forget everything I said about DiBrufa."

"Occasionally I'll review a performance. But nothing that would affect any careers. I write features, about productions mostly, and the people who put productions together. The inner workings. I'm trying to get an interview with DiBrufa, as a matter of fact. As part of a longer piece." I paused for a moment. "And Vincent's suggested I might approach you. For a different point of view."

"Have you tried to contact DiBrufa?"

"I met with his sister. Once."

"Monica? And how did that go?"

"Not well."

She laughed. "No need to explain that."

"What's the problem with his libretto?" I asked. "And don't worry. We're off the record."

"I don't think he ever conceived of his poems as a libretto. My hunch is that Monica put the idea into his head. Most of the poetry in *Sirius* follows along in a sort of narrative, more or less like Shakespeare's sonnets, but it doesn't stand up well to being manipulated into anything operatic. Our original composer has withdrawn, after struggling on his own to write some music that would make sense out of what Piero had sent him. He told me to burn his score, but I'm not inclined to do that. He did the best he could with what he had to work with." She stopped and returned both hands to the terrace railing. "God, I'm tired."

"Sounds like you're fighting a couple of different battles."

"Usually I don't mind that. Keeps me on point." She thought for a moment. "Wait a minute. Did you write that piece in *Opera World* about the Fenice opera house fire some years back?"

I nodded. "Yes. But please don't tell anyone here."

"I certainly won't. You took quite an unpopular stand. How in the world did you find your way to this gathering?"

"I came with Vincent. And I've been studying some of DiBrufa's poetry on my own. He's not a bad poet, much to my surprise. Italo Montecalvo thinks I ought to take another run at him."

"Italo's involved?"

"You know him?"

"Italo knows everyone in the city."

"I'm beginning to see that. Well, if it doesn't work, I can always go back to basic travel writing. That's how I support myself. The music is just something I love."

"Yes, in this case it probably would be more productive to write about someplace like the Eastern Desert or lively nights in Rio."

"Maybe. But it's getting interesting here. Yesterday I didn't know anyone's story. Today everyone seems to have one."

"The stories may all evaporate, you know."

"I know. But I'd certainly like to have your point of view. Anything—production, singers, even your lost composer. You wouldn't have to dwell on DiBrufa."

I saw she was shaking her head. "Too late for that," she said. "Anyway, I'm not inclined to do interviews at this point in my life."

"So you'd send me off to the Eastern Desert?" I smiled at her.

She smiled too. After a moment she said, "You're lucky. I don't have the option of retreating to the desert. I have to make this opera *work* somehow or see my career take another hit." She was about to say something further, but at that moment Margit appeared at the terrace door.

"There is coffee ready if you like. And Elaine, Della Bella is searching for you. I believe he wishes to apologize. Signor Colonna—well, I believe you must come inside. He needs coffee, and he won't take it from me."

"I'll be right there." She removed some keys from her pocket. "How would you feel about going with Vincent to take Sandro home?" she asked me. "I think it will take two people. I have keys to his car."

"Fine."

"Vincent knows how to get to his villa. Drop Sandro off, bring the car back to Perugia, and I'll retrieve the keys from Vincent at the theater. I'd go, you see, but I think I should stay here and mend some fences."

"How will you get home?"

"Someone will give me a lift, but I'll probably just walk. My apartment is right below Piazza Partigiani. Not too far. I'll go in and organize Sandro and Vincent." She started to go in but turned back toward me. "Are you always called Allyn?"

"I'm called Ally by some."

"Those who know you well, I suppose." She lifted her chin and a medallion at her throat caught the light from the interior of the room. "You're very observant, Allyn, if I don't miss my mark. Thanks for listening. I hope I see you again."

I followed her inside and went in search of my jacket.

"Thank God, thank God," Vincent said on the steps down. We were supporting Sandro between us. "Atticus is preparing to sing. We're saved."

Sandro was humming. I didn't believe he had any idea where he was or where he was being taken. In the street we began a slow procession up Via Bontempi toward the duomo. "There's a garage up here where Sandro leaves his car," Vincent said.

"Who?" Sandro asked.

"It's Vincent, laddie. And with us is the Virgin Mary. We're going to take you home."

In the distance the Priori bells struck one thirty.

"Where does he live?" I said.

Sandro stumbled on a stone in the street. "Mind your step," Vincent said. "Hold his arm a bit tighter, Allyn. He lives west of the city, on the way to Corciano. Big villa."

"Big villa," Sandro echoed.

We sped down the hill through the night streets, nearly empty now. Sandro snored quietly in the backseat. The entire interior of the car was filled with the fumes of alcohol, more like grain alcohol.

"Elaine said you knew the way," I said.

"I've been there before. Never driven it, though. We may end up in Siena."

There was still a surprising amount of activity on the *raccordo* highway, and we nearly missed the turnoff for Corciano, but eventually Vincent swung us into a long, gravel lane with fields in the darkness on either side and pulled up into the rear parking area of Sandro's villa. I assumed it was large, although most of it was in darkness above us. Sandro was beginning to recover and managed to give us emotional embraces as we delivered him to his housekeeper, who helped him inside, took the car keys, and shut the door firmly in our faces.

We looked at each other. Vincent rang the bell once more,

then knocked, and with that, the lights on either side of the door were extinguished.

"Well," he said.

"Yes, well," I responded. "Why didn't you leave the keys in the car?"

"Habit."

"Okay, what now? Does Sandro have bikes stashed anywhere?"

"Care for a walk?"

"Back to the city? How long would that take?"

"I know some back ways," he said. "Probably two hours, maybe a little less. Are you game for that? There's a half moon up."

"Do we have a choice? If you have your *telefonino*, we could call a cab. I don't have mine with me."

"Radio Taxi wouldn't come out here at this hour."

"All right, then," I said.

For a while we walked along in silence. I was finding it impossible to believe that Vincent actually wanted us to walk back to Perugia, the lights of which—as far as I could see—were not visible anywhere on the horizon. Finally I said, "Maybe some farmer will come along and give us a ride. A farmer, or anyone."

"It's Sunday now, there won't be farmers."

"What time is it?"

He was able to check his watch by the light of the moon, which was now high in the sky. "Three or after," he said.

It was beginning to get colder, and a damp mist was rising from the land around us. The wind came in chilly fits and starts, and my jacket was not keeping me warm. Vincent had turned up his collar.

"What grows here?" I asked him, as the road began to rise.

"I was surprised to run across some tobacco fields around

here once. In the spring there are glorious poppies everywhere." He pointed at the hill to the right. "Olives up there, I think. And there are always vineyards. I think Sandro rents his land out to what are called tenant farmers in Scotland. He doesn't care about tending the land himself, but he makes money from his olive oil."

"Is his mother really dying?"

He nodded in the dark. "She's ancient, but he's lived with her all his life."

"What was this *Caravaggio* opera thing all about?"

"Well, there are different opinions, as you probably noticed. Last year City Opera in New York convinced Elaine to step in and stage the premiere production of Edgardo Fracci's *La morte di Caravaggio*. You heard of Fracci? If you haven't, you'll get an earful if you mention his name to her. But she couldn't resist the challenge, even though the company was on its last legs at that point."

"I think I remember reading about this controversy. What happened?"

"It's a long story. And not very pleasant. I'll tell you sometime."

"Seems like any opera called *The Death of Caravaggio* would be an instant hit."

"You'd think that. But other forces were at play."

"You were there?"

"I offered to help her out, and eventually she took me on as her *répétiteur*. Not that there was anything consistent to rehearse." He began to cough again, and I decided not to push him further. I got the picture.

He was panting a little as we reached the crest of the hill.

"Want to stop?" I asked him.

"Not yet." He put his hands in his pockets as we began to

descend the hill. It was then that I spotted the lights of Perugia in the distance, or at least the lights from the campanile of San Domenico or San Pietro's steeple.

I pointed. "We might make it after all."

Around us the fog was growing denser. He took several deep breaths and shivered a little. As we passed in and out of fading moonlight, the fog climbed higher around us, and eventually the moon disappeared. Dimly, through the murk, the lights of a farmhouse appeared at a near distance, and we heard music and faint laughter.

"Want to stop?" I asked him again. "They might have a car."

We were approaching a stone bridge arched over a small stream, and his breathing had become more labored. "I'd rather just rest for a few minutes. I know exactly where we are. There's a little village up ahead where there's probably a phone at the police station. If it's open."

We leaned over the bridge and watched the water, which was moving rapidly along in a frigid tumble. Vincent was close to me, and I felt him shaking. I put my arm around him and drew him closer, although I wasn't much warmer.

He cleared his throat. "Sorry you got pulled into this."

"Oh, it's an adventure."

He turned and looked at me, then averted his head and coughed into his handkerchief.

"That's getting worse," I said.

He wiped his face and leaned back against the stone wall of the bridge.

"Well, here's something different to ponder. Since you've been doing some reading on DiBrufa, how would you feel about taking a look at his libretto for Elaine's opera? You might be able to give her some suggestions about how it might be made more ...

comprehensible. Just an informal opinion, of course. I think she might appreciate a bit of help."

"Well, it's nice of you to ask, I suppose, but I've got my own project on my plate. Besides, I'm not that familiar with him."

"Can you read music?"

"I can follow a score. But I know nothing at all about writing librettos."

"That's not important. But she's desperate to reshape the opera as much as she can. I just thought you might be able to open a few windows into DiBrufa's poetic state of mind. If that's possible. But we can drop it, if you'd rather."

"What's the name of this thing again?"

"*Sirius.*"

"The Dog Star?"

"The brightest star in the night sky." The moon had reappeared, and he held my arm more tightly. "It's getting colder. We'd better keep walking," he said.

"What's your history with Elaine?" I asked him. "Just out of curiosity."

"Friends. Good friends. She gave me work when I was struggling in New York. She put food on my table and made sure my rent got paid. When my friend Rob died, we got through that together. After he was gone, I just pulled in on myself for a while. No people, mostly oatmeal and lager in my larder, binge TV, the sort of life that makes all things gray. I slept, reread the Brontës, and didn't work on my music for almost six months. I lived in a shameful old bathrobe. She kept an eye on me, just to be sure I didn't jump out a window. Brought me flowers once a week. And an occasional hamburger." He paused. "That's the simple version."

"Did she bring you to Perugia with her?"

"Aye, at gunpoint," he said with a little smile. He freed himself from my arm. “Come on, let’s do this final stretch of road and get to our own beds.”

The village ahead was drenched in sleep, and we almost stumbled over the echoes of our own footsteps. A dog barked once. The little building that served as a police station was closed up tight, and there was no public phone anywhere in sight. But miraculously, an old rattling pickup appeared behind us, and Vincent flagged it down. We climbed into the rear, which was half-filled with hay, and leaned our backs against the cab, happy to get off our feet.

Then, after a while, exhaustion, the chilly night, or some other inevitability moved us closer. I think it surprised us at first, but we fit comfortably together, and I put my face against his shoulder and inhaled the traces of his cologne, now combined with steely traces of cold night air. I moved my cheek against the soft stubble of his chin and immediately thought of welts, the signora, and then of course, Senta. (Where was she now?) He turned to face me and pulled me closer to him, and for an instant I thought he was going to kiss me. At that moment, in fact, I wanted him to. But he didn’t; he just let his cheek rest against mine for a few moments, then pulled away.

“Best not,” he said.

So my body relaxed against the contours of his chest. I could feel him trembling and couldn’t guess whether it was from cold or desire—or fear. But he felt good, and we both began to warm up.

“I was married once,” he said after a little while.

“Really?” I smiled into the darkness.

“To a woman. Don’t laugh. I was young, and blissfully naïve, and had no idea at all about what to do with my talents, or if I had any. I studied piano and composition at the conservatory in Glasgow, and after that I went off to the continent for a while.

But I never seemed to click with any particular teacher. Instead I had some adventures, tried to lose my innocence, and actually did that bit quite well. Finally I met an American in London who recommended Sibylle Heilemann at the Peabody Institute in Baltimore. Are you familiar with her?"

"No."

"I'd never heard of Baltimore in my life. But we were a perfect fit, despite the fact that I was twenty-six and she was nearly sixty-eight. But she knew exactly how to bring me along. She found my métier: songs. She taught me how to write music in my own way."

"Lucky you."

"I was lucky." He gathered me a little closer.

"So then what?"

"So then she fell in love with me."

I laughed. "There's always a catch, right?"

"More than one catch in this case. I was terrified I'd lose her as a teacher, and I was also finally beginning to accept the fact that I was gay, which at that time scared me almost as much." He coughed a little and got his handkerchief out. "So I married her—which made both of her children furious and horrified her legions of lifelong friends. If I hadn't had my work, my songs, I probably would have jumped off a bridge. But she was the perfect hiding place. Not very courageous, I guess."

"Well," I said, "I'm sure you learned a lot."

"I did learn a lot. When I'm composing, she's very much present in everything I write. We stayed friends until she died. She introduced me to Elaine, who helped both of us adjust after I met Rob and decided to join him in New York. And again after he died."

"So you're a widower."

"I am indeed a widower. Twice over." After a moment he said, "Sorry. I have no idea why I told you all of that. But telling tales keeps you warm, my mum used to say."

"She's right. Interesting life you've led, though."

"We should rest," he said.

We settled down into the hay and his trembling abated. He was warm now, almost feverish. But it was comfortable lying there, close to his body, as if we knew something more could happen, but also that it wouldn't. And I dozed off.

The driver woke us just after dawn and dropped us at the station as the early shuttle from Terontola was pulling in. We had cappuccinos there and picked the hay out of each other's hair with great care. We were stiff and tired, and I felt the dampness would never leave my lungs. We drank our coffee slowly and met each other's gaze only once or twice, by friendly accident. But it was peaceful: we were alone in the station bar except for the stationmaster and a few baggage men.

"I'll call Elaine later today," he said. "So she doesn't think we've run off with Sandro's car."

"Would she?"

"Would you like to see Elaine again?"

"I'd like to see you both again."

Then he finally leaned across the table and kissed me. And it was not a quick peck.

Eventually we caught a bus and rode up toward the center of the city just as the first bells were sounding. He touched me on the shoulder and got off at Tre Archi, and I rode on to the top of the hill as if I were dreaming.

Eight

Now the city truly began to be pulled toward winter. The heavy rains came, then occasionally turned to light snow, and from within whatever tiny cupboards they had been hiding, the miniature plows appeared to clear the narrow streets and broad piazzas. Tourists who were left in the city watched the plow drivers work as if they were elves. The statues in the gardens in the upper town became frosted figurines, and the steep streets were often covered in lethal ice and dangerous to navigate by car or on foot. Thick, bulky scarves were the order of the day, and classy boots began to appear during the passeggiata, which continued as usual, with frequent stops for a *caffè corretto* or a grappa along the corso.

I had managed to pull together a rough draft about the history of Perugia and its various residents: informative but not terribly inspired. And Vincent, nursing a heavy cold, had given me a little lecture about the opera company and its current woes during a light lunch we shared the week after our night hike back from Renato's. But none of it had any meat on its bones. Without personal revelations from Piero DiBrufa and whatever operatic details I might manage to extract from Elaine, my essay would definitely lack the musical focus that usually characterized my writing. Gail Graham immediately rejected it, even in its preliminary form.

Although expected, her reaction was a bit of a blow, because it meant she would likely be pulling me off this assignment very soon. Not a good thing. I was becoming quite content in Perugia and adjusting quite well to the first conventional routine I'd kept to in a long time. I was living a life! In a city I was coming to know. And like. My living quarters were comfortable, I'd made a few friends—close friends, like Vincent, and the unsettling Elaine, who was not quite in focus but held some promise. At least in my imagination.

I was a bit haunted by the specter of unfinished business, however, and after an unproductive afternoon in front of the computer and a number of trips into the kitchen for coffee, Signora Caccini gave me an assignment—probably just to get my brooding personage out of her house.

"Signora Ally, if you will, please go to the bar down near the arch and buy some gelato for my girls. *Cioccolato.*" She handed me some euros. "I would be grateful."

I bundled up and dashed into the street. Unfortunately, I lost my footing on the ice almost immediately, and began to slide down Via Rocchi wheeling my arms and legs like a pinwheel. Some kind patrons about to enter the Bar Etrusco managed to stop my Olympic descent, but not before my head had made hard contact with the protruding bumper of a nearby parked Fiat. I was given ice and a wet napkin for the bloody cut on my forehead while the bartender called a Radio Taxi, which eventually made its perilous way down the street and picked me up. We then shot off into the night toward the *policlinico* at Monteluce, which was the nearest *pronto soccorso,* or emergency room. I was placed in a wheelchair, given a temporary bandage, and rolled into a corner. A male nurse in blue scrubs took my passport (which I always carried, for better or worse), and I peered out from under my bandage as he copied its details on an ancient machine. I'm very nervous when I'm separated from my passport, so I frowned when I saw a blurry figure remove it from the nurse's hands. Soon Vincent had seated himself by my side.

"*Brava,* Ally," he said. "Here's your passport. You fought off the Goths, I see."

I passed out then, or fell asleep, I never knew which.

"I'll stay with you as long as I can," Vincent said later, as I was lifted onto a squeaking gurney and rolled back out into the freezing night, placed in a rattling vehicle that resembled an ice cream truck, and whisked off toward another building. Vincent rode beside me and held my hand. I had a massive headache.

"What are you doing here?" I asked him, my breath forming clouds around my face, where I could still feel traces of dried blood.

"I come over here twice a week for my drugs. Be quiet now, and try to stay still."

We arrived at another building where an elevator descended floor by dark floor and deposited me into a group of basement rooms that smelled strongly of developing fluid. I was still a bit woozy and dozed off at intervals but managed to be startled by the gigantic size of what was possibly a World War Two vintage X-ray machine, which hummed loudly and occasionally groaned as it took pictures of my head from every angle possible. Vincent, who had waited patiently upstairs, returned with me to the main building, where I was subjected to the usual Italian forms of red tape and eventually admitted, much to my surprise.

No one had explained anything to me. As far as I knew, I hadn't had contact with a doctor, although my face had been cleaned up and my forehead was now wrapped tightly in a clean bandage. Two orderlies lifted me off the gurney, deposited me on the bed, and departed. I was still wearing my clothes, including, at that moment, my coat and my boots.

Vincent stood beside my bed, smiling. There seemed to be another patient present behind a curtain, and a tray of half-eaten pasta lay on the floor. "Now what?" I asked him.

"Ever been a patient in an Italian clinic?"

I shook my head, which was a mistake, for a spasm of pain shot up the back of my neck.

He pulled over a metal chair. "First," he said, "they will provide basic medical treatment, such as doctors and X-rays, drugs, a bed, coffee and rolls in the morning, and probably one main meal a day. Everything else—including soap, towels, something to sleep in, a toothbrush, even toilet paper, I think—you have to supply yourself."

"What kind of a hospital is this?"

"You're at the policlinico, in a lovely park on the way to the cemetery, just below the Monteluce church. It's on the list to be closed down soon, so you're fortunate to be having this experience now. Savor it. If you'd landed in the big new hospital on the other side of the city, things would probably be different. More organized. More modern equipment. Less quaint. Do you want something to eat?"

"Absolutely not. I'd really like some water though. And where am I going to get towels and soap and the other things? And the signora! I'm supposed to be buying gelato! I've got to call her."

"I'll scout you up some water. Do you have the signora's phone number? Where is your *telefonino?*"

I'd left it on my desk at Casa Caccini. "Here's my book of numbers. She's in there."

"I'll call her. As soon as she finds out where you are, she'll know exactly what to bring you and you'll hear her coming."

I sank back against the pillow. The unknown woman behind the curtain snored.

In my memory, the events of that night occurred like scenes in a play, and even now I'm not sure of the order in which they passed. Vincent returned with water, followed by a dark-haired female doctor wearing a long lab coat over a lovely multicolored sweater, possibly from Luisa Spagnoli. Vincent handed me the water, and she spoke with him, not me. I didn't have the strength to be irritated. The two of them talked quietly in a corner, and from time to time I heard Vincent say, "*Si, dottoressa,*" and she spoke the words "concussion" and "tomorrow" in English.

Before she departed, she approached my bed and put a cool hand on my forehead. "Signora, you will be fine," she said.

"May I introduce Dottoressa Cortina," Vincent said. "She is my primary doctor."

"*Piacere,*" I responded weakly. I did not reach for her hand.

She says you have a mild concussion," he continued, "and I can stay for a while if you like. They'd rather you didn't sleep."

"Things you need will be coming for you," the doctor said. "I know your head is painful, and you have some stitches. Look at me." She bent down with a small flashlight and examined my pupils. She smelled nicely of soap. "Please follow my finger." She moved it from right to left, up and down.

"Count backward from one hundred," Vincent said, grabbing the toes of my boots.

"One hundred, ninety-nine, ninety-eight ... do you mean in Italian?"

"Signor Vincenzo," the doctor said, "*non scherzare*. Do not joke."

"*Scusa*."

"Well, signora, for the night we would like to watch you. We will talk again in the morning. As I said before, I think this is not too serious." She turned to go. "*Buona notte.*" She closed the door behind her.

"*Mamma,*" the woman behind the curtain murmured.

"Well, that was interesting," I said. "What else did they do to me in that bunker?"

"Cleaned you up, stitched you up, and gave you a couple of jabs, I would guess. Drink some more water."

"Did you get the signora?"

"I did. She is mobilizing. Be prepared, she is bringing you dinner."

"Can I have some drugs?"

"Nothing strong enough to get you high, if that's what you're after."

"My head is pounding."

"The nurse asked if I was your responsible relative," Vincent said.

"I don't have one."

"Don't worry, I told him no. Do you think I want to get stuck with the bill? But I can stay a while. They're busy collecting the dinner trays right now."

And with that, the overhead lights came on with a flash and in marched Signora Caccini, followed by Rosemaria, her neighbor. They were carrying wicker baskets covered with colorful towels, and I could smell chicken broth and warm bread. Vincent stood up so quickly that his aluminum chair tumbled backward with a crash.

"*Aiuto! Aiuto!*" the mystery woman behind the curtain called out.

"Silvia?" The signora stopped in midstride. "*Sei tu,* Silvia?"

"Stefania?"

The signora handed one of the baskets to Vincent. "*Pastina in brodo. Pane. Acqua minerale. Momento,* I must speak with my friend Silvia."

All at once I was ravenous, and I sat up too fast. My head spun.

Rosemaria was a dainty woman, a spinster who lived in one of the adjoining apartments to ours. She bent to whisper in my ear. "Also, signora, I have here a soap, some towels, and a nightgown"—here she paused and looked at Vincent. I was happy that as a former schoolteacher, she knew enough English to get along. But I assured her that Vincent was not likely to be shocked by anything she would say, so she continued. "Also something for your teeth and other *cose femminile* that you might need." She stood up, crossed her arms over her breasts, and smiled.

"Thank you," I said. I had my eye on Vincent, who had straightened the rolling table by my bed and was setting it for my dinner.

The signora, who had flung back the curtain to speak with her friend, now closed it and took over from Vincent. "You must eat while the food steams," she said to me. "But first I remove your *stivali.*" She began to tug at my boots. "After you eat I will put you into the *camicia da notte.*"

"Nightgown, nightshirt," Vincent translated.

"I know, I know. Don't lose those boots." I had just taken a spoonful of the broth and was savoring it. Now I had the two women standing by my bed watching and nodding, and Vincent at the foot, probably wondering how soon he could make a break for it.

"I want to bring you a flower," the signora said, "but Rosemaria drives her *macchina* straight down Via Rocchi and I found no time."

"Signora," I said, "I did not buy the gelato. Very sorry."

"*Non importa. Non importa.*" She smiled. "Sleep now."

"No! No sleeping!" Vincent whispered loudly.

The signora turned and looked at him. "You are a *medico?*" she asked.

But eventually, when all the confusion was over, the plates and remaining food packed away, and after the signora oversaw my nightly ablutions and got me into a voluminous nightgown and into bed, after a nurse took my vitals and the bright ward lights were dimmed, after I said buona notte to my new friend Silvia and everyone else had departed—after all that, I was wide awake and completely unable to sleep. So I watched a soft snow that had begun to drift down, large lazy flakes with no particular purpose, and listened to the quiet sound of music from a nearby room and the regular squeak of shoes as the nurses passed by, settling everyone in for sleep. I supposed there were worse places in the world I could be spending this chilly night.

Then it was morning, and when I opened my eyes I found Elaine sitting at my bedside. I had slept and was still alive.

She smiled. "There you are," she said.

At that moment an aide arrived with a tray of hot coffee, warm milk, rolls, and cherry jam. I moved my head back and forth, testing it. I felt a bit of an ache, but the bad part of it had subsided. I was happy to see the coffee.

"I'm anxious to see that chic little nightgown you're wearing," Elaine said. "Why don't you try to sit up. I'll fix the pillows."

I swung my legs out of bed and sat on the side while I poured my coffee and milk, inhaled the steam with my eyes closed, then drank. I thought I might live after that.

"Very good," she said. "Vincent called me late last night. He was worried. He's a worrier. How's the coffee?"

"Reviving."

"I think they'll let you out today. I've already inquired."

I spread half a roll with butter and jam. I hadn't asked Elaine why she was there, almost as if I had expected her.

She shifted in her chair and loosened her coat from around her shoulders. "Vincent told me he'd spoken to you about my situation with the opera."

"Briefly." I brushed the crumbs off my *camicia da notte* and poured out the last of the coffee.

"I'd like someone who knows some Italian to take a look at the libretto. Apparently you don't feel you have the time."

"Do you really want to talk about this now? I'm not really awake."

At that moment the door to the room opened and an older doctor came in, followed by a group of interns, or whatever they're called in Italy, in scrubs. Rounds. Fortunately, they stopped at Silvia's bed first. As if in anticipation of this visit, Silvia had applied a heady dose of floral perfume, and the aroma filled the room as soon as her curtain was drawn back.

When the group arrived at my bed, the doctor took a long look at my extra-large nightgown and shook his head. "*Non è possibile,*" he said, pointing to my gown. "You must remove."

"You must remove," Elaine said to me. "They can't get at you with their instruments."

The interns, all of whom were wearing stethoscopes around their necks, stared silently at me. "I don't think so," I said with a grim look. So the doctor pulled my curtain closed with great speed and examined me himself. Since he was only interested in my head, it was all over quickly. By the time the curtain was reopened, I had located the shirt and bloody sweater I'd been wearing the night before and put them on.

Elaine had remained.

The doctor had an extended conversation in Italian with his interns and then turned to me. "If pain in the head becomes worse, or you bleed from nose or ear, come quickly to *pronto soccorso.* You must not become dizzy or fall again. This would not be good."

"I agree," I told him. "But will you discharge me now?"

He nodded, then gave me a sudden bright smile. "*Guarda!*" He gave a grand gesture toward the windows. "*Che bella giornata!* A beautiful day!" The interns obediently applauded.

"I have to find my boots," I said.

"You must return in ten days to *pronto soccorso* for removal of stitches." He handed me some forms. "Before leaving," he said, "you must visit *camera* 211."

"Do you have any cash with you?" Elaine asked me as the students filed out. "Or a credit card? I suspect that's what room 211 is about."

"I thought medical treatment for foreigners was free in Italy."

"Where did you get that idea?" Elaine said. "Did they copy your passport?"

I nodded.

"Then you're stuck."

In the end she lent me the funds that allowed me to have my forms stamped three times (by three different clerks) and walk out into the *bella giornata,* a beautiful day that was also frosty. The remains of the previous night's snowfall were crumbled along the verges of the path to the parking lot, which backed up against a grove of sleeping olive trees.

She slammed her car door and started the engine. "Let's get some heat in here," she said.

Elaine dropped me in Piazza Ansidei, just up the street from my door, and drove off to the theater looking unsettled. We'd had a tense exchange on the way about the opera libretto. "You see," she'd said, "we're having to work with the score our former composer, Giorgio Paolo, left behind after he and DiBrufa had their final flameout. Well, the flameout was really with Monica DiBrufa. He told me to burn it, but of course I couldn't, and he said, 'Use what you want,' and went off to Palermo. Now I'm beginning to realize how confusing the libretto really is. It would help if someone could take a look at it and see if it can be saved."

"And why me?"

"Well, you seem to be familiar with DiBrufa's work. I don't know anyone else who is."

"I've read his work in a very superficial way on my own." My headache was beginning to reemerge. "Do you have some aspirin or anything stronger?" I asked her.

"Not with me," she said coolly. "In any case, I don't think you're supposed to take aspirin with a head injury."

"Look, you may not remember my explanation of why I'm here in Perugia."

"You came to interview Piero DiBrufa."

"Not exclusively. I thought I made that point clear. Monica has blocked me from Piero, but I've become interested in talking to you, as well. I think you could probably give me a clearer idea of what the state of the production is and your ideas about it. If Monica changes her mind, well, that would be icing on the cake."

For some moments she focused on the activity in the piazza. Then she said, "What I asked was whether you could help me out a bit with this hopeless libretto."

"I may not be as qualified as you imagine. Why don't you ask Italo Montecalvo to help you out? Since you know him."

"Oh, they're bitter enemies, those two. Italo wouldn't touch it." She wiped her window off with a Kleenex. "This essay, or whatever it is you're writing, is focused on the production? Staging, for example, or set design? Those sorts of things? Leaving DiBrufa aside for the moment, I'd be happy to give you access to any part of the production if that would help."

"That would be entirely up to you. But I do have questions about your current problems with the production. As much as you'd feel comfortable discussing."

"It would be a one-sided point of view."

"True. So if Monica should come around and give us Piero, I would want to talk to him as well. And if he decided to go on record with his feelings about how his work had been treated here, that would be especially good to know. You'd have your chance to respond, of course."

"A dog and pony show, then."

My headache was catching up with me. "That's not how I write," I said.

In tiny Piazza Ansidei, she had pulled her car into a little space near the House of Cheese. Casa Caccini was just down the street. Although I was desperate for a cup of tea and my bed, I made no move to get out of the car.

She sat silently for a moment with her gloved hands on the steering wheel. I turned to look at her. I liked her profile, with its high cheek bones, and even her frown had a classic attractiveness to it. Her face was slightly flushed.

She turned to me. "What is it?" she asked.

"Just thinking."

"I don't think I'd feel comfortable discussing aspects of this production that are still not settled," she said. "It wouldn't be helpful to the company. Or to me personally."

"I see that. But I'm always fair. And I don't reveal controversial aspects of a situation if I'm asked not to."

She turned to face me. "There's something about this libretto that's just not right. Off the record? It's almost as if Piero wrote as badly as he possibly could just to see if he could do it. Or fool someone. I've read his poetry, in English translation, of course. Some of it is translucent; it's beautiful. Nothing like his libretto."

"I sometimes got that feeling too. But then I haven't read a lot of it. And I was trying to make my way in Italian."

"Look," she said. "Could we leave all this on the table for a while? There's a lot to think about."

"For a while, yes. But I do have a deadline." I waited a moment. "But I'm very interested in how you feel about your profession in general, your general feelings about opera as an art form, for example. That sort of thing."

"You're familiar with my recent past, I think."

"Not all of it. But that wouldn't necessarily be a focus I'd want to pursue."

She was silent for a long moment. I knew I'd ambushed her, and I'd done it without thinking. Blame it on my throbbing head, my fascination with the evening shadows on her face, my exhaustion. "I'm not convinced that sort of interview would be of general interest," she said. "And it has nothing to do with *Sirius.*"

"I might argue with you about that."

She started the car. "I think I'd better get over to the theater," she said. "Let me think about everything, and then we can talk. You'll be in Perugia for a while?"

"That's not entirely up to me, but I think I can make a case for not being sent off to Timbuktu."

"Good. Now I'm sure you're tired and you'd like to lie down or have something to eat, so if you'll tell me how to get back to the theater from here, I'll let you go."

The winter sun had fallen behind the duomo at the top of the hill, and the lights around the perimeter of the piazza suddenly lit up.

I pointed to the northwest exit from the piazza. "Take Via Baldeschi there, go straight through Piazza Cavallotti, and you'll run right into it. Thanks for the ride. And the loan."

"Don't mention it. Go get some rest and I'll be in touch. Does Vincent have your cell number?"

"I don't think he does."

She pulled a small notebook off the dash. "Write it here, then."

"Tell him hello from me. If you see him."

"I'll see him tonight. He can't seem to shake this chest thing he's got. I'm taking him his drugs and something nutritious to eat. He worries me."

Nine

Vincent called me later in the week. "Can you find your way over to the rehearsal hall in Piazza Morlacchi?"

"It's right next to the theater, I think. Why? And how are you? Elaine reports that you're still not completely well. Your voice sounds terrible."

"She exaggerates. If you're still interested in why this opera is going off the rails, get over here. War of the worlds fireworks maybe. We're downstairs. Follow the music." He signed off.

I couldn't get dressed fast enough.

The rehearsal hall was adjacent to the theater, and to my surprise, I walked right in the main entrance. It was an ancient building with high ceilings and the ghostly images of what might have been frescoes could be seen along the upper walls. One had to look closely. I followed the intermittent sound of a piano, past a woman dreaming away as she brushed the entrance hall with a twig broom.

I descended some stairs and the light grew dimmer. When I heard Elaine's voice from within a room I was passing, I stopped and peered cautiously through a small glass window in the door. The room was large, and I could see no one.

The piano began again and after a moment trailed off.

"I'm losing my patience here, Dorina," I heard Elaine say. "You're swallowing the text, and it must be understood, especially here ... So let's think about this. You're not supposed to know what his reaction will be ... This time I don't want you to sing, I want you to think the words only ... as the piano plays. Let what you're thinking enter your body and cross your face. React! But make no sound. From forty-two, Vincent, please."

The piano began alone, and after several minutes stopped. There was a tense exchange of words that I couldn't understand, then silence. Again I heard the piano, and a rich but unsettled mezzo-soprano voice lifted and wound its way upward. The piano accompaniment was lyrical and measured; against these phrases the singer's voice followed a tense, higher musical line in what seemed to be a completely different key. The tension between the two grew as they touched and came together, retreated, and came together again.

Now the piano began a variation. The singer's voice, narrowed with some violent grief, rose higher against the steady, sensuous variations of the piano, dropped down, lifted again, and the piano followed. I struggled to understand the words, or at least find some pieces of DiBrufa's poetry I recognized, but these were muddled by the door. Finally it was clear that the two lines had come tightly together but were still, in some way, moving separately, moving against each other, unresolved.

"Stop. Stop now." Elaine's voice came from just on the other side of the door, and I jumped. Then I saw her walk across the floor, pursued by a woman in dark glasses I instantly recognized as Monica DiBrufa. Elaine was carrying a clipboard. "Ten-minute break," she said over her shoulder.

I had just moved my face back to the little window when the door opened quickly and banged me on the nose. Vincent walked out. "Ally!" he said. "So sorry, so sorry." He examined my face. "Did I reopen your wound?"

"I'm fine," I said. He gave me a little hug.

"I'm off to the gents," he said. "Glad you're here. Be patient. I think the best is yet to come."

"What was that music just now?"

"A part of act two that Giorgio Paolo left behind."

"I didn't recognize any of DiBrufa's words."

"That's partly because Dorina is Latvian. Did Elaine persuade you to take a look at the libretto?"

"She made her case. But no, she didn't. What's Monica doing in there?"

"Sorry, I've really got to run." He took off.

When I returned to the window, Elaine was standing just inside with Monica, who stood slightly beneath her chin. "What's your point?" Elaine was asking her.

"That composer never did understand my brother's work. We were fortunate to lose him." She blew her nose on a large handkerchief. "What progress to find a replacement?"

"We have no time to bring in another composer," Elaine said. "We're trying to do what we can with the music Giorgio Paolo left behind. For better or worse, he did his best with the material your brother sent him. It's perfectly natural that there should be negotiations between composer and librettist along the way, but your brother has refused all negotiations and now, as I see it, we have two options: we'll consider his latest complaints about the work as it stands and try to solve them with the music we have, or we'll withdraw the entire production from the spring season."

"May we step outside, please?" Monica said.

Without thinking I moved quickly around a nearby corner. I didn't want to stumble into a confrontation with Monica before the time was right. Or appear to be stalking either her or Elaine.

"Well?" Elaine said. I could understand her more clearly now.

"Those options are not acceptable," Monica said. "Either one or two. And please remember, he has a contract."

"The issue of a contract is beside the point. Do we have an opera or not? That is the question. And by the way, I have a contract too."

I heard Elaine pacing in my direction and sat down quickly on the wooden floor. I drew myself up tightly, my arms around my knees, and prepared myself. But instead of Elaine, a large black spider crawled slowly around the corner and stopped about a foot from my left boot.

Elaine turned and went back to Monica. "Look, we're in the midst of what's already been a difficult preparation for everyone. I'm perfectly willing to allow your brother to expand the libretto in some minor ways if that will soothe him. It would be better if you could convince him to come to the theater and talk to me himself."

"Where do you suppose this composer Giorgio Paolo is hiding at this moment?"

The spider paused at my foot and put one hairy leg on my boot. I made myself completely still. My heart seemed to stop, then lurched into a rapid, rocking beat.

"He's not hiding, Monica. He's in Palermo."

The spider moved from my boot, paused again on the cuff of my pants, and moved upward. I longed to give it a violent flip, but

I knew if I moved it would run quickly, as spiders do, up onto my face or into my hair. I'd become a raving spectacle.

"Palermo?"

"He wants no part of this production now."

The spider was now crawling slowly and deliberately up the sleeve of my jacket. I could feel the weight of its body, hear its prickly legs scratching their way up toward my shoulder. I should move to get away, but I was pinned to the spot.

"You should know, signora, that I have engaged a lawyer to consult with us."

"Fine, fine, hire who you want. But the holiday season is approaching, and I've decided to send the singers home," Elaine said. "At least for now. At least until your brother and I can settle some of the difficulties with this work that aren't going to magically disappear."

"I repeat—"

"No, don't repeat anything."

There was a pause. The spider halted just below my shoulder.

"This opera does not deserve a second-class production."

"All right, then. Advise your brother to cooperate. Please. This is a very slight work, if I may say so. It's basically a chamber opera. The libretto is lyrical enough, but it does not hold together as a theatrical piece. We cannot turn it into something gigantic by Strauss or Wagner."

The spider lifted one large leg and waved it tentatively.

"Why did you agree to direct this production, Signora Bishop?"

"I ask myself that question every day. And I don't have an answer. I only know that I don't usually stage a new work like this by letting it slide along and invent itself."

Oh, shut up, shut up, I called out silently. The spider moved to my shoulder, and I could no longer see it. I waited in this nightmare for its tiny teeth to bite into the flesh of my neck.

"All right," Elaine concluded. "Tell Signor DiBrufa to expand the libretto, if he must. But not much. Make it fit the music. It's a good thing the premiere isn't until March. I'd like to remove myself from all of it, frankly, but it's too late for that. Let's go back in."

As the door shut behind them, I reached up and swept the spider off my neck and onto the floor. I rolled quickly away from it and jumped up. It seemed to be crawling after me, so I tried to smash it with my boot but missed. Finally it scurried away down the hall with surprising speed. I leaned against the wall, panting.

"What the hell are you doing, you great *eegit*?" Vincent came up behind me.

I held up my hands, unable to speak.

"All right. Want to get some dinner later?" he asked.

"I don't know if I can eat."

"Well, think about it. I've got to go back in."

As he spoke, Monica DiBrufa passed silently behind him and exited through a side door.

At dinner Vincent was laughing and couldn't stop. "You are the mad queen of melodrama," he said. "Why didn't you just stand up and knock the thing off you?"

"And why didn't I ambush Monica when I had her in my sights?"

We had come down the stairs into the old Ristorante Lanterna at the top of Via Rocchi. Despite its underground location, it had a certain class about it. The walls were of rough stone, but the tables were covered with crisp white tablecloths, and we had silver to eat with. As always, the tinny sound of radio music could be heard from the kitchen. I was simultaneously eating an artichoke salad and ravioli with black truffles and parmesan, which complimented each other nicely. Vincent was working slowly on a veal piccata. A bottle of Montalcino red (or "baby Brunello," according to Vincent) was sitting between us.

"I liked the music," I said.

"Yes, the music has its moments. Unfortunately, DiBrufa's libretto has been altered so much that it no longer makes sense with it. Giorgio Paolo got tired of trying to adjust his score. I don't blame him. I have two copies of the libretto with me, by the way, so I can lend you one of them. If you decide to get involved, that is." As he cut his veal, I noticed his hands were shaking a little, and he was wheezing the way an old cat of mine used to do when she slept. I poured us both more wine. His wheeze became a cough, which grew deeper, and he put his napkin on the table. "Excuse me," he said, and walked back toward the restrooms.

I thought about that cat of mine, the one that used to wheeze. Her name was Suri. She was black and white, and we lived together for eleven years, by far the longest and most satisfying relationship I've ever had with another living being. She was a city cat and never went out, but she didn't mind if I did, and if I left her for a weekend, with plenty of food and water, she was never mad when I returned or asked me where I'd been or asked for explanations about anything, really. We were good companions. When I read my work to her or played music, she never fell asleep; she always watched me steadily, with an occasional blink. She let me know with her eyes when she became sick, before she showed any serious signs of illness that I recognized. When the wheezing began I didn't see it as something that should be seen to until it was too late. After I finally had to put her down I wept for weeks. I betrayed her, essentially. I didn't pay attention. After eleven years that's how we ended: I didn't pay attention. I tried to think of some way to punish myself, but nothing helped. This was for a cat, not a human. I attempted to excuse myself with that thought, but I never thought it was enough. She was a cat, that was true, but she was human enough to trust me completely.

I wiped my eyes and took a drink of wine as Vincent returned to the table.

"Better?" I asked him.

His cheeks were flushed, as if he'd thrown cold water on them. "They've put red pepper in the piccata," he said.

We finished our meal and decided to go up to the corso for coffee. As we were retrieving our coats from their wooden pegs on the wall I said, "Not that it's any of my business, but what treatments are you getting at the policlinico?"

"I'm getting drugs at the policlinico, not treatments. My doctor has what she calls a surgery on Via Fiorenzo di Lorenzo, near Elaine's. For treatments or consults, I go there." He buttoned his coat up and wound his scarf around his neck. "It's complicated," he said. "Let's go."

"Do you like your doctors?"

"I like Dottoressa Cortina a lot. You met her at the policlinico."

"I'm past due to have my stitches removed over there. Some of them are even falling out."

"Oh, Margit can do that for you. For free." We started up the stairs to the street. "Here's that libretto if you want it," he said.

Ten

Early in December the Christmas lights went up, draped along the corso in spangly stars and colored twinkling lights. A large tree with blue lights went up near the Great Fountain in the central piazza. On misty nights it seemed like an apparition.

Somehow I had ended up with Vincent's extra copy of DiBrufa's libretto and, reluctantly at first, and mainly out of curiosity, I began to glance at it now and then. Since the music hadn't been included, the libretto alone read more like an extended poem, and that was the first thing I noted about it. There was absolutely no element of operatic drama to be found in it. Opera, like a conventional theatrical play, must have forward movement. The music usually sweeps the action ahead, while the libretto waits for the next aria or ensemble or taps its toe impatiently while the recitatives are delivered. In fact, Wagner is the one of the few composers who can get away with what I call "meditative ruminations" that go on and on until one's eyes become fixed. *Parsifal* is a good example. I do confess that I love that work, however, and have sat through some five-hour productions in rapt attention without suffering at all.

But DiBrufa didn't seem to have acknowledged that Giorgio Paolo, the composer, existed at all. He made no pretense of collaborating with him and showed no interest in where the music for this piece would appear from.

In any case, I was looking forward to discussing this strange libretto with Elaine, who continued to prepare for the March premiere as if it were actually going to take place. Right now, I didn't see how that could possibly happen.

Gail, of course, had no patience with reports from me about how I was spending my time. And I didn't offer many details.

"I'm coming down there," she said at one point. "I have to assess this situation for myself."

"No, I wouldn't do that," I said. "It's getting close to Christmas, and everybody will be going off somewhere else."

"Including you?"

"I have no plans to go anywhere. In fact, I'm looking forward to some peaceful days."

"I've put your piece on temporary hold at *Opera World*. You're not helping my professional reputation at all."

"You'll get everything from me all at once. You'll be thrilled."

Among the residents of Casa Caccini, I was the only one not going somewhere else for the long Christmas holiday. One by one the other tenants disappeared—to Orvieto, Taormina, Abu Dhabi—and the dark evenings were very quiet in the house. The signora was concerned about my solitary state, too much so, in fact. From time to time I had to leave the house to escape her ministrations. I went by Montecalvo's bookstore, but it was closed up tight. So I sat with the libretto in Lunabar or Sandri and nursed a coffee or a beer for an hour or two. Then later, mindful of the possibility of ice, I'd carefully descend Via Rocchi, sometimes through a light snowfall, and often found the house dark, except for a single lamp left burning for me. The Caccinis had gone off to family in Gualdo Tadino. I tried to call Elaine once or twice, but her phone went straight to voice mail.

Three days before Christmas, I ran into Vincent in the midst of the passeggiata, on his way back from the policlinico with his drugs. He talked me into meeting him later at the duomo for a performance of Saint-Saëns' Christmas Oratorio and something seasonal by Vivaldi. I was glad to have an excuse to get out of the house, but when he emerged from the crowd on the cathedral steps, he had Elaine on his arm, her body engulfed in a massive coat and hood.

"Look who I ran into," he said.

"Hello," she said with a smile. "I thought you'd be away somewhere." I held up the libretto. "This is not a night for work," she told me, and took my arm.

"Come on, let's go in," Vincent said.

The performance cheered me up. Afterward, Elaine led us toward Piazza Danti, in the direction of Sandro's garage. "You must both come for a Christmas drink at my place. I've got my car in Sandro's space, and before you ask, Vincent, I can run you home later. You too, Allyn."

I said, "Just one drink."

"Just one drink."

Elaine's apartment was on Via Cacciatori delle Alpi, just a little below Piazza Partigiani and across from the Santa Giuliana stadium formerly used by Il Grifo. To my surprise, she had decorated her rooms for the season. She'd covered the mantel with greens and holly, and there were scented candles placed about, which she set alight immediately. A crowd of Christmas cards stood about on the piano, which was sitting quietly in a corner of the living room. "Throw your coats in one of the bedrooms," she said. "I'll get some ice out."

"I'll take your coat," Vincent said to me.

I made my way through the darkened dining room into the kitchen, where Elaine was clattering around with glasses and ice trays. Her hair had recently been cut, revealing attractive curls that hadn't been obvious before.

"What will you have?" she asked over her shoulder as I came in.

"Something small and without ice, I think."

I found some Montenegro. I knew it would warm me up.

We sat in the living room in comfortable silence for a while, watching the warm shadows on the walls cast by the candles. Elaine had put on some music, something I didn't recognize, a quiet piece. I looked over at Vincent, who was carefully sipping red wine. His cheeks were still rosy, either from the cold outside or his illness, which I was continuing to wonder about.

"A very nice evening," Elaine said. "I'm glad you ran into me, Vincent."

"Yes," he said slowly. "Very pleasant."

Elaine set her glass of gin firmly on the table. "This may surprise you. I've decided to fly up to London for Christmas week. You know I've given the technical crew five days off. And the student stand-ins we're using now from the conservatory will be away until the school reopens in January."

"Why London?" Vincent asked. "It won't be much warmer up there."

"I know. I'll probably regret it. But there's another reason, of course. Patrizia Colonna, Sandro's sister, is designing costumes for the English National Opera's production of *Arabella.* It opens at the end of January. I want to speak with her. I need some advice."

"You're going all the way to London for costume advice?" Vincent chuckled.

"Costumes don't enter into it." Elaine sipped her gin and the ice clinked against her teeth. "Don't laugh. I adore London. It's sane. A perfect solution to all my current difficulties."

"I doubt it. But it would do you some good to get out of here for a while, I agree with that."

"You can stay in my place here if you like, while I'm away. It's warmer than your rooms."

"We'll see. When will you leave?"

"In a couple of days, I think. There are nonstop flights up to London from the Perugia airport. I won't even have to go down to Rome. It's not a long flight, a couple of hours. I'd ask you to come along, but ..."

"I'm not really up for it. But thanks."

"What will you be doing?" she asked him.

"I'll have Christmas dinner with Luca, you know him, and two or three others. It'll be quiet."

I went into the kitchen and poured myself another small Montenegro. It had definitely heated up my chest, but for some reason I was shivering.

"Well, Allyn," Elaine said as I reentered the room, "they did a good job on your forehead. There's only a small scar; it'll hardly be noticeable."

"Yes." I touched it lightly.

"There are some things they do very well at that clinic," Vincent said as he finished his wine. "Now." He stood up. "I'm sleepy. And don't talk about running me home, Elaine. It's only a ten-minute walk."

"Suit yourself." She turned to me. "How about you, Allyn? Want a lift? I'll take you up as far as Piazza Danti when you're ready. I won't risk driving down Via Rocchi in the dark with the possibility of ice on that street."

I looked at my watch. It was well past midnight. "Sure, if you don't mind going out again."

"I've gone out later than this," she said.

Half an hour later, she pulled into a space behind the duomo and turned off the ignition. She left the parking lights on but not blinking. There was still quite a bit of activity in the bar adjacent to the former Teatro Turreno, and its neon lights illuminated an almost completely faded poster of Gary Cooper with smoking guns.

Elaine turned to me. "Well," she said. A group leaving the bar passed close to the car. "Do you have plans for the holiday? It's almost upon us."

"I haven't decided where I'll be."

"Oh?"

"My signora's concerned. She thinks spending Christmas alone is unnatural. In fact, she's asked me to come with her family to Gualdo Tadino, or somewhere near there. In the country."

She pushed a strand of hair away from her face. "That's kind of her. Will you go?"

"I told her no. It's nice of her to ask, but it's not my sort of thing. I'm fine on my own." I shifted the libretto in my lap.

"Don't misinterpret this, but would you like to come up to London with me? Would that be a nice break for you?"

I'd had an odd sense that this invitation was coming. "It's an appealing idea, but I'm afraid I'm running low on funds."

"Technically, I'm going up on company business. And it looks like you're at least reading the libretto, so we'll call it an advance." She touched my shoulder. "No strings. Two rooms. We'll see what's going on at Covent Garden, have a couple of good meals. I'll meet with Patrizia during the day, and you'll be free to do whatever you like. Does this appeal?"

"London always appeals. But I'm sort of up against a wall with this project now. According to my editor, it's stop or go time. And Montecalvo seems to have disappeared. He's my intermediary."

"You won't get anywhere during the holidays. Monica's probably whisked Piero away to Spain or some other warm place." She smiled. "And heaven only knows where Montecalvo's taken himself off to. You might as well be in London."

I must have looked doubtful, because she continued, "I'd just like some company. Does that make you uncomfortable?"

"In a way."

"Don't make too much of it. You'd come with me as, I don't know, a consultant or something. The company will pick up the tab. I'll be at Patrizia's for Christmas Day, and we could have a light meal somewhere later in the day."

So I sat and thought for a minute or two. During that time, the Priori struck one, and the gates to the bar began to crash down. Some stragglers passed us and headed down Via Bartolo. Perugia would be a lonely place over the holidays if I chose to remain here. I imagined three or four cold, bleak days alone, having to sort out my own meals and sleep in the dark, chilly apartment. I could go off somewhere ... and then come back, but the thought of organizing a venture like that was not appealing.

"Don't make me regret asking you," Elaine said evenly. "If you'd rather not go, say so."

"I'm just thinking too much," I said at last. "If you're serious, I'd like to come."

"I'm very serious. Good." She gripped the steering wheel. "It'll be fun. You must have friends there."

"A few, yes. And my editor's based there. But I think I'd prefer to keep my distance from her at the moment."

"London's easy to hide in." She switched on the headlights and turned the car around. "Now you should get home. Today's the twenty-second. I'll try to get us a flight for Christmas Eve. Can you be ready by then?"

Eleven

We left Perugia in a cold rain and bumped over the Alps in what was possibly one of RyanAir's oldest jets. Everyone on the plane was drunk, and the one harried flight attendant ran out of free holiday miniatures somewhere over Switzerland. We landed an hour late at Stansted, northeast of London, which used to be an RAF base during World War Two and now served as yet another alternative to Heathrow or Gatwick.

"Come on, let's get out of here," Elaine said as we jerked to a halt at the gate. "I can't stand happy drunks."

She had a car waiting, and by the time we reached it, it was sleeting.

"Good grief, man, what weather," she said to the driver. "Merry Christmas."

"Not my doing, madam," the driver said. "And a happy Christmas to you."

"Hotel Washington, Curzon Street, Mayfair," she said. "That will help."

We took off in a spray of slush.

I knew Mayfair. It was not known for cheap hotels, and I had not yet made it clear that I preferred to pay my own way.

But the Washington didn't seem overly extravagant. As promised, I had my own room (although it connected with Elaine's). I walked to the window and saw the sleet had turned to a light snow. There was a real city outside. And traffic. Even with all the lights in the room turned off, it was never really dark. I liked London.

There was a knock on the adjoining door.

"In the dark?" Elaine said as I let her in. "I've got to make a few calls and take a shower. Then would you mind if we ordered room service? I don't have the strength to deal with the restaurant downstairs, and it's too messy to go out. Did you bring the libretto?"

"Yes. And as it happens, I'm a great fan of room service."

"Good. I'll see you in an hour or so."

Later we sat in her room (which was larger than mine) with the remains of our meal around us. I'd ordered a ham sandwich on toast, which was all I wanted, but with it came a zesty potato salad, a selection of cheeses, a little dish of tart mustard, and some pickles. Elaine had ordered a bottle of Pinot Noir, and I was thinking I'd better not have another glass. The libretto lay on one of the beds.

"Tired?" she asked me.

"Red wine makes me relax, gives me a big headache, and then makes me sleepy."

She nodded. Then, "Forgive me, but how old are you?"

"Old enough to drink." I smiled. "Forty-five. And a half."

"You look younger. I thought forty-five-year-olds were all

fixed with settled-down spouses, settled-down houses, teenaged children."

"I'm sure a lot of them are." I reached out and put my hand on the libretto. "I've just looked through this once, but it will take a miracle to make this libretto work as an opera. I'm not even sure it's possible. I'm not even sure a miracle would help."

"We don't need to get into this tonight."

"DiBrufa's simply cobbled twenty-one of his poems together, taken longer bits from some of his other works, and inserted them as transitions. There's no particular dramatic conflict that I can pick up. I guess you could imagine reappearing characters, but no one could ever believe that these poetic figures were involved with one another in any way. Or cared. It doesn't go anywhere."

"Well, what else? As long as you've started."

"In a way DiBrufa seems to be trying to copy *Pelléas et Mélisande*. It's simply one extended dream sequence after another and no plot to speak of." I picked up the libretto. "This, as it stands now, might make a nice song cycle with the right composer, and parts of it are occasionally lyrical, but it's not opera material. That's my take, but I'm not a pro, remember."

She sighed. "Well, in defense of *Pelléas,* you know Debussy was handed a libretto that he hated. He had no use for external drama. Or any real arguments between his characters. And our Giorgio Paolo was no Debussy, keep that in mind. She rose from the little table and crossed the room to one of the armchairs. "I'm not making excuses, of course." She sat down. "Or maybe I am."

She remained in the chair in thoughtful contemplation of something, I couldn't guess what. So I began to put the plates and glasses back on the trays and gathered up the trash. I placed everything outside in the hall.

"Has the snow stopped?" she asked finally.

I returned to the window and looked down at the street. "Yes."

She stood up and stretched. "A long day, wasn't it?" A taxi horn sounded from below. A couple emerged and ran down Half Moon Street toward Green Park, their scarves flying out behind them. "Well, thank you," she said. I turned around to face her. "You've done exactly what I asked you to do. You've confirmed the feelings I've had for nearly half a year now." She yawned. "I'd like to hear more of your ideas, if you have any left, but I've got to get to sleep. What time is it?"

"Twelve thirty. Merry Christmas."

She walked to the connecting door and opened it. "Yes, Merry Christmas. I'm glad you're here."

"So am I."

As I passed her, she took my hand and held it for a moment. "Good night," she said then, and closed the door behind me.

In the morning I woke to the invasive call of bells. And a loud siren. For a moment I thought I was back in Perugia, but soon a pounding came on the door and a male voice ordered me to get out of my room. A fire alarm had gone off.

It was a false one, as it turned out, but all of us milled about in the street in boots and gloves, some in coats thrown over pajamas, waiting to be readmitted. The sun was pouring down, and most of the snow had disappeared. It was a jovial group, everyone exchanging Christmas greetings, and even the firemen were laughing as they re-coiled their hoses. The curve at Curzon Street was completely blocked off to traffic. Eventually several of the waiters from the dining room brought out flutes of champagne on brilliant silver trays, and a sort of party began. I looked around for Elaine but didn't see her, and when I returned to my room I found a note from her slipped under my door.

I've gone for brunch at Patrizia's. I'll be back in time for a Christmas dinner this evening, unless you have other plans. I've managed to get good seats for "Fledermaus" at Covent Garden for tomorrow night. It's not what I might have chosen, but at least it's not "Hansel and Gretel." —E.

I took a long, fragrant bath and prepared to go out and find something to eat. I don't usually pay a lot of attention to what I put on my body, but it was Christmas after all, so I decided to make an effort. The black ankle boots I had splurged on in Florence—at the insistence of Ines—my slim Jil Sander trousers (knockoffs, but still a splurge), a loose white silk shirt under a nicely-cut black jacket, and for some color a blue and green silk scarf I'd picked up on the corso. I felt unusual, possibly like a flight attendant.

I headed for Shepherd Market, a couple of blocks away, to find brunch. I was happy to discover Da Corradi not only open but packed. A waiter found me a table on the lower level, and without glancing at the menu, I ordered creamed spinach over two poached eggs with half an avocado on the side, its hollow center filled with a tart, in-house vinaigrette. I did not feel alone, or even lonely, sitting there with my delicious meal in a room of cheery celebrants who were already, at eleven o'clock, on their way to becoming falling-down drunk.

That evening Elaine and I made our way by cab through an early darkness to Café Carlyle in Chelsea, which she described as "sedate, but swinging." An oxymoron, but I didn't point that out.

She had reserved a corner banquette, which kept us away from some of the babble.

"What a day," Elaine said. "I thought Patrizia would be alone, but instead she invited half the city." A waiter stood by attentively. "Would you like a drink or some wine?" she asked me.

"Vodka rocks with two olives," I said. Vodka-infused olives sounded like a delicious treat at that moment.

Elaine raised her eyebrows. "Plymouth martini up, very dry, with a twist," she told the waiter. "And some of those hot cheese puffs you just delivered to the table over there." When he had departed, she asked, "Did you have fun today? What did you get up to?"

"I found some brunch, and then I walked it off."

"London's a good walking city, isn't it? As long as you can find a taxi when you need one." The drinks arrived and the cheese puffs followed. "Cheers," she said, raising her glass. "To a happy holiday."

"*Salute.*" I allowed the fiery vodka to warm my throat before I asked, "Patrizia is Sandro's sister?"

Elaine took a deep breath and put down her glass. "I'd just like to say, or to ask, could we possibly relax a little bit? I'd just as soon not spend the evening making small talk, if it's okay with you. For example, let's stay away from our current opera snarl, although I will say that last night you gave me a solid confirmation of most of my doubts about this—thing—I've allowed myself to sign onto. Thanks for that." She took a sip of her gin. "What else occupies your mind? You've done some travel writing, or so you mentioned at Renata's. In addition to your musical critiques. Tell me where you've been. What are your favorite places?"

A waiter appeared. "Would you like to order, madam?" he asked Elaine.

"Well, yes, we'd better," she said. She looked at me. "What would you like?"

I'd been reading the menu while Elaine was talking. "Prime rib," I said. "Medium rare. Potatoes dauphinoise. Brussel sprouts. A salad after."

"Make that two," she told the waiter. "And please open a bottle of Merlot for us. You choose. It needs to breathe a bit." She handed him the menus. "Our arteries may never forgive us," she said to me.

"The salad will save our arteries."

She put her glasses away. "Has it been exciting, your traveling life?"

"Well," I said, "I haven't climbed Mount Everest, like Jan Morris. Or roamed around Havana at night like Pico Iyer. That's real travel writing."

She gave me a look.

"A lot of my travel pieces have just been extended sidebars to wherever I've landed to interview a music director, for example, or write about a particular production."

She gave me a patient look, which made me a bit uncomfortable. People tend to think travel writing is exotic when it's anything but.

"But I was eventually able," I remarked in a self-deprecating way, "to write a very colorful piece about my hot and humid luncheon cruise down the Brenta Canal in Venice. And what followed, which was the worst case of food poisoning I've ever experienced."

"You don't say."

"One small shrimp, one dollop of tainted mayonnaise. A night from hell."

"Electrifying."

"Oh, it was tremendously electrifying."

"I wasn't asking for your professional history."

"What, then. My personal history?"

Interestingly, we weren't conversing in tones of anger or irritation. Not at that point. It was more like affectionate bantering, as one would do with a friend with whom one had a long history.

"Good grief, I wouldn't dare. Not now."

We laughed a little.

"I'm a bit too curious, I guess," she went on. "All right, just tell me one thing about yourself that might surprise me."

"What would surprise you? I don't know you well enough to take a guess."

"Your book maybe?"

"Why would that surprise you?"

"It didn't, to tell you the truth. In fact, I'd like to read it. What's the title?"

"*Boarding Passes*. Selections from my travel writings."

"Tell me about it."

"Glimpses of unusual corners of the world. Personal views. You'll still find collections of them stashed in some long-haul British Airways flight lockers. They used to give them away."

"And your Perugia article?"

"That's developing into a much longer piece, much to my surprise. And the focus has changed. But it's coming along."

"Has that been an onerous task?"

"At first it was. But the city's been growing on me. I lose my way, and then suddenly find myself on the brink of some breathtaking view. Or at the door of a tiny restaurant I probably would have overlooked. I love the light. There aren't any glorious piazzas there—or only one; no Campidoglios. But they have a Raphael, and the other Piero, and a fascinating history of crazy families and bloody massacres in the night. The city itself is an opera."

I was tired of hearing myself talk. "Now I either need food or another drink."

Elaine caught the waiter's eye, and the Merlot was quietly delivered and left to further expand its lungs.

"Well, I wish I shared your enthusiasm. You see its charms, and all I see is a place I'd like to get out of," she said. "Too many steep streets."

"When will that Merlot be ready to drink?"

"When the meal arrives. Soon, I have every hope." She finished her martini. "Is our Christmas celebration beginning to bore you?"

"Not at all. I'm not easily bored. There's always something to speculate about."

"Yes," she said. "I believe being bored shows a lack of imagination."

"Maybe. Or it could just be restlessness."

"Tell me what doesn't bore you then. What you like."

"You know, we could talk about you for a while. That would be a nice change."

"Aha." She smiled. "Now you know why I'm cautious about interviews."

I took a deep breath. "All right. What I like. Hotel bars. Arriving at new places. Certain familiar books. Breakfast in the cockpit of a beautiful sailboat. Shakespeare. Piero della Francesca. Opera, when the house lights dim and everything gets breathlessly dark, and you know what's coming. Looking down at the world from a window seat on a plane. Sitting on the corso in Perugia with a *caffè corretto*, watching the passeggiata."

She looked at me thoughtfully. "You know what all of those things have in common?"

"What, possibly."

"They're solitary experiences. You don't need anyone else to complete the picture."

"I think I'd prefer to have someone with me in the sailboat." I gave her a self-satisfied smile.

She didn't return it. "I've watched you," she said. "You wait for things to happen. You like to look. What in the world do you do with all you see? You can't put it all in magazine articles."

"You know what? We don't know each other well enough to be having a conversation like this. I don't like playing defense."

She was almost smiling.

After a moment I added, "Yes. I like to look. I like to see. I shouldn't have to explain that."

"It's an excuse. Generally."

"An excuse for what?"

"For not participating."

"I participate. I just choose my times. What point are you trying to make? And please don't act like a bully. It doesn't suit you," I said.

And then with a great whoosh of white linen and a soft clattering of plates, our dinners were delivered. By two waiters.

"Could you pour the wine, please?" Elaine said politely to the older one.

Later we sat over the remains of our salads and finished the Merlot. The wine had been a complete waste, at least for me. I had quickly downed two glasses, and those, on top of the vodka and my unnerving conversation with Elaine before dinner, had definitely affected my enthusiasm for the meal. We had exchanged comments about the beef, which was almost tender enough to cut with a fork, and the potatoes, which she said she'd never tasted before.

Eventually a large, loud group of revelers was seated near us, and conversation of any sort became difficult.

She poured the final drop of wine into my glass. "Will you have dessert?" she asked.

I shook my head. "Absolutely not, thank you." My head had begun to pound.

"Coffee, then."

"Not even that."

"All right, I'll finish my wine and get the check."

"Good idea."

She sipped her wine with particular care, as if she were making it last as long as she could, and finally said, "If I've offended you, I'm sorry. It wasn't intentional."

"You haven't offended me."

I don't think she believed me. The waiter passed, and she raised her arm.

Outside, it had grown much colder, and happy groups passed us, some singing, enjoying what was left of the holiday. I thought I might possibly throw up and used every physical device I could muster to keep myself from doing that before I got into my own bathroom. But by the time we got to the hotel, I no longer felt the urge. Perhaps the night air had helped. So I threw some cold water on my face, removed my clothes, and changed into pajama bottoms and a sweatshirt.

Elaine knocked on the connecting door and called out, "Do you have any Perrier in your little fridge? I'm out."

We sat in the armchairs with our glasses of Perrier. It was nearly two. The night was finally quiet.

"I guess it must have seemed like I was attacking you," she said finally. "I apologize. Lately that seems to be the only way I can get anyone's attention."

"You had my attention."

She rapidly changed the subject. "Vincent is your biggest fan, you know. He seems to have figured something out about you, but he won't say what."

I sipped my water. "I like him. And I like his music."

"Vincent appeals to everyone."

I curled my legs up under me. "Is he very sick?" I asked her.

"He's struggling. Whatever treatments they're giving him seem to have stabilized his symptoms, at least for the moment."

"What does he think about the opera?"

"He agrees with you, for the most part." She walked to the bed, took off her shoes, and propped herself up against some pillows. As I said, it was very quiet, and I waited for her to go on. But she didn't, not for a few minutes. "You know," she said finally, "when you look at an opera program and see the word 'Production,' that usually refers to the stage director. Theoretically, he's the head honcho of the creative team. He's given the score and libretto, over which he has no control, and the singers are often selected by someone else, maybe someone who's financed the production. The singers themselves will move in and out of consideration, or withdraw, and you don't know who you'll end up with. Conductors present another type of challenge. So with all that ambiguity swirling about, the stage director is expected to arrive with a creative vision or concept. Unless you're someone like Robert Carsen, for example, or Francesca Zambello, who have starry reputations. Then productions are built around them. As they should be. But the rest of us are expected to *impose* our visions—I've actually been accused of that on more than one occasion—on everyone involved."

"Sounds like you're not happy with your work."

"On the contrary, I love my work. And I'm good at what I do. Very good. Usually I get a long look at the score and libretto, if I'm not familiar with it, have some preliminary talks with the composer, if he's alive, and even the conductor if I'm lucky. Then I meet with the lighting people, the costume people, and the set designer. So by the time the singers get involved, the production team is already at work. It may sound straightforward, but it can take years."

I wondered where she was going with this. I was drifting off.

"This production in Perugia should have been way past the development phase a year ago. I've been pulled in and given seven months. I can't think of one reason why I shouldn't withdraw. Or rather there are reasons, but I'm wondering how important they are now."

She appeared to be talking to herself at this point, so I repositioned myself on the chair and closed my eyes.

"My agent can probably get me out of my contract, under the circumstances. I haven't heard from my usual team of technicians in several weeks. I don't blame them. I have no so-called vision to offer them. The set designer can't design a set for a staging that's in constant flux, and a lighting scheme can't be plotted for a set that hasn't been designed. Not to mention that our original composer threw in the towel the day I arrived!" I opened my eyes quickly. She was looking directly at me. "And the entire opera world is waiting for me to fall on my face again."

"The entire opera world?" I asked. I hadn't meant for this comment to sound snide, although it probably did. I could see she was upset now, but I didn't think it was with me.

"Yes. Probably. And don't be dismissive; be happy you don't know the whole story."

"I didn't mean to sound dismissive. I'm very sympathetic to your situation."

"But you can do nothing about it." This wasn't said in an accusatory way; it was simply a statement of fact.

"I can't do anything about the libretto, you know," I said. "I've never imagined writing one. I've been reading some of DiBrufa's poetry and I know opera and love it. I'm trying to absorb all the Italian I can. These are the only qualifications I have."

She was holding her head in her hands. "Could you possibly bring me the bottle of Tylenol that's in the bathroom on the basin?"

In the bathroom I was immediately enveloped by her scent. So much so that my knees weakened, to my surprise. I looked for the Tylenol and found my own face in the mirror, unnaturally flushed and marked by a crease from the chair cushion I'd been resting against. I needed sleep. But now my body was awake.

I picked up the Tylenol and grabbed one of the bottles of Perrier I had brought over from my room. When I arrived at her bed, I thought she'd been crying.

"Thanks," she said.

There was no reason for me to sit down beside her, but I handed her a Kleenex and sat down anyway.

She blew her nose and took the pills with the Perrier. She looked tired, washed out, but strangely younger, and definitely more attractive, without most of her makeup. She smiled. "Were you awake for that entire diatribe?"

"Most of it. And I was wrong. It sounds like you love your work."

"Oh, the work, yes. But I've been very foolish in this particular case. I think I signed on for the wrong reasons."

We looked at each other expectantly for an extended moment,

as if a question had been asked and we were waiting to see which one of us would answer it. At last her eyes softened and she reached up and touched my face and moved her hand across my shoulder and down my arm. I could hear her breathing. Or perhaps it was it my own. She took my chin in her hand and said, "When I first saw you I thought you were Scandinavian."

I smiled. "You did?"

"You've got a nice dusting of freckles on your cheeks. You're a true blond."

"You've got a perceptive eye. My mother was Danish."

"Really. Well, lucky you. Do you speak Danish?"

"Not much. *Jeg taler kun lidt Dansk.* That's it. I only speak a little Danish, that means."

"Well, we won't speak Danish, then." She took my hand. "None of this will show up in that profile of me that you hope to write," she said with an amused smile.

"I can't say. Nothing's happened yet."

"Something's happening now, I think."

Something was happening now. But I couldn't bring myself to speak.

"Is it the age thing?" she asked.

"No. Not at all."

"I'll be fifty-four next August. Is that too frightening?" She laughed a little.

"It's not the age thing."

"It frightens me from time to time. The age thing. I don't know how I got here. That gives you a bit of an advantage, I suppose."

"Why would I want an advantage?"

She shrugged. "It's a matter of control, I guess. Gives you an out."

"I see. Should I want one." I put my hands on her shoulders and pulled her closer and kissed her and finally the talking stopped. For quite a while. Until we came to rest facing each other and tried to catch our breaths.

"Could you do something with those long legs?" she laughed. So I wrapped them around her. She pulled me closer. "I'm not a bully, you know," she said. "Not in ordinary times."

"Good." I pulled myself up on one elbow and then, as if it were inevitable, I lowered my head and kissed her again. "You took a chance," I said against her ear, "bringing me with you."

"No, I didn't. You were easy. But you're all wired up with explosive devices. One has to be careful."

Now I laughed.

"I guess that was what I was up to at the restaurant," she said. "I was trying to defuse you. In a very clumsy attempt. And you exploded anyway."

"There are easier ways to defuse me," I said.

"Look," she said, "I've got to get out of the rest of these clothes. I'm smothering." She kissed me quickly. "Would you like to sleep in here tonight?"

"I think," I said as I sat up, "I need some time to recalibrate. And I definitely need sleep." I got to my feet and immediately sat back down. My knees had buckled.

She finished unbuttoning her shirt. "What you mean is, let's see what happens in the harsh light of day."

"No, what I mean is that I need to sleep. Right now I feel hungover, and all my joints are out of whack. I don't know if I can walk."

"Okay, I'll see you at breakfast then."

But when she pressed against me at the connecting door, I almost changed my mind. It seemed as if I'd made a decision: chosen—something—and I could take as much time as I wanted and it would remain. Possibly change, but not disappear.

At first I slept well. Then just before dawn I wandered into a dream in which the face of a former involvement named Lois appeared, a psychotic photographer who had left me for a former Anglican nun who now called herself Bree. She noisily began to set up her tripod and unpack her cameras, making quite a bit of racket. I woke up quickly after that because it was clear the noise was coming from the connecting door to Elaine's room, and she was knocking with some insistence and calling my name.

"Why did you lock this door?" she said.

"Habit," I muttered. I had leapt into my jeans to let her in and now sat on the side of the bed with my head in my hands, slowly reacquainting myself with my aching brain.

Elaine had remained by the door, and although she didn't seem angry, I could see she was disturbed.

I looked up. "What's wrong?"

"Something's very wrong," she said, and came over to sit next to me. "I got a call from Luca, a friend of Vincent's, very late last night. Very early this morning, more like." She rubbed her temples. "Vincent was rushed to the hospital yesterday evening. Luca was excited, and I didn't get everything straight, but apparently Vincent began to cough and then bleed from his mouth and nose, and they couldn't stop it. So they called a Radio Taxi and took him off."

"Aren't there any ambulances working in that city?"

"Taxis are quicker. And it was Christmas night."

"Where did they take him? Not to the policlinico, I hope."

"No, no. To the new hospital, down near San Sisto." She took a breath. "They've put him on a ventilator, Ally."

"Oh, no."

"Acute respiratory distress, Luca told me. He couldn't breathe."

"Has this happened to him before?"

"Not exactly like this."

I waited a moment. "What can we do?"

She took my hand. "I think I may have to go back. You can stay on if you want. But first I'm going to call Renata. She'll know who to call to get some accurate information. I don't want to jump in prematurely. But ..." She turned toward me. "I don't want him to be alone."

"Of course not." In spite of her anxiety, in spite of the late night we'd had and little sleep, she now looked, not beautiful but striking. Her hair was tousled, her cheeks slightly flushed. I embraced her. She was still warm from sleep. "I'll come with you. He's my friend too. Not like you, but still."

She turned her head and kissed me on the cheek. "Good. Good. I'll go call Renata and let you know what she says. She'll have to call me back, but I'll take a shower while I wait."

"Should I order up some breakfast?"

"Why don't you call room service; use the phone in my room. Order me coffee and toast. Maybe some bacon." She walked toward the door. "Please don't lock this," she said.

We went back out to Stansted and managed to change our tickets to a midafternoon RyanAir flight down to Perugia. The traffic was light. It was Boxing Day; I had forgotten. The day was cloudless, bright, and there were whitecaps beneath us on the channel and fresh snow on the Alps. On the plane we held hands casually, possibly to remind ourselves that we had unfinished business. She was thinking of Vincent, but I might be part of these thoughts now, I didn't know.

However, as we left the mountains behind us and began our descent into a purple dusk, I thought about yesterday and last night and began to wonder if I'd read too much into it. I looked out the window, wondering whether those might be the lights of Bologna beneath us. I remembered Senta, and how in Bologna someone—Ciro?—had persuaded her to put a slice of lemon in her white wine. She did enter my thoughts at the oddest moments.

I took a quick glance at Elaine and saw her eyes were closed. She seemed cool and remote. Yes, her thoughts were of Vincent and mine should be too, but instead I began to consider a scenario in which I would be completely written out of whatever events were to come. I thought I'd made my case about the libretto, perhaps too thoroughly, which might remove me from that project altogether. If Vincent survived—and I was unable to imagine that he wouldn't—Elaine would doubtlessly take him to her place after he was discharged and nurse him until he was back on his feet. Between them they would figure out how to deal with the opera, DiBrufa, everything. There might not be a role for me in that plan. And there shouldn't be. I was not part of their creative world. I had my own situation to work out, exactly as it was before Christmas. My brief—very brief—physical encounter with Elaine would no doubt be filed away as a pleasant holiday diversion.

These ruminations were clearly meant to keep the horrifying image of Vincent on a ventilator out of my conscious mind. Under normal circumstances my instincts would have been to pack up and move on. I had come to Perugia to put a human face on an eccentric librettist. That effort had stalled and might never move forward, but a more attractive alternative had moved into its place. Elaine had revealed more of herself on this brief journey than I ever expected. But every revelation was fraught with complications that had now become unnervingly personal. At this point one of these complications was Elaine's hand, which still lay in mine. So as the plane banked steeply over the lights of Assisi and began its final approach to the Perugia airport, I abruptly detached myself from her and began to rummage through my carry-on. Nothing was going to be simple.

At that time, as today, there were no jetways at Saint Francis of Assisi Airport, and as we walked across the tarmac toward the terminal, I said, "Look, I think you should go on to the hospital by yourself."

"All right, if you like. But why?"

"If he's in real trouble, he'll just want to see you."

"Ally, he won't be seeing anyone. He'll be sedated, I'm sure."

"Give him my best, then, when you can."

In the early evening darkness, I saw her shrug. And with that shrug I realized there was a real possibility that I wouldn't see her, or Vincent, again. This realization quickly turned into a defensive petulance, and I didn't welcome it. It never occurred to me that she might need any support from me at all.

Outside the terminal I politely asked her to let me know how much I owed her for the trip, but I didn't give her much chance to respond. An empty taxi appeared, I jumped in, and closed the door before she could join me. The driver took off at great speed, and I didn't look back.

A friend of mine once cautioned me, "Don't become a character in your own drama." Her advice seemed sound at the time, but becoming a character in my own dramas, whatever they were, had always been so attractive a proposition that it was advice I seldom heeded. So here I was again at the bottom of the birdcage, among old seed husks and poop and ragged feathers, looking up at a self-absorbed parakeet pecking at his reflection in the mirror. I recognized the parakeet, and the cage, even the mirror, but I was unable to step away.

Twelve

On the evening of my return from London, I was surprised to find that more than half the household had returned and the entire Caccini family was back from Gualdo. I passed Ercole on the stairs, on his way to work at the Brufani, and he wished me a happy St. Stephen's Day. He pointed up to the next landing. "*Vai! Vai!*" he said, smiling. "*C'è un gran festa nella cucina!*"

It sounded like the "*gran festa*" was already well underway. I had forgotten that in Italy St. Stephen's Day, December 26, was a much livelier celebration than Christmas Day itself. People were back in the streets, and groups tended to go out for dinner and make pilgrimages to see the *presepi,* or nativity scenes, that had been set up in various churches around the city. So when I entered the apartment, I was greeted by a loud cheer from the Caccini daughters, and the signora bore down upon me bearing a glass of prosecco, an unusual drink for her to be carrying about. Ines had bought it, as it turned out, and as I dropped my bag in my room, the little girls presented me with a plate of Asiago and prosciutto *bruschette,* which I was happy to sample. Anita and Ines followed, tenants whom I didn't know well, and with some enthusiasm told me they were going out for dinner. Would I join them? The scene at the airport was still playing uncomfortably in my mind, but I knew I needed food and accepted their invitation before I could change my mind. The little girls were singing and dancing in circles, and the signora finally herded them back to the kitchen, where she was brewing coffee. I took another glass of prosecco, and after I'd washed up a bit and changed clothes, the evening got underway.

London faded into a mental mist, as if it were a fairytale, not real in any way.

We linked arms as we walked along the corso. Including English, there were three native languages among us—Ines spoke a mysterious Argentine dialect and Anita was from Mexico City—so we conversed in Italian as best we could. We turned downhill into one of the dimly lit streets off the corso—Ines had a particular destination in mind—and by a circuitous route arrived at Trattoria Mandorla, near the Mandorla Gate. It was nearly full, but the *padrone* found us a table near the back and immediately produced mineral water and a carafe of the house red without being asked.

I spied a beautiful blue and white flag hanging behind the bar and immediately recognized this establishment as the one where Greek inhabitants of the city habitually gathered to drown their homesickness and debate among themselves about political matters. I had even mentioned this place in my city article. The Greeks I had met were convinced that their country was currently perceived as a politically corrupt wasteland, and they would sit late into the night at the Mandorla and sing and drink and eventually there would be much weeping. I wouldn't have chosen this place for dinner, but according to Ines they served very good beef, which she had been missing.

We were all hungry. I began with a bowl of spaghetti carbonara, and we each had a *bistecca*. The red wine quickly disappeared, and Ines ordered another carafe. Greek music began to filter in from somewhere in a back room as I consumed my meal, seemingly feeding a part of my body that had been overtaken by the *idea* of food. I seemed to be feeding a starving monster. I was distracted by the sound of a familiar voice, and when I looked up there stood Jo, flanked by a pair of handsome Greeks. The youth brigade. Everyone pulled up chairs, and Ines ordered another carafe of wine but for unknown reasons switched the order from red to white. An unfortunate decision. The Greek music had increased in volume, and Jo began to explain—loudly—where she had been and how she had discovered where we were. (I suspected Signora Caccini had played a role.) The two Greeks quietly observed this scene and slowly drank their beers. Yanni was one, dark and intense; Georgios sported a drooping Fu Manchu moustache and was the larger of the two.

At some point a particular song began to play and a large number of people stood up, including the two Greeks at our table. The music didn't sound like a national anthem, so the rest of us remained seated, but soon all the male customers who were on their feet began to sing and sway back forth, their eyes closed. As the music concluded, they lifted their glasses and shouted, "*Viva Grecia!*"

The answering shout came from all around us: "*Eviva!*"

Yanni and Georgios resumed their seats and looked around at those of us who had not joined in this toast. Yanni, in particular, became visibly disturbed. Georgios, on the other hand, had decided to put the moves on Jo, and at that moment was kissing her hand and slowly moving his mouth up her arm. He seemed to be a big friendly guy. I was not worried about him. Yanni was another matter.

Yanni fixed his black eyes on Anita and me. "You do not drink to the glory of Greece?" he asked us.

I lifted my glass a bit and said calmly, "*Viva Grecia.*"

"I do not hear you," he said to us.

"*Viva Grecia,*" Anita and I called out in unison, lifting our glasses.

"You must stand up. On feet."

"Oh, please," I said. "We're tired."

Georgios was finally diverted from his attempts to kiss Jo's ear. He turned to Yanni and spoke to him firmly in Greek.

The noise in the room had grown deafening, and I thought perhaps there was some additional commotion inside my head. I heard a combination of radio static, waterfalls, breaking glass, and honking horns. Above this racket I imagined the hissing sound of an air pump, breathing like a dark blanket over our table.

Yanni stood up. Now he was looking only at me. Under the table Anita clasped my hand. Jo had put her head down and seemed to be asleep. Still it went on. "Up. Stand on feet," Yanni said with a hard look. "Salute *Grecia.*"

All right, I thought. I got to my feet unsteadily. "No, Allyn, no; not important, not important," Anita said to me in Spanish.

"He's just a little boy," I said, from what I thought was the advantage of great age.

Georgios continued to speak to Yanni urgently in Greek, but he was deaf to whatever Georgios was saying. He raised his glass and waited.

The room was whirling about me like a carousel. I had a quick vision of the hotel room in London, Elaine's face as I had leaned down to kiss her.

Then I forgot what I was supposed to do. I remembered a toast. So, supporting myself with one fist on the table, I raised my glass and shouted, "*Viva* America!" I recall being satisfied that I had said "America," because that would include Ines as a South American and also Anita, who had recently reminded me that Mexico was considered a geographic part of North America. (As is Greenland, to my surprise.) I didn't expect to hear an enthusiastic response to my toast.

But "*Eviva! Eviva* America!" came the happy chorus in the room. And with that, Yanni leaned across the table and spit in my face.

I sat down hard on my chair, and Anita poured some mineral water on her napkin and began to clean off my face. Ines was now on her feet. "*Sporco Greco!*" she shouted viciously at Yanni, followed by some untranslatable words in her native dialect. Georgios, to his credit, bid the still sleeping Jo a reluctant farewell and grabbed Yanni by one arm and pulled him to his feet, his face still disfigured by rage. "Good night, *buona notte, vaya con dios,*" Georgios said with a smile as he dragged Yanni away.

I was still astonished. I wanted no more wine, no more food, no music, no more of this place. I didn't know if I could manage the hike back up the hill to the corso, and for some reason this made me very angry. I could not think of how to get home. I imagined home to be in a far distant place. How to get there?

As I was pondering this situation, there was movement beside the table, and when I looked up, Elaine was standing there, a fatigued but amused smile on her face.

"Oh, hell." I closed my eyes.

"Time to go," she said. She looked at Ines and Anita and down at Jo, who had raised her head groggily. "Ladies, may I offer you a ride? Allyn will be coming along with me."

Thirteen

A great many hours later, I opened my eyes into a dim, shuttered room. Walls ascended into angled moldings and dark corners. I heard no sound of activity, but a noisy, brilliant light was perceptible beyond the louvered shutters. I felt it shatter against my eyeballs. The bed I was in was enormous, a *letto matrimoniale*, which accommodated my long legs deliciously. I was on my back in the center of it, surrounded by space and quilts. But when I lifted my head the room spun, so I closed my eyes and went back to sleep.

Sometime after that I felt someone sit down on the side of the bed, and it was Elaine, of course. She placed a steaming cup on the bedside table. "Chamomile," she said. "Be careful, it's very hot."

I had no intention of swallowing that or anything else at that moment.

"Can you look at me?" she said. I did try, unsuccessfully. She resettled herself and was quiet for a while. "You can't handle your liquor," she said finally.

In this case, that was true.

"And it's not the solution anyway."

"Empty stomach," I croaked, startled by my own voice.

"Yes. Mine was empty too. I got a sandwich at the hospital last night. And a cup of ghastly coffee out of a machine."

I remembered Vincent then, and opened my eyes. "How is he?"

"He's still intubated, but the doctors may remove it later today. Right now he needs it to help him breathe, but they want to get it out as soon as they can. His body had begun to resist the drug regimen he's been on, that was part of the problem, as I understand it. So they're talking about other alternatives." She patted my cheek. "Now I'd like to see if you can sit up and drink some of this tea. Can you manage that?"

I slowly pushed myself into a half-sitting position. "Where am I?"

"In my bedroom." She handed me the cup.

I breathed the fragrant steam and took a sip. Its warmth descended reassuringly through my chest. "Thank you." I drank again. "Did Ines and the others get home?"

She nodded. "Right to their door. I challenged Via Rocchi. Don't you remember?"

"I guess not."

"Anita will take care of the signora. And I spoke with her earlier as well. She knows you have a friend who's very ill. She's eager to help, in fact." She took my cup and put it on the bedside table. "You have a very loyal landlady."

The tea had settled my stomach somewhat; now I needed water. And probably a hot shower. I closed my eyes again.

"Don't go back to sleep," she said. "Need a shower? Towels are in the bathroom, through that door. And a new toothbrush. Your clothes are on the chair. And your bag is on the table."

"What time is it?" I asked.

"Noon," she said as she left the room.

After my shower I felt partially revived, but I had doubts about the substantial brunch that Elaine had laid out on her dining table. Coffee, warm bread with butter and jam, scrambled eggs, and some prosciutto. I was delighted to see a full glass of tomato juice at my place. Half an hour ago I probably would have had dry heaves at the sight of this feast, but now it looked pretty good. I started with the juice and quickly put it down.

"Not to be ungrateful, but the Italians can do everything with tomatoes but make juice," I said.

"Drink a little more, then eat the food," she said, and I began to do that.

"Tell me more about Vincent," I said to her over my second cup of coffee.

"He'll be in ICU, or whatever they call it, until they get him off the ventilator and his condition stabilizes. I don't know how long that will take. You have to understand, Ally, he's fighting a terrible battle. Much worse than he ever let us know. His lungs nearly shut down on Christmas night."

"Did you see him?"

"I sat by his bed for a few minutes. He's deeply sedated."

"Did you say anything to him?"

She smiled slightly. "Yes. A few words. I told him where he was and that we were here. I told him we loved him. I hope that was all right."

"Of course it was. Could I see him, just for a few minutes?"

"You wouldn't want to see him, not the way he is. Anyway, they probably wouldn't let you in."

"How did you get in?"

"I'm his next of kin. So I told them, and so they believe." She walked over to the window. "Such a nice day," she said. She went into the kitchen and turned on the water in the sink, then shut it off. "I'll go down to the hospital later."

I began to clear the table. Memories of our brief encounter in London continued to ambush me at odd moments.

As if reading my mind, she said, "Just soak those plates. I'll get to them after a while. What I'd like is for you to come and lie down with me. We can talk or we can nap. When we were in London, you spoke about recalibrating. That sounds like a good idea, for both of us."

My understanding of recalibration was that it was done in order to set a new course. At that point I didn't think I could plot one, even with a compass.

At first it was like making love with a stranger, and I wasn't surprised to find that part of it exciting. She had a firm, attractively athletic body, and her passion was quick, as if it had been waiting. This was not like sex with Senta, who had been youthfully coltish and would fall away into sleep almost immediately if we should rest for a moment. Elaine and I seemed to respond to each other as if we had long been lovers, and if we drew back to take a breath, a touch brought us back to another beginning. Sleep came and went, and eventually, when I looked, evening had fallen outside her windows. We were quiet, both of us on our backs. Even her relaxed presence beside me remained stimulating, although physically I was nearly unable to move.

She lifted herself up on one elbow. "Who are you?" she said in an amused voice, "and what the hell are you doing in my bed?" I turned toward her and saw she was smiling. "Someone asked me that once. Seriously. It makes me laugh." And she did laugh. I wasn't sure how to respond. "Would you like something to drink?"

"Water," I said. "Lots of it."

She walked naked out of the room, and I closed my eyes and fell into a doze. Just for a moment, I thought. Eventually, there was the sound of water running, and then she was back in bed beside me.

"Have some water," she said. "Then we'll sleep a little."

Later I helped her clean up the kitchen. "Are you sure you want to go down to the hospital at this hour?" I asked her. "It's nearly ten."

She was wiping off the stove with a sponge. "I'm sure," she said. "I need to go. They let me come in at any hour. I'll run you up the hill first. Unless you want to wait here for me. If you'd rather not, that's fine."

She was all business again, and now I was thoroughly at sea. A week ago I might happily have said a casual good-night and walked out the door without looking back. I had never been keen about complicating sexual encounters with immediate analyses, agendas, or discussions of plans for the future. But now I wanted to ask her, "What happens next?" and I hated that: well, *hate* is too strong a word. But our encounter had been so surprisingly satisfying that "What happens next?" was, despite my pessimistic ruminations on the plane, a question I wanted to ask.

She dried her hands on the dish towel and hung it over the back of a kitchen chair. "So, what's your decision?" she asked me.

I definitely needed some distance.

She gave me a friendly kiss and then embraced me. "I see you worrying," she said. "Look. What happened this afternoon was between us. And we're the ones who will work out where it goes."

I nodded. "Well, I should check in at Casa Caccini, I guess." I felt a little let down. I do have weak moments when I need to be reassured. Childhood breaks through the armor. An event to be avoided. If possible.

"Okay then. I'll run you up to Piazza Danti." She took my face between her hands. "Don't overthink this," she said. "Relax. It was lovely."

Fourteen

I was bombarded by the sounds of activity as soon as I entered Casa Caccini. It was Christmas week, after all, and everyone was up despite the late hour.

"Signora Ally!" the signora cried out, coming toward me with her arms outstretched. "I have fear they kept you at the *ospedale!* Come, come, I have food for you!"

Jo emerged from the hall by the kitchen and dragged me down to her room by one arm. "I need your help. Seriously."

The signora stuck her head out of the kitchen door. "Come, Ally! *La piccola cena è pronta!*"

"*Vengo subito!*" I called. "Can this wait?" I said to Jo. "Let me drop my things in my room and take off my coat." There was lively dance music coming from the room now shared by Anita and Ines, and I could hear the little girls singing.

"I think Yanni is after me," she said in a loud whisper.

I looked around my room. "Where is everybody?" I asked her. "Where is Shaima? Did she go off to Abu Dhabi?"

"She's sleeping at her dig. Down by the Etruscan tombs."

"Allyn!" the signora called.

I rubbed my eyes. I needed sleep, and soon. "Why would Yanni be after you?"

She put her hand on my arm. "He's a fucking maniac. He's wants to hurt someone, and I think he's aiming at me."

"Why you? You were asleep on the table. I'm the one he spit on. Where has your soccer guy gone? Can't you call him?"

"He's useless; he's always traveling with the Grifos, and now he's obsessed with his knees. He's afraid he'll hurt them or someone else will hurt them and he'll be kicked off the team."

I was getting impatient with all this youthful, heterosexual melodrama. "All right. Georgios is a nice guy. Let him take care of Yanni. That's his business."

"Allyn!" The signora came to the kitchen door. "Cena for you!"

The little girls burst out of Ines and Anita's room. "Mamma! Mamma! C'è gelato?"

"What is it you want me to do exactly?" I asked her. We began to walk down the hall toward the kitchen.

"Georgios has a Greek friend. A medical resident at the hospital. A little bit older. Perfect for you. If you could come with us ..."

I stopped at the kitchen door. "Jo, this isn't my problem. I don't want to be a target, if that's what you had in mind. Thanks, but no thanks. Ask Anita. Ask Shaima whenever she comes back. Just remember that almost every available female in this house is too old for your guys."

She put her fist over her mouth and ran back down the hall.

After I'd had something to eat, I returned to Jo's room to try to calm her down. I brought her a glass of wine. "You don't have any reason to be nervous about Yanni," I said.

"He thinks I'm pulling Georgios away from the Greek force in the city," she said. I've seen him on the street once or twice. He looks at me with those black eyes."

"Is there a Greek force in the city?" I asked her curiously.

"Oh, who cares!"

I thought for a moment. "Tell me how a double date with the older Greek resident would help your terrible situation."

Her face brightened. "It's for New Year's Eve. The fireworks, if we can find them. Whatever parties we run into. There will be huge crowds, and I don't want to always be looking over my shoulder. Know what I mean? It would be easier with four people." She moved to the mirror and began to brush her hair.

This sounded like a night from hell to me. But it had a possible upside.

"What's his name, this elderly Greek doctor?"

"Odysseus."

"You're kidding."

She fluffed her hair. "I know it's odd, but he was named after that book. He's very nice, though."

Elaine and I met for coffee at Sandri the following afternoon. It had grown bitterly cold. We sat at a table behind the steamed-up windows. It was lovely to be in this bar during the weeks most of the students were away.

She unwrapped her scarf from around her neck and opened her datebook. "I'm having dinner with Sandro tonight. I have to explain in believable detail why this production is doomed."

"Well, don't say *doomed*, to begin with. Come up with another word."

"It's a most appropriate word, I think."

I sipped my coffee. "What about Vincent?"

"They removed the ventilator tube late this morning, thank God. And he's slowly coming off the sedation. They seem to be treating him very conservatively. He tried to speak to me before I left, but his voice is terribly hoarse. He knew who I was, though."

"I don't suppose I could see him now."

"He's still in ICU." She finished her tea. "What are you doing New Year's Eve?"

"Well …"

"Because I'm having a little get-together at my place. Sandro suggested I ask some of our major donors and some company board members and a few others who stayed in town. Nothing fancy."

But I knew it would be a lot more than fancy.

"Why don't you come?" she went on. "Square it with la signora and you can stay over." She smiled.

"I'm going with some of the signora's other tenants to watch the fireworks, wherever they are."

She shrugged. "Well. All right." She leaned across the table and took my hand. "Can you come by later?"

"We'll see. But you can handle public relations on your own, and very well, I should think."

"All right then." She released my hand.

"Where will you and Sandro have dinner?"

"I'm not sure. He has a couple of places he likes. I'd like to find someplace quiet, so we can talk. But we'll probably end up at La Taverna."

"Umm. Get the baccalà to start."

"Wrong time of year."

"It's always on the menu."

"Are you being deliberately disagreeable? Or just flirting."

"Oh, I dunno." I looked into her eyes and felt a frisson of physical memory. I gave her a little smile as she stood up. "The adventure begins, I guess." Her eyes softened a bit, and I had a quick urge to kiss her. Providentially, the door opened at that moment, admitting a chilly whoosh of air, and several early passeggiata strollers rolled up to the bar, rubbing their hands.

I stood up beside her and looped her scarf around her neck. "Stay warm. I'll call you tomorrow."

"I'll be at the theater from about ten on."

"On New Year's Eve? Why? Vincent's in the hospital and your pro tem singers are still on vacation."

"There's always work to be done. And I think better at the theater." She put on her coat. "About the libretto. Your decision is final? You won't help me out?"

"It's not mine to save, Elaine," I said. "I'm sorry." I didn't like myself very much at that moment. But I had some other ideas I wasn't ready to share with her.

Fifteen

We saw some flurries on New Year's Eve day, but they weren't serious enough to stick, and by evening it was slightly warmer, something to do with a particular wind from Africa, Ercole told me. Before our outing I stuck my head into Jo's room to see what she was wearing. Tight jeans and a form-hugging red sweater, short leather boots with two-inch heels. She smelled divine. She was standing in front of the mirror putting on makeup.

"I'm wearing my hair up," she said, "and my neck will probably freeze."

"Where are we meeting them?"

"On the steps of the duomo. Nine o'clock."

If I had expected Odysseus Lianis to resemble his classical forbear, a world-weary sailor with a scruffy beard, I would have been off the mark. This Odysseus was tall and lean, with clear, inquisitive eyes behind steel-rimmed glasses and confident, well-tended hands. He was somewhat older than the other Greeks I had talked with in Perugia, a second-year resident already at the new hospital complex down near San Sisto, specializing in cardiothoracic problems. He did not seem to be obsessively morose, like the other Greeks. He was quiet, self-contained, and spoke excellent Italian and English. I instantly surmised that he, like I, had been coerced into this New Year's date in order to enable Georgios to further his personal agenda with Jo.

The four of us began to amble through the crowds on the corso in search of wherever the fireworks were to be set off. Georgios hadn't taken the time to find out, and Odysseus, I suspected, had been on duty at the hospital. Jo did offer, "I think there's a Ferris wheel in the Carducci Gardens ..."

But Georgios turned us down Via Priori, which was still ablaze with Christmas lights. Several social celebrations had already spilled into the street. When we turned left toward Via della Cupa, I knew Georgios was heading for the Mandorla bar, where all his Greek pals were no doubt waiting for him to appear with his sexy *americana.* Jo shot me a pleading look. I had not spotted Yanni in the streets along the way, but if he were to cause trouble anywhere, it would be at the Mandorla. I had no desire to return there.

"Stop," I said. Odysseus, who had taken my elbow to guide me through the crowds, dropped his hand. "Georgios, if you're heading for the Mandorla, I'd rather not."

"But why? All our friends will be there."

"All *your* friends, I think."

"There will be music at the Mandorla," he said plaintively. "It will be the New Year! *Capodanno!*"

"It will be New Year everywhere in the city," Odysseus said. "Come, we keep walking, find another place for a drink. On the way we will find a beautiful view that I know, and maybe the fireworks will be below the Etruscan wall."

"Thank you," I said, as we continued on, our breath clouding around us. "I had an uncomfortable evening at the Mandorla not long ago."

"It is full of weeping Greeks," he said with a little smile. "Not good for New Year's Eve."

Georgios pouted for a few minutes, but Jo diverted him by whispering into his ear and by the time we got to the main section of Via della Cupa, he had leapt up onto the level top of the Etruscan wall that followed the curve of the street and was strutting along, balanced like a high-wire artist. This particular section of the ancient wall dropped steeply down to a small park that lay near the entrance to the Kennedy Tunnel, far, far below. The view to the west was indeed lovely, but a fall down to the park was not one that could be survived.

Odysseus moved quickly to pull Georgios off the wall, while Jo clasped her hands in mock terror. We all peered over the edge of the wall and agreed that no fireworks were being assembled in the little park.

"I know a bar back up the hill," Odysseus said. "Off Via Bonazzi. No one knows it's there, but I like it. I studied there sometimes when I was in medical school."

"There is music?" Georgios asked hopefully.

"There is a jukebox," Odysseus said, "with very good music."

At Café Bonazzi, Georgios was restless. He didn't like the music on the jukebox, there were no snacks available that pleased him, and the bartender was eyeing him in a suspicious way. And where were the people, the celebration? The place was indeed quiet, and one could have a normal conversation without yelling. I liked it. I ordered some wine, and the bartender threw in a plate of very good Fontal cheese and some toasted bread. But quiet was not what Georgios wanted, and Jo wanted to be with Georgios. So when he stood up and announced he was moving on to the

Mandorla, Jo, who by that time had put away two large glasses of wine, shrugged and said she would go too.

Odysseus and I looked at each other. I could tell he would agree to whatever I suggested, and I also knew that Georgios probably didn't care whether we came along or not. But I liked Georgios, so I said, "I want to sit here with Odysseus for a little while. We'll see you at the Mandorla later."

Georgios threw an arm over Jo's shoulder, and they made a noisy exit.

"I hope you don't mind," I said to Odysseus. "I was beginning to feel like an old maid chaperone."

He smiled. "I don't mind. I am an elder statesman myself. And I've just come off a thirty-six-hour shift."

"Oh, too bad," I said. "Do you want to call it a night and go home to sleep? That would be all right with me."

"No." He smiled. "It's good for me to get out." He got up to fetch us more wine.

Now I was having doubts about my plan. Odysseus was a nice guy, he'd been working for thirty-six hours, and what I was going to ask him to do might not sit well with his medical superiors. He returned with the wine and a bowl of nuts and sat down. After a moment he said, "Do you have some plan in mind? I think you do."

"As a matter of fact, yes. I need to visit a patient in your hospital who's in intensive care. What is that called in Italian?"

"*Rianimazione. Terapia intensiva.*"

"Right. And I'm not a family member, so I don't think they would let me in at any time. But now it's night, everyone is somewhere else celebrating, and I'm wondering if there's any way you could get me in there to see him, if only for five or ten minutes. He's just come off a brief experience with a ventilator, and I think he's probably had a couple of transfusions. I don't have any harmful objectives, believe me. It wouldn't be for long." I paused and took a drink of wine. "I know you're tired, so if you say no, I'll completely understand."

"It will be difficult for him to speak, you realize. And he may be partially sedated still."

"Yes, I know. I just have some things to say to him, and there won't be any need for him to talk."

He finished his wine and looked at his watch. "We'll go," he said, "and make some tracks, as they say in America."

I remember the trip down the hill to the hospital as a journey through an alien planet. Strobe lights assaulted us from darkened doorways, blasts of music were present and quickly gone, and on the corso and into the gardens beyond—where there was, indeed, a Ferris wheel—small firecrackers sounded and an occasional rocket lifted into the sky. We retrieved Odysseus's car from under Piazza Partigiani, and he drove us swiftly down the hill by backstreets, making sure to avoid hitting pedestrians who leapt out at us, twirling fire batons and shouting messages I didn't understand. We finally took the turn around the station and dove into the newer area on the southwestern side of the city. We arrived at the Silvestrini hospital ten minutes later.

I was stunned. I had been expecting something like the policlinico. Instead we entered a parking area that resembled one of the airport terminal complexes at JFK. In addition to the collection of buildings, a herd of bulldozers and backhoes and several large cement mixers was presently at rest.

"They are still finishing construction," Odysseus apologized. "*Quasi finito.* Almost done."

"I'm impressed," I said.

He parked and turned off the ignition. "First, I must know your friend's name. We go in through *pronto soccorso.* Then you follow me to a locker room. I will give you a scrub jacket and a clipboard if I can find one." He settled his glasses on his nose. "It is important you do not speak. I am hoping someone I know will be on duty at the unit desk. I will find his bed number. You will follow me in. I will lead you to his bed, and I will stand there. I will give you privacy, but I must stay. Please be very quick, talk to your friend five minutes, no more, and then we will leave. If someone is at his bed giving care, we must go and that will be the end of this." He looked at me through the darkness. "*Capito*?"

"His name is Vincent Norrie," I said as I opened the car door.

His plan worked better than I had imagined, and in the end the dramatic subterfuge was probably unnecessary. My experience at the policlinico had prepared me for the strange ways of Italian clinics, but this was a large, multistoried city hospital, in capital letters. If you behaved as if you had a purpose, no one would give you a second glance. And no one did. The emergency room was already active with the results of holiday car crashes and celebratory mishaps, so we were able to go directly to the staff locker room with no questions asked. He took his own white jacket from his locker, with ID pin attached, tossed me a clean green scrub top, and we went quickly on our way. Before I knew it, I was standing in the semidarkness beside Vincent's bed. He was in a long ward with a few other patients, dozing by a little light.

"Begin," Odysseus said, and moved to the end of the bed.

"Vincent," I said in a low voice. I took his hand. "Vincent, it's Ally."

He opened his eyes and made a hoarse noise in his throat, which I finally understood was an attempt to say my name. His face was washed out under the reddish stubble of his beard, and several different lines were plugged into his arm.

I bent down and kissed his cheek and then pulled a small metal chair up to his bedside. "Listen. I can't stay long."

He lifted his head slightly and looked at Odysseus.

"Yes, that's Odysseus. He's okay." I took his hand and held it against my cheek. In spite of the clear evidence of his medical battles, there was still a sweet boyish innocence about his face.

He rubbed his cheek against my hand.

"Vincent, where is your copy of the William Trevor book, the one you're adapting for your opera? Can you remember? Please think hard."

He frowned a bit.

"Do you understand? I need to find your annotated copy of the Trevor book. Where is it?"

"Why?" he managed to say.

"Oh, please, Vincent, I don't have enough time to explain."

"Elaine ..."

"No, not for Elaine. For me. I'm going to write you a libretto. As good as I can make it."

He shook his head weakly. "Won't work," he tried to say. "Elaine ..."

"I can't do anything to save her opera. I want to help you finish yours."

He shook his head and closed his eyes. And I heard him begin to wheeze a bit. So I stood up. But he continued to grasp my hand. I knew he wanted to say something, but he didn't seem to know how.

"Is it at Elaine's?" I took a guess. "It's there?"

"Don't," he finally whispered. "Don't try." He took several

deep breaths. "Help her." His arm had become tangled in one of his lines, and I straightened it out.

"Allyn," Odysseus said from the foot of the bed, "you must come now."

I put both my hands on his cheeks and kissed his forehead. "Don't you dare go anywhere, Vincent," I said. "Don't leave us. I mean it."

"Ally," he whispered roughly. "Please. Help her." He closed his eyes.

I switched off his little light and walked out the door. Odysseus caught up with me at the elevator, and still wearing our hospital garments, we walked right out the emergency room doors into a night filled with rockets and explosions that seemed to be coming from all directions. As if we had stepped into a country at war.

"Ah," Odysseus said. "The arena at Santa Giuliana. That's where they are."

I put my arms around him and gave him an embrace. "Happy New Year," I said. "And thank you for this."

Sixteen

The sound of the family telephone finally woke me. After a while, when no one picked it up, I crawled out of bed and went down the hall to answer it.

"Is that you?" Elaine said into my ear. "Check your cell phone. I think it's dead." I stood there groggily in a sweatshirt and pajama bottoms. "Never mind. Meet me in the Brufani bar in an hour. Can you manage that?"

"Where?" I said.

"The bar at the Brufani. Hurry up."

The house was unusually silent. I knocked on Anita and Ines's door and looked in. Beds neatly made. Nobody home. I was concerned about Jo, but when I checked she was out cold, barely breathing, her clothes slung about on various chairs. Shaima's bed had not been slept in. I was beginning to think of her as a ghost.

I assumed the Caccini family was away again as well, so I used the time to sneak in an illegal shower while my cell phone charged. Still in a state of semi stupor, I made my way up the hill toward the corso. The sun appeared and then disappeared above a thin scrim of fast-moving gray clouds.

At the Brufani, Elaine was sitting at one of the leather banquettes and had a cappuccino ordered for me, plus a cornetto with butter and jam. There were folders and what appeared to be ledger books spread out around her. The few people who were up and about on this first day of the new year seemed to have migrated into the hotel dining room for a late breakfast.

"Well," she said as I sat down, "happy New Year to you."

"Yes. Happy New Year." I poured myself some coffee.

She rested her chin on her hand and gave me a look. "You look sleepy. Up late last night?"

"Ah. You've been down to the hospital."

"Yes, I have. Vincent's got a new room."

"That's good news." The coffee entered my veins with a resounding jolt.

She was looking at me in a steady way, and I waited for her to begin to question me about the night before, but for a long moment she said nothing.

"What is it?" I asked finally.

She refilled her coffee cup. "DiBrufa is dead."

I placed my cup down carefully on its saucer.

"Last night," she said. "He got into the theater, forced my office door, and completely demolished the place looking for scores, copies of his libretto, who knows what else. Anything he could destroy. Tore everything to shreds and smashed some of the set miniatures to boot. He put his contract on my desk, torn into pieces, fell on the floor, and died."

"You mean suicide?"

"They don't think so. Stroke or heart, probably. One of the theater security guards identified him by the ring he was wearing with the family crest. He's at the coroner's office, wherever that may be. I'm not sure what he had in mind, but it seems his excitement about this adventure caught up with his heart or his brain before he could escape." Her words were measured, not particularly upset, but shock takes many forms.

"Do the police know?"

"Of course. The security guard called them. He actually came to my house last night, in the middle of my little gathering—which is of no importance now—and told me. After he called the coroner, he also called the theater manager, but it was New Year's Eve." She shrugged. "Who knows if anyone's even been over there yet."

"And Monica?"

"The police were on their way out to the family villa in Beata Colomba to bring her back to the city. That's all I know. I haven't spoken with her yet, and I'm not looking forward to it."

"Good grief, what next."

"Yes. There goes your interview."

"That's not what I meant. Did you tell Vincent?"

"Briefly. He was a bit out of it. When I arrived they were wheeling him to his new room. I didn't give him many details because I thought the news might confuse him. But it didn't. He's speaking a little better today, at least well enough to give me a rough idea of your New Year's Eve visit." She looked at me steadily with eyes that probably hadn't closed in twenty-four hours. "Whatever were you thinking of?"

"I just needed to see him."

"I think it was a little more than a loving visit in the middle of the night."

"Could we talk about it later?"

"Why? Is there a crime involved?"

"No, but you'll probably be upset, and I don't want to deal with that right at the moment. Anyway, the DiBrufa situation will trump anything I have to say."

"Now I must hear. But I need more coffee." She waved at the bartender, who brought over a fresh carafe.

"I wanted to ask Vincent where the Trevor book was. His annotated copy."

She nodded. "I thought that was what he was trying to tell me. It's on a table in my living room. Why didn't you just ask me?"

This was going to be tough. "I want to write a libretto for him. Or start one. So he will have *something,* something to come home to. To work on. His music."

"So this would be like a ... benevolent gesture."

"I don't care what you call it."

"You who have never written a libretto in your life."

"That's not important at the moment. He needs words. I want to give him words."

"Well, that's what you seem to do best. You use words to avoid issues. Or because you're bored. Or in this case, because your interviewee has just dropped dead."

"I don't deserve that."

"No, you probably don't." She reached over and touched my hand. "Well, I'm exhausted right now; I don't think I have the energy to argue with you. Or even if this idea is worth an argument. You've already decided that you won't help me out with *Sirius* and, frankly, that issue might be moot, once the lawyers, Monica, and everyone else gets involved. It's going to be a real mess."

"Elaine, I could not have saved DiBrufa's libretto."

"You've made that point."

"Do you think you'll go ahead with *Sirius?* After what's happened? Couldn't you just withdraw it?"

"Oh, believe me, once the lawyers get involved ..."

"But what do you have? A score by a composer who abandoned the project and went off to Palermo? And a useless libretto by a poet who's now dead."

"Yes," she said. "But we're still legally contracted to produce it, in whatever way we can pull it together. Monica will insist on that, make no mistake." She rested her forehead on one hand. "Sandro should really be dealing with this, but in his current state, I can't always trust him to be rational," she said finally. "I'll have to handle it."

"They won't hold you responsible for DiBrufa's death, will they? How could they?"

"I won't be accused of killing him, no. But I had a well-documented antagonistic relationship with him. People may think I drove him to it. A large part of the creative world respects this man, even those who know all about his irrational behavior. They consider him a brilliant creature of mystery." She was silent for a long moment. "What a way to start the new year."

"Was Sandro at your party?"

"He was there and actually sober. He thinks we should just back off and consider the entire situation a lucky escape. But legally I'm not sure we can. His contract may stand, whether he's living or dead."

"He was just the librettist, Elaine. Operas belong to the composer mainly, don't they?"

"DiBrufa has a seventy-one page contract. I'm sure Monica has hundreds of copies stashed away in various places. The opera 'belongs' to Piero, living or dead, and to the composer, who at the moment is living it up in Sicily with two gypsy women." She finished her coffee. "I don't know where to start."

"What exactly are you supposed to do? You're the stage director, not part of the management."

"That may be, but I do have an honorable commitment to our

supporters and their contributions, which have been very generous. And I have personal relationships with most of the singers now. I have to tell them something."

"Did he leave any sort of note?"

"If he did, the police haven't told me. I haven't been into the office yet, but I doubt I'll find one there. He just got fed up with the entire project, probably, and decided to end it himself. But he didn't live long enough to enjoy the results." She allowed herself a little smile. "Monica becomes the problem now."

After that, I discovered I was ravenously hungry, and I thought Elaine could use something to eat too, whether she knew it or not. I asked the man behind the bar if he could get us some eggs, bacon, bread, anything at all to eat. He had been watching us and seemed to know that something significant was going on. On a hunch, I told him I was a tenant of Ercole Caccini, and his face lit up. "*Si, si, signora. Subito!*" He rushed off toward the kitchen.

When I returned to the table, she said, "I think there's an issue that you haven't really considered here."

"And what would that be?"

"How far along are you with your Perugia piece?"

"Well, I don't have my DiBrufa interview. But ..."

"Yes, but look what Piero's left you. This story's just taken off. Am I right? It will be bigger than any interview you might have come up with." She sat back. "Let me see: Insane poet destroys production of opera featuring his long-awaited first libretto, then drops dead."

"Monica might have something to say about that."

"Never mind her. Make it as melodramatic as you like. You can even add something about the composer who's presently in Palermo, and to top it off you can discuss my recent operatic disaster in New York if you want to hurl that in. What a scoop!

And in the midst of this, you want to get in involved in developing a libretto for Vincent?"

I could do nothing but let this run its course.

"I hoped you might hang around Perugia for at least a little while, but you're going to be a busy girl, no matter where you are."

At that moment a waiter arrived with a tray of eggs, some sort of potato hash, warm bread, and a fresh carafe of coffee.

"I don't know where I'm going from here," Elaine said. She moved her folders and ledgers to the side and picked up her fork. "But food is as good a place as any to start."

An hour and a half later, we were back at her house, burrowing into her unmade bed. We had made an uneasy peace while we ate—I think she had exhausted herself—but the climate was still unsettled.

"Sorry if I went off like that," she said as we settled in. "But the scheme you've dreamed up about Vincent has no basis in reality. You can't just move in and start acting like Mother Teresa, no matter how compassionate your intentions are. Vincent is still very, very ill. For the moment, he's out of the picture."

"I can work without him. Until he feels better."

She rolled over and put her hands on my shoulders. "Listen to me. I don't know how much better he will ever feel. No one's mentioned his prognosis, except in general terms. But no one's suggesting that he make any long range plans, either. You've got your scoop, and I'm happy for you. Really. Be satisfied with that. Now I want to sleep."

I moved onto my back. Elaine was right. Despite all the uncertainties, Piero DiBrufa had left me the story I'd been waiting for. If I'd been debating whether to stay or go, I had my answer now.

And I should turn my full attention to Monica, as unpleasant as that prospect might be. My interview would have to be with her.

But Elaine had nailed the headline, whether in jest or not: "Insane poet destroys production ..." She had the complete view of the entire situation. Yes, I did need to interview Monica, but for what point of view?

The answer was eluding me. If Vincent wanted me to "help Elaine," he'd have to show me how.

Outside, snow was falling lightly, and the streetlights below were casting odd, disorienting shadows on the bedroom ceiling. I turned away from them, curled up against Elaine's softly breathing body, and fell asleep.

Seventeen

The next morning was unsettled from the beginning. I rose first—at ten thirty—and made coffee. I knew I had to touch base with Gail Graham, but she got to me first. "Thank God you're still there!" she began. "I've just heard."

"Listen ..." I began.

"No. I'm tired of this dilly-dallying. You listen to me."

"I just wanted to say that I'm sorry I never got to Piero. Circumstances ..."

"Ally, forget him! He's dead now. Out of the picture."

"But his opera isn't. In fact, it's going to turn into a legal mess."

"Perfect. We'll get to that. Besides the lawyers, who else is hanging around?"

"Well, the original composer left in a snit. He's down in Palermo with some gypsies."

She gave a hoot of laughter. I heard her fingers clicking away on her computer. "And the dreaded sister?"

"Oh, she's here. But cloaked in black."

"And your old guy who's your contact with her? Monteverdi?"

"Montecalvo. He's disappeared completely. But Vincent seems to think he'll be back."

"And Vincent is ..."

"He's a younger composer I met, who's become a good friend. But he's very ill, in the hospital, in fact. He's trying to finish his own opera before something worse happens to him. I've promised to help him pull together some sort of libretto."

"How many operas are we talking about here?"

"Well, two."

"And you're involved with both?"

"It's complicated. I was never involved with the DiBrufa opera. Not directly."

"Who was in charge of that?"

"We've talked about this. Elaine Bishop was head of production. She was at loggerheads with both DiBrufas, and now she's going to be caught up in the legal mess that's heating up."

"Bishop? She's still there? Jesus, Mary, and Joseph, Ally! You're sitting on top of an exclusive!"

"Well, I thought I might find a way to get something out of Monica ..."

"You'll use her and you'll use Elaine Bishop. You'll use them both. Parallel stories. Bishop is no dummy; she's got a creative brain, in spite of her recent professional bad luck. Who would know better the inside details of the DiBrufa opera? And this Monica person could give you everything you would have wanted to ask Piero DiBrufa, including the reasons for his melodramatic exit."

I took a deep breath. "Nice try, Gail, but I don't think either one of these women will want to cooperate."

"Don't think you're up for the job? Want me to fly down there?"

"That is the last thing I want."

She laughed. "Yes, get your back up. That's the old Ally I want to see."

"You have no idea."

"What I'm going to do is adjust your contract and send you an additional advance. You get to work, make your contacts, talk to Elaine, locate your contact with Monica DiBrufa. You know how this works!"

"It's more complicated than you think, Gail. And it's not going to happen overnight."

"Ally, you've been in that city since last September. What in the hell have you been doing?"

"Well, if I was a smartass, I'd say I was cultivating my sources."

"I know what that means. You're either thinking—again—of making a career change, or you're involved with one of the principal players."

"You'll have to guess."

"That's not my job. I'm telling *Opera World* to expect an exclusive," she concluded. "And remind Ms. Bishop that her professional life needs a boost."

"I will not."

"Don't make me a liar." She beeped off.

At that point Elaine walked into the kitchen barefoot, her hair wrapped in a towel. She glanced at my phone. "So, it's started already," she said. She unwrapped her towel and gave her head a vigorous shake. "You look tense," she said to me as she sat down with her coffee.

"You look lovely. You should leave your hair like that."

Then her phone rang from the pocket of her robe. She turned it off and tossed it on the table. "That's what I think about phones at the moment," she said.

I found my mind in an odd state of reverie. I looked ahead, imagining the various roads I would have to take to bring even one of these projects to fruition. I wondered whether my thoughts before sleep last night were an intimation of Gail's explosive call this morning. I had been wandering toward the same conclusion, but of course I had more direct knowledge of the characters involved, their quirks, and my responsibilities to each of them. There were questions I would not ask, areas that I would not enter, but the idea of parallel interviews was one I had thought of first. And I was responsible for it.

Where to start?

"Vincent's got TB, doesn't he," I asked Elaine finally.

"Yes. You must have figured that out." She finished her coffee. "And the TB, on top of his immune issues, is what's causing the trouble now."

"TB's mostly curable now, isn't it? If this were 1924, he'd probably be sent off to a sanitarium or someplace quiet for a long rest. If we lived on a magic mountain, that would be the appropriate treatment."

"Don't be disingenuous. This isn't 1924. *The Magic Mountain* is ancient history now, from a medical point of view. And there are other complications."

"You keep referring to his immune issues. There's no need to be evasive. I've guessed that he's HIV positive; I'm not blind to that. I'm familiar with it. And I can guess that HIV complicated by TB can't be easy to treat."

"It isn't. Christmas was a serious crisis for him. Or they wouldn't have put him on a machine. He's lucky it was only for three days." She finished her coffee. "That's as much as I want to say right now, Ally." She stood up. "At least before breakfast. Should I make more coffee?"

The following days were cold and snowy on our mountaintop.

Vincent, with the help of some different drugs, began to regain his strength, and Elaine became busy with extended daily meetings with Sandro, the president of the opera company board, the general manager of the theater, the conservatory director, and three or four major donors, Renata Grillo among them. The lawyers were already lurking around the stage door.

Montecalvo remained mysteriously "away," which was troubling. I missed our regular conversations in the Brufani bar, and I very much needed his advice about my current editorial dilemma. I was also counting on him to convince Monica to agree to what Gail was now calling a double-barreled interview. I wasn't responding to her urgent requests for updates and prayed she wouldn't suddenly step off a plane at St. Francis of Assisi Airport. Elaine must agree first, and that was my responsibility.

In what remained of my "free" time, I began to look through William Trevor's novel, in search of scenes that Vincent might eventually be persuaded to score.

Several days after our magic mountain conversation, I met Elaine at the old Falchetto restaurant for a late lunch. It was one of those cold, damp winter days when the light begins to go by three o'clock. The black remains of snow were crusted against the buildings along Via Rocchi, and a bitter wind slapped at me as I reached the top of the hill and turned down Via Bartolo.

The Falchetto, however, was cheery and warm. Elaine had ordered a carafe of Torgiano white and was paging through a folder of notes. I unwrapped myself from my coat, scarves, and hat and hung them on one of the wall hooks.

"Just one moment," she said. "Pour yourself some wine."

Finally she gathered her folders and replaced them in her briefcase. She put her chin in her hand. "Hello," she said smiling. "I've missed you."

"Good. It's been an entire day and a half. An eternity."

"Don't make fun of my attempts to be romantic." She tapped the side of her water glass with her finger.

"I wasn't."

A waiter appeared and we ordered without consulting the menu. All I wanted was a large bowl of pasta fagioli. I poured myself some mineral water.

"So, what's going on?" she asked.

"Any attempt to contact Monica will have to wait for Montecalvo's return, whenever that happens."

"You don't want to wait too long. Someone else might grab your story. Why wait for him?"

"I know that. But my editor is doing her part to keep it on hold. And burning my bridges behind me."

She raised her eyebrows. "Nice."

"I'm counting on Montecalvo to nail Monica down. They're old friends."

"You'll have to cast a magic spell to do it. She's in deep mourning. In full black, with a veil."

Our meals were delivered, but mine was still too hot to eat. "Elaine, do you remember a conversation we had last year, well, a couple of conversations really, around the time you took me home from the hospital?"

"You mean when you shot down my attempts to pull you into the DiBrufa libretto crisis? Yes. Are you reminiscing?"

"Not exactly."

"He broke one of the windows in my office. Did I tell you that? I've never had an experience with someone who disliked me so much."

I began on my pasta. It occurred to me that she'd probably been more affected by DiBrufa's death than she would care to admit. She was now in the uncertain position of not knowing whether she would have to move forward with a work that would surely be a catastrophic failure—despite her reputation for working miracles—or hoping the lawyers would allow her to withdraw it altogether. Either way, the results would not do much to pull her career out of the chasm of bad luck it had recently fallen into. Maybe I should feel at least a little guilty about that. Especially since my offer to write a libretto for Vincent might be viewed as a betrayal of sorts.

As if reading my mind, she said, "Regarding Vincent's opera. If you managed to pull together some sort of working libretto for him, or even organized his scattered collection of arias so he could do it himself, what purpose would it serve? Other than to give him the 'benevolent gift' of getting him back to the piano?"

"But wouldn't that be enough? Does it have to have an ulterior purpose? Work, work one loves, can be a great healer."

"Very New Age. And I agree with you, up to a point. However—I don't really know how to put this—events here are moving forward quickly, Ally. Say you do some writing for Vincent, give him some text to compose for, and eventually there are two outcomes: he finishes his opera, that's one possibility. And then what? It's not likely to be produced, so where does he go from there? The other alternative is that his diseases catch up with him, he's unable to work, he's pitched into a gloom of despair and dies a very unhappy man. Which outcome would you prefer to deal with?"

"I don't think much of the second option."

"Both have their downsides." She took a drink of wine. "Or maybe we're trying to do too much, that may be my point. It's your decision, of course, yours and Vincent's. I don't need to be putting my two cents in at every juncture."

“But—”

“Yes, but. I will say this.” She waited a moment. “This will be hard for you to hear, but I don’t want you to lose sight of the fact that Vincent may very well not win the physical battles he’s fighting. I’m sorry, but at some point you’ve got to accept this fact. Because he already has.”

“Is that true?”

“He and I have talked, once with Dottoressa Cortina. Vincent is very clear about what he does not want. He does not want to linger on and on with these episodes that continue to put him in the hospital, each time worse than before. He’s very courageous, Ally. I think he’s reconciled to losing his life; it’s his music he can’t let go of. I love him completely, and I want to see him die with his work finished. Or at least substantially longer than it is now. But he can’t do it without a libretto. At the same time, I don’t want you to ...”

“Bite off more than I can chew?” I thought about what lay ahead of me. “Sorry. It’s too late for that.”

“Maybe not. You know your way around words and you’re more than simply familiar with opera. That may be enough to chew on. If you can use these assets to help him in any way, after he’s recovered from this latest bout, it would be a wonderful gift. More than just benevolent. But you must go into it with your eyes open, and with as much courage as he has. And with as much honesty as you can bear.”

I looked across the table at her, at a loss about how to respond, and realized there was no other place I’d rather be at this moment than right here with her. I had never been involved with anyone quite like her before. I had never looked for reasons to stay, or stay involved, with anyone. Our personalities were sometimes alarmingly at odds, but she had a sense of herself, of who she was, that drew me toward her. A sense of what others needed, without being compelled to give them everything at once. I liked who she was. She made me want to take myself seriously, which had always been an uphill climb.

"Elaine, there's something else I need to ask you about."

The waiter arrived with the check; she glanced at it and handed him a card.

"No time today, darling. Vincent will be released day after tomorrow. I'm taking him to my place, so you have time to think about all of this." She signed the check for the waiter and pushed back her chair. "I'm not a devious person," she said. "I'm not looking for ways to talk Vincent—or you—into making one decision or another. Especially one that might weigh too heavily on his health. But don't have any doubts about whether I want you to stay on in Perugia. For whatever reason you can come up with. And I don't want to argue with you about this, in case you're wondering."

"Don't you have a meeting or something to go to?" I asked her.

"Yes, I do. In fact, I'm late." She stood up and reached for her coat, which she had flung over the chair beside her.

I walked around the table and put her scarf around her neck. Then impulsively embraced her.

She picked up her briefcase and departed, walking straight and sure up Via Bartolo toward the duomo.

I was unexplainably happy as I watched her go, even with Vincent, the elephant in the room, standing close beside me.

I headed along Via Bartolo toward Piazza Danti through an evening that had become densely foggy. As I turned toward the downward slope of Via Rocchi and home, I bumped full tilt into Odysseus, who had just reached the top of the hill. We both backed away in surprise, then he put down his briefcase and shook my hand. "Sorry," he said. "The fog is bad."

"Yes. My mind was miles away."

"I'm happy to see you," he said with a smile. "Where are you going?"

"Home." At that moment the clock in the Priori struck five thirty. "You're far from the hospital this evening."

"In fact, I'm going there now. I didn't want to drive my car in this fog, so I was on my way to take the Minimetro down the hill."

We stood uneasily together for a few moments. Then I said, "Do you have time for a coffee somewhere? Or a drink?"

The passeggiata had proceeded as usual in this unpleasant weather, but we found a table at Sandri, and Odysseus pushed through the crowd at the bar to get me a caffè latte and himself an espresso. He brought back a plate of little toasted sandwiches as well.

"Forgive me," he said as he sat down, "but I must eat something. I won't have another chance for many hours." He bit into one of the sandwiches, which smelled like it was tuna. "Have one," he said.

"I've just eaten, thanks. I'll leave them for you."

He took a sip of his coffee, then finished the rest in one swallow and wiped his mouth with the little paper napkin. "I notice your friend is better," he said.

"Yes, I think so. He was moved out of—rianimazione."

"I checked on him. He is still very sick. But yes, better."

"He'll be discharged soon, I think."

He ate another sandwich. "You are friends for a long time?"

"I met him here in the city." I finished my coffee. "He's a composer, you know."

"That I did not know." Without asking, he got up and bought us two more coffees.

"How is Georgios?" I asked him as he returned.

He shrugged. "He is in love. Perhaps in vain." He smiled. "So

I will say that he is happily miserable. His friend Yanni failed his primary level exam."

"He did?" I paused. "What will he do?"

He took another sandwich. "I don't know. He is busy being very angry right now. He wants to leave Perugia, but he will not go without Georgios."

"And Georgios wants to stay here."

"Yes. Georgios is serious about his studies. And ..."—Odysseus smiled—"there is the American girl, of course."

The coffee had fired up a bit of a buzz in my head. I began to search through my bag for my wallet. "Let me pay, Odysseus," I said. "For both of us."

"No, it is my treat." He put his hand on my arm. "I must say something more about your friend. You know his illness is serious."

I stood up. "Yes."

"Has he spoken with you about it?"

"I know he's being treated for tuberculosis."

"You should talk with him. Even in these modern times, certain types of tuberculosis can be quite contagious." He met my gaze steadily. "But that is not his only battle."

I had the sense that he was attempting to caution me about something. "I'm aware of Vincent's illness. Most aspects of it," I said, "so don't worry."

He stood up and shrugged himself into his jacket. "Good. Good. Keep him happy now, while you can."

What an odd thing to say. I shook his hand. "Greetings to Georgios."

Eighteen

Vincent was at last discharged and installed in Elaine's guest bedroom. I let him get his bearings for nearly a week, then went down the hill to see how he was faring. Elaine had departed for the theater but left the front door unlocked. I found him sitting amid the pillows in blue and green striped pajamas and a sweater. A book was open on his lap. He was dozing, with his glasses down on the end of his nose. I watched him for a minute, then knocked on the door frame.

"Hi, my friend," I said.

He opened his eyes. "Ah, at last it's you," he said. There was still a gravelly hoarseness about his voice.

I took off my coat and threw it on one of the chairs. There was a faint medicinal aroma in the room that I did not associate with Elaine. Or Vincent.

"I keep nodding off," he said with a frown.

"Sleep, if you need to. Is there coffee?"

"She made some, I think," he said slowly.

"I'll get it, then. Anything for you?"

"Just more water. Bring the bottle."

A bit later I was sitting in a chair beside the bed with my new briefcase open. I had splurged on this purchase at one of the post-Christmas sales because my large book bag was beginning to fall apart.

He coughed a little bit into a handkerchief and motioned for me to move my chair farther from the side of the bed. "Just to be safe," he said. "I'd hug you if I could."

"Well," I said, "should I ask how you're feeling?"

"I'm just glad to be out of that hospital."

"I'm happy they let you go. I don't think I could manage any more midnight visitations."

He laughed a little. "Aye. She was furious about that."

"Don't remind me."

He took a long drink of water. "Did you find the book?"

"I got it."

"And now you want to find me some words."

"We'll see."

"I hope you're not part of any little plan of hers."

"I'd like to see you back at the piano. So would she. That's not exactly a plan."

He put his head back against the pillows and closed his eyes. He was still wearing his hospital ID around his wrist. "I will get back to my music," he said. "But I can't jump out of my hospital bed onto a piano bench. It won't happen that way."

"I'm not here to push you."

"What's going on with your own writing?"

"It's stalled. I need to nail down an interview with Monica before someone else gets to her. And discover where Italo Montecalvo's hiding so I can persuade him to intercede with her. His bookstore is all closed up."

"He's in Morocco, where he always spends the holidays. Ercole, at the Brufani bar, told me that. Before Christmas, I think."

"Really? Well, that's helpful to know."

He scratched his face. "I know you don't want to hear this, but Elaine's in one hell of a mess. She's going to have to pull this production together herself, it looks like. And DiBrufa's libretto cannot work."

"Don't go there, Vincent."

"I'd help her out myself if I had the strength."

"Something new has happened with my work. I've been more or less ordered by my editor to change my approach to this assignment. When DiBrufa made his exit, he took the possibility of an interview with him. But his death made news, and *Sirius*, with all of its complications, has become part of that interest. So what my editor wants now is a double interview: one with Monica and the other with Elaine. Monica would fill in the gaps about Piero and the development of the opera—and possibly his state of mind—and Elaine would take a broader picture, addressing the preparation for *Sirius* and its problems but also her ideas about modern stage direction and her own experiences. Maybe giving her a chance to right her personal lifeboat, which has been caught in a tempest over these past years."

For quite a while Vincent was silent, although he had opened his eyes. Finally he said, "Are you completely out of your mind?"

"*Opera World* is already on board."

"Ally, the DiBrufa opera is still very much alive. That's part of the problem. For the moment Elaine is legally stuck with it, or the company is, and you'll never get her to go on record about any part of that situation. Have you talked to her about this plan?"

"We've talked around it, but she manages to head me off whenever I try to approach the subject."

"Not surprising."

"And yet, in an indirect way, she seems to be encouraging me to help you out."

He took another long drink of water.

"I'm not going to bully her or you, Vincent," I went on. "I'm not qualified to fix DiBrufa's libretto. That much is settled, at least in my mind. And even if I were, I don't feel pulled to do it. I do feel pulled to help you out a little on your work if I can. I'm familiar with the Trevor book, and I have the composer sitting right in front of me. I might find scenes for you to set, something like that. But I also have a responsibility to my editor, who has made some sort of deal with *Opera World* to produce this feature article—for which I have already been partially paid—no matter what form it takes. I'm experienced enough to interview Monica without stepping on her toes or the memory of Piero. Elaine might be more difficult."

"You can count on that. She's been shafted by the critics so often over the last couple of years that she prefers to keep her distance from the press."

"My objective would not be to shaft her. I'll make that clear. I don't know why she would imagine that anyway. The ground rules would have to be solid, and I'm fine with that. But Vincent, when Elaine and I were in London, we had several long conversations about the very ideas I would be asking her about. She was eloquent, quite open with her opinions, which to my mind were intelligent, well-thought-out, and although they touched on the DiBrufa situation, they never strayed into any self-serving or petulant hysterics. My point is that a Monica/Elaine double piece might be difficult but worth trying. If we could just get started."

He sighed, and I knew he must be thinking about his own work, how that fit into the picture, if he could take it as far as he could without being overtaken by the demons that were chasing him.

"Well, you'd better approach her about this idea," he said. "And don't put it off. It might take a while to bring her around."

Finally I got up and said, "I'm going for more coffee."

In the kitchen I took my time, even rested for a few minutes. I took a new bottle of water out of the refrigerator and noticed that Elaine had left some lunch for us—some sandwiches wrapped up, and a salad, waiting to be dressed.

When I returned to the bedroom, he said, "Let me just point out that you're going to need some information about how librettos are created and sometimes how they fail. You're going to need to know this if both of your subjects will be discussing the creation of an opera. I can help you there. And we might as well start now."

"All right." I got my notebook out of my briefcase. "Whenever you're ready."

He removed his glasses and said, "Generally, the librettist matters most to the composer, and fades into the background when the opera is completed."

I watched his body slide down again against the pillows. He had begun to sweat a little. "A conventional novel's the hardest thing to write because usually everything has to be described—or at least suggested: states of mind, what actions the protagonist takes, what he's thinking, and on and on. But when you're writing an opera libretto, the depiction of states of mind, just as an example, is often taken over by the music; it can suggest emotions that often make words unnecessary. And one can *see* what actions the characters take, so no descriptions are needed."

He paused. "This is stuff you probably already know."

"Okay, talk about something I don't know."

"The librettist has to remember that it takes about three times as long to sing something than to speak it. For example, if the tenor wants to say 'I love you, let's go away for the weekend,' it might take him a ten-minute aria to do it. With lots of repeats. But we expect those ten minutes to be full of glorious music that reveals his emotions—even though he doesn't actually say a whole lot. His words have to push the action forward without getting in the way of the music. DiBrufa's libretto doesn't have a clue about forward movement. That's one big reason why it doesn't work. He wanders off into dream worlds or writes about the structure of a linden leaf, while Georgio Paolo has composed rapturous music for a love duet." He took a breath and suddenly began to gasp.

"What should I do?" I said. I quickly opened the new bottle of water.

He held up his hand and continued to try to catch his breath, and at last took several deep breaths and reached for the water bottle. Then we both were quiet and eventually he settled down.

"Sorry," he said in a little croak.

"Maybe we should stop. For now." I got a small towel from his bathroom and wiped his face and neck.

He lay quietly, breathing carefully. Growing paler.

Finally I asked, "How about something to eat?"

"No, not now. If you could just turn off the light for a little bit, I think I'll rest."

I took up my briefcase, along with his copy of the Trevor novel. As I got to the door, he said quietly, "Don't worry. I'll get back to the piano when the time is right."

He was asleep before I closed the door.

I got one of the sandwiches from the refrigerator and poured myself a glass of Vernaccia from a bottle Elaine had thoughtfully uncorked. I settled down with Vincent's copy of *My House in Umbria*, which he had heavily annotated, and half an hour later, deep into the text, I came upon the episode in which two of the principal male characters begin to make plans for the creation of a garden in a small corner of the grounds of an ancient Umbrian villa. Their idea is to please Amelia, an eccentric writer of romance novels, who has allowed her home to be used by a few recuperating victims of a recent terrorist explosion. Down among the weeds, their horticultural imagination springs to life and prompts them to dance about, shouting, "Here, azaleas!" and "There, fuchsias—red and cream! Basil, rosemary, lavender! A sundial! And there, small trees—peach and pear!" It is a small break from tragedy, although the wounded victims have not yet realized that the terrorist himself is recovering among them. But in the garden, the story has moved forward, expanded.

I raised my head, wondering whether Vincent had already set this scene, then took my pen and wrote "waltz" in the margin of Vincent's book. And underlined it.

After that, I put my head down and fell asleep myself.

It was not a real nap, for when I lifted my head again, only half an hour had passed, and what woke me was the sound of water running in the guest bathroom. For some reason the sound alarmed me, but when I made my way down the hall, I found Vincent standing in his pajama bottoms gazing into the bathroom mirror. The room was full of steam from the hot water faucets in the sink and in the shower. When I spoke, he jumped.

"You mustn't creep up on me like that," he said. When he turned toward me, I saw his chest was flushed and his eyes were bright, as if he were about to cry. The hair above his forehead had formed curling locks.

"I'm going to turn off these faucets," I said, moving past him. "What's with the sauna?"

He rubbed his chin. "I'm trying to soften my beard. I need a shave. It's scratching me." He turned to face me again and said, "Could you give me a shave, do you think? The other day I tried, but my hands weren't steady enough. I nicked myself." He paused. "And I don't like electric razors."

I nodded. "Sure." I put one hand on his chest and reached around him to grab a towel. He closed the toilet seat lid and sat down, and I put a pillow from the bed behind his back. "Turn your face up," I said. I lathered his beard with the lavender shaving cream from his kit, which was resting on the sink. "Now hold still."

"Still as the grave," he said, his eyes closing. And then, "This is nice."

It was nice. The remnants of steam lingering, the scent of the shaving cream, the whiffs of peppery sweat that occasionally emerged from under his arms—it was very peaceful. I was careful, softly tracing the hollows of his cheeks and jaw with the razor. And the fine lines of his upper lip. I managed not to draw blood.

I washed off his face, patted it dry with a towel, and handed him a mirror. "What do you think?" I asked. "All right?"

He opened his eyes. "Yes. Much better."

"*Acqua di colonia,* signore?"

"Why not."

I fetched the cologne I had seen on a table in the bedroom and patted some on his cheeks and neck, cleaned his razor, and closed up the tube of cream. And then, perhaps aroused by the familiar aroma of his cologne, I put both hands on his cheeks and leaned down and kissed him. "Back to bed," I said.

This project had exhausted him. He put on his pajama top but didn't button it and made his way back into the bedroom.

At that moment I heard the front door close loudly. Then Elaine appeared in the doorway, still in her coat. "Well." She smiled. "Someone's had a shave."

"Is it an improvement?" he asked.

"Yes. I'm going to have some wine. Come with me, Ally."

Vincent closed his eyes and lay back against the pillows. "I'll just rest," he said.

In the kitchen I put my arms around her waist from behind. "Thanks for the lunch you left."

She took the open bottle of Vernaccia and poured us both a glass. Then she turned around and pulled me gently against her. "Ah," she said, inhaling deeply.

"Nice, isn't it," I said.

She handed me my glass and kissed me quickly on the mouth. "Very." She stepped to the kitchen door and called, "Can I bring you something, *caro?*"

"He's probably asleep again," I said.

"We're on our own, I guess. I'm going to change my clothes." I followed her into her bedroom. "Did you have a productive day?" she asked me as she unbuttoned her shirt.

"I'll let him tell you about it. It wasn't a long one."

She went into her bathroom. "I'd like to hear it from you."

The water was running, so I waited to respond.

"Did you hear me?" she asked as she returned, toweling off her face.

"I talked, he talked, I listened, he slept, I ate lunch, read for a while, shaved him, and you came home."

She pulled on some warm flannel pants. "All right. I'll get it from him."

I finished my wine. "Now I think I need to go back to Via Rocchi for a while."

"You won't stay for dinner? I have some cutlets."

"Not tonight."

"You're thinking about Monica."

"Among other things."

"Well, sorry you won't stay. Where's your coat?"

She bundled me up and knotted my scarf and pulled my hat down forcefully over my ears. "It's colder out. I'd give you a lift, but I've put my car under the piazza so it won't freeze up."

I stuck my head into Vincent's room, but he appeared to be sound asleep. "Tell him I said goodbye," I told her.

At the door she said, "I'm not going to the theater tomorrow, so why don't you come down in the morning."

"Late morning. I need to do a laundry." I kissed her and departed. Halfway up the block toward Piazza Partigiani I stopped. Why had I left? The laundry could wait another day. Whatever work I had to do on my own project would certainly not move forward tonight.

But it was too late now to change my mind.

Nineteen

Late the next morning, I sat with William Trevor's novel once more, this time at the Lavanderia Splendida on a small street off Via Pinturicchio. Across the road loomed another tall section of the Etruscan wall. I had my eyes on the washing machine, however, which was moving rhythmically to music only it could hear.

My book was open, but I was drawn to the activity in the machine, as people often are in laundromats, spellbound by the regular movement of the clothes, clockwise, then counterclockwise, while water rose and fell and the heart of the machine hummed and paused, hummed and paused. As I watched, a pair of blue underpants flashed by in the circular window, followed by my green and blue checked shirt. My red pajama bottoms lingered for a long moment, followed by several intertwined T-shirts, and after that a collection of socks that seemed to be wildly arguing. All caught up in the ceaselessly turning metal drum from which there was no escape.

I put the book down on the bench beside me. At that moment the machine gave a lurch and stopped, and for an instant there was an ominous silence, as if an unexpected disaster were about to occur. Life inside the machine took a hesitant breath, not aware of where it was or what horrible event was about to overtake it. Then with a great scraping sound, everything was thrown into a violent metallic spin, and the clothes were hurled against the sides of the drum as the exiting water spun out, gurgling as if a dam had broken. What had been a graceful ballet of dancing colors disintegrated into a great roar of chaotic noise as socks, shirts, pajamas, and leggings were pressed against the violently spinning cylinder, tangled in an explosion of terrible turbulence. As I fixed my eyes on the circular window, I saw nothing but blackness.

I waited until this event had subsided and the clothes inside had sunk into an exhausted, injured pile, until the rinse water had gently begun to enter the drum, before I took up my notebook and pen. If such a thing had been possible, I could easily have believed that each article of clothing had been calling out: *Where am I? What has happened? Who is caring for me now?*

There it was. A new beginning for Vincent's opera had emerged out of a washing machine. The opening scene should not be on the train, and the terrorist explosion should appear musically, as part of the overture, and not depicted in any way. The opera itself should begin quietly, in a dim hospital ward. *Where am I? What has happened? Who is caring for me now?* A quartet for four survivors. And although it was probably too late to make a difference, and although I was once again stepping into a creative arena in which I had no business, I began to write.

After a while I closed my notebook. I already knew: too many verbs, too many conjunctions. Too many articles, even. Too many words! This must be a quartet, but each character must be understood, in uncomplicated but feverish song. Frantically, I threw my damp clothes into one of the giant dryers. Coins, coins.

They bounced and rolled around on the floor, several lost forever under the dryer itself.

Then I sat with my notebook in my lap, watching my clothes turn as if I didn't have anything better to do. And of course, that was the problem: at the moment, I *didn't* have anything better to do. As if I were waiting on an empty station platform for a train that was parked on a siding—within my sight!—carrying the crucial elements of my real work, but—without an engine—unable to arrive. Monica DiBrufa was in deep mourning. And I hadn't even begun to deal with Elaine. My double engines. I could not make a move without them. Instead I was in a laundromat creating a scene for an opera that in all likelihood would never be completed. Work that had no point. And observing an electric dryer as if it were the Delphic oracle.

I reopened my notebook and ripped out the offending pages. A large green trash can was waiting for me by the entrance door. I stood beside it watching the midafternoon traffic move by and a group of students, who headed into the bar next door. My fist was full of crushed paper that I couldn't bring myself to toss away.

Twenty

Half an hour later, I rang Elaine's bell, my damp laundry in a sack over my shoulder, my breath steaming. "Is that laundry?" she asked when she opened the door.

"Not quite dry. Is Vincent awake?"

"Give me a hug, at least. I'm just cleaning up the dishes. Lunch is over, I'm afraid."

Vincent was out of bed and in his jeans and an undershirt. He was banging his toothbrush rhythmically on the bathroom sink as I came in. "Is it cold outside?" he asked me.

"Of course it's cold; it's February."

Elaine appeared at the door with a tray of coffee and warm milk. "I'll just put this down on the table," she said. "You can help yourselves. I'll be back in a few minutes."

Vincent put on a long-sleeved white shirt and pulled his old blue crew neck sweater over his head. "Maybe I'll stay up for a while," he said.

"Good," I said. "Good." I felt a small hope trying to revive itself, like a hesitant weed. Hope is difficult to banish; one wants it to stay so much.

I watched him throw his bed together, not exactly make it, and then pour himself some coffee and milk. He looked at me, smiling. "Want some?" he asked.

"Yes, okay."

"What's in your sack?"

"My half-dry laundry. I'll go put it in."

When I returned, Elaine was straightening up the room, putting Vincent's desk in order, squaring up his piles of papers, stacking his scores. "I should vacuum in here," she said as she worked. "You're a really messy guest, Vincent."

"You do have a cleaning person, don't you?"

"Yes, but I straighten up a bit before she comes. You know. Silly, really."

I set my cup down shakily on its saucer.

Vincent and Elaine exchanged a look. "What's the matter?" Elaine asked me. "Did you have a dramatic morning at the laundromat? Was there a ghost in the machine?" She smiled as if we were sharing a private joke.

My frustration finally found a voice. "Yes, in fact. Your opera, Vincent. I had an idea about a new beginning."

"Do you have my Trevor book, by the way?" he asked quickly.

"Yes. I wanted to look at your marginal notes."

"Just so I know where it is. Elaine, are there any of those little pastries left?"

"I think you ate the last one after dinner last night. I'll pick up some more."

"Something's happened," I said.

"Well, in fact ..." Elaine began.

"A week ago you were predicting the end of the world because the DiBrufa opera was unstageable. You nearly convinced me, Elaine, that your professional life was more or less finished. Now everyone's focused on pastries and vacuuming. I sense a mood change."

"Well," Vincent said thoughtfully, "a week ago I thought I was going to die." He took his coffee and moved across the room to his desk chair. "Go on, Ally, tell me about your idea for the beginning."

Elaine held up her hand. "We've all been carried away a little, I think," she said. "Let's get this unpleasantness over." She sat down on the bed and motioned for me to sit down beside her. "The situation's been confusing for everyone. But now it looks like the business with the DiBrufa lawyers won't be finished for a while. Certainly not before a March premiere." She took a breath. "And Vincent can't be sure at this point about what parts of his opera he might be able to pull together, even for a workshop performance. Which I'm not in favor of anyway."

"I wasn't aware that a workshop performance was being considered."

"Well ..." Vincent began.

"That was my idea," Elaine said. "It was just part of a casual conversation I had with Vincent."

"After I talked to him at the hospital," I added. I immediately recognized this casual conversation as part of her plan to get Vincent back to the piano. "Vincent, did you talk to Elaine about our conversation yesterday?"

He thought for a moment. "I think so."

"He did," Elaine said. "And it might have been a nice exercise for you to try, Ally. You and Vincent working together, setting some of the major scenes."

Ringing in my ears were Elaine's comments about "benevolent gifts" and "biting off more than I could chew." Well rehearsed, I suspected now. The three of us seemed to be wandering separately through an intricately constructed maze, not knowing who, or what, might be encountered around the next corner. That's how I felt, at least.

"He would have needed some sort of text even for a workshop production, wouldn't he?"

"Yes, of course." Elaine paused to gather herself together. And she must have sensed that I was more than a little irritated, because her voice became very gentle. "There have been changes. Late last night Sandro called to let me know that the lawyers on both sides had reached a preliminary agreement about the DiBrufa opera. Monica was part of the decision, and it looks like she's agreed to let us withdraw *Sirius* from its spring premiere. There's a lot still to be worked out, but let's just say that a big hurdle has been jumped."

"What a relief for you, then."

Finally, she took my chin in her hand and turned my head so we were facing each other. "This is my point, dear Ally. *Sirius* is *finito.* And with it the entire spring production. The opera will remain in limbo, for the immediate future, at least. Perhaps forever, if we're lucky."

I removed my chin from her hand and said evenly, "Good decision. *Sirius* has been your real problem all along. But now you and Vincent have decided there's no way he can have anything ready to take its place, so you're leaving musicians, singers, backstage workers, donors, everyone in the lurch."

"Yes. That happens sometimes. It's not the best of situations. But that's why contracts were invented. Most of these folks do have contracts, and we'll work with them. Do you think I'm happy about that part of it?"

"I guess I'm out of the loop. For example, I didn't know anything about a workshop performance of Vincent's opera until ten minutes ago."

"That needn't disturb you at all. I have to point out that although you are a brilliant commentator on the operatic world and its artistic productions, you have never worked in the machinery, the nuts and bolts involved in pulling a production together. Situations like this occur more frequently than you imagine. Professional workers are used to last-minute catastrophes, singers who cancel because they don't like the weather or give birth in their dressing rooms. Or die singing onstage in the middle of an aria. You learn to do what you can and move on." She paused. "I'm not being difficult here. Do you understand?" She reached over and touched my hand.

Vincent had bowed his head in an abashed gesture.

"I'm sorry, Vincent," I said. He turned his body slightly away from me. "When we talked yesterday, I thought you might be serious about finishing your opera. It didn't sound as if you'd given up on anything, not then."

"There's no need to be unpleasant, Ally," Elaine said.

"She's not being unpleasant," Vincent said. "She's disappointed. So am I. But I'm not abandoning my opera. I want to finish it. I just can't pull anything together by March." His voice had a hollow sadness in it, and I felt my initial irritation begin to abate. "It's just bad timing," he added.

I moved away from Elaine and walked across the room. But she followed me and put her hands on my shoulders. "There's no reason why you can't help Vincent continue, in whatever way you can. Give him some words to work with. But you may find that your kind of writing isn't a natural fit for libretto work. And I fault myself for not seeing this sooner. I pushed you too hard about the DiBrufa mess."

"My kind of writing? How would you know anything about that?"

Vincent got himself more coffee and returned to his bed. His hands were trembling. I was in need of coffee myself, but I wanted Elaine to answer my question first.

"Because I called Patrizia after we got back to Perugia and asked her to locate a copy of your book in London. She found one in a used bookstore and mailed it down. I've spent some time with it. *Boarding Passes.* A nice title."

"I'm surprised she could locate a copy."

"I liked the parts of it I read. It's difficult to write believably about particular places without veering into personal sentimentality. You've avoided that. I don't even know whether I'd call it a travel book, not in the generic sense. Your essays are really lyrical meditations on all types of journeys."

I realized she'd managed to change the subject. "It's airplane reading, Elaine. Most of those pieces are extended sidebars to longer articles about opera houses and productions and singers."

"That may be, but they're very close to being creative narratives of some type, I think, as they stand. Without the novelistic nostalgia that some writers fall prey to." She paused. "Now, you could possibly pull an opera libretto together, or even parts of one, but I would guess that in the end it would be a struggle and you wouldn't feel comfortable with it. I'd stick with the path you're on. It suits you. I loved all your brooding ruminations. Your love for music just winds in and about the place you're writing from and evolves into an affectionate portrait of both. Very moving, very immediate."

Brooding ruminations? I couldn't tell if she was being critical or attempting to flatter me out of my bad mood.

Now I did get myself more coffee. I'd felt a twinge of pleasure at her words, but I had to be careful. Elaine specialized in ulterior motives. "And you got all this from spending a little time with my book?" I asked her.

She laughed. "You challenged me," she said. "In every way. In London and back here in Perugia. I admit it." She was now pacing back and forth between the desk and the bed. Vincent had closed his eyes and was possibly asleep. "Sweetheart, if you tried to write a libretto, you'd go nuts in very short order. Even with the composer sitting right in front of you. I didn't realize this until I read some of your essays. And—what might be worse—you'd lose your own voice, lose your style. A libretto requires a very constricted type of lyricism. It has a formal grid. It's for writers who can work fenced in, if you get my meaning. In the end, the composer rules the roost."

Vincent gave a tremendous sneeze and sat up. He blew his nose loudly.

"Do you have something to add?" I asked him.

"I'm very sad," he said. "About everything."

Elaine walked over to the bed. "Is there blood on that handkerchief?" she asked him.

"No."

"Would anyone like a drink?" Elaine went off toward the kitchen. I heard the release of the ice trays.

"She's giving us time to talk," I said to Vincent. "Are you feeling awfully let down?"

He shook his head. "Not really. She's the one who'll lose the most with the DiBrufa cancellation. Remember that. Not me. And certainly not you. You've got something almost ready for the presses."

"You're being optimistic."

"Ally, you've got to talk to Elaine about the double interview. I mean right away."

"It's all I have left."

"It may be all you have left, which I doubt, but it's what you want the most."

I nodded.

"And what new idea did you come up with for the beginning of my opera?"

"I think I had some sort of sexual encounter with a washing machine."

"She said some nice things about your work. She's a perceptive critic."

"She has her motives."

"She doesn't want you to leave. And neither do I, really. Couldn't I hear about your laundromat experience?"

"Sometime. I've probably just boarded the wrong bus again." I sat down beside him on the bed. "What will she do now? If she doesn't have a production?"

"Well, the DiBrufa investigation will probably go on for a while, in its Italian way, and she'll have to work with Sandro to pay some people who had contracts. Since Monica was part of the decision to withdraw the opera, her lawyers will have to deal with any issues she has."

"But Elaine?"

"I'm not sure if there's another production on her calendar before the fall, to be honest. I hope there is." He took my hand again.

Elaine entered at that moment with her glass of gin and a newly uncorked bottle of Vernaccia. "Here's some wine. Would anyone like something else? Whoops! Forgot my lemon peel. Be right back."

"Irritatingly upbeat," I said.

"Let her be. She's whistling in the dark."

I could see he was worn out. And he was getting hoarse again.

Elaine reentered, waving a curling piece of lemon peel. "You haven't poured the wine!" she said.

"I wonder," Vincent said, "if I could have a nap now."

"Of course," Elaine said. She dropped the lemon peel into her glass. "Ally and I will go into the other room and leave you be. Bring the wine please, Ally."

I released his hand and followed Elaine out into the front part of the house, closing the door behind me.

We sat down in the dining area, which was filled with late-afternoon light. The snow on the distant Apennines was glittering and looked bitterly frigid. I could almost feel it. "I don't know why I prefer sitting in here," Elaine said. "It's a better view, I guess. And I haven't taken down the Christmas decorations in the living room." She smiled at me. "Are you awfully down about this? Are you still angry?"

"Well, I do have a plan B," I said. Her face grew serious. That had been an unkind point to make, and I quickly regretted it.

"You blame me entirely for this, no doubt."

I poured myself more wine. "I'm not sure blame enters into it."

"Using parts of Vincent's opera was a lovely idea, if that's what you had in mind, but I could never have seriously considered it. I do love his music, but I'm not new to this game. I've staged productions of all sorts, and I even started out in musical theater, which is where his piece belongs, I think. On a sophisticated level. His music leans toward the operatic, but it's not quite full-blown opera. It's so wonderful though, that I was almost ready to consider it, for a day or two."

I wondered.

"DiBrufa's death shocked me, I don't deny it. Even though I never laid eyes on the man. I never wished him harm, but I'm relieved he's gone. The production would have been a complete disaster." She went into the kitchen and fixed herself another gin.

“I need a cigarette,” she said as she returned. She looked around. “Would you mind?”

“Go ahead.”

We sat quietly for a bit, while the early evening drew quickly down into the city and the smoke from her cigarette eddied above us.

“How long will you keep Vincent here with you, do you think?” I asked her.

“Until he’s stronger, until he can shop, cook for himself, get to his medical appointments on his own. Until the wind changes, as Mary Poppins would say. Until he stops endlessly coughing in the night.” She leaned back in her chair. “I’m not going to toss him out.”

“Of course not.”

We were quiet for a few moments. The light was fading quickly.

“You used the DiBrufa libretto as a lure, didn’t you?” I said. “To get me to London. Even when you thought the opera would probably be withdrawn.”

“I’ll just say that the libretto wasn’t the only reason I asked you to come with me.”

“You should have known that bribes weren’t necessary.”

“How would I know that? You don’t give much away. I was afraid you’d finish up your writing and head off to someplace else. I’ll apologize for my motives, if you like, but I don’t think it’s necessary.”

“You could have just said, ‘Stay a little longer.’”

“I thought I had.” She looked at her glass. “I’m going to have another gin. Just a small one. Give yourself more wine if you like.”

I thought I’d had enough wine.

She was stirring her gin with her index finger as she returned.

“Do you have any other productions lined up?” I asked her.

"Not until the fall. I was planning to take a break after Perugia, and now it will be an extended one, it looks like. But there are still things to settle here."

I was a bit lightheaded because of the wine, and in great need of food.

"Hungry?" she asked me.

I nodded.

"It's too cold to go out. In a minute I'll see what I can rustle up. Vincent will need something too." The radiator clanked as steam began to move up the pipes. "Do you forgive me?" she asked.

"For?"

"For spoiling your opera dreams."

"They were never serious. They gave me something to do while I waited for Monica, that's all." I could detect the remains of bitterness in my voice.

She leaned over and put her palm against my cheek. "When will you grow up, I wonder?" she said.

"I am grown up, unfortunately."

"What, in dog years?" She smiled.

"Dog years suit me."

She looked at her watch. "Come and lie down with me for a while. Then I'll throw some dinner together. Pasta and whatever else is there."

"I should get my clothes out of your dryer."

"You know where it is."

We seemed to get along better in bed, whether sex was involved or not. Sex had just been involved, but of a leisurely kind, and I was relaxed beside her, half asleep. She pulled me closer and rested her chin on the top of my head. "Are you worried about your financial situation at all?" she asked after a while.

"Not yet. The major payment will come at the end, when my piece is submitted. And I get royalty checks every now and then. From the book and other articles."

"Still getting royalties?"

I rolled over on my back. "They keep coming, fortunately. But lately my editor's been pushing me to finish up in Perugia and head for a spring music festival in Malaga."

"So you do have a plan B."

"My editor has a plan B, let's say. But Plan A isn't over yet. In fact, it hasn't begun."

I felt her stretch and begin to pull away. If I wasn't quick about this, she might drop off. Or even get up. So I held on tight and explained the entire deal.

"This is your usual pillow talk routine?" she said, after I had laid out Gail Graham's plan.

"No diversionary tactics from you this evening. You can't start the car or change the subject."

"I had a feeling this was coming, you know."

"I know. But I didn't push, remember that."

"The last time I was profiled was for *Opera News*. A couple of years ago. This was for the disaster-in-waiting *Caravaggio* at City Opera. An entire photo spread."

"Well, I can't promise that. But they'll probably want some photos."

"And Monica and I would not be interviewed together."

"Absolutely not."

"And you would be writing the piece."

"Yes." She was silent for a moment. "Elaine," I said, "you can pretend we're back at the Hotel Washington on Christmas night. You were eloquent. You were entirely focused on the state of modern opera production. You talked about Debussy and his aversion to conventional librettos, you talked about the role of the stage director. I wouldn't expect you to discuss anything that made you uncomfortable. It would be nice if you could explain something about *Sirius,* go as far as you wanted or nowhere at all. It would be entirely up to you."

"And Monica? What will she have to say?"

"I hope Montecalvo will be able to get a sense of that when he goes to see her."

"You mean she hasn't said yes?"

"He hasn't even approached her! He's in Morocco. Ercole Caccini may know when he's due back. Soon, I have every hope."

She laughed a little. "As long as we don't have to meet."

"Well, brace yourself. You may both be on the cover of *Opera World.* Separate shots, of course."

"So when would this interview take place?"

"Soon. They want this for their April issue." I waited. "You'd see the final copy before I sent it off."

"Have you discussed this with Vincent?"

"Yes. He's very protective of you. He suggested I move with caution."

"Really. And you said?"

"I thought you could take care of yourself."

"Would you mind if I talked to him about this deal?"

"Not at all."

We were interrupted by the sound of the piano.

"What ...?" she said.

I laughed. "Vincent's back at the piano. 'Glitter and Be Gay,' if I'm not mistaken."

"So it is," she said as she rolled out of bed. "I'd better get out there. He's started dinner and he'll let the garlic burn."

I left Elaine's a couple of hours later feeling a little better. My emotional response to the events of the earlier part of the afternoon would probably resurface as I was trying to get to sleep. Vincent had walked me to the door at Elaine's while she began to load the dishwasher.

"Don't forget your laundry." He smiled.

"I've got it."

We stood in the darkness by the door. "I've got a doctor's appointment tomorrow," he said.

"Will Elaine go with you?"

"No, she's spending the morning with some committees at the theater. For a while I thought I might cancel with the doctor, but I think I'll try to make it."

"Do you want me to come along? Just for company?"

In the kitchen Elaine slammed the door to the dishwasher and I heard the surge of water as the cycle began. "Thanks," he said. "But I'm going to try it on my own."

He put his arms around me and pressed my head against his chest, where I could feel his heart bumping rhythmically along. He smelled deliciously of garlic and peppery arugula. We stood there for a few minutes, just holding each other. Finally he put me at arm's length. "You want to meet me for lunch somewhere? Then you can make sure I get started home in the right direction."

"Sure."

"I don't see the doctor until eleven. And it may take a while."

"I'm going to see if I can find Montecalvo in the morning. I'll meet you in Piazza Italia at one. At the top of the scala mobile. Can you get yourself up the hill?"

"Sure."

"If I'm not on time or you get cold, go into the Brufani bar. I'll find you." I said.

Outside, I fought the wind on the way up to the scala mobile, and few people were out. I loved this city at night. Lights in windows somehow made me feel that the world was a place full of calm and order. Unexplainable thoughts, from outside looking in.

It was earlier than I thought when I unlocked the door to Casa Caccini. The signora emerged from the kitchen carrying a hammer. The little girls were watching something on television, and there were several guests in the kitchen. "Follow me to the *sala da pranzo,*" she ordered, and we entered the darkness of the formal dining room, where the aroma of the recent fire still lingered. She pointed to a chair, and we both sat down. She placed the hammer on the table between us.

"*Allora,*" she began. *Allora* is an imprecise Italian word, to foreigners at least, that has a variety of meanings. It is often used in storytelling ("and then," for example) to indicate that a new part of the tale is about to commence. It is also very happy to stand alone. Usually classed as an adverb, it can also be an adjective, although I've never known how. I'm learning to love this Italian word, because no matter how one uses it in conversation, it is rarely incorrect. As usual, its meaning depends on the situation.

When the signora said "*allora,*" I thought she probably meant something like, "Now then." Or "All right now," indicating that she was about to begin a definite line of conversation. So I sat in the darkness and waited.

"You have not confirmed," she said in a low tone.

I made a dismissive gesture, as good as a comment, perhaps, in Italian.

"It is late and you have not confirmed if you will keep your bed. Our contract is for three months. These are long finished."

"Oh, that," I said. "*Perdonami*, Signora Caccini."

"The bed, Signora Ally."

I took a breath.

She reached across the table and took my hand. "We love you here in our house," she said in careful English. "You are a good friend to my girls. You bring calm to this home." She withdrew her hand. "If other places call you, I understand this. You must live in your life. But I must have the answer."

Moved, I responded without a thought. "I hope to keep my bed, signora, with your consent." How else to reply to an operatic gesture such as that? In an instant, what other choice? "But I cannot tell you how long I will stay."

"No?"

"I will be working. On an assignment." I watched her consider what I'd said, and I tried to explain in the most exotic of ways. I thought she would respond to exotic, and I was right.

Her eyes grew wide when I mentioned Monica's name. "Monica DiBrufa?" she said breathlessly. "You must bring her here, to my house. For a festive drink."

"I don't know how it will go," I hedged. "I'm hoping Signor Montecalvo will help me."

"Italo!" She stood up. "Ercole, *mio marito,* is a friend. He will help you!"

"That's a generous suggestion," I said. "I'll talk with him if it's necessary."

She nodded. "All will be well."

"But signora, my schedule may not be regular. There may be nights when I must be away. This will not mean I have departed. Or injured myself again. *Ha capito?"*

"Si, si, capito bene, Signora Ally."

"And I have my bed?"

She walked around the table and hugged my shoulders. "You keep your bed. We go month to month. I am most happy. *Sono contenta.* My house is full. Now I go to speak with Rosemaria." She picked up her hammer and departed.

In my room I undressed in the dark, put on my freshly washed pajama bottoms and a T-shirt, and crawled under the blankets. At that moment, at least, I was contented too.

Twenty-one

As I began my walk up the hill the following morning, I sensed something unusual about the air: it was laced with the aroma of spring. I thought I smelled freshly turned earth, and there was a hint of sweetness in the breeze. It was familiar: in Boston we called it a "January thaw," when the temperature rose from five above zero to fifty-five degrees in the span of a day or two and stayed there—often for a week—while the filthy ice and snow began to gurgle down into the storm drains and people threw open their windows, imagining the unlikely appearance of budding trees. Although the flower shoots that sometimes pushed up during this brief respite from winter usually met cruel fates, our spirits were lifted for these precious days, which were generally followed by a blizzard or a paralyzing ice storm.

As I climbed up the street, I saw housewives leaning on their window sills hailing friends in the street below, and there were gatherings outside the open doors of bars. The proprietor of the House of Cheese had dragged one of his wooden stands out into Piazza Ansidei and filled it with beautifully packaged cheeses, actually anything colorful he could find on his shelves.

To my great relief, I found the lights on in Montecalvo's book emporium and the door standing open. "Come in! Come in, on this fine spring day!" he called to me from the back of the store.

I deposited my briefcase by his desk. "Glad to see you back. You missed a lot of excitement while you were in Morocco."

"Coffee? Pull that chair up." He poured two cups from the pot that was balanced on one of his filing cabinets. "No sugar, I'm afraid. I have not had time to shop."

"You look healthy and tan."

"The beach was lovely, yes. I spent much time at the beach." He smiled at me with a twinkle in his eye and drained his cup.

"Were you upset to hear of DiBrufa's death?"

"Surprised, I would rather say. I did not know he had enough imagination left to go out with such dramatic flair. I salute him. Of course I will miss him. He was a formidable adversary."

I set my cup on its saucer with some force.

"But you," he continued, "you are more interested in Monica now, è vero?"

"Well, there have been some radical changes." I explained the current situation in some detail.

"Many changes indeed," he said. "Signora Bishop has agreed to this plan?"

"She's considering it. But I hope she'll agree, if Monica can be persuaded. My part in this is that I'll now have to write about DiBrufa instead of interviewing him, and I'll need Monica's input to do it. Will that be completely impossible?"

He poured himself another coffee.

"I understand she's in deep mourning ..." I continued.

"He held up his index finger. "Mourning, perhaps. But one must remember that Monica is always aware of the dramatic moment. For now she will play the grieving sister, but under the veil she is no doubt thinking of the role she will step into next. She does have a story to tell."

"About Piero."

"About Piero and about herself."

I gave him a look.

"No," he laughed, "nothing to do with unnatural acts."

"But will she talk to me?"

He shrugged. "If I'm not mistaken, she is ready to speak to *someone.* And the prospect of sharing a feature story with the illustrious Elaine Bishop, who she's been challenging for many months now, will be very persuasive."

"I would not be talking to them together, you understand."

"That would not be recommended."

"Would you be willing to negotiate a meeting for me? I don't think I'd get very far on my own."

"I'm certainly on better terms with her than I was with her brother."

At that moment a group of three customers entered the front of the store.

"Allow me to consider my approach," he said, rising to his feet. "Come back in two days. We will speak again."

I found Vincent standing on the edge of Piazza Italia with a beatific smile on his face, which was turned toward the early-afternoon sun. He was leaning on a cane.

"Isn't it wonderful?" I approached him and took his arm. "Smell the air."

"Heavenly," he said.

"What's with the cane?"

"Let's find someplace to sit down and eat. Do you feel like a pizza? Soup? Or a big meal?"

"Oh, a pizza, I think."

"My favorite pizza place is about halfway down Via Priori."

"Can you deal with Via Priori? It's steep."

He waved his cane. "Of course."

He didn't make a big deal about using the cane. But since it was such a nice day, I didn't mind slowing my pace.

We sat at a streetside table. I ordered a *quattro stagione* and Vincent got a *salsiccia e cipolle*, sausage and onions.

"Are you sure about that?" I asked him. But as soon as the food arrived, I grabbed a sausage slice from his plate, and he took an olive slice from my *quattro stagione.*

"How was your meeting with the doctor?" I asked him.

He took a slow drink of beer. "No surprises. She thought a cane might give me more stability on the icy streets, but the ice is gone! At least for the moment."

"What else did she say?"

He stood up. "I think I'll get another beer. Want one?"

I shook my head.

When he returned and had filled his mouth with food, I said, "Why don't you talk to me about what's really going on in your body, Vincent. Don't you think it's time?"

"Could I possibly have one of your prosciutto slices?"

"You can have any of my slices except the mushroom one." Then I got up and went inside to get a beer after all.

"I know I should have talked to you before," he said as I returned. "Maybe I thought that if you didn't know everything, I could keep at least one sanctuary of normalcy. Pointless, really."

"I've figured out a lot of it. I'm not blind."

He nodded. "Well, it looks like I should stop looking for another love of my life. That's one thing."

I looked at him across the table. "You're beginning at the very end. It won't help." He shifted his gaze to a point beyond me. I reached across and put my hand against his forehead. "Your fever's up."

He took a slow drink of his beer. "I think I mentioned my partner Rob that night we walked home."

"Yes."

"He died of a virulent form of PCP, full-blown AIDS. It was a horrible death, but he was brave and made a good fight of it. Although as it turned out, I didn't play much of a role."

"How long were you together?"

"Nearly seven years. I'd known him for longer than that, so it seemed like a lifetime to me. I didn't sleep around during that time, but he did. And I knew it. But we made compromises. And I did love him. He was diagnosed positive about the time they were discovering ways to control it, so we both tried to look on the bright side."

"Take your time. It's just me you're talking to."

"I was beginning to get a small reputation as a song writer in New York, and whether as a diversion or whatever, I became completely involved in my expanding career and all its accoutrements and simply stopped paying attention. To him. No other way to say it. I just assumed if he took his drugs, he wouldn't get worse. And life would go on. Of course I got tested, but I was negative, time after time.

"But then a recital of some of my songs got a single good review in the *Times* and suddenly I was the newcomer in town, on everyone's musical want list. I grew a wee moustache and a monstrous ego and began to hang out with some weird folks. I partied—a lot—and just turned into a self-absorbed idiot. A proper beast. And while I was busy getting too big for my boots, Rob was slowly getting sicker and losing weight, and I didn't even notice. Or I chose not to see. His friends were looking after him and taking him to appointments, and I was just—absent. Until finally I couldn't avoid what stood in front of me. He went into the hospital with what turned out to be his third bout of PCP, and one of his closest friends ambushed me one night in Chelsea, slammed me up against a building, and made me look at what was going on. Two weeks later, Rob was dead."

"What ..."

"Let me finish. I had those two weeks to make up for a year and a half of neglect, and it wasn't enough. Oh, I was a constant partner for those two weeks, but by then he was delirious half the time and didn't know who I was. He died with a bunch of people around him I didn't even know. I was glad he wasn't alone, but I was standing on the outside of that circle. Exactly where I belonged."

"I'm so sorry," I said.

"I thought he was safe," he said. "I thought we were safe."

"It wasn't a unique situation, Vincent. It's a nasty disease."

"That's not the point."

"So what's happening with you now?"

"Well, the moving finger writes. What goes around comes around, whatever cliché you want to use. Four months after Rob died, I was diagnosed with HIV. I considered it payback."

"How did you—"

"It doesn't matter how I got it. Or who gave it to me."

"Sorry."

"But it was controllable, so the doctors said. They had the perfect cocktail for me. Eat well, get your rest, and so forth. Keep those T cells up." He paused.

I felt a heavy weight pressing on my chest, that I didn't think was the result of the pizza. Life was moving very quickly.

"If I finish this tale now," he said, "I won't ever have to go through it with you again. Right? No more questions?"

"I'll do my best."

"Okay. I got tested regularly, I tried to live a healthy life. I began to relax. Then what comes in the back door but something else. I've got TB."

"Yes, I know. Elaine did tell me that."

"Elaine knows everything."

"TB is treatable," I said.

"Wake up, Ally. People with HIV can still die of it. For us, it's still an opportunistic infection. Not always so easy to treat. There are two kinds: latent and active, or TB disease. People with latent TB don't have symptoms usually and don't feel sick. They're not infectious. But they're susceptible to developing active TB, and people with HIV are at particular risk. I started out latent and then over Christmas the axe fell, and I've now switched sides. I'm being treated for active TB. It's a mild case, they say, but still."

"How are they treating it?"

"Drugs. In addition to my HIV cocktail. And rest. It's long-term therapy. Very long-term. And there are no guarantees it will work." He took a breath. "My appointment with Dottoressa Cortina today was just to confirm the result of my third TB test. Positive. So she's changing my drug protocol. In addition, she doesn't want my HIV to mutate into full blown AIDS. Which may happen anyway. And when it happens, it happens fast." His eyes had grown watery. "So. Satisfied?"

For a long while we sat there while life moved on around us, the pizza plates hardened with crumbs, the empty beer glasses began to stink. The noise increased. Someone behind the bar dropped a glass.

"How can I help?"

"You can't help. Just don't get too close if I'm coughing. Or sneezing. The germs are airborne, and they stick around for a while. And you probably shouldn't have kissed me the other day. I should have moved out of the way."

"That's helping me, not you. What do *you* need now?"

"Please go somewhere," he said, "to the policlinico or another clinic, and get a TB test. Or even my doctor. Actually, that might be a good idea. I'll call and see if she'll test you." He gave me a little smile. "Just in case."

"Has Elaine been tested?"

"Twice. Negative."

"Why didn't she say something to me?"

"Well, she wouldn't. She felt it was my place to talk to you. She kept after me to fill you in, but I put it off, irresponsibly. The opera situation got in the way, and then everything else. And selfishly, I guess I was afraid you'd take off if you knew."

I pushed my chair back and stood up.

"You're angry," he said.

"I'm not angry." I put some bills on the table and anchored them with a glass. "It's not like we ever had sex, Vincent. Well, not really."

He used the cane to help himself up. "Maybe I just dreamed we did," he said. The moment had become very tense. I was about to reach over and touch his arm when he added, "I just think you should be tested, that's all. See where we stand." He lifted his chin and smiled at me. "Could we possibly continue this later? I'm feeling shaky all of a sudden. I'd better get home."

"Should we get you a taxi?"

"I'll be fine."

The Priori struck three, and we slowly started up the hill. It was an abrupt conclusion to an afternoon that had begun so beautifully.

Twenty-two

"When are you having your test with the dottoressa?" Elaine asked me one day at lunch. Vincent was napping.

"Tomorrow morning."

"She's very nice, very thorough."

"Has Vincent been coughing much?"

"He's always coughing. Last night was particularly bad. He was up and down a lot."

She reached across and took my hands. "I'm wondering," she began, and then stopped.

"What."

"I hate this idea, but I've been thinking that he might be better off in some sort of care facility. I don't mean a hospital. Nearby, not far away, but a place where he could be looked after by people who are familiar with his sickness, who could feed him what he needs, who would have the drugs ... any drug he might need. Maybe a wing for patients who might be contagious? And he would have people to talk to."

One part of me knew she was right, but it was not a path I

would want to follow, had I been Vincent. "Have you talked to him about it?"

"He was the one who brought it up. I think he's lonely. What does he do all day? I'm at the theater, you're preparing for *Opera World*. He did have friends from the conservatory who came by from time to time, but he's been brutally honest with them about his situation, so I haven't seen them in a while. He gets up to try to work at the piano, but he always ends up back in bed. It breaks my heart."

"Is there a place like that around here?"

"There must be. I'd thought about asking the doctor."

"How much would it cost?"

"Quite a bit, I imagine."

"Because he couldn't afford it. And I'm in no position to help at all."

"Don't concern yourself with that part of it."

"And you don't think he'd be able to take care of himself if he went back to his own rooms?"

She shook her head. "I don't. And I wouldn't send him back there. He called the conservatory and cancelled his tutoring sessions, by the way."

"When?"

"I'm not sure, exactly. I was at the theater."

"I don't understand. When we had lunch he had a fever, but he was able to get around."

"Yes, well, after that lunch he made it as far as the Hotel Rosetta and had to get a taxi to take him the rest of the way. He couldn't even negotiate the scala mobile."

"He did have a couple of beers that day. Small ones."

"I don't think that had anything to do with it. Although I

really don't know anything about the new meds he's taking, what shouldn't be combined with alcohol."

"I should have walked him home."

"The most immediate thing is to talk to his doctor about places in the area. I can do that."

"I'll be seeing her in the morning ..."

"No, this is for me to do. But really, do you think this would be the right way to go?"

"I would talk to the doctor first. But I think it would be worth investigating, as long as he's in on it." We looked at each other. "I hate this," I said.

At that moment a door closed softly in the hall.

"What was that?" I asked.

"His door." She rose and went into the kitchen.

I remembered Dottoressa Cortina immediately from my night at the policlinico. She was a tall, graceful woman who wore her dark hair pulled back and secured at the nape of her neck with a silver barrette. I guessed she was around forty, but her lovely, smooth skin did not reflect her age. She wore a lab coat over a colorful wool sweater and dark trousers.

She sat with one hip on an examination table and made notes on a form. "How is Vincent?" she asked me, without looking up.

"He seems well enough. But he's always tired. And his fever is with him more often." I waited for her to look up.

"And how are you feeling?"

"I feel fine."

"No after effects from your head injury?"

"No."

She crossed the room and sat down before the computer, entered a few notes, then turned around to face me. "I'm curious about why Vincent feels you should be tested for active TB," she said with a little smile.

"He must have explained."

"I'd like to hear what you have to say."

"Well, I suppose because we were working closely together for a while on the opera ..."

"Of course."

"Also we're friends, we see each other socially ..."

"You see, I understand why Signora Bishop should be tested. Vincent is living in her home, and she has been caring for him quite closely. There is every reason to suspect that she might have been exposed, even though Vincent's case is mild. But you ... you don't seem to be quite so close." She regarded me calmly.

After a very long time, I responded, "It's a complicated situation. Could you just give me the test?"

"Signora Crosbie, I am not what they call born yesterday." Even she laughed a little at that, and I tried to join her, without much enthusiasm. "But my schedule is full this morning, so please do talk to me while we have this time."

"Your English is very good, very formal."

"I have run the New York marathon twice. In New York I made some British friends who helped to smooth my English. Now please speak to me. You can use Italian if you prefer."

Now I did laugh. "I'm not sure I can explain in Italian," I said. So I composed myself. "Elaine, that is, Signora Bishop, and I are ... intimately involved. We're having an affair. It hasn't been going on for long, but Vincent introduced us, and the three of us have spent quite a lot of time together."

"And ..."

"And what? If she's been exposed, it stands to reason that she might have passed it along to me."

"I'm sure there's more to say, so please go on. I can deal with complicated."

"Late last year Vincent and I became physically closer for a period of time. And we've had some intimate contact even since Elaine and I've been involved."

"You had sexual relations with him?"

"No. Not in the conventional sense. And before you ask, I'm aware of his HIV status as well as his tuberculosis. But we've never slept together. He must have told you that."

"It's not so unusual."

"I'm glad you think so."

"Is Signora Bishop aware of this situation?"

"It's not a situation." I took a breath. "I haven't shared every detail with her, no."

"Well, I understand these complications, as you call them, and I will test you. But I'd also suggest that the three of you sit down and have a candid discussion about what's happening. Especially if you and Signora Bishop intend to continue your relationship."

"Of course," I said. "But regarding Vincent, emotions aren't contagious, dottoressa."

She was preparing some instruments. "Well, there I might argue with you." She smiled at me over her shoulder. "Please roll up your sleeve. Would you permit me to test you for HIV as long as you're here?"

"All right."

I had to sign a permission for the HIV test, after which she drew my blood into several vials and sealed them off. "Now I will ask you to spit as much saliva as you can into this container," she said.

After I'd done that, I asked, "Are we finished?"

"Call my office tomorrow or the day after and we will have

results for the TB test. The HIV will take longer. I would also like to repeat the TB procedure in two weeks. Can you return?"

"Yes." I put on my coat. "I'll have to pay you in cash. Is that all right?"

She nodded. "Speak to my assistant." She held out her hand. "If you must see Vincent, do not get too close. He will know why. You might want to think about limiting your visits, sorry to say."

I shook her hand and left.

Outside a light snow had begun. I made my way up Via Fiorenza past the old prison wondering whether the phenomenon of the January thaw was related in any way to what is called a "false dawn." I had looked that up once out of curiosity and found that a false dawn was nothing but reflected light from interplanetary space dust illuminated by the sun on the other side of the world. I thought it might have had some magical meaning. It seemed like the proper term for certain situations.

In any case, the January thaw, whatever it had been, had ended, and February was in its third week.

Some days later I came home to Casa Caccini for lunch and the signora handed me a sealed envelope. A note from Elaine invited me to dinner and asked me to pick up a bottle of Grechetto. This was oddly formal. I wondered why she hadn't called.

"Come in, come in," Elaine said later, and kissed me firmly on the mouth. "Did you bring the Grechetto? Good. I'll give it a quick chill in the freezer."

I took off my coat. "It got chilled on my way down the hill," I said. "Is Vincent up and about?"

"No. He was tired, so I gave him his dinner early and sent him to bed. He'll probably wake up later."

We stood and talked in the kitchen, where a cutting board was strewn with a fragrant mix of chopped tomatoes, olives, peppers, and basil. There was also a small pile of sausage, presumably leftover from another meal. "Nothing fancy tonight," she said. "I was going to do a risotto, but I didn't realize I was out of porcini."

"I'm more interested in wine," I said.

"Ten more minutes. Did you visit the good dottoressa?"

"Yes, a couple of days ago. The TB test was negative. She also tested me for HIV, but those results are still out."

Her chopping ceased. "HIV? Why?"

"Routine, I suppose. This was my first visit."

After a pause she continued her chopping. "I had a talk with her about Vincent's situation, and she agreed that a care facility might be a good idea. She knows of a good one nearby."

"Is there a medical staff there?"

"Yes, some live-in, some not. They have X-rays and a CT scan, and also a lab, but if there's a serious need for treatment, they take people into the big hospital down near San Sisto, where Vincent was before. It's only twenty minutes away."

The timer gave a loud ding.

"Good," I said. "I'll open the wine." She took the wine bottle from me and gave the sauce a healthy splash. "It's in an ancient villa south of Perugia, completely modernized. On a high hill, beautiful grounds, a swimming pool, and it's part of a working farm, vineyards and olives and sunflowers."

I sipped my wine. "It sounds more like a resort."

"I thought you might say that, so I brought home a couple of the brochures she had in her desk." She stirred the sauce and tasted it.

"Who owns it?"

"I'm not sure. Somebody owns it, owns the land, the farm.

The care facility I expect supports itself, maybe rents the land, I don't know. Is that water boiling? Throw the linguine in, will you please? And set the timer for eight minutes."

She left the sauce bubbling and took a salad out of the crisper and dressed it. "No bread either," she said. "Sorry, I haven't shopped in days." She wiped off the kitchen table and put down some table mats and a bowl of parmesan. "Let's eat in here. I'd rather not wake Vincent, if he's still asleep."

We didn't return to the subject of the care facility until we were mostly finished eating. "How much would it cost?" I asked finally.

"It depends," she said, "on the patient's condition and how much care he needs."

"Would his doctor be able to treat him there? He seems to like her, and he's been seeing her for a while now."

"I don't know. Since she recommended this place, I would assume yes."

I asked the question we had both been avoiding. "How long would he stay?"

She looked at me and rested her chin on her hand.

"I mean," I went on, "would it be day-to-day, week-to-week, or what? He's told me that treatment for HIV complicated by TB is long-term. And there's no guarantee of anything. Is there light at the end of this tunnel?"

She rubbed her forehead. "I get my information from him. What he tells me and what I observe. If he's coughing up blood, he's hiding it now. I know he takes his drugs, especially his new ones. I make sure of that in the morning and the evening. But the midday dose—who knows? He's having trouble sleeping, except at irregular times of the day, like right now. But he's always exhausted. Sometimes while he's in the shower, I grab his sheets to do a quick wash and they're soaked in sweat." She paused. "So please don't ask me about lights in the tunnel. He needs to be in a place where someone can care for him better than I'm doing. In this facility or someplace like it. But it should also be nearby, so we can go to see him." She looked at me. "And now maybe I have to worry about you too."

"Whatever for?"

"Why did the doctor think she should test you for HIV?"

"I told you. My guess would be routine first-visit examination. I signed a permission. And I've been tested before."

"She didn't test me."

"If you're concerned, ask her about it. I told her about you and me, by the way."

"Did you now. Was that necessary?"

"It seemed to be the answer to some questions she was asking."

After a long pause, she asked, "How intimate were you and Vincent before this recent illness of his? Physically, I mean. And don't be coy and pretend you don't know what I'm talking about."

"I know what you're talking about, and I'm not very good at being coy. If you mean are we sexually involved now, the obvious answer is no. Last fall, if the circumstances had been different, the situation might have gone another way. But emotionally, yes, we've become closer." I looked at her. "It happens, Elaine."

"I know it happens. It's happened to me. It's called flirting."

"It's not anything like flirting. We're friends. I don't flirt with friends."

"I've always had a feeling that something happened on that night walk back from Sandro's."

"In the hay truck? Something almost did. But he stopped it. Now I know why."

"Meaning ..."

"At that point I don't think he was sure about how sick he really was. Or with what, in addition to HIV. I was disappointed, because at that particular moment—well, I wanted something to happen. Physically. It wasn't like a gigantic forest fire; I know what those feel like. But in the end I went to sleep, if that helps you out."

"But did you continue to think about it?"

"You mean did I want to try again? Not really. The moment had passed. But I do think of him differently now. We're easier being physically close. We're perfectly aware of our own sexual preferences; we aren't trying to fool each other. But there are different kinds of intimacy. And different ways to experience it. Sex is the easiest way, or so I always believed, but that's not the road we took."

"But there's something exclusive between you now."

"Maybe. But I could say the same thing about the two of you. There's a particular closeness there that I don't share. You have a history. I know that." I stopped. "We're not getting touchy about Vincent, are we? Because that would be ridiculous."

"Of course it would." She sighed. "Okay, I'm sorry if I pushed you. My nerves are shot. I don't want to argue with you or Vincent or anyone right now."

"Good."

We sat quietly for a while. At one point I looked over and wondered whether my feelings for her might be changing gears. I was trying to be completely candid with her, and it was a new and oddly pleasurable sensation. I was even looking for a way to bring up the *Opera World* decision.

"So where do we go from here?" she said. "You and I."

"You mean, what are my intentions? After you quashed my operatic career?"

"You must always joke." She smiled.

"All right, think of our circumstances. I've got *Opera World* to take care of. You've still got complications at the theater to straighten out. So you'll be in Perugia for a while, and I'll be here too, for at least a bit, so maybe we could, I don't know, date, I guess."

"*Date*? You mean like dinner and a movie? Sweetheart, we're way past dinner and a movie."

I touched her hand. "That was another joke."

"Well, stop it." She turned her head toward the hall. "Meanwhile, we have a mutual project, and I think he just flushed the toilet." She went into the kitchen and began to rinse the dishes under the hot water tap.

I followed her. "Have you talked to Vincent about this care facility?" I asked her. "And can we please stop calling it a care facility? There's got to be a better name."

She shut off the water. "I let him look at one of the brochures. He seemed interested."

"And my *Opera World* proposal? Have you been thinking about that?"

"Yes. But I did say that I would wait until I heard Monica's reaction. Have you heard from Montecalvo?"

"He needs a couple of days more." I shook my head. "Obviously he's making a plan. And it will have to be perfect."

"Listen to this, Vincent," I said half an hour later. We had moved to the dining room, and Vincent was eating a late supper of pasta and Elaine's warmed-up sauce. He was wearing his old robe over a T-shirt and sweatpants.

He rubbed one eye and took a sip of mineral water. "What?" he said.

"'Opera must draw tears, terrify people, and make them die through singing.'" I was reading from an old copy of *Opera News.*

He smiled at me. "That's Bellini, but I can't remember who he said it to." He took a small forkful of pasta and pushed his plate away. "Is there any gelato left?" he asked hopefully.

"I think there's a little stracciatella," Elaine said.

When she was in the kitchen, Vincent said quietly, "Have you looked at that brochure?"

"Not yet."

"It seems like a practical idea to me. It's not fair for me to stay on here with her. She *worries* so much."

"You need a haircut," I said with a smile. "Your locks are starting to look a little bushy."

He ran his hand through his hair. "I think they would probably have a barber at this place, don't you?"

"If they don't, I'm sure they can arrange for one."

"And maybe a piano?"

"It seems likely."

"Look at one of those brochures for me, could you? And let me know what you think. My head's not always on the right rails these days."

"Okay."

"And the cost ... I don't know where ..."

Elaine returned with a small bowl of stracciatella. "This is all of it, I'm afraid."

After he finished his gelato, Vincent made his way back to bed.

"It's a little late for you to go back up the hill," Elaine said as she loaded the dishwasher.

"It's not too late, but it's cold and I'm really tired."

She switched off the kitchen light. "Good," she said.

In bed, under the quilts, we wrapped ourselves around each

other and rested. The wind was particularly fierce and wailing dramatically against the shutters.

"This is a nice way to spend a winter night," she said.

"Yes." My head was just beneath her shoulder; I was already half asleep.

Then we heard Vincent begin to cough. Elaine sat up and I rose on one elbow. "Should you go to him?" I asked her.

"He doesn't want that. I'll just wait for a few moments."

It was not a small cough. It came from deep within his chest and didn't stop for quite a long time.

Twenty-three

We had decided to refer to it as the villa, not a "care facility," and Elaine drove us over to look at it the following weekend. There had been a light snow during the night, but the day was sunny, and most of the snow on the roads was gone. The frosty vineyards stood in lonely rows, their outstretched limbs askew like deserted crucifixes.

"This probably isn't the best time of year to visit this place," Elaine said.

"Well, we can skip the swimming pool, as far as I'm concerned." Vincent spoke from the backseat, where he was bundled up in a muffler and his heavy jacket.

"Cross the Nestore over a wooden bridge, then look for a roadside coffee bar. Turn right and head up the hill," I read aloud from the directions Elaine had received on the phone.

The road was steep, and as we swung past the *casa di riposo,* the old folks home, the few who were out and about on this cold morning waved as we spun past. As we ascended, the road began to twist, and the sleeping vineyards and olive groves fell away beneath us. Elaine's car began to encounter patches of ice, and we slid to the side a couple of times as the cypresses rose beside us. From time to time, tantalizing views of the massive villa began to appear high above us as the road turned one way, then another.

At last we pulled up before some great iron gates, and one of the caretakers waved us through. We approached the villa by way of a lane canopied by the leafy arches of what probably were laurels and crunched across a gravel parking area toward a gentleman in a well-cut dark suit who seemed to be there to greet us. The oft-restored stone front of the "parking entrance façade," as it was called in the brochure, extended in wide wings, and at each distant termination was a tall tower topped by a loggia. I had read that several sections of the walls on the lower grounds had been erected two hundred years before the birth of Christ. I was curious about these, but of course we weren't here to sightsee.

"Wow," Vincent said as he slowly pulled himself out of the car. "Wow."

I saw that Elaine was introducing our small group to the *direttore*, if that's who he was, and getting our inspection underway. As Vincent and I approached, he was apologizing for the winter state of the grounds. "The gardens are all asleep," he was saying, "and there is a cover on the pool, but we will show you what we can."

Before we entered the villa, I noticed a beautiful little chapel slightly beyond the western wing, which featured a small rose window of modern design above the entrance. To the side, in the remains of the snow, two workmen were planing an object that was resting on a couple of sawhorses. What they were making was a coffin.

We had an extended tour of the first-floor facilities, Elaine following the director and asking the questions. I hung back with

Vincent, who was maneuvering slowly with his cane. It was clear that this villa had once belonged to an illustrious family, perhaps more than one, and great care had been taken during various restorations to preserve the original state and beauty of the rooms. Frescoes remained near the upper reaches of several walls, and the stone surrounds of the windows had been intricately carved. The few common areas we were allowed to see had crystal chandeliers hanging near the ceilings. The card room featured studded emerald-green leather walls.

For some reason Elaine asked to see the kitchen, and I was glad she did. It was immense, with a bright fire ablaze in the *pietra serena* fireplace. A massive walnut table stood in the center of the room, where several cooks were at work preparing what would probably be the midday meal. There were two large six-burner gas stoves, where pans and large pots were producing copious billows of aromatic steam. Elaine stuck her head into the back room and called to me, "Three refrigerators."

Our host explained that the utilities and diagnostic medical equipment were all below us, in what he did not call a basement. "X-rays, scanners, a *laboratorio,* all laundry facilities, a root cellar, wine storage, etcetera, etcetera."

"I think we'll forgo the lower regions, Direttore," Elaine said, "if you don't mind."

"*Va bene,* signora. I will show you the view to the north, then." We filed back through the hallway and exited the building on the opposite side from the parking entrance. The view to the north, even on a cold February morning, took our breaths away. We stood at the crest of a wide lawn, which stretched grandly to the west and east and fell away to stone walls that stood above a descending path lined with olive trees, below which, I assumed, was the pool, as advertised. To the east stood the snow-topped

Apennines, stretching northeast and south at this point, and in between stood a village or two, smoke curling up from distant chimneys. We were very high up, and as our mountain continued to gently descend, we were able to see field workers far below, busy with the winter pruning of the vines.

"In the warmer months, of course," the director remarked, "those who are able spend much of their time outside, and we take meals in the loggia just there." He then stepped forward and pointed directly northward. "And we see Perugia, on the mountain there, perhaps thirty kilometers away. At night she glitters like a forest of lights."

"That is my home," I heard Vincent say quietly behind me.

As I attempted to remove thoughts of *The Magic Mountain* from my mind, I turned and took his arm. "Perhaps we could see one or two of the bedrooms," Elaine said to the director. "We don't wish to delay you."

"Certo, signora. Please follow me."

As we reentered the house, Vincent said to Elaine, "Do you mind looking at the rooms yourself? I spotted a common room, just here, actually, and I think I'd like to rest awhile."

"Fine," Elaine said. "You can rest here, and I'll go on upstairs. Ally, want to stay with him?"

"Come on, Vincent," I said, "we'll go in."

We entered through a glass door and found a large, comfortably furnished room, with soft rugs over red Italian tiles. A fire of olive wood was ablaze in yet another deep *pietra serena* fireplace. One or two of the other occupants looked up and smiled as we came in but went back to their reading or writing or headsets.

"Look," I said to Vincent in a low voice. "A piano."

"I saw it," he said. He sank down onto a sofa.

I sat down beside him and finally removed my jacket. We sat

together for a while, just resting, absorbing the quiet of the place, and the spectacular view, which was still partially visible through the large northern-facing windows of the common room.

"Could you be happy here?" I asked him.

"Couldn't anybody?" He took my hand. "Sorry. I guess I should say that if this is the end of the line, it's a pretty classy one."

"The line doesn't end here."

"I don't know why Elaine's brought us over here. I mean, look at it. It's for rich retirees from Rome or Milan, exiled Middle Eastern shahs, wealthy British widows. There's no way in hell I could fit in here."

"I don't see any shahs," I said. "But *non si sa mai*. You never know."

"I want to go back to Perugia."

"We'll go soon. Would you like some coffee or water?"

He looked at me with his beautiful eyes and leaned his head back. "I don't mean to be unpleasant," he said.

"You're not."

"I know something has to change, but please don't let Elaine take over. I love her to death, but what's happening to me is out of her control and she doesn't like it."

"I don't like it either."

"That's different."

The door opened softly and a young man with handsome curls came in carrying a tray of coffee, steamed milk, water, and a plate of sweet cookies. "The direttore asks me to bring this in," he said.

Vincent sat up. "Why, thank you," he said with a smile. "*Grazie.*"

"*Prego,* signore. *Stai attento*. The *caffè* is hot."

"We'll be careful," I said. "Thank you very much."

I poured Vincent his coffee and added the milk. "You've brightened up," I said.

"There might be a few advantages to living here," he said as he watched the young man depart.

Afterward, on our way down the hill, Elaine pointed toward the east. "It's snowing in the mountains," she said. "The clouds are dark."

Vincent had dozed off.

As we turned onto the highway back to Perugia, she said quietly to me, "I'm going to drop him off at my house, but I'll run you up to Piazza Danti before I come back and park the car. I want to talk to you."

"How were the rooms?"

"Oh, elegant, some of them. Others ordinary, but comfortable enough. Most with bathrooms. A sort of nursing station on every floor. Very clean, all of it."

"He's afraid to come here, you know."

"I feel like a traitor. Please don't make it worse."

"He knows he has to come, Elaine. Just don't push him."

She squeezed my hand. "Wait. We'll talk later."

Later we sat in the car behind the duomo at the edge of Piazza Danti, our usual spot, and did our best to keep warm.

"It's staying light a little longer," she said. "It always raises my spirits when I realize this."

"We could all do with a bit of spirit lifting."

"Just listen." She took a breath. "Something's happened that may make a difference. I've been wracking my brain about how to finance Vincent's stay at this place, if we can get him to agree to go. I have some funds stashed away in various accounts, and the company still owes me a large chunk for the work I did on the DiBrufa opera that will never be. We've been working on that with the lawyers, but I'm not counting on much. The singers and musicians should be paid before anyone else, and after that's done, there's not likely to be a lot left for the rest of us."

"You said something's happened."

"I'm getting to that. I was at the theater last week and Renata came in—you remember Renata Grillo, surely."

"Of course. Her dog bit me."

"We went for coffee. This whole business with Vincent was on my mind and it just spilled out of me. I told her all about it."

"I'm not sure how Vincent would feel about that."

"Oh, he's quite close to Renata. She and Margit let him compose on their baby grand, even arranged for his tutoring job at the conservatory. They're very fond of him. I didn't think Vincent would mind."

I surreptitiously glanced at my watch.

"She knows this place well, where we were today. Apparently they have a fine reputation. It's much more than a retirement community, despite what Vincent thinks. She's on good terms with some of the doctors, including Vincent's lady doctor, and contributes to it in a small way."

"All good to know."

Elaine turned to me. "Are you suddenly in a bad mood?"

"I'm just tired."

She drew herself up. "All right. She's offered to pay for a year's stay in the villa for Vincent, if he'll agree to go."

"What?" I placed my hand on her arm. By this time the car

windows were completely steamed up, and I lowered my window so I could breathe.

"She'll pay all expenses for Vincent to stay there for one year. And when one pays for that, everything is included: room and board, all medical treatments, drugs, laundry, the whole package."

"Good grief," I said. "How much money does she have?"

"A lot. She can afford this. She asked me why I hadn't approached her before."

I hugged her enthusiastically. "That's wonderful."

"Put that window back up, darling," she said, laughing. "Night has fallen."

"I just needed to breathe." I sat very still. "What a generous offer."

"She's very generous. There are groups in the city that don't like her, I don't know why. Maybe because she's a bona fide contessa, because she's used to getting her own way, because she lives with another woman, because she's wealthy, because her dogs are allowed in the Brufani dining room and in the cafés and they sometimes bite people. I like her very much."

"Even so, you may have a hard time persuading Vincent to go. He thinks he won't fit in."

"He must fit in. Mostly right now, he needs to rest. That will keep his TB from getting worse and his other diseases from taking over. I think his best option is to accept Renata's gift and thank her by allowing himself to be cared for. His doctor may help us with that part."

"What's she told you?"

She rubbed her forehead with her fingers. "His new treatments are beginning to help the TB, but now the HIV has become more active. When one disease pauses for breath, the other takes over. He's losing the ability to resist both of them. I think this villa place will give him the best chance to feel better, but I don't think anyone's mentioned the word 'cure.'"

I looked out through the steamy windows. "I don't want him to imagine we've dropped him off there to die."

"Why would he think that? We'll be over there as often as we can."

"And how often would that be?" She looked at me through the early-evening light. "He said going there would be the end of the line."

"The end of the line is a dramatic figure of speech. I think he might come to like it."

"He knows his own body pretty well. He's not stupid, Elaine. He watched his own partner die."

"Yes, and a lot of what he thinks, and sometimes says, is based on this horrible guilt he's been carrying around since that happened." She took my hand. "I thought you'd be pleased about Renata's offer."

"I am. Have you given up on him, though?"

She frowned. "Given up? Of course not. What could be more important?"

"Finding new work, maybe. Perfectly understandable."

We sat in silence for a few moments. I knew I'd thrust into a vulnerable spot. A place that would hurt her. And once again I wondered why I would become so quickly defensive. I should have aimed this thrust at myself. I was idly biding my time waiting to complete an assignment that might possibly jump my professional career up a rung or two, but what could be *less* important at this point?

I opened the car door and the cold swept in.

"Come back in here," she said.

I slammed the door and turned to face her.

She took a Kleenex and wiped off her side window. "Let's not argue," she said finally. She rubbed her forehead again; she must have a headache on the way. "I will say this, though. Don't make assumptions like that until you know me a little better."

I felt the cold in my bones and put my arm around her shoulder. "Sorry. I know better."

She put her head down against the steering wheel. "It's been a long day," she said after a moment. "And we never got anything to eat."

My hand remained on her shoulder as she sat up. "For now, let's just say that Renata's offer is very good news," I said, "and you—probably—should get the dottoressa more involved. Another chore to add to your list; sorry about that."

"It's not a chore." She raised her head. "I'll also ask her to encourage Vincent to accept Renata's offer. I hope she will, and we can get that part rolling."

We sat there for a while in silence while the cold intensified. She seemed to be trying to tie up a lot of loose threads. All at once.

"And I guess we'd better start thinking about an interview, Ally. So you can finish up your piece. No point in waiting for Monica. I don't know why Montecalvo is dragging his feet about her."

"I've put together a sort of outline of how I'd like to work, what points I'd like to cover."

"Let me take a look at it then. I'll check my date book when I get home."

"I'll send it over when I get back to my computer. If we can get your part done, then I'd be all ready to go when Monica joins the party."

She laughed a little. "I wouldn't expect a party, if I were you."

"Oh, I won't."

I got the strange feeling that she was waiting for me to leave, so I opened the car door and a blast of neon-infused night air rushed in once more.

"Ally," she said.

I turned back. She leaned across the seat and kissed me. "I wish ..." she began.

"What do you wish?"

"Oh, I'm just tired, I guess. I'll call you later."

"Right." I shut the car door and began the descent into Via Rocchi. When I turned around to look, she was still sitting there in the darkness.

Twenty-four

I'd been thinking about how I might approach an interview with Elaine. When I tried out some of my ideas, she vetoed several points I was hoping to pursue, which made me a little nervous. I was aware that she would be a reluctant subject. But my main points I knew she could handle; how she chose to expand on them would be out of my control. She also agreed to let me use my tape recorder, which was a relief.

I called her one day as she was about to leave the theater for a meeting with donors. "I think I'll go down and see Vincent," I told her.

"Yes, why don't you do that. We're just waiting to see if the villa has a room for him. You'd better call him first."

"Oh, yes, come on down," he said. "But bring your own lunch."

"Nothing for you?"

"I'm not too hungry these days. Do you know what it's like to spend day after day looking at fog?"

"Well, yes."

"Come cheer me up, then. I'm not doing anything but playing Bach on the piano and taking naps. I'm trying to keep my fingers from falling off for lack of exercise."

"Okay. I'll buy myself some lunch and come on down."

I decided to eat my lunch in the dining room. I'd brought a container of pasta salad, cheese, and some slices of roast chicken. Vincent brought me a half-finished bottle of Torgiano white from Elaine's refrigerator.

After watching me eat for a few minutes, he said, "Could I have just a wee taste of the pasta salad?"

"Of course. Get yourself a bowl."

He took quite a large helping. And ate it all. I'd brought enough for both of us, but I thought he might have preferred the chicken. "I was getting tired of *pastina in brodo,*" he said as he put down his fork. "I didn't mean to eat so much."

I looked over at him. "She's a terrific cook. Surely she's feeding you more than gruel."

"She does her best." He chewed on a crust of bread and then brushed his hands together. "Come on," he said. "I'll play some Bach for you." He stood up and took off his robe. He was wearing jeans and a faded green sweatshirt, both of which hung loosely against his body.

I've always loved the Goldberg Variations and never quite known why. They are intricate and calming, and each one concludes so decisively that it seems to answer questions you hadn't known you'd asked. He played four or five of them, and when he stopped, my eyes were damp.

He came over and sat down on the couch beside me. "Are you upset? What's going on?"

"I want the sun again, that's all."

"I hope you're not thinking of moving along to some place with better weather."

"I think about it all the time."

He took a deep breath. "What do you think I should do?" he asked.

I hoped he was referring to Renata Grillo's offer. I didn't think it would be fair to tell him it was his decision, in order to remove myself from the awful hurt of sending him away. But he'd asked, and I had to answer.

"I think you should say yes," I said. I saw him shudder and got up to retrieve his robe. "Here, put this back on." We returned to the dining room table, and I began to clean up the remains of lunch.

"It would be like giving up, wouldn't it?"

"What, exactly would you have to give up?"

"Hope, mainly. Not about life and death, those I can deal with. They're familiar companions. But my music is there, hanging like a loose thread. I want to finish my opera, as much of it as I can. What if they won't let me use the piano in that place, for example?"

"Have you been able to work on it here?"

"I can't seem to focus on it. It confuses me sometimes. Sometimes I don't know how to mark the music. I can't even *read* it sometimes!"

"You're recovering, Vincent."

We were quiet for a while, then he said, "If I'm going over there, it should be very soon." His face had flushed, and I could see drops of sweat on his forehead. Fever.

"Vincent ..."

"It won't help to ignore that fact."

I took the dishes to the kitchen and put them in the sink.

"No. It won't," I said as I returned to the table. "But you'd better make it clear what you mean by 'soon.'"

"As in, the sooner the better." I brushed some crumbs off the table and gathered them into my hand. "And what will happen to us, do you think? When that day comes."

"You and me? You might see more of me than you want to," I said.

"And you'll get over there how—by donkey?"

"Yes, if necessary." I was not smiling. I got to my feet and embraced him from behind. I could feel him shaking and I knew he did have a fever now.

"I have to excuse myself," he said after a few minutes. "I think I'm going to get teary or something worse, and I need privacy for both." He left the room with his robe billowing out behind him.

At that same moment I heard the distant sound of the main door thudding closed three flights below and guessed Elaine was on her way up. I wiped my eyes and blew my nose and hoped there was more wine. I still had the crumbs grasped in my hand.

Elaine enveloped me in her arms and said, "Oh, good. You're still here."

I inhaled the scent of her, the cold evening, and the wood smoke. She turned away for a moment and dropped her coat on one of the chairs. "Where is he?" she asked.

"In his bathroom. Or in bed."

"I need a drink of something. Come with me."

"I'm afraid I finished the Torgiano."

"No matter. There's more of everything." She stopped short as we walked into the kitchen. "Aha. You've been to the deli. Were there beans in that pasta salad?"

"Small ones. Full of protein."

"No wonder he's in the bathroom. But not to worry. That issue will soon be solved." She took my face between her hands. "You'll stay for the night, won't you?"

I thought of her big bed, the clouds of soft comforters, the scent of her sheets. I thought of sleep. "Do I have a choice?"

"No. You don't." She patted my behind. "Now fetch the gin for me please from the liquor closet. I'll open another bottle of wine for you."

"Hello, there." Vincent came into the kitchen in his sock feet and touched her shoulder.

"Why are your eyes so red?" she asked him. "And you have a drop of blood under your nose."

"Have you eaten?" I asked her. "There's some chicken left."

She dropped some ice cubes into a glass and picked up the bottle of gin. "Maybe after a while. I had something to eat earlier. Ahhh," she said as she took a drink. "Let's go into the dining room. I have something for you to see, Vincent."

We sat around the table while Elaine retrieved a file of papers from inside her briefcase. She divided them into two separate little stacks and placed a fat pen between them. "Vincent, dearest, it's all been approved," she said. "You're in."

"I thought he might have been happier about it," she said later as we were getting into bed. "They said yes to everything." I had thrown my clothes into a pile on a chair; she had taken the time to hang hers up.

"He was happy," I said.

We both slept deeply. I woke only once, to use the bathroom, and made my way back across the chilly tiles to wrap myself around her again. Returning to bed in the depths of a winter night, to someone who is warm, sleeping, keeping your place from getting cold: a profoundly peaceful feeling. Someone wrote about that once, not precisely in the same way.

I got up first the next morning and found Vincent at the dining room table surrounded by the forms Elaine had brought home. He had made coffee and poured himself a large glass of blood orange juice.

"So what do you think?" I asked him as I sat down.

He looked at me over his glasses. "She wants me to sign this right away?"

"Are there specific dates mentioned on the forms?"

"I'm not sure." He went through the papers. "It looks to me like Renata's already paid. Everything. She's signed, Margit's signed, Elaine's signed, and my dottoressa has also signed. There are big spaces for my signature in a lot of different spots, but it looks like I could go over anytime I wanted."

"Well, read it carefully. Figure out what they're offering you—will the dottoressa be paid separately, your room, the piano business, and so forth."

Elaine swooped in, wearing slacks and a turtleneck. "Getting advice from your lawyer, Vincent?" she said, and kissed me on the cheek.

"This is moving along so fast," he said.

She got herself some coffee and sat down next to him. "It can move along as fast or as slowly as you want," she said, exchanging a glance with me.

He removed his glasses. "But faster is better."

"You and I've been over this." She ran her fingers through her hair. "You need better care than I'm able to give you right now, I'm very sorry to say. And we've known each other too long for me to make excuses for that. Frankly, I think it would be helpful for you to be around people other than just this neurotic stage director. They'll move the piano into a private room for you, did you read that part?"

"Yes."

"And," Elaine went on, "you're sure to get more nutritious meals than I've been providing."

"I'm not arguing with any of that," he said.

"Are you nervous about the change in your routine?" Elaine asked him. "Because that would be a perfectly natural reaction to have. Your life will be very different. But better, I hope."

"Elaine," I said, "do they have any small rooms where a guest could stay, maybe for a night or two?"

"There are three of these rooms," she said. "A bed, a chair, a table, and a little wardrobe. A small sink. No bathroom; it's down the hall. Very nunlike. And they would feed you—or whoever the guest might be."

"Well, there you are," I said.

There was silence while Elaine went into the kitchen to fix some toast.

"Don't worry," I said, putting my hand on his arm. "It's such a beautiful place. It'll be glorious in the spring."

"I'm not going for the flowers."

"Right," Elaine said, returning to the table. "Who wants toast?"

I looked at my watch. "I want to drop in on Montecalvo."

"Hot toast," Vincent said, tossing it up in the air. He eventually went off to shower, and Elaine brought my coat to the front door.

"Don't push him," I said to her.

"Ally, I must, a little bit. He's signed now, and they'll be expecting him."

"Is there really a need for this absolute rush?"

She put her hands on my shoulders. "Every day when I walk out of here, leaving him alone sometimes for more than ten hours, it's torture for me. I worry all day about whether he's fallen in the bathroom or coughed himself to bloody death in his bed or simply if he's lonely. He has to be lonely here. I know Renata has come by a couple of times, but that's not who he wants to see."

I put on my gloves.

"But you're right about one thing," she added. "That place will be glorious in the spring, and in the summer too."

"Are things about to wind up at the theater?"

"Oh, with all the lawyers involved, it may go on forever. But I think my part of the drama may be drawing to a close."

"Good."

She smiled and kissed me lightly on the mouth. "You're going to Montecalvo's?"

"Yes."

She opened the door and a brisk whoosh of cold air came swirling in around us. "Well, let me know what he says. And keep your phone charged. Maybe dinner over the weekend?"

"I'll call you."

On my way up to the *centro* on the scala mobile I felt a tap on my shoulder, and I turned to find Odysseus Lianis, whom I hadn't seen in several weeks. Or more.

"Hello to you," he said with a weary smile.

"I'm happy to see you," I said. "You must be coming up from the hospital."

"I'm having visions of some soup and my bed. But now I have thirty-six hours off, so that is something." He adjusted his scarf against the chill of the tunnel.

"How have you been?"

"Working hard. Very many sick people. Much pneumonia, I am sorry to say."

"How is the Greek contingent?" I asked him, as we began to climb through the tunnel toward the next set of moving stairs.

"Georgios is doing all right. Yanni went off to Germany, very angry at him, at all the Greeks. Making many terrible threats, about the Greek police and so forth. Hot air, I think." He gave me a small smile.

"I'll tell Jo," I said.

We reached the top of the second set of moving stairs and the climb became steeper. The walls of the old fortress seemed to loom over us.

"I was hopeful a couple of weeks ago," I said. "I thought spring might be coming."

"You really didn't."

"For a moment maybe."

We had reached the top of the penultimate set of moving stairs but were still underground in the medieval environs of the former homes of the Baglioni family, its mysterious streets disappearing into dimly lit gloom. "Where are you going?" he asked, as we stepped onto the final set of escalators and felt the first touches of chilly air from above.

"I'm on my way to check on a friend. Via Oberdan."

"Come with me first. I have something to show you that may make you feel better." He took my arm and guided me through Piazza Italia toward Via Baglioni.

"Where are you taking me?"

"Just wait."

It was very late morning now, and there was a pre-midday passeggiata feeling stirring about in the streets. "Are we going for a coffee?" I asked as we passed through Piazza Matteotti. "Because I could use one."

"*Pazienza,*" he said. We paused in front of the Mercato Popolare at the east end of the piazza. "Now here I will ask you to cover your eyes."

"We're shopping, then. All right." I covered my eyes with my hands, and he guided me into the store. I smelled oranges first, before I could see them. The unmistakable fragrance of blood oranges.

"Now," he said. "Remove hands."

My eyes opened upon a pyramid of blood oranges, one cut in half to reveal its rosy inner fruit. Around the walls were pails of fresh asparagus and spring wildflowers. Stacked in the center of the store were large piles of gracefully arranged tomatoes, about midsized, and plump artichokes. Fava beans. There were even some baby lettuces, but as I marveled at them, a woman grabbed two, shouldering aside someone who'd tried to push her out of the way.

"*Dica,* signora!" the young woman behind the deli case called to a customer. Meaning: tell me what you want! And then: "*Altro!*" (What else?) The smell of roasting chicken was pungent in the air, and I also detected the aroma of some cheeses I hadn't encountered since late last summer.

I turned to Odysseus in astonishment. "What's happened here?"

He gave me a big smile. "Sicilia," he said. "Sicilia has happened. Sicily is sending up her early crops, and if you want anything, you'd better move fast."

I grabbed plastic bags and collected as many tomatoes and oranges as I dared, flung two entwined bunches of asparagus together, collected some wildflowers for the signora, and threw some fava beans into a bag. I then went to examine the cheese. The baby lettuces, unfortunately, were *finito.* Odysseus stood in the doorway and laughed. He took off his glasses and wiped his eyes.

"*Dica,* signora!" the deli girl called to me. I'd had too much chicken lately, so I declined that and bought some soft robiola cheese instead. "It's like Christmas!" I said to Odysseus as I joined the line to pay. In the street, as I tried to organize all my bags, I said, "You're right, the weather has changed. It's spring!"

And as I said that, a few flakes of snow began to fall. I didn't care. I could smell the wildflowers, the fragrant skin of the oranges, the sweet aroma of the tomatoes, the tangy robiola. The bread I had purchased was still warm. "Thank you, Odysseus," I said to him. "Not for the first time, you've saved the day. Can I buy you a coffee?"

"I would say yes, but I have not slept for almost two days. I am a walking zombie, I think they say. I must go to my bed." He gave me a hug around the shoulders. "Perhaps another time."

"I don't think I know where you live," I said as we began to descend Via Rocchi. "Nearby?"

"Now I am living with friends in rooms off Corso Garibaldi. But soon I will move to a place of my own closer to the hospital. This going back and forth is wasting my time. And if I take the Minimetro, there is a long walk at the end. Sometimes I am sleeping in the hospital for many nights in a row."

"You deserve a good meal for this shopping spree. Please call me when you're free. Oh, I have a new telefonino now."

"Say your number. I would enjoy a good meal with you."

I said it, and he took his pen and wrote it on the back of his left hand. I noted there were other figures there as well, a series of numbers, the names of several drugs. I laughed. "Don't wash your hands," I said.

We stopped in front of Casa Caccini, and he handed me the bags he'd been carrying for me. "I must ask," he said, "how is your friend doing? Your sick friend."

"I think, I hope, he's about to go and live at Villa Vibiano, over near Mercatello. They've admitted him, and I'm hoping they'll give him the rest and treatment he needs ... but doesn't seem to want."

"I know it," he said. "It's a good place. He will be happy there, I think."

I shuffled my bags around in my arms. "I'd better go in."

"Ciao, Allyn."

He went off down the hill toward the Etruscan Arch.

The signora collapsed in a chair when she saw the wildflowers, the beans, the tomatoes, and all the rest. "*Gioia!*" she cried. "*Mille grazie,* Sicilia! And Signora Ally! Teresina! Maria Rosa! *Venite qua! La cena è qui*!" As I watched her glowing eyes, I tucked a couple of oranges and a few tomatoes into my coat pocket, because I knew I might never see the rest again.

The signora put her hand on my arm. "*Momento,* Signora Ally." She pulled me into the dining room. "You have a guest waiting. For one hour he is waiting still."

"Who is it?"

"You will see. I think now I must ask him to stay and enjoy the gifts you have given me."

As we left the room, the imposing figure of Italo Montecalvo emerged from the kitchen, led by the two Caccini daughters, each holding a hand.

We sat down in the darkened dining room. He was carrying a glass of white wine.

"I've been looking for you," I said.

"My mission took more time than I expected."

"Were you successful?"

He sighed deeply and took a sip of wine. "She is a difficult woman. My approach had to be carefully constructed. But I immediately saw that she was growing a little bored with the role of grieving sister and I became hopeful. For years, you see, she was in charge; no one could get to Piero except by way of her. She was the guardian of the gate, but the fame usually went to him. So maybe she is tired of this."

He was taking the long way round. "So?" I asked him. "How did you approach?"

"First, I asked her to remove her veil. I wanted to see her eyes. She did, to my surprise." "Go on."

"I simply suggested that it might be time to step into her rightful place in the DiBrufa family firmament. Time for her to speak the truth about her brother, to talk of his youth, his disappearance into a life of complete seclusion. Including, of course, his final work, the opera that will never be produced. Thanks be to God. And then at last to speak for herself, for the first time."

"And what did she say?"

"Nothing. At first. She poured me a glass of very fine Brunello and served with it some excellent cheese from the Valle d'Aosta." He thought for a moment. "A bit too strong for the Brunello, but very good nevertheless."

"And then ..."

"Then we sat quietly and watched the evening descend over the Tiber Valley and some brave birds searching for shelter from the cold. She lit a fire in the fireplace."

I couldn't bring myself to urge him forward again.

But he finally went on. “At last she said, ‘I do have a story to tell. And the time has come to tell it. How shall I proceed?’”

“And you replied ...”

“Of course I replied. Afterward I kissed her hand, which was a mistake, but did not affect the final outcome. She has asked me to accompany you, and I am happy to do this. I should confess that I have an idea about the tale she will tell, but it would be unfair to prepare you. It is hers to reveal.”

“Curiouser and curiouser.”

After an extended pause, he said, “I feel there is still some resistance there on her part. Some reluctance to speak about her private life. This is just a caution. You must treat her with great courtesy.”

“I intend to.”

“We must now set a date.”

The signora was not a selfish woman, as I have noted before. She cooked for us all that evening, and it was a feast. Jo wandered in, and Ines and Anita, and we pulled in some extra chairs. Montecalvo stayed for a while and squeezed in where he could. The signora remained on her feet. The entertainment was provided by Teresina and Maria Rosa, who recited lessons from school and sang a couple of songs having to do with bears in the woods and birds who built their own houses (as opposed to nests).

After the meal we tenants passed the hat and sent Teresina downstairs to buy some gelato from the bar across the street. She brought Shaima back with her and sadly announced that it was snowing again.

After Montecalvo departed, Anita and I did the dishes while the signora readied the girls for bed, and things quieted down quickly. I lay on my bed for a while enjoying the aftertaste of the evening. It had been a relief to relax for a while among people who knew nothing of my current personal concerns but were simply sharing a meal with others who were glad to be together. It seemed that by complete accident I had been swept up into a very happy place.

Twenty-five

It hadn't exactly been spring, but even without looking at a clock we could tell that the days were slowly lengthening. Of course, March was nearly upon us, neither spring nor winter, fish nor fowl, as they say. A single day might begin with a chilly rain, which would stop for the duration of the midday passeggiata, when a pale sun would sometimes appear. And if we were lucky, we'd sometimes be treated to a blood-red sunset toward the end of the day, and the aroma of freshly turned earth might be carried in on an evening breeze. By nightfall, however, the breeze could become a fierce windstorm. I was walking home along the corso one night when a violent gust came down the street from nowhere, whirling pieces of trash and grit ahead of it, thrusting pedestrians against glass doors and store windows. Cries of "*Terremoto! Terremoto!*" were heard as many ran into the duomo for cover.

But it was not an earthquake—the earthquake came after lunch the following week. And although the epicenter was not in Perugia but down near Norcia, it was close enough. I was at my desk when it began, and it shook most of my papers to the floor and my jar of pens. A picture fell off the wall. I managed to catch my little laptop before it slid off my desk and ran to stand under the doorframe, which we had been advised to do. The entire house seemed to be undulating under my feet, as if I were walking on a wave. It lasted maybe forty or fifty seconds. Afterward the signora came into my room, casually carrying her large vegetable knife.

"Terremoto," she said.

I nodded.

She put her hand on my shoulder. "A small earthquake, Signora Ally. Here we are safe."

My phone vibrated in my pocket then, and I knew who it would be. Elaine would be nervous about Vincent.

"I can't reach him," she said. "I'm pretty sure my building is okay, but where could he be?"

"He probably slept through it."

"I'm in the midst of a final meeting with the set carpenters, and I can't run home. Could you possibly go down there and check on him?"

"I don't have keys to your apartment."

"Daniele Pulci on the fourth floor has a copy of my keys."

I waited.

"Ally, please. Vincent's not answering his phone."

There didn't seem to be much damage in the center of the city. People were milling about because it had been an event, after all, and must be discussed. Would there be aftershocks? The plate glass window fronting one of the dress shops on the corso lay shattered in the street, and I heard more than a few security alarms wailing, but for the most part, people had stopped for coffee or a drink, and it looked like the evening passeggiata would begin early.

There were crowds of people on the scala mobile, but most

of them were ascending into the city and not fleeing it, so I was able to take the descending stairs two at a time. As I approached Elaine's building, I noticed a familiar black Alfa parked in front, but I was intent on getting up to Elaine's and forgot about it immediately.

I had some trouble opening her front door. As I shoved in, I saw that it was blocked by several large suitcases, some boxes of blank scoring sheets, and two thick briefcases. There were ten or fifteen loose books scattered about on the couch. A murmur of male voices came from down the hall.

"Hello!" I called out. "Vincent?"

The murmuring ceased.

"Vincent, it's Ally. Are you all right?"

"Oh, Ally!" I heard his voice. "Good! Come join us."

I walked into his bedroom to find it almost completely stripped. Empty closets, empty bookcases, and the large table he'd been using as a desk was completely cleared off. He was standing in his bathroom with his shaving gear and some other bottles in his hands.

Sitting in a chair beside the bed was Sandro Colonna, who rose to his feet as I entered the room. He bowed slightly and said, "Signora Crosbie."

I opened my mouth to speak but was interrupted by the buzzing of Vincent's telefonino, which he had placed on his bedside table. He made no move to answer it.

"That is Elaine," I said. "Would you talk to her please? She's concerned about you." He continued to collect his bottles and jars in the bathroom. "If you don't answer it, I'll have to."

"Be my guest. I can't deal with her right now."

I moved around Sandro and picked up the phone.

"Who's there?" Elaine asked.

"It's me," I said. "I'm here, and he's perfectly all right."

"Well, put him on."

Vincent shook his head vigorously.

"He's in the bathroom right now."

Sandro took the phone from me. "I will speak," he said. He walked out of the room.

I took Vincent's bottles from him and put them on the bed. "Well, maybe you can explain what's going on," I said.

"I have to sit down." He had rolled up his shirt sleeves and I noticed a gauze bandage in the crook of his elbow, dotted with a drop of blood. He sat down on the bed, then lay back, his arm across his eyes.

"You're going ..."

"I'm going over to the villa tonight. I called Sandro because I wanted to move out before Elaine got home."

"That's not fair," I said. "She was frantic. You could have picked up your phone."

"She would have come straight here, and then things would have turned complicated." He coughed into his handkerchief.

"What do you mean?"

"She has a lot of conflicts about whether or not I should make this move. We start to talk about it, and she gets agitated, and then things get unpleasant. It hurts, Ally. I don't want to argue with her or anyone. She doesn't mean to cause hurt, but she does."

I leaned down and put my hand against his cheek. In a way, I was relieved that he'd made his decision. What I didn't like was being left to deal with Elaine.

"All the papers are signed, I have my room waiting, and Sandro's spoken with whoever's in charge there. I can arrive anytime this afternoon or tonight."

"Have you told your doctor?"

"Yes. I called her."

"It's okay," I said. "I can help Sandro load the car."

He sat up and blew his nose. "It's just the leaving. It has to be done quickly."

He was right: It *was* the leaving. It was always the leaving.

Sandro walked back into the room. He was smiling a little. "She is upset, but she will recover. It is the right thing to do. She knows this. It is best if we go now, Vincenzo."

"I'll carry some things down," I said to him. "Have you packed your opera score up, Vincent?"

"In the car already," Sandro said. "I will begin with the *valige*."

"Finish packing up your beauty products there," I told Vincent.

We were now standing close together, and he bent his knees to look directly into my eyes. "Will you come to see me soon?"

"Of course. And I want you to call me tonight, no matter how late." It was happening now, and now I really didn't want to let him go. Twenty miles seemed half a world away.

Together Sandro and I got his bags and the rest of the boxes into the car and left Vincent alone upstairs to say goodbye to the house and turn off the lights and lock up. We stood on the grass beside the curb. "Was she very upset?" I asked him.

He nodded. "Yes. More than usual."

"Will she be coming home soon?"

He glanced at his watch. "I think so."

Vincent appeared then and gave me a long hug. "*Ciao, cara.* Don't forget me." He dropped his keys into my hand. "I don't suppose I'll be needing these any time soon.""Call me," I said.

Everything else went very quickly. I closed the car door firmly. I put my hand on the window, he covered my hand from within, and then they drove away, the red tail lights of the Alfa disappearing into thickening traffic.

To the west the sky had cleared, and it had become a lovely early evening.

I suspected Elaine would be in a mood when I called her later.

"It's so strange here," she said. "So empty."

"It's a very courageous thing he's done."

"I suppose it is. But it hurts."

"It does hurt."

"I've just had something to eat. I'm tired. They broke up parts of the set today."

"How about setting a time for us to go over my talk with you."

"Why did he leave this way? I could have driven him over."

"He's anxious, Elaine. Sometimes action helps."

"There wasn't any need to involve Sandro."

"I think there was."

There was a long pause, and I heard the ice clinking about in her glass. "I don't suppose you'd want to come down here for the night."

"I'm almost asleep right now. But I want to wait for his call."

"All right, then. Can we go over your interview plans for me at lunch tomorrow? Maybe Sóle?"

"Okay. I'll be there as close to one as I can."

"Ally ..."

"You know, if you want to know how things went with Vincent, why don't you call Sandro?"

"I won't bother him tonight."

"Do it in the morning."

My phone vibrated under my pillow sometime after midnight.

"You've just now gotten settled?" I answered sleepily.

"It's me, Ally."

"Elaine? What's happened?"

"You couldn't have come down, even just to sleep?"

This was the gin talking. "Vincent hasn't called yet?"

"He called around eleven thirty. I told him I'd phone you."

I rolled onto my back. "What did he say?"

"He had an agreeable dinner—so he said—and his room has a nice view. He thought he might be put in semi-isolation, but apparently the doctors decided it wasn't necessary."

"That all sounds positive. Do you feel better about this now?"

"Not really. I'm acting like a lonely old woman, I suppose. I'm just rattling around this place tonight."

"When will we see him?"

"You can go over whenever you want. There's a bus that will drop you at the foot of the hill. You'll have to hike up. But if you want us to go over together and spare yourself the climb, then you'll have to wait for the weekend."

"That sounds like a better idea."

"I love you, you know," she said then. I was so surprised that I made no immediate response. "So I'll go off now to sweep this day away to some other place," she continued brightly. *"Buona notte, cara."*

She signed off before I could answer.

Then, of course, I couldn't get back to sleep. I thought of Vincent in his single room, his single bed. It would be cold now on his mountaintop. I wondered about his view, if he could see Assisi's lights, if he could see the late night glow of Perugia, ready to call it a day. Where I was. Where Elaine was. Under the same stars, wherever they were hiding. I wondered if he was thinking about his new life. His new home. Whether he might die there.

Twenty-six

We did have lunch at Sóle the following day. I was ten minutes late because I'd been on the phone with Montecalvo. Monica had decided she would be pleased to receive us tomorrow. Tomorrow!

"No warning," I said to him. And I could imagine how Gail Graham would react.

"She made up her mind. Then she moved quickly."

"Well, I'm ready for her. But I did want to have my hair cut."

"Childish worries, my dear. She will not be concerned with your hair."

"Still ..."

"Come to my shop at one. We'll take my car."

So that call delayed me, and I was late getting to Sóle. The day was chilly, and an oncoming storm seemed to have stalled in the west, over the lake. Elaine and I were both uncomfortable at first. With Vincent gone, our bearings had shifted slightly. We'd been left unprotected in a way and put in the position of beginning from a different point on the compass.

When I told her about my appointment with Monica, she raised her eyebrows. "Well," she said, "she's trying to upstage me?"

"You said you wanted her to go before you."

"I did, yes."

"But you know I can't actually brief you about what she's said."

"Of course."

We began our meal. She ordered perch. I had a risotto with bits of beef and truffles in it.

"I won't be completely specific about my queries," I said, "but I'm not deliberately setting out to surprise you."

She inclined her head.

"I'd like to talk a bit about modern-day stage direction, how certain directors like Francesca Zambello and some others, including you, have experimented staging certain familiar operas in obscure settings."

"I wouldn't say 'obscure' always."

"Well, setting *Rigoletto* in Las Vegas would be considered obscure certainly, or *Das Rheingold* in the American West and the oilfields of Azerbaijan."

"Since this isn't the actual interview, I think I'd rather wait to comment."

"Fine. I don't want you to comment now."

"Francesca Zambello versus Franco Zeffirelli."

"Wherever you'd like to take that conversation."

She had finished her perch and was sitting thoughtfully with the last of her wine. "What else?" she said.

"I'd like to conclude with a longer discussion about *Sirius*."

"You know there's a lot about that situation that I can't talk about."

"All right." I put my notes in order. "You realize that this won't be a conventional interview. I'll be writing a profile, using some of your words, but the point of view will be mine. I may shift things about a bit after I talk with Monica, but you'll see the copy before I send it out. Do you see any problems?"

"None that I can't avoid."

I was relieved to have that part of it out of the way. I knew she might avoid issues that became too personal, but I also knew that she was fair. And honest. And that was good enough for me.

We didn't discuss Vincent's departure at any great length. We had a couple of espressos, and as we stepped out into Via delle Rupe afterward, I felt some sprits of rain against my cheek. She remarked that if the weather turned bad over the weekend we might have to reconsider our plan to visit Vincent. When we parted at the top of Via Oberdan, we embraced briefly, and she headed off across Piazza Matteotti. I turned up the collar of my coat and began to think about tomorrow's weather.

Twenty-seven

"You do not need a haircut," Montecalvo said as he carefully maneuvered his vintage Alfa Giulia around the curves past the vast Lungarotti vineyards east of Torgiano.

"Too late now, in any case," I said, my briefcase open on my lap. "But it looks like you washed your car."

"It was covered with bird droppings."

"Do you have any advice?"

"Don't let her intimidate you."

"That was your advice about Signora Caccini."

"That was a different game. But the same suggestion applies."

I hadn't decided whether to interview Monica on tape, use my laptop, or take notes by hand that I might be unable to decipher later. As we arrived in Beata Colomba, Montecalvo said, "Don't confuse the situation by bringing electronic devices into the picture. She dislikes performances. Take your pen in hand and make as few notes as possible. I will be your memory, if necessary."

The DiBrufa villa was large, but not grandly so, and we were shown into a tastefully decorated salotto, where a fire was burning brightly in the stone fireplace. She made us wait, and by the time she entered, tea and other refreshments had been placed on a side table. With her dark hair loosened around her shoulders, and without her sunglasses, she was not as imperious as I recalled. She was all in black, of course, but her sweater was cashmere, her skirt expensively tailored, and her pearls were real. The veil was gone.

She said, "Signora, a pleasure to see you again," and shook my hand.

She shook Montecalvo's hand a bit more warmly and took her place in an antique armchair near the fireplace. Montecalvo stood up and asked, "Shall I pour tea?"

"Unless Signora Crosbie would prefer wine or something stronger."

As I shook my head, my notebook and some loose papers dropped to the floor with a thud. Not a good start.

"Where should we begin?" she asked as I reorganized my notes.

I wanted to make eye contact with her, in order to establish some control. This I managed to do, more or less. Although her look was not completely unfriendly, she was not smiling. "I should ask," I said, "if you would prefer to have our conversation in English or Italian."

"Oh, English. It will be printed in English, è vero?"

"Yes."

"English, please."

"I should also remind you that whatever I write may be picked up by other publications; that is, your information will be in the public domain."

"She has several lawyers," Montecalvo commented. "And she thinks before she speaks."

Monica raised her hand. "We will not be shifting the universe here," she said.

"*Magari,*" I remarked under my breath. If only. "All right. I'd planned to focus this part of my essay on your brother's role in the creation of the opera *Sirius.* Since he can't be with us to provide this view, perhaps you can talk about how he got involved with the project. Tell me a bit about him."

She drew herself up. "It may not be necessary to go beyond Piero," she began. After a dramatic pause she added, "To begin, he never wrote a poetic word in his life."

Montecalvo rose and refilled her teacup.

Monica's story was not what I expected. I imagined she might reveal a sordid tale of incest or some other dark family scandal, but it never approached the tawdry. Nevertheless, if her account could be verified, it would send an elite group of musical and literary scholars into a state of complete confusion. Monica, of course, was the poet in the family and had been since a very early age.

"I never had a desire to publish any of my own writing," she said. "I find the obsession for recognition a distasteful preoccupation. But Piero was born expecting it. I'm not quite sure what mischief my mother was up to while he was in the womb."

She sat thoughtfully for a moment, then turned to Montecalvo. "Can you find me a cigarette somewhere, Italo?" she said.

Montecalvo provided her with one of his and lit it for her.

She smoked quietly for a while, and I resisted my inclination to push her forward. She finally recrossed her legs. "Piero's delight in his youth was dressing in my mother's elegant collection of medieval battle garments, heirlooms she treasured and kept in various trunks. For a while he imagined himself to be a reborn *condottiero.* Then his mind became fixed on Grifonetto Baglioni of Perugia, the beautiful young warrior who organized the slaughter of certain members of his family in 1500."

"So beautiful that Raphael immortalized him in his *Deposition of Christ,*" Montecalvo commented.

"That fact is of no consequence here," Monica said.

"Hanging now in the Galleria Borghese," Italo quickly concluded.

Monica gave Montecalvo a look and went on. "As he grew older, he would occasionally appear in the streets of Beata Colomba armed with an ancient crossbow and waving the DiBrufa family *bandiera.* I don't know why my mother didn't stop him, although they did share a love of the clothing. People thought him odd, but harmless."

She considered this statement for a moment, then continued. "His behavior suited me, however. It gave me the freedom to pursue my writing, and my parents left me alone to do that. Perhaps they thought it would—what is the English word, Italo?—*temperare*—the more serious side of my personality."

"Moderate, I believe is the English word. Soften your sterner side."

She nodded. "I was content with that side of myself, though. I rushed every day from school to my desk, which overlooked our orchards and the vineyards that spread out toward Bettona and the mountains beyond. I was happy there and produced a vast collection of poetry—who knew how much? At night I read to refill the well." She put her cigarette out firmly. "I had very little to do with my brother—until it became impossible to ignore him."

"And when was that?" I asked.

Montecalvo gave me a frown and shook his head.

"It's all right, Italo. It was a petty prank, but an omen of things to come. At age seventeen Piero was arrested on the runway at the Perugia airport—he and some others tried to steal a small plane in order to fly up and down the Tiber Valley and shoot flaming arrows at cars on the E45 highway. The young men were severely warned. Their families were also cautioned. My father, Luigi DiBrufa, exacted a more severe punishment and confined Piero to the grounds of the villa for half a year."

"*Conte* Luigi DiBrufa," Montecalvo interjected. "Make a note."

She waved his comment away. "Piero sulked around the villa, sometimes in battle dress, sometimes not, looking for trouble. When he was not wandering in and out of my quarters, he was chasing the kitchen maids, and finally got one of them with child. When the girl's father appeared at the gates of the villa, accompanied by a group of citizens with torches, my father's patience reached its limit. He put Piero to work in the vineyards tending the vines, always with—how do you call it?—a 'watcher.'"

"Like house arrest," I said.

"Ordered by my father, not by the court. With my father, there were no second mistakes." For a moment Monica seemed caught up in emotion and unable to go on.

Montecalvo stepped in. "I will speak of this time now, Monica, because I was there to witness it. Some years passed, and there was continuing unpleasantness at the villa here. One, I remember, was a fire set in the vineyards as a diversionary tactic—unsuccessful, fortunately—that Piero imagined would camouflage an escape. The damage was minor. At last, one evening at dinner, Conte Luigi fell face-first into his plate of capon and roast potatoes and died, exhausted. Monica's mother, Ariosta—a most lovely woman—followed after several months. And, in what was perhaps the wisest decision of his life, the count left administration of the villa and its finances, all control of the products of its fields and other fortunes, in Monica's hands."

Monica shook her head. "Foolish man."

"No, indeed he was not," Montecalvo said. "Piero received a small stipend, virtually nothing, and, thanks to an arrangement between Conte Luigi and the town magistrate, he was permitted to stay on at the villa. But not to leave it. If he attempted to depart, he would be stopped and immediately arrested."

"Was that legal?" I asked. "I mean, his crimes were troublesome, but they weren't felonies, were they?"

"It was for his own protection. There were many waiting for what American gangster films call a 'piece' of him. And by this time there were serious questions about his mental state."

"I will continue now," Monica said, "and I believe this last part is what Signora Crosbie has come to hear. First, some wine. Italo?"

Montecalvo poured us each a small glass of white wine.

"Grechetto," Monica said. "From our vines."

By this time I was on my third pen and was searching for a fresh notebook, but I was happy to pause for a moment with the Grechetto.

"I ran the villa with success," Monica went on, "but from time to time I was required to leave my writing desk to attend to my new responsibilities, and it was during one of those moments that Piero, still very angry at his situation, entered my room and stole a volume of loose sheets of my poetry. You see, Signora Crosbie, his longing for acclaim continued; the fire had not gone out. He began to submit these pages to journals under his own name. Whether to spite me or my father makes no difference. His mind was no longer rational. These submissions became increasingly well received and his admirers more prestigious. So, to shorten this tale, after some years his success in this scheme finally brought him the renown he had longed for. And the situation worked out very well for me because it kept him out of my way and allowed me to continue with the only work that mattered: my writing. Public notoriety is anathema to me."

"You must tell her about the code," Montecalvo urged her.

"No, that I will not do. I will only say that there is a way I can identify these works as my own, should there ever be a need. The matter came up when Piero was asked to appear in public for the first time, to accept some prize or another. If he had attempted to leave the villa, the entire charade would have been brutally exposed, of course. He confessed his theft to me, I warned him about the code, and we negotiated an arrangement. I appeared in his stead, and so afterward—on all necessary occasions—I continued. I signed all contracts, accepted all awards, in his name. From time to time I gave him pages to submit and allowed his prestige to grow. And I have not betrayed him. He is the reclusive poet in residence, and I became known as the 'keeper of the flame.'" She exchanged a glance with Montecalvo. "That part I find very silly. I want to write my poetry, nothing else."

I took a breath. "And the opera ..."

"Ah, yes, the opera. Your arrival in Perugia, Signora Crosbie, could not have come at a better moment. But you were almost too late. On New Year's Eve, a very dark night, if you remember, my brother finally broke from his senses completely. With the cooperation of two kitchen maids, he eluded his watchers, took a bus into Perugia—disguised as a friar from the monastery at Assisi—and broke into Signora Bishop's office. After causing a great deal of serious damage, he fell over dead. His heart or his brain, either or both, collapsed from a surfeit of excitement. A most appropriate exit, in my opinion. I identified him by the signet ring he wore—and his costume—and claimed his body. And before you ask, I will not reveal where he rests today. I would not want hordes of critics trampling through our fields."

"But why all the destruction?" I asked her. "Was it really necessary?"

"He was determined to take some action of his own, I suppose."

"I must point out that he was not living much of a life," Montecalvo observed in a low voice.

"Also," Monica continued, "he was blindly focused on Signora Bishop, who he believed was blocking his path to true glory. So he did get his adventure in the end; it was just too much of one." She gave me a small smile. "The family, of course, is making full restitution to the opera company for the damage he caused." She brushed some ash or lint from her shoulder.

"One last question," I said. "The opera libretto. According to Signora Bishop, it was far below his usual lyrical standards. Of course, since you wrote it, those would be yours. Can you explain that?"

She brushed her hair away from her face. "I am acquainted with this director. Her eyes are shrewd. *Sirius* was doomed to failure from the beginning. By deliberate design—my own. It was never meant to be an opera. Someone wrote to Piero with the idea when I was distracted by another matter. When I realized I'd agreed to this fanciful proposal, I knew I could not, in my position, allow the family name to become attached to any part of it. So my plan was to gather together some of my poetry already in print—under Piero's name—reorganize it as unimaginatively as I could, and submit a libretto in complete disorder. Piero never realized, of course. I hoped the company would withdraw the production, and the company wisely did. It would have ruined them and everyone involved."

"But all that work for nothing," I said.

"Not so for you, Signora Crosbie. You grew more fluent in Italian, you've had an adventure or two, and now, I presume, your story will set the opera world back on its heels, as they say. I would not call that nothing."

I looked up. "How much of this may I use?" I asked her.

She glanced at Montecalvo. "I have given you several stories, Signora Crosbie. Sort them out. Use what you wish. You must choose which road to follow. I would like to see your final version before you submit it, of course."

"You're aware that my article may alter your life dramatically."

"That depends," she said, "on how you reveal it." She rose to her feet. "But I've told you everything about myself—and my brother—that needs to be said. Now I am finished with talking, and I am expecting guests for dinner. May I offer you more wine?"

Montecalvo and I politely declined.

I shook her hand. She, at last, had spoken the truth. Some sort of truth. And that, as they say, was that.

We drove back into the setting sun.

"That was hardly an interview," I said to Montecalvo. "It was more like a soliloquy. Do you believe her story?"

"Does it matter?"

"Of course it does."

"Because if you have any hesitation at all, you must decide how much of it you really need to publish. It seems to me, and of course it is my opinion only, that the complete physical destruction of a new opera at the hands of its celebrated librettist would be story enough. Most especially if details of Piero's early life and his disappearance into seclusion are included. He has a ready-made reputation for bizarre behavior that you would not have to embroider. As for Monica, my sense is that she might prefer to simply continue as the 'keeper of the flame,' publishing, of course, the now-posthumous writings of her brother. She is a remarkable woman, perfectly capable of living two lives."

"What you're suggesting is that I avoid mentioning the fact that she is the actual poet. The most intriguing fact to emerge from this tale."

"I'm suggesting that your story will be just as effective without that part of it. Monica has great poetry yet to write. It would be a shame to put an end to that part of her life, one that brings her such satisfaction. And if the complete story were revealed, I doubt she would continue. Pride, you see. The downfall of many an Italian."

"So Monica DiBrufa runs the family business, and the estate of Piero DiBrufa continues to release his elegant verse."

"Both with great success. And who is hurt, after all? My guess is that the tale you will tell about Piero, his unorthodox life, and especially his operatic death will not suffer from the omission of particular facts that might cause some unhappiness. He will certainly be given a grand memorial service at some point, which may include a complete performance of the Verdi Requiem. Why spoil this by inserting pointless controversy? The world is happier with the poetry of Piero DiBrufa in it. And Monica is happier writing it."

He was slowly winning me over, but I was clinging to the explosive revelations I was already composing in my head. He was suggesting that I turn those into what might become just an ordinary story. Something I could write in my sleep. "I'm going to have to think of a good explanation for why he attacked Elaine Bishop's office."

"I'm sure that is not beyond you."

I turned sideways in my seat. "Monica didn't have to reveal

every part of that story. Although I'm glad she did. I was only after material for a simple profile. And I'm well aware of her opinion of journalists. So why did she do it? The story will be difficult to control, whether I write up the whole thing or not. Someone, somewhere, will eventually want to dig into it. Think of the Elena Ferrante controversy."

"My dear, I have given much thought to Elena Ferrante. Her life is quite a different mystery. She wants to conceal her true identity for very different reasons. But Monica's association is with you. You persevered after her initial rejection. You have come to love Piero's city. I believe after all that effort, she wanted to give you the truth. And trust you to do the right thing."

"Have you discussed this with her?"

"Indirectly."

He swung the car onto the E45 highway and headed north, back toward Perugia. As he did, a low-flying Cessna passed overhead on its final approach to the Perugia airport. I quickly glanced up, for a moment imagining a flaming arrow en route from its fuselage.

"Do you suppose Monica would agree to having her photo included with my interview?" I asked him.

"Giammai!" he said, giving me a horrified glance. "Never!"

Twenty-eight

Elaine and I went over to see Vincent the following Saturday. She drove silently over the road heading south out of Perugia and finally said, "Well, I'm glad to learn that my intuition was on the money. You say she thought I had shrewd eyes?"

"Shrewd, yes."

"Well. I'll take that as a compliment."

"I'm wondering about this interview. If I use Monica's complete story, my piece will have a completely different focus now."

"Does that mean I'm off the hook?"

"Absolutely not."

"Do you have a contract?"

"Not really. My editor controls my assignments. She's sent me more of my advance. I get my payoff at the end."

"It's your work, though. You organize Monica's words, write my profile, and choose what to submit."

"That's the drill."

She shifted gears as we descended a hill. "You've built a nice little life here, haven't you," she said.

"Meaning ..."

"Well, look at you. You've made friends, you live with a happy family. You go blithely on your independent way, and now, with Montecalvo's help, you're probably going to publish the piece that will jump your career into the mainstream."

"I'm not counting my chickens. Lots can go wrong still."

"I think it belongs in something like *Vanity Fair,* by the way. Not in *Opera World.*" She slowed at the turnoff sign for Spina. "Is this where we turn?" she asked.

"No, keep going straight, then follow the signs to Mercatello."

We bumped across the wooden bridge over the Nestore River and shortly after that started up the steep road to the villa. After a mile or so, she pulled off to the side and stopped. We passed a few minutes without speaking, watching the beautiful late winter landscape around us, the cypresses swaying in a wind we couldn't feel, a cottage chimney farther down the hill issuing graceful spirals of white smoke we couldn't smell.

Finally I said, "I have made a life here of sorts, that's true. But I've always thought of it as temporary."

"Temporary's where you feel most comfortable, I think."

She had something on her mind that was bothering her, and I decided to wait and see what it was. I hoped it wasn't about me. She was understandably troubled about her uncertain professional circumstances, but I was in no way responsible for those. There was also the issue of my friendship with Vincent, who, until I arrived, had been her personal domain. And there was also Vincent himself and his illness. At the moment, she had no control over any of these situations. Or my future plans. Maybe that was the real issue.

"Did you say your agent was coming up to see you?" I asked.

"Yes, this evening, tomorrow, Monday—I don't know exactly when. She's in Rome now, and I don't want to miss her."

"I don't think we need to stay long today." The sun briefly emerged. "How do you expect to find Vincent?"

She restarted the car. "Ally, whether you choose to accept this or not, he may never leave this place."

"He wants to finish his opera. I don't think he cares where he writes it."

"Does he really? When he was living with me, I thought he'd given it up. Despite what he's saying now."

"I think it's what's keeping him going. The possibility of it, maybe."

"You haven't lived with him, darling."

After a few moments, she pulled the car back onto the road and we continued up the hill. I stared silently ahead.

The dark-haired young man who had served us coffee on our previous visit let us in. "Signor Vincenzo?" he said. "He is just now gone down to the laboratorio to give his blood for a test. But he will return soon. Please be comfortable in the salotto. I will bring you coffee." He opened the door to the large common area. "I am Antonio," he said. "I remember you."

Through the arch at the far end of the room, we could see several staff members preparing a dining table for the midday meal.

"Anywhere, I guess." Elaine shrugged off her coat.

We seated ourselves in nearby armchairs. "Smells good in here," I said.

A smiling woman in a colorful dress and a bit too much makeup had followed us in and sat down at the end of a nearby sofa. She was carrying a copy of *Gente,* the Italian incarnation of *People* magazine. "It is the aroma of the *filetto di maiale* we will eat at one o'clock," she said proudly, as if she were preparing it herself.

"Ahh," I responded. "Pork loin. A favorite."

She leaned toward us, exposing glorious cleavage. "You are visiting?" she asked me. "You will join us?"

I felt Elaine growing restless. "Excuse me," she said, and got to her feet.

"Down the hall," our companion said to her in a loud whisper, pointing toward the end of the room. Elaine went off in the opposite direction.

"We're visiting someone," I said. "A friend."

"This day is not good for visiting. Too much winter still." She extended her arms toward the large glass windows that gave onto the great lawn, which was slumbering under a colorless blanket of melting rime. "How I am longing for *primavera!*"

I looked up and spotted Vincent, smiling, standing at the door with Elaine.

"Excuse me," I said to her. "My friend is here."

She seemed to have collapsed into a dream, and I departed quietly. At the door I hugged Vincent, trying to ignore the feel of his bones against my body. "I see you've met Floria, our resident diva," he said to me.

"I rescued him from the basement," Elaine said. "Now I've told Antonio to take our coffee to Vincent's room, so let's go catch up."

We followed her to the little elevator.

Vincent's room was good sized, and he had made it comfortable for himself in simple ways. His view was toward the mountains. His papers were stacked on the corner of a beautifully carved cherry desk, and Antonio had placed the tray of coffee and hot milk near them.

I picked up the carafe of coffee. "I'll pour."

Vincent had immediately flopped down on the bed and

propped pillows under his head. "Sorry," he said, "but they took away half my blood." He stretched out his legs with a sigh. Elaine carefully removed his shoes and then went to sit by the window with her coffee.

I put his cup on the bedside table. "Did they move the piano for you?" I asked him.

He nodded. "It's in a small room downstairs."

I made room for myself beside his feet.

We all drank our coffee and waited for whatever would happen. For a while nothing did.

Then Elaine said, "Are you eating well? Is the food good?"

"The food is all right. I haven't felt like eating much." He paused. "But I can go into the kitchen at any hour, if I want, and get something to drink from one of the refrigerators. Or any leftovers from dinner. They don't mind. Whatever's there."

"Good," I said.

He pulled up the sleeve of his shirt and removed the gauze bandage from the crook of his elbow. "I'm well taken care of," he said, closing his eyes. "Don't worry."

After a few minutes, we realized he had fallen asleep. I exchanged a look with Elaine. "Now what?" I said. I presumed this was not her idea of "catching up."

She took a deep breath. "I wanted to speak to the direttore at some point," she said. "I may just go find him now." She placed her cup on the tray and walked to the door. "Back soon."

After a moment I quietly moved to the chair by the window she had vacated. It was very peaceful here. Aside from occasional footsteps in the hall, there was no sense of anyone else's presence.

I sat and watched him sleep and let some time go by.

"Ugh," he muttered at last, and opened his eyes. "How rude of me. Very sorry." He rubbed his chin. "Where is she?"

"She went in search of the director."

"Aha."

"How are you doing, Vincent?"

"I'm getting a stem-to-stern workup on Monday. After that I'll let you know." He waited a moment, then asked, "How long can you stay today?"

"Not too long. Her agent's in Rome, and she'll be arriving tomorrow, probably."

"Blimy. Sally. That's not good. I have a feeling she'll be bearing bad news."

"What—in particular?"

"I think she's going to tell Elaine there's no new work for her. Not for the summer, anyway."

"How do you know that?"

"I overheard some phone conversations while I was at Elaine's. She needs work. I don't know what will happen if there isn't any."

"She's on edge."

"She's anxious. She saw this coming as soon as DiBrufa died."

I returned to the foot of his bed. "Surely no one's blaming her for that."

"Who knows? People are strange. She's convinced he didn't kill himself, except maybe accidently on purpose, but it's had the same effect. How did your get-together with the sister go?"

I planned to talk to him about my meeting with Monica, but I didn't feel like going through it today. "I'll tell you about it when we have more time."

"And now you have to write about Elaine." He laughed a little.

"It won't be entirely about her."

He took a tissue from a box by the bed and blew his nose.

I poured myself a little more coffee. "You haven't given up on your opera, have you?"

He closed his eyes. "I miss it. I miss working on it. Sleeping with it in my head." He looked at me, knowing the questions I wanted to ask him. "But my body is driving the bus right now, Ally. Right now I have the energy to sleep and have a meal now and then. I dream a lot. But the doctors here have confirmed that the TB is either taking a breather or in retreat. It's left some serious wreckage behind, though. So we have to deal with that."

"How can I help?" I asked him.

He raised himself on one elbow. "You can come back."

"You know what I'd really like? I'd like to hear you play some of your own music again."

"Well, we could do that one of these days."

We heard footsteps in the hall. Elaine came in and said, "We have to go soon, Ally. The direttore was in the middle of his meal, so I just had a moment to speak to him. He did *not* ask us to stay and eat," she added.

"Were you expecting that?" Vincent asked.

"It doesn't matter. We have to get back to Perugia. Sally Kepler is coming up from Rome. Did I tell you?"

"Is this just a friendly visit?"

"Friendly? My guess is no. Listen, Vincent dear. Can you promise me that you'll make an effort to eat more regularly? Come downstairs with us, and go on into the dining room. That pork loin smells wonderful." On the way to the elevator, she asked, "Has Sandro been back to see you?"

"Not yet. Renata and Margit came by, but I was asleep."

"Too bad."

On the ground floor Elaine stepped out of the elevator and headed for the front door.

"This wasn't much of a visit," Vincent said softly to me.

"I'll come over alone next time. Now go and eat."

"Take care of her. And call me."

"Come on you two!" Elaine called out.

On the way down the hill, I said, "Will they continue with his new treatments here?"

"Right now they're concentrating on rest. And good food, which the direttore informs me he isn't eating. Or not much. Plus his regular medications. On Monday he gets an extensive workup."

"We didn't stay long enough today."

She gave me a look but said nothing, and shortly after that we joined the main highway back to Perugia. As we approached the station, I said, "Do you want me to stay with you until Sally comes? If she comes today?"

"She hasn't called, so it probably won't be today. Let's get some dinner somewhere, then you can go on home."

I could tell she was terribly tense, swinging in and out of traffic as we climbed the hill, blaring her horn at buses. She parked her car in Sandro's garage, and we had an early dinner at Borgo San Francesco, a small restaurant on Via Priori we had recently discovered. After dinner she walked me to the top of Via Rocchi, and we stood there surrounded by people passing us, going up or down the hill. My hand was on her waist. It was again a moment when there was either too much to say, or what could have been said was inaccessible.

"Come for dinner tomorrow," she said. "You might enjoy meeting Sally, if she's here. If she's not, well, you'll have to be content with me." She actually smiled, for the first time that day.

"What's a good day for our interview? And can we use your office? We really need to finish this."

"After Sally leaves. She won't stay long, I hope."

I gave her an affectionate kiss and left her standing there, alone in the crowd.

Twenty-nine

I had one brief encounter with Sally Kepler, Elaine's agent, who insisted on taking a suite at the Brufani, smoked like a chimney, and drank even more than Elaine. She could not seem to carry on a conversation unless she was pacing up and down, her earrings swaying wildly. I met them at the hotel, and after an hour in the bar listening to them talk about opera houses and their general managers—which house was doing what, who had been let go—interspersed with gossip about people that I did not know, I excused myself, pleading time to work a little, and departed. This was Elaine's business.

I was ascending Via Rocchi the following morning when my phone gave a trill. Elaine spoke quickly. She and Sally would be flying up to Brussels that afternoon to speak to the *intendant* of the Theatre Royal de la Monnaie about a production of Handel's *Alcina* that had just been inserted into the fall season—minus a stage director. Sally thought it would be a perfect vehicle for Elaine.

"This is sudden," I said. "I thought you had something set for the fall."

"I do. I'll have to withdraw from that if this works out. Handel isn't my cup of tea, but I know *Alcina,* and I think I can do something interesting with it. Even on short notice. It'll be a nice challenge." I heard the relief in her voice.

"What about our interview? We were going to try for Monday."

"I've been thinking about that."

"We can't put it off. I've got everything else ready to go."

"When I'm finished in Brussels, I'll be right back to Perugia to get packed up. We'll do it then."

"Or I'll come after you." I was not convinced. "Seriously."

"Now you must listen. I'll leave my car keys on the dining table. If you still have my spare house keys, let yourself in and get them. If you don't, get the keys from Signor What's-His-Name upstairs again and hang on to them. My car is in Sandro's garage, and I'll take care of paying for that. Use the car to see Vincent or go wherever you want. Or even stay at my place if you'd like that. The company is taking care of the rental fees until I move out."

"You should call Vincent."

"Yes, I know. I will. Now, what have I left out?"

"When will you be back?"

"Soon. I'll be in touch. Call me whenever you want. Now I have to finish packing. Sally's checking out right now." She paused. "I know this is unexpected, lots of strings left untied, but try to understand, sweetheart. My life has collapsed into a pile, like Humpty Dumpty, and this may be a way to start putting it back together."

"I understand. And the Monnaie is a prestigious house. Good for you."

"Please don't run away anywhere, Ally. I need to know that you'll be there. Take care of Vincent, and if you need serious help, call Renata. And me, of course. Now goodbye, goodbye, love you, love you."

“Safe trip,” I said into a dead phone.

Two days went by, and I heard nothing from Elaine. I called Vincent. “Has she called you?”

“She called once while I was with the doctor. Her message said she’d call back, but she never did. Are you worried? Don’t be. She’s engaged in what she does very well: negotiating. She’s in a familiar milieu, she’s probably met some old friends, and Sally’s probably driving her crackers. I see this is as a good tonic for her.”

“What were the results of your stem-to-stern exam?”

I could hear him talking to someone who had apparently entered the room. Then he responded, “Look, when are you coming over?”

“Well, soon, I guess. Friday maybe? I’ve done all I can with the Monica interview, and Montecalvo will take a draft over to her today or tomorrow.”

“How about staying Friday night? In one of those little rooms. I could arrange it.”

I thought for a moment. “Okay. Why not?”

“Good. I think my phone’s about to cut out here. You’re breaking up.”

“You’ve got to keep it charged, Vincent.”

“Will you be here in time for dinner?”

“I doubt it. It’ll be later. After eight. Do you need anything?”

“Will you bring me some nice soap?”

Elaine did call, finally, as I was preparing for bed that night.

“I miss you,” she began.

“How are things going up there?”

“They’ve offered me *Alcina* for late fall, and I think I’ll accept, although I may live to regret it. I’ll be playing catch-up, but they’re borrowing the sets from another company, fortunately, so it won't be a completely new production. I'll have to wrap my own ideas around what's available."

"Looks like you'll have to learn to love Handel."

"Well, he does have his moments. But it's a relief to have it settled. I'm going to have to shut down my Perugia life and leave the remaining legal business for Sandro to take care of, if he can. I've got to settle down in Brussels and immerse myself in the eighteenth century. A daunting prospect."

I knew how she felt about daunting prospects: she loved them.

"And of course I must find a place to live here. Oh my God, I also need some of my files from New York." There was a pause while she presumably wrote something down. After a moment she said, "Are you wondering how you might fit in?"

"Not yet. I have other things on my mind."

"It will all work itself out. I want you to think about joining me. Coming up to Brussels."

"You mean right now?"

"They've offered me a handsome fee. You could finish up your work here, my interview, your galleys, whatever it is you need to do."

"Well ..."

"Ally, what's in Perugia now that you absolutely can't leave?"

"There's Vincent, Elaine."

She took a long moment to answer. "Of course. But he'll understand why I have to make this move. I can always fly back to Perugia in two or three hours if it comes to that."

But I couldn't leave Perugia yet, and Brussels was probably not the place for me, in any case. And not only because I didn't want to leave Vincent. There was nothing immediate for me in Brussels. Except Elaine was there. I was missing her now and trying to fight it off.

"So, I'm serious. How would you feel about coming north?

That would solve the interview problem. Or am I jumping the gun?"

"You're jumping some sort of gun. And I'd rather do the interview here in Perugia. All my papers are here. Plus, it's more appropriate."

"Ally ..."

"And Vincent is only part of it. When will you come down to settle things in Perugia?"

"As soon as I find a place to live here, which has to be soon. The company is working on it." She took a breath. "You think I'm deserting Vincent, I suppose."

"Not exactly. He doesn't want either one of us standing at his bedside, wringing our hands."

"So you won't be running right over to the villa to take up permanent residence?"

"Why don't you find somewhere to live, and then let me know when you'll be coming down. Do you want me to tell him?"

"No, no. I'll call him." She stopped to blow her nose. "I'll be in Brussels all summer," she continued. "You might consider that. It could be nice. And Paris is right down the road."

"Yes."

"I do miss you, Ally. I miss us. More than I expected."

"You sound happy."

"I'd be happier if you were here."

The next day I bought Vincent some lavender bath soap, to match his shaving cream, and a little bag of Perugina Baci. As I passed the kitchen on the way to my room, I noticed the signora was sitting alone at the table peeling potatoes. I knocked on the doorframe. "Signora, *permesso,*" I said.

"*Avanti, avanti,* Signora Ally. *Prendi un caffè*?"

"No, *grazie,* Signora Caccini, but I'd like to speak with you." I proceeded to tell her, with as few details as possible, about the circumstances of my upcoming visit to the villa on Friday night.

She was immediately sympathetic. She shoved the potato peelings aside and took out a dog-eared notepad, licked the end of a pencil, and began a list. "*Allora,*" she said. "I will prepare some few things you will take to your friend in this place." I started to object, but she continued. "He will need good bread, some of my minestrone I will place in a jar, and what *frutta* I will find. I will put extra pasta in the soup."

"Signora, he is fed there ..." I began, but she was adamant.

"Feeding, but not enough. People are in beds starving there. It is well known."

It would have been ungracious to refuse her.

"When do you go?" she asked me.

"Friday evening."

"It will be ready."

Thirty

By Friday evening the temperature had moderated somewhat in the city, but it was still chilly on Vincent's windy mountaintop, where his new home was ablaze with lights. I was happy to see a roaring fire going in the fireplace of the main salotto, where several of the residents were sitting with after-dinner coffee. The aroma of the evening meal lingered in the air; it had been fish, I guessed.

Vincent met me at the door, looking dapper in his jacket and a crisp white shirt. "Hellooo!" he said brightly, his Highland lilt even more pronounced. He gave me a quick hug, then reached behind me and pushed the front door closed with the end of his cane.

"I actually drove Elaine's car," I said. "Her dash has as many bells and whistles as a 747." I stepped back and looked at him. "You've had your hair cut. You look like a young lad just out of school."

From behind him a familiar face appeared. "Signora!"

"Oh," Vincent said, startled. "Floria. You remember Floria, Ally?"

"Of course," I said.

He smiled at her and took my arm. "Allyn is my guest tonight, Floria. You'll see her again."

I could have agreed with Elaine's description of the little guest room as a nun's chamber, but since it was Italian, it had some style to it. One single bed, check; one small wardrobe, check; one comfortable chair by the window, a small sink in the corner, a writing table and chair, check, check, check. On the floor lay a colorful area rug, and on the walls were a couple of small watercolors that possibly depicted Umbrian scenes. The walls themselves were painted a restful pale rose.

Vincent turned on a couple of lamps. "Did you eat?"

I placed the signora's wicker basket of food on the table. "Yes, but the signora's convinced you're starving to death, so she sent you something extra. I may try some of that. It smells good."

"Kind of her. I can get us some wine, if you like."

I hung up my coat in the wardrobe. "Maybe later."

He sat down in the chair by the window, and I perched on the side of the bed. "Do you want to go down and sit by the fire?" he asked. "These rooms can get chilly. And there's coffee too, if you'd like some."

"Relax," I said. "You don't have to play the host." I leaned forward. "Are you settling in? Feeling a little easier?"

"The new medications they've given me are doing nasty things to my intestines," he said.

"How unpleasant. Are they helping?"

"I'm in the mood to work again, that's new. But I don't think it has much to do with my intestines. The food is okay, when I feel like eating, and there are a few people around to talk with. I can sleep as much as I want, on my own schedule. And that is the report—all you're going to get." He leaned his head back against the chair.

For the moment it was all I needed. "All right, then," I said. "How do we get the wine?"

He used his cane to push himself up. "Let's go up to my room. It's bigger, and I have some glasses and a few bowls there. I'll get Antonio to bring us some wine. What did your signora send to save my life?"

I checked the basket. "Minestrone, bread, fruit. There may be more."

"Well, I'm not hungry now, but you can have something."

"Let me get a sweater from my bag and we'll go up."

"I should warn you."

"What?"

"Elaine may call later."

"For which one of us?"

"*Chi lo sa*? For both of us, maybe."

Vincent exchanged his jacket for a heavy sweater and his trousers for sweatpants, then crawled under a quilt to watch me consume a small bowl of the signora's excellent minestrone and a glass of wine. We'd ventured into the kitchen downstairs to heat up the soup, and the clean-up staff paid us no mind other than to offer assistance with the microwave. The signora had included two slices of vanilla cake filled with several kinds of candied fruit.

"The cake doesn't go with the wine," he said. "But just as well. I have some meds to take."

I wiped my mouth. "How do people spend their evenings here?"

"There are little groups that stay up doing different things. They watch TV, they read, play cards, sit and talk, listen to music.

There's a rotating chess game that's been going on for months apparently. When it gets warmer, people will take walks, I suppose. Those who can." He paused and thought. "I haven't joined any particular group."

"It all sounds very congenial." I pushed my bowl to the side. He began to line up some vials of medication that were on his bedside table. "Do you want to be alone to take those?"

He shook his head. "I just have to figure out which ones I can take now, and which ones have to wait until my stomach has something in it."

"Should I rinse off these dishes somewhere?"

He threw some pills into his mouth and took a swig of water. "Put them on the tray there, and Antonio or someone will pick them up."

I seated myself in the more comfortable chair. "This is good wine," I said.

"Grechetto. From the estate."

"Have you been playing the piano?" I asked him.

And at that moment, my phone trilled.

"Aha," Vincent said. "She called *you,* lass. Should I leave? I can take the tray down."

"No. She'll want you too." I grabbed my phone.

"Ally, I've got good news," Elaine began. "We may have snagged Isabel Castagna to sing Ruggiero."

"Brava. I thought she was retiring her trouser roles. How's it going?"

"The opera? Oh, the damn opera. It's full of magic spells and flying horses and characters turned into singing rocks. Very un-Handel. The plot line is laughable. At night I lie awake pondering whether to stage it as a farce or set it in some imaginary time zone. But some wonderful music. How are you, sweetheart?"

At that moment Vincent, who was attempting to organize the tray, dropped the empty soup bowl and it rolled under the bed. He swore loudly. Elaine was silent. Then she asked, "Are you with Vincent?"

"I came over for the night, and we've just finished eating."

"Did you use my car?"

"You did suggest it."

"Any trouble?"

"None at all. It could drive itself."

"I don't suppose you can say how he's doing."

"Not really. Well, in fact, I don't know. You'll have to ask him."

"And you have your own room?"

"I do. Small, but comfortable."

"I see." She took a breath. "Well. Can we still do the interview business if I come down the first of March? That's ten days."

"All right."

"I think I'll come down then and get it out of the way. Renata's finding me a mover. Most of the furniture isn't mine, so it will stay. The apartment will be paid up until the end of May, if you change your mind about using it."

"Thanks. I'm set where I am."

She sighed. "I'm very busy now. Oh, I've got a place to live. Two bedrooms, two baths, plus a study. An interesting neighborhood. I think you'll like it. Whenever you decide, you know, to visit."

"Good." I loved her voice. I'd almost forgotten how much.

"Put Vincent on for a moment, will you, if he wants to talk."

Vincent had returned to bed, and I handed the phone to him. "Be right back," I whispered as I left. "Bathroom."

I took the slow way back to Vincent's room and walked around a bit more, up and down the quiet corridors. When I opened his door, I found him holding my phone against his chest and snoring lightly.

"Hey," I said as I came in. "Time to let you sleep?"

He yawned. "I don't have a regular schedule. I just drop off from time to time, for ten minutes, an hour, doesn't matter." He stretched and sat up. "Why did you run off? Elaine expected to talk to you again."

"Bathroom. I said that."

"I have a bathroom." I didn't respond. "I should have left you alone with her," he said. "You were talking to her as if she was a foreign dignitary."

"I was? What does that mean?"

"You didn't sound happy to hear her voice."

"I was very happy to hear her voice. But I'm not good with phones. I like to look at people when I talk to them. Why? Did she make a comment?"

"No. I just noticed."

"I think she wants me to come up to Brussels now. And I can't do that."

"Well, she misses you, probably."

"She's busy." I poured myself half a glass of wine and returned to the comfortable chair. "And I'm busy. Or I should be. Monica's piece is finished, waiting for her okay. I thought she would be the difficult one. But now Elaine's run off. I understand why she wants this job in Brussels, but I need to finish up this interview with her quickly. She doesn't seem to understand that."

"She's never been good with public relations."

"This is different from shaking someone's hand and saying, 'Nice to see you.'"

He turned on his side to look at me. "Is this a clash of careers you're talking about? That's dangerous ground. Or who cares the most? Is that what you're thinking?"

"I don't think so. Why would you say that?"

"She's easy to misunderstand. You have to pay attention."

"And you mention this because ..."

"Just following a line of conversation."

I turned to face him more directly. "What's bothering you about my attitude? For what it's worth, I don't think of her as a foreign dignitary. Is there something else?"

"Look. I've watched her fall in and out of love for years now, never very seriously, always on her way to someplace else. You walked in, and suddenly she's got long-term on her mind, or that's what it sounds like. You're definitely not in a fling category."

"Are you trying to reassure me about something? It's not necessary, you know."

"She stayed in Perugia with that DiBrufa travesty for you. In case you hadn't figured that out."

"But she's gone now, isn't she. And left me in the lurch with no interview. Which I could probably write myself now. What point are you pursuing, Vincent? And I'm nowhere close to figuring her out, by the way. I feel like I'm standing in a darkroom watching a photograph develop. That's how our relationship seems to me now."

He rolled onto his back. "I don't know which one of you is more inscrutable."

"Also, dear Vincent, you're the reason she didn't leave Perugia, and she'd made that decision long before I got here."

"I wish you'd just go after her."

"It's not that simple. She's got an agenda. Well, we both have agendas." After a moment I added, "She doesn't need your protection, Vincent, at least not from me."

"Hell's teeth," he said. "Give me a little of that wine, if you've left any."

The wind was beginning to push at the windows. I handed him his glass. "This is the situation. Elaine and I are both ... in transit, more or less, right now. And we haven't had enough time together to figure out how to deal with each other's issues. The revealing ones. It can become too intimate, and we're not there yet. Maybe that's what you're picking up on."

"You have entirely missed the point."

"Enlighten me, then." I finished my wine.

He waited for a long moment. "You and I, for example," he began. "You and I know how to do this. We know how to let each other in. Struggling or not. We know how to allow ourselves to be vulnerable, about how necessary it is ... for ..."

Please don't let him say "love," I thought.

"Understanding," he finished.

For a while we didn't say anything.

Finally, I said, "Our relationship is different, Vincent."

"What you mean is that we have less to lose."

"That is not what I mean. We all have something to lose here. That's part of the problem. And I'm not the one to lecture anyone about loss. I don't like it. I don't handle it well. I protect myself from it if I can. The fact that I can say that to you says a lot about how I feel. About you. Get it?"

He rubbed his eyes and nodded.

"I understand why you want to get everything, everyone, settled, especially now, and I wish I could move things along for you, wherever they're going. But you and Elaine have a history; yours and mine has just begun."

The wine was gone, and I began to gather the glasses and plates together and stack them on the tray with the soup bowl. I turned to face him.

"You know, Vincent, she got to me right away, from the moment you introduced us. I knew I wanted something to happen. But there were too many distractions. From the get-go. The libretto was a mess, you were sick, I was obsessing about the DiBrufa family—there was no time for the air to clear."

His eyes had grown watery, but he watched me seriously.

"In London, it almost turned into something else. Something else could have begun. Something really nice."

"And then I nearly bled to death."

"You were only a part of it. After we got back I sort of fell down the rabbit hole for a little while. And on New Year's Eve, my original story collapsed."

"But something better took its place. You have to admit."

"Yes. Thanks to Montecalvo."

"Odd bird, that one."

"No odder than you." I smiled.

His face relaxed a bit.

"I couldn't imagine myself with her or without her," I went on. "Of course, it didn't help that I idiotically tried to insert myself—and your opera—into her production. I don't think the three of us ever glued ourselves back together after that fiasco."

He lay back and finally said, "You tried to involve yourself to stay close to us. I saw that. In fact, it made me happy."

"I'm relieved to hear it."

"You remember our hayride?" he said. "That night in the

truck, with you curled up against my chest? The night air, the moon, as it finally went down? It's the last peaceful memory I have. After that night I lost my balance a bit myself. I was afraid I'd given you something ghastly, and I wasn't sure what to do. I was getting sicker, more than anyone knew, and I kept remembering Rob, and here I was, heading down the same path."

"Not quite."

"Close enough." He sighed and shook his head. "Now I worry about what will keep you two together when you don't have me around."

I almost laughed, but then I realized he was serious. I went over and sat down beside him on the bed. He'd just exposed an uneasiness of my own that had been there, unacknowledged, for a while probably. Eventually I took his hand, but then I realized he'd dozed off again.

After about ten minutes, he woke up coughing. And confused. "What is it?" he said, looking around. "Is someone knocking?"

I handed him a clean handkerchief. "No. Are you ready to shut down for the night?"

"Oh. Soon." He pulled his blanket up around him. "But first, tell me about London. If you can."

So I told him about Christmas night, after dinner, back in the hotel room. How close Elaine and I had become, so quickly; how open she had allowed herself to be. And sensing that, how I had let down my guard. Maybe I was trying to reassure him. Or remind myself of that night.

"And then I hemorrhaged all over my Christmas dinner. Am I doomed to always get in the way?"

"Stop indulging yourself about that. I wanted to come back.

And not only because of you. I wanted to come back *with* her. Together."

"And you did. But what the hell happened? London was happy for both of you, it sounds like. But when you got back to Perugia, you were like aliens from two different planets."

"It seems ridiculous now. We'd almost begun an affair in London, but on the trip back I began to imagine scenarios in which I'd be written out of her life, your life, your life together, I think. It was all going to just disappear, including the music."

"Why would you ever think that?"

I shook my head. "It's an old habit, I guess. It preempts disappointment."

"What a self-destructive fantasy life you have." He wasn't smiling.

"If it makes you feel any better, the night we got back I ended up drunk in a bar with lots of Greeks. One of them spit in my face."

"Don't blame me for that." He slid deeper beneath the blankets and adjusted his pillow. "Well, like you said, you imagined you were going to lose both of us."

"I should have been able to get past that."

"But there's no need, Ally."

"Stop trying to fix things. Please."

Quite suddenly I recalled that on the very next day Elaine and I had made love for the first time. In spite of everything. I chose to keep that to myself.

"So what do you think, in this little drama you've manufactured. Will Elaine be the loser here?" he asked.

"Does someone always have to lose? I can't imagine her as a loser, no matter what the circumstances."

"Well, she might possibly think she could lose you. Think about it. She's let you see part of herself that she knows you could just walk away from."

I frowned. "Has she?"

"Well, think about it."

"Since you keep bringing it up, I have to." I took a breath. "And I have no idea how to answer that question."

"I get that. But the way to cross that pond is one stone at a time." He laughed a little. "It's called trusting your own feelings. Trusting hers." He paused. "Like you and me."

"You and I have never talked about that, have we."

"No, we haven't." He reached for his handkerchief and patted his forehead.

"Fever?" I got a cloth from the bathroom and wiped off his face and neck. He looked up at me, blinking, his eyes damp, then reached for his water glass. I helped him drink. "You're tired," I said. "Matchmaking can wear you out."

After a long moment, he asked, "Ally, if I'd been less cautious, would something more have happened between us, do you think?"

"Maybe."

He closed his eyes. "I've always wondered, that's all."

"I thought about it," I said. "In fact, on that one night it might have been wonderful. But we both would have regretted it, I think. We'd have lost her, wouldn't we."

Somewhere in the villa, beyond his door, a clock struck an early hour.

"Time to sleep," I said. His eyes were already closed.

I turned off his lamps and departed.

Thirty-one

I didn't sleep well Friday night. I tossed about in a confused tangle of unfamiliar sheets while the wind battered a shutter along the north side of the villa as if it were knocking on my door. When light finally crept in and I could see a collection of gray clouds that seemed to have impaled itself on the pointed tips of the cypresses outside, I dressed and went downstairs in search of coffee, which I could detect like an aromatic echo in the hall. Breakfast was apparently a buffet affair, which made sense, and I took a large caffè latte and some rolls and jam over to a table near the fireplace. The olive wood was already ablaze. There were a few people about, including a group of three medical personnel in lab coats, who were conferring quietly in chairs by the window.

I was in a somnolent state of fatigue, my brain muddled by images of the night I'd just passed. It took me a few moments to realize that Antonio was standing by my elbow holding carafes of coffee and steamed milk.

"*Buon giorno,* Signora. You slept well?"

"Hello, Antonio."

"More coffee?"

"Yes, thanks. Have you seen Vincenzo this morning?"

"It is early." He consulted his watch. "I take him his coffee in half an hour."

I glanced out the window. "The weather looks unpleasant today."

He gave me a look of distaste. "*Brutto,*" he said. "*Fa brutto tempo oggi.*" Then he smiled. "But very comfortable inside. Others will be coming to join you for breakfast."

When I arrived at Vincent's room after my shower, the door was ajar and I could see several figures moving around inside. Antonio exited quickly with a tray of bowls and glasses from the night before and an empty coffee cup. He closed the door behind him.

"Is something wrong?" I asked him.

"Signor Vincenzo is not good this morning," he said. "I regret, Signora, you cannot enter at this moment."

"Something serious?"

"The doctors are inside."

We walked together down the hall toward the elevator. "When should I come back?" I asked.

He pushed the elevator button. "I do not know." His voice caught slightly, reminding me of how young he probably was.

In my room I found the bed straightened but not completely made. It was nine thirty, not so early anymore. As a gust of rain hit the window, I retrieved my phone from the bed table and pressed Elaine's number on speed dial.

No answer.

I got into Vincent's room a little later, just after his medical team—or so I was coming to think of them—filed out. The last in line said to me, "He is very weak, Signora. Do not stay long."

Vincent lay propped up on a couple of pillows. He was ashen, except for two bright pink areas on his cheekbones and a purple bruise on his left temple. I pulled up a chair and he opened his eyes. For a brief while we simply looked at each another and did not speak.

"What's happened?" I asked him finally.

"Nothing much. I fell down trying to find the bathroom."

"You mean you passed out?"

"Not for too long. I hit my head when I went down."

"You didn't eat much last night. That cake was all. And the wine."

"Low blood sugar, you're suggesting. No, not that."

"Maybe I should go on back to Perugia."

He looked out the window. "It's such an awful day."

"Brutto, Antonio told me at breakfast."

"Yes." He took a sip of water. "I think I'll go back to sleep now," he said, shifting one pillow aside and sliding down in the bed. "But I'm wondering. Could you stay another night? Would that be a problem?"

"If you want me to stay, of course I will."

"I told Antonio to speak to Signora Lidia. She's in charge ..." He was drifting off. "In charge of things like that."

I stood up. "Just sleep for now." I tucked the covers up around his shoulders. "See you after a while."

As I switched off his lamp, the wind shook the window fiercely, as a lion would shake a doomed prey, to break its neck.

I'd left a message for Elaine when I called earlier, and as I walked into my room to get my books, my phone trilled.

"It's Saturday," she began, "but I *am* working. Just so you know."

"I didn't call to chat. I won't keep you long."

"Are you back in Perugia?"

"I'm still at the villa. I wanted to let you know that Vincent fell during the night, or passed out and fell, I'm not sure."

"And ..."

"And the medical people have seen him. He's sleeping now."

"Is it a concussion? He shouldn't be sleeping if he has a concussion. Did the dottoressa see him?"

"I didn't see her. But I talked with him later. He's weak, tired."

I think she expected me to go on, but I didn't.

"Is there something you think I should do?" she asked.

"Well, the doctors aren't going to give me any details. You're his next of kin."

"I'm hundreds of miles away. I'm not sure how helpful I can be from here. I'll call Vincent later."

"He shouldn't be falling and spending the night on the floor."

"Ally, if it was serious, the direttore would have called me right away." I heard her take a breath. "He's asked you to stay another night, hasn't he."

"Yes. And I will. He wants company, I think." Earlier I had wanted Elaine to sense that I might need some reassurance from her. But that didn't come. "If the situation doesn't bother you," I said, "maybe I shouldn't be concerned."

Her voice softened a bit. "Things have been confusing, haven't they?"

"You might say that."

"I was hoping to tell you about what's happening here, about my new apartment, the production. But I guess this isn't the right moment."

"Probably not."

"Everything sounds so meaningless going back and forth on these damned little phones." She laughed, and I remembered that laugh. Against my shoulder. Her arms around my waist.

But I was disturbed by her matter-of-fact reaction to the news of Vincent's fall. I wanted more. She took control of events much better than I did, and I needed to feel that control. But she'd lost some control of her own life in recent months; maybe she was reluctant to get involved in a situation that might remove even more. This was different, however. Vincent was not a "situation." Vincent was someone she loved.

"You'll be relieved to know that I've spent some time with your interview points," she said. "The ones you talked about before I left. I think we can take care of that business pretty quickly when I'm there."

"I hope you're right."

Too late I noticed my low battery light blinking furiously, and my telefonino went suddenly silent. I looked at it as if she had cut me off. Maybe she had. After all, she still had control over her phone.

Because I was hungry, I did join the others at the dining table for the midday meal. The aroma of roast pork drew me in. My plan was to eat quickly and go back upstairs, but Floria got to me first and took my arm.

"You will join us, Signora? Come, sit here by me." She patted a chair. "You will meet some friends."

The group gathered around the table was right out of a Fellini film, people who had opinions about literature, space aliens, growing tomatoes, music of all sorts, politics, and of course medicine and its miracle cures (for example, the benefits of iodine). And my companions at the table weren't shy about arguing their points.

"People overlook Mascagni," Floria said to a gentleman with handsome sideburns who was sitting across the table. "Being

Russian, you may not find him on your personal list of great composers." She took off on her favorite topic, a lecture he had no doubt heard before.

"Dostoevsky," he interrupted her.

"No, no, Herr Rostov," she said. "That is someone else."

"I am not a Herr," he said to her severely. "Not German. I am a proud son of the Steppes."

"Stairs?" she inquired with raised eyebrows. "La Scala Milano?"

I was attempting to translate while negotiating a bowl of what I feared might be a turnip or rutabaga soup. But then the roast arrived, encircled by crisp potatoes and small artichokes, and I put the soup aside. Bottles of wine and mineral water had appeared at strategic positions at the table. Vincent would like this meal, except possibly for the soup. We shared a dislike for root vegetables. I wondered whether Antonio or someone else had taken him a tray.

"Signora," Floria said, "you must tell us your name. Before *insalada* arrives."

"Allyn," I said.

"Eileen?"

"Allyn. Call me Ally if that's easier."

"Signora Ally," Herr Rostov said, "I understand you are a friend of our composer, Maestro Vincenzo."

"Yes. He's not well today."

"Ah. I am unhappy at this news."

"Oh why, Herr Rostov?" Floria asked. "Illness is our companion here. Always."

"Please allow me to be unhappy," he said firmly.

I looked around the table, thinking I'd never seen a healthier looking bunch of invalids. Of course, there were many upstairs, I supposed, who were not able to come to the table.

But Floria turned back to me. "We have heard Maestro Vincenzo playing the piano. Alone in the room down the hall there," she pointed, "on the way to the card room."

"Yes," I said, pouring myself a little more wine. "He's finishing his opera."

Floria's eyes widened. "An opera?" she exclaimed. "He has not said!"

I kicked myself for mentioning it, but just then the table clearers appeared and a discussion began about dessert and coffee. As I turned away from Floria, I spied Vincent's dottoressa pass by in the hall, headed briskly toward the elevator. She was bundled up in a coat and a heavy scarf.

I stood up. "Please excuse me," I said to the table in general. "I have to catch the doctor."

"You must stay for the fruit, Signora," Herr Rostov said, half rising from his seat.

"Not today. Perhaps another time."

The elevator had departed by the time I reached it, so I went back for my briefcase and took the stairs.

I caught Doctor Cortina in the nursing station removing her coat. She smiled. "Signora Crosbie," she said. "Are you here for the weekend?"

"He's had a fall," I said. "I suppose you know."

"The direttore telephoned." She sat down at the computer and began to scroll through the charts until she found Vincent's. I stood respectfully by. "But this is good," she said after a moment. "He has had a tray of soup and some of the roast." She looked up at me. "This is very good."

"I agree. But he fell, Dottoressa Cortina. In the night. I'm afraid I kept him up late talking ..."

She held up her hand. "That had nothing to do with his fall. He got out of bed, became disoriented, ran into the door, and fell." She returned to the chart.

"But he did hit his head when he fell."

She nodded. "He was taken for a scan this morning, early, after one of the aides found him. No immediate evidence of concussion."

"So it was all right for him to sleep."

"No need to worry." She closed the file. "But now I will see him."

"Would you have time to speak with me afterward?"

"Certainly. But I have other patients to visit also."

"I understand. I'll wait for you downstairs."

She picked up her medical bag and went off toward Vincent's room.

I was again by the fire in the main salotto, mostly deserted now. It was nap time, I supposed, and it was a good day for a nap. The wind had eased a bit, although the oaks were still tossing their naked limbs angrily against it. But the rain had stopped. There was no sign of human activity. I took the printout of my interview with Monica out of my briefcase with every intention of tightening it up, but I soon nodded off myself.

I was awakened a little later by the doctor, who stood with her hand on my shoulder while Antonio placed coffee and a plate of little cakes on the table.

"Would this be a good time to talk?" she asked.

"Yes, of course," I said, sitting up.

Antonio moved to the fireplace and knelt to add more wood.

The doctor took a seat and poured us both small cups of espresso. "The rain has stopped," I commented, still a bit groggy from my nap.

"Look there," she said, pointing to the west. "That thin line of gold on the horizon. The clouds are breaking. The weather will clear overnight."

"How is he?" I asked her.

"The food has helped. You can see him when you like."

"Good." I stirred sugar into my cup. "Can you explain why he fell?"

"As I said before, he became disoriented on the way to his bathroom and ran into the open door. He lost his balance and fell."

"But he was unconscious."

"Yes. He was." She smiled and took one of the little cakes.

"If he fell in the night and wasn't discovered until morning, wouldn't that be considered unusually long to be lying there unconscious?"

"It would, yes. But Vincenzo told me he was not unconscious for long. Maybe several minutes. He was dizzy and decided to rest on the floor until Antonio or someone came to help him up. He pulled a blanket off the bed and put a towel under his head."

I frowned. "That sounds very strange."

"The scans were negative. There was no stroke involved. He was definitely disoriented, as he sometimes is these days. It is part of his sickness now. The drugs cannot control everything."

I still felt the scenario was troubling. "What, exactly, is his condition now?" I asked her.

"It changes from day to day. You may have heard this from Signora Bishop. We have the TB under control, or mostly, but his brain and some of his organs have been compromised. His struggle with tuberculosis has weakened him, made it difficult for him to defend himself against his secondary disease, which is—what is the English word?—battering him at this point."

"Forgive me, but does he have full-blown AIDS? Are you allowed to say?"

She sighed. "I can say that we are doing our best to prevent that from happening."

"Would another transfusion help?"

"The transfusions were to replace the blood he lost during the worst periods of his struggle with tuberculosis. Now he is in a different situation. A transfusion will not help."

"So ..."

"At this point we treat his symptoms, keep him comfortable. He is not in pain, and when he is fully alert, his mind seems clear enough."

"It was clear enough the other night."

"As long as he takes his medications and has enough rest, he may lead a comfortable life for a little time." She paused. "He knows what is happening."

That sounded like palliative care to me. I finished my coffee. The cakes did not tempt me.

The doctor refilled her cup and sat back in her chair. "You must understand about the course of this disease he is fighting. His death, when it comes, may not be unpleasant or painful. His body will continue to shut down at its own pace."

I felt the breath pull out of me. She was *expecting* him to die. In some hidden part of me I'd imagined he would walk out of here at some vague future date.

"He has spoken of several things he would like to do—soon, of course," she went on. "He's been thinking of an evening of his music, for one thing; a few songs, perhaps some brief excerpts from his opera. That, I am sure, would be something to stay alive for. I am working on a plan."

I was astonished. I'd thought all performance plans for the opera had been abandoned. "This would be for the residents here?"

"For the people here, yes. It's very uncertain. All aspects of it. But"—she shrugged—"there is no reason not to plan. This afternoon, for example, he is a little stronger. You could speak with him about this idea."

"So it's a matter of keeping him alive."

She smiled. "That is for him to do. With our help." She stood up. "Now," she said, "I must return to Perugia, to the hospital. Vincenzo is being well cared for, do not worry. You may find a different attitude about illness and death here, but his needs are not ignored."

She extended her hand and I shook it.

"I'm staying tonight," I said. "I'll speak with him. Will I see you again?"

"Help him lift his heart," she said, wrapping her scarf around her neck. "That, you can do. And now, *arrivederci.*"

She was quickly gone.

I returned to my room, which had once again been straightened, wastebasket emptied, bed now fully made, and fresh towels. Unsettled by my conversation with the doctor, I sat down in the chair by the window and began to go over the chain of circumstances that had brought me to this day, this particular view, overlooking an expansive landscape that was struggling toward spring. When I left Rome back in September, I had expected to have a quick week in Perugia and depart as soon as I could. And yet, here I was.

On the day I arrived, was Elaine already in Perugia? Was Vincent seated at the contessa's piano, or walking over to the policlinico for his drugs? Was Senta asleep in a library somewhere in Milan or sitting in Piazza Maggiore in Bologna, near the statue of Neptune perhaps, drinking white wine with a wedge of lemon? Who had been sleeping in my bed at Casa Caccini? Was the contessa considering party menus while Margit sat with the dogs in a dark corner of the terrace, smoking? Was Sandro perched dutifully by his mother's sickbed, holding her hand in the late-afternoon sun?

The answers to these aimless ponderings seemed to lie in a vague territory that existed before I was born. These people were part of my life now, people I had come to care about, people—for once—that I didn't want to walk away from. And I found that realization almost as impossible to comprehend as, say, the life of the human heart, which can beat away for ninety-nine years without more of a rest than a pause between beats.

It was nearly five thirty: time to turn on the lamps. I chanced a look out the window, and just as the doctor had predicted, the clouds on the western horizon had lifted to admit the glow of the descending sun.

"So, did you enjoy the rutabaga soup?" I asked Vincent later. He was dressed and sitting in the chair by the window. I was at his desk.

"Root vegetables? Nay. Such an ugly name: rutabaga." He frowned. "There were turnips in that soup too."

We looked at each other and burst out laughing. His eyes were brighter, but his cheeks had acquired an unnatural rosiness that made him resemble a clown. I wondered if drugs had been involved or if he actually felt better. I realized he was wearing gloves.

"What have you been up to today?" he asked me. "While I was sleeping."

“Nothing much. I had an interesting midday meal with some of your fellow residents. I also had the soup.”

“They could have mashed up the vegetables,” he said. “That might have helped.”

“I had a talk with your dottoressa. And with Elaine. She called.”

“And what came of that?”

“It was a little rough. As we were saying goodbye, my phone went dead. She may make something of that.”

“And my doctor?” He coughed a little into his handkerchief.

“She tells me you’re interested in putting together a musical evening.” He gave me a look, his eyebrows raised. “Is that true?”

He rubbed his gloved hands together. “She suggested that, yes.”

“She said it was an idea of yours.”

“It was, I guess, when I was feeling better.”

“Well, she says she’s working on a plan.”

He used his cane to push himself to his feet and walked to the corner of the desk where I was sitting. He rummaged through some papers and extracted a folder of sheet music. “Eight songs,” he said. “Not all new. That’s what I had in mind. I had quite a lot of time to think about it when I was on the floor during the night.”

He had dropped his cane, so I picked it up and helped him back to bed, where he sat down, music sheets in hand. “The truth is, I’d done a lot of restructuring already, without recognizing it. And the music’s coming more easily now, more naturally. You started me off, really. That garden scene. Einar and the major planning their garden. You wrote ‘waltz’ in the margin of my book. A happy waltz. I’ve already roughed it out.”

I was relieved because I realized his innate musical sense had brought him back to a decision he’d made long ago that hadn’t worked. And he was now on a different path. "Anything else?" I asked.

"The other one still needs work. It's a tenor aria for Einar, the young terrorist. He's singing about his own death, which he's expecting will come soon. Please don't cringe. It's not dark; it's joyful. Something like Britten's Billy Budd in the moonlit brig, the night before he's hung from the yardarm. 'Billy in the Darbies,' Melville's poem set in the most heartbreaking way. Almost at the end of the opera."

"Yes, yes. I know it." I thought for a moment. "This all sounds right to me," I said. "You should run into doors more often."

"I knew I was right. I lay there on the floor, and it just poured into me. An angel must have been there."

"Maybe an angel was." After a few moments, I said, "Would you like to go down to the piano? Let me hear what you've done?"

He opened his eyes. "We might." He sat up. "First I'd like you to look at the text I wrote for Einar. Can you bring me my briefcase?" He went through more papers and removed a sheaf of pages covered with his scrawl. "This is a rough text. Take it somewhere, somewhere away from me, and read it through. Does it work? Is it lyrical enough? Would you like to hear it sung?"

"How long do I have?"

He gave me a smile. "If it doesn't work, lass, you should tell me quickly."

I stood up. "Okay. I'll do it now. When will dinner be over?"

"I have no idea what time it is."

"Nearly six thirty."

"Oh, they haven't begun. But they'll all be in the salotto. Better take it to your room."

It didn't take long to read. Afterward I sat quietly for a few moments, until the ticking of my watch reminded me that I shouldn't get stalled.

I'd interviewed composers often enough to understand that in writing vocal music, the words usually come first. In opera, words are the scaffolding, and the music joins them and gives them life, changing both into a completely new life form. Right now, the text Vincent had created was in some sort of anteroom, waiting for its music. On its own, it was full of tantalizing hints of brilliance. It wasn't Melville, it wasn't "Billy in the Darbies," but he was clearly headed in the right direction.

After a while I gathered the sheets together and prepared to return to Vincent's room. I thought about where to begin. But the problem was solved for me. As I approached his door, I heard low voices in conversation, and when I entered, I found Sandro sitting in the comfortable chair by the window.

"Ah," he said, rising. "Signora Ally. Buona sera."

"I'm glad to see you, Sandro."

Vincent had remained fully dressed, although he was back under the blankets. The gloves had disappeared. He took off his glasses and smiled. "Should I call Antonio for some wine?" he asked.

"I will go down," Sandro said. He was dressed in his usual combinations of elegant blacks and grays; this evening, however, he was wearing a blue and red patterned tie under his black sweater vest.

He shut the door behind him.

"I thought you were never coming back," Vincent said. "What took you so long?" He got out of bed and took off his sweater. "Never mind. I should put on a clean shirt. What do you think about pink?"

"I'm not a big fan of pink, but I like pink shirts."

He decided to change his undershirt as well, and as Sandro returned he finished buttoning up.

"Antonio says wine will be waiting downstairs," Sandro said. "They are setting up different foods on a long table."

"Oh, right," Vincent said. "The evening meals on Saturday are a bit of whatever's around." He began to straighten up the papers on his table. I stood at the window, thinking about Vincent's opera, and wondered whether something miraculous had happened.

Vincent began to tell Sandro about the musical evening his dottoressa was urging him to put together, and I heard him say that Antonio was a tenor, studying at the conservatory.

I turned around. "Could he sing a couple of your songs?"

"Someone will have to, I guess. If it goes forward." He put on his blue jacket again. His face had grown more flushed. "Let's go downstairs," he said. "We'll find some food and eat in the piano room."

Sandro and I exchanged a look. I thought this might be a bad idea after all, but I was weary of constantly checking on Vincent's health and receiving indirect responses, if not outright lies, as answers. "Okay," I told him. "Where's your cane?"

"Don't know. Under the bed?" He gathered his music sheets into his briefcase. "You still have the text?" he asked me.

I held it up, and we moved toward the door. "How is your mother, Sandro?" I asked him.

"*Poco meglio,*" he said. "Better. A little. Thank you for asking."

Vincent stood outside the door and banged his cane on the floor. "Hurry up, Ally!"

In retrospect, it is difficult to imagine how I could *not* have been prepared for what happened during the hours that followed.

Vincent's fever continued to rise. Most of the ambulatory residents had decided to celebrate the departure of what they hoped was the last big storm of winter by imbibing whatever wine, spirits, schnapps, and even beer the staff had brought out. We could hear their joyful shouts from within the elevator as we descended. In fact, I still heard some singing when I returned to my room several hours later.

The hour the three of us spent alone in the piano room confirmed Vincent's own assessment of the radical shift that had occurred in his own work. It had assumed an assured lyricism that was a little shaky but mostly in his grasp. The "little waltz," as he called it, for the garden scene, even with an incomplete text, was fresh but not sweet, occasionally dipping into the atonal, but resurfacing with distinctive bursts of playfulness. It was clearly Vincent's musical voice, difficult to describe but completely recognizable. And Einar's darker solo, with Vincent half singing, half speaking the text I had just read and playing music he was possibly working out as he went along, was almost there. It all needed some work, but the direction in which he was headed was the right one.

Vincent then played a few of his older songs, until in the midst of one, to the text of Elizabeth Bishop's unpublished poem "Breakfast Song," the piano room door burst open, and we were engulfed by a group of semi-intoxicated residents who had been listening from the hallway. They demanded an encore of the selections from Vincent's opera, then moved on to demands for particular favorites of their own. The evening quickly turned into a circus. The staff brought in extra platters of what was left of the pork roast, marinated potatoes, and cheese—and wine—which I was happy to see. Vincent's cheeks had acquired a more dangerous flush, however, and I could see beads of sweat streaming down into the neck of his pink shirt. He had removed his jacket, which Sandro was holding with a worried frown on his face. But he was obviously having a delightful time and playing with great flourishes of his arms.

After Vincent had accompanied Floria's quavering rendition of "*Non ti scordar di me*" for the second time, I had heard enough. I quietly told Sandro that I was heading upstairs, and he promised to get Vincent back to his room before he pushed himself too far. "Try to get him to eat something," I added. "I'll see him in the morning before I go."

The sounds of applause and laughter followed me up the stairs, into the bathroom, and lingered even as I stood at my window looking out into the night. It had cleared finally, and there must have been something of a moon because I could make out the dimly lit windows of houses in the valley.

But look: through the port comes the moonshine astray! It tips the guard's cutlass and silvers this nook ... Fathoms down, fathoms, how I'll dream fast asleep ...

I tried to imagine old Melville writing poetry as lovely as this. And Vincent recalling it now.

As I lifted my head, the grand spectacle of Perugia appeared, glowing on its hilltop to the north, its tangled streets and alleyways no doubt alive with Saturday night mischief. And hundreds of miles farther north, Elaine might be preparing for bed, knowing nothing of the angel who had given Vincent what might be his concluding moments of happiness.

I left Vincent around ten the following morning, just after Antonio had delivered his coffee, which sat cooling on his bedside table. I was troubled to see that the flush on his cheeks had not faded. Or not much.

He propped himself up on his pillows. “I’ve driven you away,” he said. “All that ridiculousness last night.”

“Of course not. You knew I had to go back today.” I sat down by his bed. “Last night was a success. Your opera has had its first performance.”

“Not exactly.”

“Well, I think of it that way. I’m glad I was there.”

He rubbed his chin. “What will you do today?”

“I have to take Elaine’s car back to the garage.”

“That’s it? Sounds like a dreary Sunday.”

“But look, the sun is out.”

He coughed a little and wiped his face with a small towel. “When will Elaine be here?”

“Next week, if she doesn’t change her mind.”

“Then Easter, then after that, Pasquetta.” He took a sip of coffee. “And the days go on.”

“And the days go on. And so do you.”

“I need to work on Einar’s music.”

“Not too much. You’re almost there.”

He shook his head. “I try to hear my own music, but there’s so much static now in my brain. I can’t always grab it.”

I stood up. “You still have a fever, Vincent. Your pajama top is soaked. Do you want me to find you another?”

He squinted at me. “Now?”

“Yes. Now.”

“There’s too much light in here. It hurts my eyes. Can you fix it?”

I turned off his bedside lamp. “Better?”

For a moment he didn’t answer. Then he said, “I’m not afraid, you know, Ally.”

“Of what?”

"Of not knowing. That's what scares most people."

"If that's true, you're luckier than the rest of us."

"I *am* lucky," he said, as he settled into his pillow. "I'm here in this land where life and death are natural occurrences, like weather, like the changing seasons. Like the summer evenings coming that are so *sweet* that if you were to die right then, if you could simply allow yourself to float away, formless, into the air, it might be the most natural act of your life. Like when twilight becomes evening, almost as you blink your eye. The line between spirit and mortal flesh would simply dissolve. Fear has no part in any of that."

"How elegant. Is that from the Trevor book?" I asked him.

He turned his head. "No. I wrote it. It was part of Einar's aria, but I cut it."

"Why?"

"It's too long. And it's not Einar's voice."

"No, it's not. It's your voice. It's like 'Billy in the Darbies'; it inserts some lyricism into what otherwise might be a very somber scene. You might want to rethink cutting it." I walked to the window and looked out. There were a few people strolling about on the lawn now in the late morning sun, and a leftover breeze was making the tips of the cypresses move about. It was only an inkling of spring, but like a hologram, one could imagine the whole from just a small part.

Spring this year would be all about Vincent, I guessed, in ways I couldn't predict, and I had more than one small part of him. I had those brief moments with his music during that first evening at the contessa's, music that had made me stop breathing. I had his graceful interpretations of Bach's musical variations; I had our arms around each other in the chill of the hay truck. I had his laugh, his courage, his hope, his honesty, his work, and the sure compass direction of his spirit, not at all like the swinging weather vane that was more accurately a description of my own. And in some unexplainable way, I had his love for Elaine—and hers for him—that were strengthening my ability to care for them both.

When I turned around, he had removed his pajama top. He pointed to his wardrobe, where I found a short stack of clean ones. When I'd managed to get him into his familiar green and white striped top, I said, "I'm off now, Vincent."

"All right, then." He smiled. "Thanks for the visit. I'm going back to sleep."

I was holding his damp pajama top. "Where should I put this?"

"Just leave it on the foot of my bed." He slid down under the blankets and closed his eyes.

I bent down and kissed his forehead, putting both hands on his cheeks.

"Go on now," he said sleepily. "Don't forget the signora's basket."

"I've got it," I said at the door.

He turned on his side and faced the window, giving me a little wave over his shoulder.

I found Antonio at the door with a tray. "He's asleep now," I said to him. "Can you come back later?" We began to walk toward the elevator. "I understand you're a tenor," I said.

Thirty-two

It was slightly warmer back in Perugia, and the edge had left the wind. As I had guessed, the signora had not been concerned about my extra night away, only asking whether she had sent enough food. She handed me a couple of messages, one from Odysseus, who had called on the Caccinis' house phone, and another, surprisingly, from Senta, who had reappeared and once again "knocked at the door."

"She was weary from travel," the signora said, shaking her head. "I give her some coffee. She will stay with the sisters in Via della Cupa, where you must go to find her."

"Did she leave a phone number?"

"She has no telefonino."

I finished my coffee. "Well, I'll say goodnight, signora. My friend Vincenzo thanks you for your gifts. The minestrone was especially good."

She nodded. "I am happy to help his recovery."

I heard music from Jo's room and realized it had been a while since we'd talked, but I was too tired to meet that challenge tonight. Senta's reappearance disturbed me a little. I had a few ideas about what she might want, but those speculations would have to wait as well. I washed up quickly and went straight to bed.

Late Monday morning I headed over to the residence of the Oblate Sisters to see whether Senta was actually there. If she needed money, I had little to spare. If she wanted a meal, I could just about manage that and some advice, if that was required.

A pretty young nun ushered me through the massive front door and told me Senta was helping prepare the tables for the midday meal. The sisters provided an excellent midday repast for anyone who chose to come in: students, homeless people, wives who were on the run, druggies, women of dubious repute or with fatherless children, just anyone who needed food and friendly company was welcome.

Senta was setting the long rows of tables. She looked punched-out and a little bedraggled and was moving slowly. She didn't hear me approach.

"Hey," I said, putting my hand on her shoulder.

She jumped, then turned and threw her arms around my neck. Some forks clattered to the floor. "Where the hell have you been?" she mumbled into my shoulder.

I drew back and looked at her face. "What are you doing here?"

She sat down in one of the chairs. "You want to stay and eat?"

"Are you allowed to offer?"

"There's plenty of food." She ran her fingers through her hair. "You're looking good," she said. "Better than me, probably."

There was a glass of thin breadsticks on the table, so I sat down and helped myself. "Did you finish the novel?" I asked. "Or are you back to labor unions?"

At that moment a group of nuns in aprons marched in carrying enormous bowls of steaming gnocchi, platters of salad, bread, fruit, bottles of wine, and water. They were chattering loudly.

"I've got to finish these tables," Senta said.

I helped her. Then the crowd flowed in.

After the meal we made our way back up to the corso for coffee. It was too chilly to sit outside at Lunabar Ferrari, so we found a table inside and I bought us both espressos. I watched her as she stirred two full spoons of sugar into her cup. Her hand was shaking.

"I'm glad you're still here," she said finally.

Her tale was not too complicated. She had rejoined Ciro and his family in Naples after she left Perugia, and in very short order his mother died and Ciro went off his rocker. He moved to her gravesite, where he slept, ate, and wept in operatic fashion until his father took his army rifle to the cemetery and told Ciro he was no longer welcome in the family home. Senta, who had never been liked by *papà* because she was American, also got the boot, and she and Ciro, now ostracized by most of his family, took to the streets.

It was at this point in the story that my telefonino rang and I heard Elaine's voice through a connection that was beset by dropouts.

"Where are you now?" Elaine asked.

"I'm at Lunabar on the corso having a coffee. Can I call you back?"

"All right. I just wanted to let you know that I'll be arriving next Saturday. I'm flying into Perugia on RyanAir. From London."

"What time?"

"Midafternoon. Don't meet me." Her voice began to break up. "Taxi ..." came through.

"I'll wait for you at your place," I said in a loud voice.

"Food!" she shouted.

I understood that she wanted to be sure her place was provisioned. Yes, that would be possible.

Senta got to her feet. "Do you want another coffee?" she mouthed at me.

I nodded. I opened my wallet, but she shook her head.

"Who's with you?" Elaine's voice was suddenly clear.

"I'll call you later. Vincent was in a strange way when I left him yesterday."

"Yes, yes, I know. The direttore finally telephoned." I waited for more information, but she volunteered nothing. "I'll see you Saturday, then." Once again the reception was crackling. "Ally?"

"Yes," I said. "Saturday."

"Saturday! And I don't expect ..." Then I lost her completely.

"Here we go," Senta said, arriving with the coffee.

"So what's your plan?" I asked her. "Where is Ciro, by the way? Will he show up here?"

"Gone. He signed on to a freighter in Naples and went off to South America. Happy to see him go." She scraped the sugar around in her cup with her spoon. "I was really sad about his mother, though. She was good to me."

I watched her and said nothing.

"My plan?" she said. "My plan is to fly home. There's no place else to go now. I boxed up all my papers and books in Naples and mailed them to my sister, so I'm traveling light."

"Why are you here, then?"

"I had some time. I wanted to see you again, I guess. Before I left."

"I can't give you any money. Or not much. How will you get home?"

"I don't need money. My sister sent me enough to cover a flight to JFK."

I looked at her and saw a raggedy waif. I remembered her face on the pillow beside me. The night view of Assisi from her room. We had been part of each other's story for a little while. A good part. We run into these people as we go along, if we're lucky.

"One thing," she said. "Do you have access to a washing machine?"

"Wow," Senta said later as we entered Elaine's apartment. "This is a classy place."

"The washer's off the kitchen." The apartment was chilly, and I began to look around for the thermostat. We'd picked up pasta and a big salad at one of the takeout places for dinner later, and the pasta would probably need to be warmed up. I wandered around the house as the pipes began to clank and checked Elaine's bedroom—for whatever reason, who knows? Just to get the scent of her again. Despite the rush of her departure, she'd left her bedroom neat and tidy, no clothes strewn about, or papers, and it looked as if she'd swept everything off her bathroom shelf into a travel bag probably. She was very much present, and I stood breathing her in while watching the reflection of her bed, her wide *letto matrimoniale,* in the mirror. I made a mental note to change the sheets.

As I was looking at the bed, I noticed a folded piece of paper that had fallen just under her desk. I carried it toward the wastebasket, but it looked like a torn off section of a letter, or a note, and I unfolded it to see if I should save it for her. It was definitely part of a letter and read, in her familiar hand, *I want commitment with the possibility of escape, eternity without sleep, work without struggle.* My first thought was that it was part of an aria, but I recognized the tone as that of her voice. I stared at it for a long moment, trying to think of who might have been the intended recipient, and even briefly imagined it might have been part of a farewell note to me. But before I could follow this disturbing line of thought, I heard Senta approaching, so I folded the note and put it in my pocket.

"I'm not sure if I did it right," Senta said, as she came into the bedroom. "But I punched buttons and poured soap in, and now it's sloshing around."

"Good. Let's eat. It's warming up in here. We can take off our coats soon."

"Who is this friend? Do you ever stay down here?"

I put the pasta in the microwave. "She's someone I got to know after you left. Can you look in that cabinet by the door and see if there's some red wine?"

"Will she mind if we drink her wine?"

"I'll replace it."

After dinner we sat finishing the wine. Senta had transferred her clothes to the dryer, which was much quieter than the washing machine. The apartment was now quite comfortable. She poured the last of the wine into her glass. "So is this serious with her, or what? And what's her name, if I'm allowed to ask."

"Her name's Elaine. And we're working on serious."

"But she's run off?"

"She's got a new job in Brussels. She'll be back on Saturday to start packing up her things." So then I felt a little guilty. "I'm sorry I just walked away, Senta. I don't regret any part of what happened with us."

"I'm glad to hear it."

"In spite of Ciro. Your other diversion."

"Ciro never meant anything serious to me. It was his mother I was in love with. If you hadn't been doing your damned writing, I would have stayed in Perugia."

After I washed up the dishes, I collected the empty wine bottle and the napkins and the food containers and put them into one of Elaine's trash bags. Hung the damp dish towel over the back of a chair.

"Leaving no trace," Senta said. She put her arms around my waist. "What if we went to bed? I wouldn't mind spending the night in that huge bed."

"That's not going to happen. Do you have to be back in the convent at a certain hour?"

"They gave me a key, but they like you to be in by eleven."

"It's ten fifteen now. We can just about make it." I gave her a quick kiss.

She put her hand on my arm and pulled me closer to her. "I really did come up here to say goodbye. Please consider that important."

"I do." I put both hands on her cheeks and kissed her. And again for a longer moment. She was still a temptation. "Okay," I said, with a little reluctance. "Want me to help you fold your laundry?"

"Nothing to fold. I just jam it into the bag."

I looked around the apartment one more time. "When do you fly out?"

"Saturday afternoon, from Fiumicino. I'll go back down to Rome tomorrow."

As Senta was taking off from Rome, Elaine would be landing in Perugia. Senta and I would probably never see each other again, but one never knows. You meet people who've been part of your life at surprising moments, even after you, or they, have moved on.

I locked up and we walked peacefully up the hill toward Via Parione, which would lead us to the Santo Spirito church and then through a warren of streets to Via della Cupa and the nuns. We didn't speak. It was still a little chilly, but there was a *soupçon* of sweetness in the air that enlarged my spirit. I took her hand.

Before I went into the Caccini apartment, I gave Vincent a call. It wasn't too late. But a strange woman's voice spoke into his telefonino.

"Signor Vincenzo *non è qui,*" she said tentatively.

"He's not there? Where is he?"

"Gone for new blood, Signora. I am cleaning the room now."

"A transfusion?"

"*Non so.*"

"Did he hemorrhage? *Un'emorragia?*"

"*Mi dispiace,* Signora. *Non lo so.*"

I put my phone away and stood there in silence. I would not call Elaine. If it were something serious, the director would call her. And then, surely, she would call me.

I had programmed Odysseus's number into my phone, and very early the next morning I called him, having no idea where he would pick up, at home or at the hospital.

"Odysseus," I said. "It's Allyn."

"Yes," he said sleepily.

"Where are you?"

"At the hospital. I was taking a short nap."

I took a glance at my watch. "Sorry. I'll be quick. Do you know any of the doctors over at the villa well enough to ask them about a patient?"

"Yes, one or two. But ..."

"I'm trying to contact Vincent, my friend from New Year's

Eve. When I called last evening, a cleaning person answered his phone, in his room, which is very odd because he would usually have his phone with him. She told me he had gone for new blood, whatever that means. Maybe a transfusion. But his doctor told me there would be no more transfusions. Would it be possible for you to call—"

"Allyn, wait a moment."

"To call one of the doctors there who might know what's happened to him? I just left him yesterday morning. He was weak, but he was going to rest. So I was hoping ... Do you think ..."

"Allyn, stop. Stop."

I heard the tone in his voice and took a breath.

"I know where he is," Odysseus said. "He is here. At the hospital. I was in *pronto soccorso* when they brought him in. Yesterday evening, about eleven. He has had another hemorrhage, yes. A bad one. And unexpected. The doctors have put him into a sort of coma, but he is alive. Resting deeply."

"In *rianimazione?*"

"No. In a private room."

"Is he back on a ventilator?"

"They are still giving him blood." That was a not an answer. "I'm sorry to give you this news. I was going to call you later."

"The signora gave me your message. Was that about Vincent?"

"No, no, that was something different. I wanted to ask you for coffee or a drink. She said you were at the villa."

"Should I come down to the hospital?"

"He's not conscious, Allyn."

"But someone should be there ..."

"The nurses and doctors remember him. They are taking good care of him now." He paused. "If there is a crisis, I will call you. All right?"

"I guess so."

"Allyn, I want you to hope—of course there is always hope—but he is a very sick man. It's not just TB now, or the pneumonia; it's everything. You had your talk with him?"

"Yes."

"So you know all the details."

"All I'm allowed to know, I think."

"Okay. Now I must go."

"*Ciao,* Odysseus. Thank you."

Now it was time to get in touch with Elaine. I expected her to know everything by now.

And of course she did.

"I'm on my way," she said. "I was going to call you after I settled my flight."

I told her about Odysseus's news.

"Yes, I heard all that from the direttore. But a coma can be anything, Ally. It can be a protective response from the body. Doctors may have put him into one deliberately, to allow the body to recover if it can. But ..."

"He lost a lot of blood apparently."

"He's had a transfusion. That should be finished now."

"Why was a transfusion necessary? I thought the TB was under control."

"It may not have anything to do with TB. He was in acute respiratory distress. That's all I was told. We'll have to find out."

"When will you get here?"

"Tonight, I think. I'm waiting for confirmation. I'll text you with details. A friend has offered to drive me down to the airport in Charleroi, and I can get a RyanAir nonstop to Perugia from there. I won't have to go through London."

"Should I get your car and meet you?"

"No, a taxi will be quicker. But I'd love it if you could go down and turn up my heat. And get some food in the house. I left enough gin, but check on the wine, and something to make pasta sauce. Salad things. Bread. Cheese. Eggs. Coffee. Milk. Whatever you think."

I remembered then that I'd forgotten to turn down the thermostat last night. "Fine." There was a moment of silence. "I'll see you at your place, then."

"This was bound to happen, Ally. It's a natural progression. We'll deal with it."

"There's nothing natural about it."

"All right, I have to get going. See you tonight."

"Safe trip."

A moment more of silence, and then the connection was broken.

Almost with the speed of light, the day passed into late afternoon, and I found myself once more at Elaine's, cleaning up the small mess that Senta had left in front of the washing machine. I gradually realized that I was attempting to remove all evidence of our visit here the night before, but I had no idea why. Possibly I feared Elaine's imagination, which was almost as creative as my own.

After speaking to Elaine that morning, I had returned to the signora's to get some clothes and to bring her up to date about my plans. I diplomatically managed to convince her that Vincent would not need another basket of food at this moment; perhaps later would be better. I checked that task off my list and headed for the Mercato Popolare, where I discovered that some early strawberries had arrived—from what part of the world I couldn't imagine. I knew they would please Elaine.

Finally, around seven thirty, I looked around and decided I'd done all I could do. Odysseus had not called.

I had thought there was nothing left to do but to wait for Elaine. But Gail Graham got to me first. And it was not a friendly conversation. She gave me an ultimatum, and I made no serious effort to explain my stalemate. And agreed to her terms, with no real hope of success.

Thirty-three

I heard her say, "Just put the luggage there, thanks. Here's something extra for you." The door shut firmly, and I heard her coat land on the back of one of the chairs. I'd dozed off on the couch with a copy of the *International Herald Tribune* on my chest. Somehow I hadn't wanted her to find me asleep in her bed.

"Ally!" she called as she walked toward the kitchen.

"I'm here." I sat up. Then got to my feet.

"Where?" She started down the hall to the bedroom.

"Right behind you."

She held me for a long while without saying anything, while I reacquainted myself with the contours of her body. She had the aroma of travel on her, the stale confines of the plane, probably a drink or two, along with traces of her familiar scent: a day on the run. Finally she leaned back. "God, what a day. I've been up since five. Come into the kitchen, I need a drink. Have you eaten?"

"I bought some cheese, fresh Asiago. It came in today. I had some of that. There's bread and the other things. And strawberries."

"Strawberries! Wonderful!" She cracked open an ice tray and

threw some cubes into a glass. “Can I fix you something?” She unscrewed her bottle of gin.

“In a while. I’ve been asleep. What time is it?”

“Around nine thirty. Or ten. We were late. Come into the dining room.”

“Maybe I’ll have a little more of the Asiago.”

“Good. I’ll have some too. I had an airport hamburger, of all things, at Charleroi. A hamburger and a beer.”

“Where is Charleroi?”

“About thirty miles south of Brussels. Come in and sit down. Bring the cheese. And some bread.”

I decided I did want some wine, so I went to the refrigerator and grabbed a bottle of the Vernaccia that I’d purchased.

“Have you heard anything new?” she asked as I sat down.

“Nothing. Odysseus said he would call if anything changed.”

“Odysseus is ...”

“He’s a friend, a resident at the hospital. He knows Vincent from when he was there in December. I told you about him.”

She smiled. “Oh, yes. From New Year’s Eve.” She cut herself a small wedge of cheese.

“I’m glad you’re here,” I said.

“Where else would I be?” She got up to refill her glass and touched my shoulder as she passed.

“Will you go down to the hospital tonight?”

“Not unless someone calls.” She returned, stirring her drink with her index finger. “He’s sedated and sleeping. Tomorrow will be soon enough.”

We sat there with our drinks, the cheese and its knife between us. Elaine had returned, and every eventuality I had been imagining had become disturbingly possible. Including Vincent’s death. I wiped my eyes and blew my nose. “Sorry,” I said.

"We can talk, sweetheart, I want to talk, but I must have sleep first." She gave me a small smile, then reached across and took my hand. "So much has happened. It's just ... like moving through fog. Different things keep getting in the way. If you understand that."

"I do."

"I'm worn out. Not just from the trip down, although we had ghastly turbulence. I hate that." She held my eyes for a moment.

"We could go to bed," I said. "To sleep. I put clean sheets on the bed."

"That was thoughtful." She sat there for a moment, her face pale and drawn. "Before we do that, let's have some strawberries."

I stood up. "I'll fix them."

As it happened, we took our bowls of strawberries with us to bed. I had a taste of mine while Elaine took a quick shower, and when she joined me, she'd washed the plane and travel tension from her body, and the tendrils of her hair were damp and curling.

"These are so good," she said. "Where did they come from? Sicily?" She placed her half-empty bowl on the night table and slid down under the quilts.

"Greece maybe? Or Spain."

She turned toward me and pulled me close against her.

"Vincent's opera had its first performance while you were away," I said.

"What?" She raised her head.

"Parts of it. A couple of arias. A waltz."

"Where did that happen? At the villa?"

"With quite an appreciative audience."

"Well." She turned onto her back. "Sorry I missed it."

"It wasn't planned. He and the dottoressa had been talking about pulling together something for the patients. But it just ... happened."

"And what did you think?"

"He's moving in the right direction. He's had some sort of epiphany that involved an angel. I believe him."

"And there was an audience?"

"A small one. But yes. And enthusiastic."

She turned toward me again. "Maybe that will be enough."

"Do you think so?"

But she was quickly asleep, barely breathing, the way she is able to do.

Sometime during the night the weather changed, and a soft rain began. I got up to close the window a bit. When I returned to bed, Elaine's body was still turned toward me, and I moved back into her arms without disturbing her. We slept on, while the fragrant aromas of fresh strawberries and sweet night rain eddied above us.

Just before dawn, my phone vibrated under my pillow and I answered without speaking.

"Allyn," Odysseus said. "You should come. He's awake."

Thirty-four

Odysseus met us at the main hospital entrance and took us into a large coffee bar, which was beginning to fill up with the departing night staff and those arriving for the day shift.

"Are you one of his doctors, then?" Elaine asked him, as he delivered three small cups of espresso.

"No, Signora ..."

"Please, Elaine will do," she said.

He gave her a weary smile. "His doctor is with him now. With some others. They wait for the respiratory therapist."

"Does that mean a ventilator again?"

"Not necessarily. Last night I might have said yes."

"When did he wake up?" I asked.

"Just when the rain began. Almost exactly at that moment."

Elaine finished her coffee. "Who decides about the ventilator?" she asked.

"You should speak with the doctors about all of that. I understand you are *il parente piu prossimo*. The responsible relative."

"So it seems," Elaine said.

The hospital corridors looked very different in the daylight. And it was noisier, with intermittent announcements and occasional calls from within the rooms and the incessant sounds of the machines. As we approached Vincent's room, two doctors emerged and headed toward us. One of them was Dottoressa Cortina. Elaine stopped to speak with them. I took a quick look into Vincent's room, then went to sit in a small waiting room nearby. Eventually Elaine and the doctor joined me.

"He seems to be asleep again, or still asleep," I said to the doctor as I shook her hand.

She smiled. "Be patient. He'll be back. He moves in and out. And they've given him some drugs. Now he is just sleeping. When he wakes, his mind may be perfectly clear for a while. But eventually he will sleep again, for longer and longer periods." She shrugged. "Or not. It is an unpredictable situation."

"Are they considering a ventilator?" I asked her.

"We'd rather avoid that if we can. The respiratory therapist will be here soon."

"If his lungs aren't functioning," Elaine said, "it may be necessary, Ally."

The doctor put her hand on my arm. "It's difficult to think about, I know. But he is breathing a little easier at the moment. We're watching him closely. Now I must do some charting at the nursing station computer. Please excuse me."

"May I stay?" I asked her. "In his room?"

"It is better if only one person sits with him at a time. Take a seat in the waiting area. Signora Bishop can call you in if necessary."

She walked away.

Elaine took the seat I had vacated. "I'll come and get you after a while. We'll share the load."

"It isn't a load," I said.

The waiting room was comfortable but could not block out the clatter of passing gurneys, the squeak of nurses' shoes, the serious murmur of voices, all particular to what hospitals are supposed to do, which is to keep people alive. Or possibly make dying easier to bear. Those who serve there roll patients into surgeries they may not survive, soothe moans of pain, deal with irate or frightened families, and respond to the urgent electronic summons of those whose bodies are in distress. I suppose doctors and nurses adapt themselves to these alerts and learn to judge where to go first and when to move quickly. Hospitals are private cities, with their own hierarchies and rules of engagement.

I went downstairs and got myself a caffè latte, and when I returned I took a look into Vincent's room for a moment to be sure all was well. He was still asleep. Elaine had posted herself at the window, lost in thought or possibly sleeping on her feet. I didn't disturb her.

Waiting in a hospital for something inevitable to occur, or even for news that an unexpected miracle has happened, is a long business. I had brought along nothing to read and eventually became the sole occupant of this anteroom to the unknown. Time slowed. I finally turned my head to the side and dozed off.

I woke a little later and found Elaine sitting on the small couch by the door. She had let me sleep.

"What's happened?" I asked quickly.

"Nothing. The doctors are in there again. They're doing something, I don't know what."

"Was he awake?"

"More or less. He seemed to be aware of where he was and

what had happened, and he knew who I was. He asked me if my new apartment had space for my piano." She smiled slightly. "Not what I expected."

"Do you want a coffee or something to eat?"

"What I really need to do is make a couple of calls. I suppose I should go outside."

"Go ahead. I'll stay."

When the doctors left and Elaine had gone to make her calls, I went into Vincent's room and found him rubbing his eyes. "Hello there," he said slowly. And then, as if he were learning to talk, he said, "I was hoping you would come."

I tried to get close to him, but he was in the midst of a jungle of lines. Completely unreachable. So I squeezed his toes, or rather his socks, and he smiled a little.

"Could you raise the blinds a bit for me?" he said. "I'd like to see outside."

I raised the blinds a little and the mountains appeared under a light blue sky.

We sat in comfortable silence for a while. "I've been somewhere," he whispered finally.

"You've been asleep."

"I mean somewhere else." He was breathing slowly. "Could you manage to pass me some water?"

I negotiated the labyrinth and found his glass with the bent straw. I held his head while he drank a little. This seemed to exhaust him.

I sat and watched his face, which seemed beautiful and peaceful to me.

"Elaine told me you found strawberries," he said.

"Those early, small ones. Very sweet. They hardly need sugar at all."

"Talk to me," he said. "Tell me things."

"Well, I'm waiting for Monica's final approval of our interview. It was anticlimactic in a way, but it turned the piece around. Piero DiBrufa never wrote anything, Vincent. It was all Monica's work. Deliberately confused."

He smiled. "There's a story there, I'll bet."

"There's a lot that won't be told." I walked to the window where Elaine had been, looking toward the mountains in the east as the sun fell to our west. The light blue sky of early spring was acquiring the lavender shades of evening. "The bigger problem is my profile of Elaine. My ideas about this thing are shape-shifting by the hour, and I'm afraid I'm going to lose them. We're having trouble finding time to sit and talk. But we have to soon."

"She may surprise you," he said.

I rubbed my eyes. "She's working again. And I think it's made a difference. She's got her strength back. Or she's refocused. Or something."

"Does that bother you?" His voice was growing hoarser and more fatigued, after just these few minutes.

"Truthfully? I'm relieved to see it. I may have met my match, Vincent. I want to stop fighting myself. Although where that will take us is anyone's guess."

He shifted his position in the bed, moving carefully. "It's about time. Try to be happy about it." He started to laugh but choked on his laughter and began to cough. And it was not a good sound. "Help me," he said, "help me sit up." As gently as I could, I pulled him up and let him rest against his pillow while I untangled his lines. His face had turned ashen, and he was weeping from his efforts to breathe.

"Should I ring ...?" I began.

"No, no. Just a minute. Just wait."

"You shouldn't talk," I said.

After a little bit, his breathing became more regular, and he opened his eyes. "Sorry, love. But I think you ought to go now. This is an ugly business."

"Now?"

I'd been gripping his hand, but he released me and reached underneath himself and felt the sheets. "I think I've wet the bed. Or my catheter's pulled out maybe. On your way out, could you ask one of the nurses to come in?" He took a hesitant breath. "And the Italian word for catheter is *catetere*."

"*Catetere*. Am I on my way out?"

"Yes. You are." His voice had fallen into a deep whisper.

"Please don't, Vincent. It's me. I'm here."

"I'm so tired," he said.

I put one hand on his cheek and kissed his forehead. His skin was dry, like parchment, and despite his brief moments of laughter, his shallow breaths were struggling against the awfulness in his chest. Still, the sweetness of his smile was there, impossible and heartbreaking.

"I ..." he began.

"I know," I said, close to his ear. "I know. I love you too."

"See you in the morning, then?"

"In the morning, maestro."

When I returned to the waiting room, Elaine was writing in her notebook. I sat down across from her and said nothing. I had no desire to say anything more today, in fact. Grief affects one in odd ways, even the premonition of grief, during the moments and hours before it actually begins. I felt a little lightheaded.

Elaine finally slapped her notebook closed and slid it into her briefcase. She put her hands on her knees and leaned toward me. "We should get some dinner," she said.

"Are you going back in to see him?"

"I'll look in. But I won't stay."

"Did the doctors say anything significant?"

"They said his body was slowly shutting down. They were quite blunt."

"What I want is for him to get out of bed and come with us for dinner. Wouldn't that be nice? But that won't happen, will it."

She smiled a little. "No, sweetheart, not today."

"Should we leave, then?"

"If we go, we may miss the moment." She reached across and took my hands. "Would that trouble you? If it happened?"

"What you're saying is that we could possibly sit here for the next week."

"That's what they implied, in fact. He just goes into a deeper and deeper sleep."

Fathoms down, fathoms, how I'll dream fast asleep ...

"But I have a more productive idea," she continued. "You have unfinished business with your editor. Or your editor and your readers. Let's go finish it." She held out her hand. "Come on. I haven't been entirely idle. Monica's given you the entire story of her life with no prompting at all. I think it's my turn to speak a little. You won't get my life, and there are some matters I won't discuss, but I think I can put this operatic fiasco to bed in its proper place."

We settled in at her dining room table with some deli takeout—soup, cheese, salad, bread—and there were still some strawberries left for later. I was a bit overwhelmed by this rapid turn of events, so it took me a while to get my papers organized. But she was fully prepared: two or three pages of notes that were neatly organized into paragraphs and sections—very like her.

I took out my little tape machine. "You'll see a copy of this before it goes anywhere," I told her.

"Of course. More wine?"

"I'll wait."

Elaine's ground rules were simple: she had only two. She would not discuss her personal relationship with Piero DiBrufa or comment on the role Monica DiBrufa had played in the preparation of *Sirius.*

To begin, I took a deep breath and asked her if she thought that opera was the most complete art form. And she began by correcting my grammar relative to 'most complete.'

We laughed and went on from there.

And my part wasn't difficult to write. Her responses were simple and clear. I had the piece mostly finished anyway, based on notes to myself and on the computer, and memories of her voice talking about her sense of the operatic art form, its difficulties, its spectacle, its entertaining catastrophes. The use of her unique artistic vision to shape the creation of productions that were entirely her own was the unwavering focus of her professional life. The collection of her commentaries that I had gathered for nearly six months now was clear proof of that. Her own words created her profile. My personal contributions dealt with the things she couldn't say, such as her struggle with a libretto that nearly destroyed her belief in her own vision, and how she fought for this vision in order to ensure that opera in Perugia would continue on another day. It would not be beaten by the exotic whims of a confused dreamer who had lost his way long before she arrived. She fought an honest but frustrating battle with him, and I don't think I would ever say that it was one she had lost.

I included a couple of descriptive paragraphs about the city, but I wanted to keep Perugia for myself. The city was mine now, and I didn't want to share it.

Thirty-five

These calls always seem to come at night, and this one was no exception. It was long before dawn. Elaine took her phone into the bathroom and talked quietly for what seemed to be too much time, and during those moments I drifted back to sleep.

I woke again when I heard her phone beep as she turned it off. She went out to the kitchen and returned with a bottle of water. "Take a drink," she said.

"Elaine?"

She eased back under the quilts and pulled me against her. "He's gone," she said.

"Who called?"

"The dottoressa. I'll talk to you about it in the morning, but she said he went off to sleep soon after we left, and at about eleven one of the nurses responded to an alarm and went to check on him. He wasn't breathing. No heroic measures were taken, as she put it. Which is what he wanted."

I took another drink from the bottle and set it on the night table. "What happens now?"

"They want me down there in the morning."

An ache that had bloomed in my chest seemed to be falling into some vast area below my heart. I tried to tell her this, but the words weren't there.

She just held on to me, and after a while the pain eased. What remained was a massive, empty space, a door he had closed behind him on the way out, and the bitter awareness of what would never, now, be experienced.

The street outside was completely still: no rain, no wind, and for once, no traffic. Then in the distance I heard the bells of Santo Spirito begin, ringing the early hour. The church was up above Porta Eburnea, just north of Piazza Partigiani, and normally we weren't able to hear these lovely bells. But the city was quiet tonight. It had paused, as if to allow us to hear them clearly.

As they rang, the last of winter slipped into true spring. And that was how I got through the first hour.

Thirty-six

For a while I thought this tale might end without having a real conclusion. Sometimes this happens. In fact, most of the significant events in our lives, especially those that involve someone's death, do not really conclude, because having actually experienced them, we cannot send them back to the place where they existed only as possibilities. Our recollections of them stay with us, and although they sometimes shift in perspective as we grow older, they remain until our own death at last allows them to disappear with us.

I thought about that sometimes during those first days after Vincent's death, although I wasn't able to put any particular reactions in real order during that time. I seemed to be "up in the north pasture," as my mother said once, speaking of loneliness. And the north pasture was not a place from which I wanted to return, at least not immediately. There was a vast sense of absence that lingered in Elaine's apartment, in certain corners of the city, in music that floated out of windows as I passed by. Someone was missing. For the living, that's what death is: the absence of a particular life.

Elaine planned no service for Vincent, although—counting friends he had made in the city and at the villa—it would have been well attended. But that issue had been settled between them. She'd pulled a few legal strings to have him cremated in Italy, an issue I didn't pursue, and also said that he wanted his ashes scattered in certain corners of the Umbrian countryside. At first I thought I'd leave that pilgrimage to her: I didn't want to encounter him as a handful of dust. But in the end I realized that Vincent would not have wanted her to go alone. So I went with her.

And so the question remained—the one Vincent had posed: what would we be now, Elaine and I, without him?

Spring was arriving all around us. We opened the windows, and the air was full of sweetness, the wind gentle. "What's the weather?" I asked Elaine during a break in packing up her apartment—a pointless query, for I could have looked out the window directly at it.

"It's spring, Ally. Can't you smell it?"

At last the afternoon came when we stood in front of Elaine's building and watched the moving van lumber up the street toward Piazza Partigiani, take a wrong turn, and head downhill in a direction that would quickly get the driver completely lost.

"What the hell." Elaine laughed. "I don't know where I'm going to put most of that stuff anyway."

She took my arm, and we went upstairs to finish up whatever food we could find in the cupboards and drink as much of the wine as we could tolerate. Elaine had picked up yet another roasted chicken too, just in case. She would leave tomorrow on a late morning flight to London or Charleroi, I didn't know which.

I would remain in Perugia to conclude the business I had left to do. I was pleased enough with what Elaine and I had created together, but Monica had yet to give me the green light about her own. And Gail Graham was suddenly so confident in my work—and my ability to produce it—that she was already talking about sending me directly to a spring song festival in Malaga as soon as the text of the Monica/Elaine article had departed on its electronic journey to her computer. And although we hadn't spoken about it, I knew Elaine had her return ticket to Brussels, or Charleroi, already confirmed.

So if I had thought for a moment that Vincent's death would settle the particulars of my life, I would have been completely wrong.

That evening we had a little bit to eat and sat at the dining table with our wine. We didn't talk much. The sun was setting, and we watched the light fade on the tiled roofs of the houses behind hers that fell away toward the street below and listened to the sounds of evening as they drifted in—the closing of shop gates, the calls to dinner, occasional music. We'd done a lot of work, and we were tired.

"I have something for you," she said after a while. She went into her bedroom and returned carrying an envelope. "Now, I don't want you to be upset," she began.

"That's a terrible way to present a gift."

"Well, it's not exactly a gift." She handed me the envelope, which had my name written on it. "From Vincent," she said. "He didn't want you to have it until after he died."

I held the envelope in my hand and finally put it on the table and finished my wine. "I'll read it later," I said.

"He wrote to me too, but I haven't looked at it." She reached over and tucked a strand of hair behind my ear. "I wonder what we're afraid of."

I didn't think I felt afraid. I just couldn't imagine what more he could possibly have to say.

"More wine?" she asked me.

We had to begin somewhere. I was uncomfortable with conversations that involved decisions I hadn't yet made, which was the situation I sensed stumbling toward me. I was better at flying by the seat of my pants, but the time for that maneuver had probably passed. Perhaps I could discuss the chicken, just to begin. But she took the lead.

"So what's next?" she asked. "Have you thought about Brussels? Should I expect you at some point? Soon? Next year? Christmas? Ever?"

"Strange," I said. "I've only been to the train station in Brussels. Just for an hour. On the way to some other place."

She lifted her eyebrows to acknowledge that I had avoided her question. "Is there something about Brussels that's putting you off? Of course, it's not Tahiti or Kathmandu, is it? Or some other exotic place. Or maybe you just don't like Handel."

"Nothing like that. Exotic places encourage shallow reactions."

"Always ready with the *bon mot,*" she said.

I sat quietly, watching my empty wine glass.

"Well," she said, sitting back, "maybe we'd better just decide that after everything that's happened, it's simply not the right time for us. Under any circumstances. I had great hopes; in fact, I'm reluctant to give up on them even now. But we may not be headed in the same direction, and that may be an insurmountable impediment. So maybe, in fairness to both of us, hope had better be shown the door."

This talk was so like her. She met reality eloquently, and it was just a month ago that I was wishing for her reassurance about the right road to take. But she had sensed my hesitation, my uneasiness, and the road that lay divided at my feet.

"I miss Vincent," I said suddenly.

She smiled. "Yes. I do too."

"He was worried about you and me, what would happen to us without him."

"He was right to be concerned, I think. He was at the center of our relationship, yours and mine, from the beginning. Both of us had him to turn to when the going got rough. Instead of to each other."

She was right, of course. But I remembered how perilous turning to her had seemed to me.

"Vincent was my best friend," she said. "I loved him very much. Your relationship with him was more complicated, I think. So you may be having a harder time."

"Maybe."

"You know, I really wouldn't have been surprised if you'd slept with him. My concern was with his illness, and your susceptibility. It would have disappointed me, but I didn't want both of you sick."

"I know that now. He did too. When I was at the villa, he asked me—once—what might have developed if we'd slept together. Because for a brief while that could have happened."

She watched me, her eyes careful. "What did you say?"

"I told him we both would have regretted it. Because we'd have lost you. He wanted me to see that for myself, I think."

"Did you feel you had to choose?"

"I chose you in London, Elaine. Although I didn't know what to do about it then."

"Did you tell him that? At the villa?"

"I didn't, but he knew. That didn't mean I loved him less. Then after London I stupidly convinced myself that I'd lost you both. And talked myself into a very unsettled state of mind."

"I wasn't exactly presenting any reasonable alternatives."

"I wasn't exactly ready to make a move."

"Are you ready now?"

"I think I'm ready to consider the possibilities."

She smiled. "Talk to me then."

"Realistically, I need to get back to work. The Perugia piece will be out of my hands soon—I hope—and I'll have no control over it then, or what will happen after. My editor is pushing me toward Spain. There's a festival of Spanish song at the Teatro Cervantes in Malaga, and right now that might be the simplest way for me to get back in harness."

"That would be when?"

"End of May, I believe."

"Is that something you want to do?"

"Well, it's my job, whether I want to or not. I'm not sure how I feel." I looked at her. "I'm not the same person I was six months ago."

She nodded.

"But," I said, "I'm thinking about going over to Spain by the overnight ferry from Civitavecchia to Barcelona. Then getting a car and driving south, unwinding as I go. That's my hope."

At that point she went into the kitchen for more wine. "Why would you want to take an overnight ferry?" she said as she returned. "Go down to Rome and fly directly to Malaga. It's only an hour or so."

She refilled my glass, then her own.

"Anyone can fly. I like to write about alternative choices."

"Sounds too slow for me."

"I need slow right now."

"*Chacun à son goût.*"

"Of course, that doesn't mean everyone has to go that way."

She rested her chin in her hand. "Happily, that's true."

"If I go to Malaga, I want to stay someplace on the coast, not right in the city. Because I need the sea. I've missed it. I want to hear it and breathe it and eat with it at my feet. And at night let it sing me to sleep."

"A poetic sentiment."

"And then after the festival I think I'll get away from the Costa del Sol; everyone writes about it. I think I'll take some off-the-map routes, find some lovely places to stay in the hills, walk the smaller streets in Andalucia." I stopped. "This will be a different kind of chapter."

"It will. It sounds good."

"I'm already rereading Lorca. I might write something focused on him."

"Ah, yes, Lorca." She thought a minute. "*For love of you, the air, it hurts—*"

"*And my heart, and my hat, they hurt me,*" I continued.

It was clear that we were talking around issues that, if they were not settled at this exact moment, would move forever out of reach.

"Why don't you take a break from Brussels, then, if you can work it out," I said, "and join me in Malaga for a week or so? You might enjoy the festival, in fact. You'll probably even know some of the singers." My voice caught somewhere in my throat.

She turned her head aside with a half-smile.

"There are flights every day to Malaga from Brussels—or from

Charleroi, if you're hankering for another burger," I said. "Two and a half hours, nonstop. I checked. And meet me ..."

She turned to face me. "Where?"

"Hotel Torre del Mar, just east of Malaga. A small place. On the sea. Large, quiet rooms. A fountain in the lobby. A little restaurant. Big shrimp. Good wine."

"You've been there?"

"Never. But I've spent some time with it online. Call it a place to escape to, if you like. I don't think I can promise you eternity without sleep, but I do know about some ways to escape."

"Oh." She let her head drop for a moment and then lifted her chin. "I wondered where that scrap of paper had disappeared to."

"Were you writing to me?"

"I'd rather not say, if you don't mind."

"I don't mind." I took a breath. "And as a trade-off, I might try to suffer through four hours of Handel in the fall, just to experience the singing rocks and flying horses. If I'm lucky, I might even wangle an interview with the stage director."

"Let me just get my schedule book." She went off toward her bedroom.

We talked for a while until she finally closed her date book.

"Was that so hard?" she said.

"It was more like a business deal. No offense."

"That was only to keep things clear. The next part will be easier." She rose and took my hand and led me down the hall toward her familiar bedroom. And as it happened, we drank no more wine that night, the cupboards were not cleaned out, and the aroma of roasted chicken was left to float away through the house and out through one of the windows open to the spring night.

We made love with relief, loosening the emotional knots that had been tangling us up. Despite the decisions we had made, our freedom still felt fragile. But there were, finally, very few defensive boundaries left. We weren't entirely free of those, but we found tantalizing ways to maneuver around them, much as a trout will dance through water to avoid a net. We slept and woke, and talked and then we didn't talk. Each of our descents into sleep was longer and finally went deeper into a mutual darkness.

Just before dawn I woke, desperate for water. In the kitchen I put the poor chicken to rest in the refrigerator and drank about half of one of the last little bottles of Pellegrino as the soft, peach-infused light of day grew beyond the mountains east of Assisi. Back in the bedroom I impulsively shook some water from my fingertips over her breasts, and she smiled as she woke and said, "Lovely." Then I finished the bottle and we returned to sleep.

"Should we have chicken for breakfast?" she asked a little later.

"That chicken is destined for my signora," I said, without opening my eyes. "What time is your flight?"

She grabbed the clock. "Oh, God! You'll have to drive me to the airport." She kissed me quickly and threw back the covers. "We have to leave here in an hour. Can you take care of the food later? And the cupboards? Thank God I'm packed. I've got to shower."

I stretched and decided my shower could wait. And the food. And Vincent's letter even. But I managed to get her to the airport—only just—and our time on the way was taken up with the usual instructions about keys and garages and where to put the garbage. "And keep your phone charged," she reminded me.

We skidded up to the departures entrance.

"Don't come in, don't come in," she said. She was carrying two Louis Vuitton suitcases and a couple of coats thrown over her arm, but she dumped the coats on top of the luggage and reached for me with one eye on her watch. Then she was gone, leaving only her familiar scent in her wake. All departures should be exactly like that. I thought I would probably get used to them.

I was tempted to wait in the parking area to see her flight lift off, but I headed for the highway back to the city instead, hoping the mechanics in Sandro's garage had not decided to close down for the midday passeggiata.

When I arrived at Casa Caccini later, the signora met me at the door and beckoned me into the dining room. "*Messaggio* for you," she whispered breathlessly, drawing herself up. "From Montecalvo. He says I must tell you that Monica DiBrufa has approved the writing. You must visit him at his store today." She smiled triumphantly.

I sat down at the table. "That is good news," I said.

"Does this mean she will come to my house? What day? I must clean! I will prepare a special meal."

"I wouldn't be at all surprised to see her," I said.

That evening, after the signora had calmed down a bit, she cooked a grand meal for all of us (with the little chicken taking pride of place). Afterward, I retired to my room with the remains of my wine and opened Vincent's letter.

My dearest Ally,

According to a director friend of mine, there is a particular way to exit the stage. "You're not simply walking out the door," he said. "You must move as if you have a particular place to be going, something in your mind. A purpose.

A story. A destination." A libretto, if you will. Well, here is mine.

I'm in a silver plane, high above the lights of this city that now belongs to both of us, held aloft by wings lifted by the night winds from the hills. I'm flying away to someplace new, toward Jakarta, let's say. Soon the dawn will come, and I'll smell the coffee, and the cabin lights will come on and people will yawn and go down the aisles, stretching their legs. The window shades will slide up and the sun will be rising over orange and pearl layers of cloud, and beneath me will be a grand ocean, perhaps, or a land of heroic colors. I'll feel the plane bank and begin its descent gently, from its great height, and I will be arriving somewhere! My odyssey will be over. And this arrival will be happy, because although I'm in a different world, a familiar joy will still be with me and I can rest at last. Thank you for that.

And when I rise from sleep, I will throw open the windows and see a place I may not recognize but one that's been waiting for my return all of my life.

Someday maybe I'll meet you there.

Always with my love, Vincent

I turned off my lamp and sat there in the fading light for a while. People were coming home; the little girls were laughing in the bath, the signora was cleaning up the dishes. There was intermittent applause from a television somewhere and the pleasant aroma of coffee. I rose at last and opened the shutters wider. I rested my elbows on the sill, a customary position for the women on my street, and leaned out into the spring evening.

Later the Priori bells would ring midnight, then one. The streets would empty. The waiters on the corso would gather up the empty beer glasses and wipe off the tables; the last lovers would wander home, down ancient lanes dimly lit. But the glow from the centro would remain through the night, lighting the way for an Etruscan ghost or two, or a wandering foreigner perhaps, looking for a place to rest his head.

Meanwhile, the rest of the world would move on toward the next day, where, in Jakarta, the sun had already risen.

Acknowledgments

In Perugia, I'm indebted to Dorine Kunst, photographer and painter extraordinaire, who was always the first to welcome me back to the city and was able to turn any event—even a cup of coffee on the corso—into a celebration. COVID has restricted my travels for several years, but she has served as a loyal link to all matters Italian during this dark time. I thank Professore Giovanni Battista Moretti at the Italian University for Foreigners, who taught us much more than simply how to speak and read Italian. And, finally, the Giovanni Pulci family of Via Rocchi, who opened their home and their hearts to me and always brightened my spirits.

In Boston and points west, a short list of readers who have stood by me as I managed to write three complete versions of *Libretto*—with three different titles—would include Dori Hale, Pam Hoyle, Lynda Leahy, Jane Nussbaum, Catherine Roberts, and Betsy and Jerry Mandell. They have accompanied me on a variety of journeys—by plane, train, car, boat, subway, funicular, taxi, vaporetto—and each of them has enriched these travels with their good humor and intelligent company. As readers, they improved my text in individual and collective ways, whether catching errant commas or spotting ridiculous figures of speech. As opera lovers, they endured an endless number of *Rosenkavalier* productions in my grateful company and many an afternoon at Metropolitan Opera performances in Boston and New York. And finally, they were patient during those times when I turned my laptop off and chose to binge watch *Call the Midwife* or *Downton Abbey* instead of getting down to work. One or two of them were always there to press the power key and get me going again. My thanks to all of them for sharing the journey.